Praise for *This Is Why I Need You*

"An intimate portrait of female friendship in all its messy, complex, beautiful glory, *This Is Why I Need You* is an unforgettable story full of humour and heart. Alecsandra Kakon writes with uncanny empathy and insight and has created characters who will feel like your best friends by the end of the book. *This Is Why I Need You* is a remarkable debut, and Kakon is a writer to watch."

—Amy Jones, author of *We're All in This Together* and *Pebble & Dove*

"Kakon writes about female friendship with a sweet clarity that is bound to resonate with so many. I cried, I laughed, I reflected on my own relationships—all while rooting for the love tying these four flawed, yet lovable characters together. An endearing, sparkling, sexy book that redefines what relationships we prioritize. It will make you want to pick up the phone and reach out to your friends."

—Mai Nguyen, author of *Sunshine Nails*

"I can't wait until *This Is Why I Need You* becomes the next great Canadian love story."

—Anne T. Donahue, author of *Nobody Cares*

"The perfect blend of romance and women's fiction, *This Is Why I Need You* is a heartwarming examination of friendship and forgiveness that's filled with the kind of multilayered characters that feel like your own lifelong best friends, the kind who remind you that you're worthy of being loved even when you're at your messiest."

—Bianca Marais, *USA TODAY* bestselling author and cohost on *The Shit No One Tells You About Writing*

ALECSANDRA KAKON

This Is Why I Need You

A NOVEL

Published by ECW Press
665 Gerrard Street East
Toronto, Ontario, Canada M4M 1Y2
416-694-3348 / info@ecwpress.com

Editor for the Press: Kenna Barnes
Cover design: Thomas Hayman

LIBRARY AND ARCHIVES CANADA CATALOGUING IN PUBLICATION

Title: This is why I need you : a novel / Alecsandra Kakon.

Names: Kakon, Alecsandra, author.

Identifiers: Canadiana (print) 20250319780 | Canadiana (ebook) 20250319810

ISBN 978-1-77041-857-8 (softcover)
ISBN 978-1-77852-566-7 (PDF)
ISBN 978-1-77852-565-0 (ePub)

Subjects: LCGFT: Novels.

Classification: LCC PS8621.A4648 T45 2026 | DDC C813/.6—dc23

This book is funded in part by the Government of Canada. *Ce livre est financé en partie par le gouvernement du Canada.* We acknowledge the support of the Canada Council for the Arts. *Nous remercions le Conseil des arts du Canada de son soutien.* We would like to acknowledge the funding support of the Ontario Arts Council (OAC) and the Government of Ontario for their support. We also acknowledge the support of the Government of Ontario through the Ontario Book Publishing Tax Credit, and through Ontario Creates.

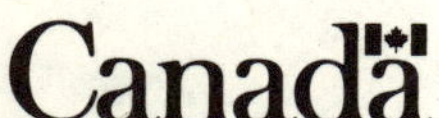

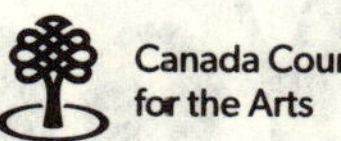

PRINTED AND BOUND IN CANADA

PRINTING: MARQUIS 5 4 3 2 1

To Lauren, the bestest friend who always has my back.
If I saw me the way you saw me, I'd be unstoppable.
Isn't that the true power of friendship?

To my Serge, forever and always.

"The truth will set you free, but first it will piss you off."

—GLORIA STEINEM

PART 1

The Trip

Zinnia

NASSAU, FEBRUARY

THE SOUND OF MY POUNDING HEART DROWNS OUT THE ECHO OF my flip-flops clapping against the white marble floor as I cross the hotel lobby. I catch a glimpse of her sitting by the bar, sliding her finger around the rim of what I know is Pinot Grigio. The driest one on the menu, no doubt.

I stop on the doorway and look out at the hot Bahamian sun setting through the floor-to-ceiling glass walls, casting a light glow around Fay: petite, but lean and long, mostly legs. Thick, shoulder-length, dark hair and deep-set brown eyes that she's thinly outlined in black liquid liner, same as she's done ever since we were fourteen. Her dark skin often gets mistaken for Middle Eastern blood, which makes us laugh since I'm the Lebanese one; she's French Canadian through and through. Everything about her face is sharp, except the dimple in her chin, which was a souvenir from our failed attempt at sneaking backstage at a Dave Matthews Band concert when we were in high school. Cut to Fay falling chin-first over a chain barricade (in front of many, *many* people). Instead of fan-girling with Dave himself, we ended up spending the night giddy from Gatorade, blasting "Ants Marching" with the nurses in the ER. The scar is small, but it deepens every time she laughs and reminds me that we make life good regardless of the forces that try to stop us.

And now this.

A serendipitous chance at having some alone time on what was meant to be our annual girls trip. Two friends shy of our foursome, Fay and I have three uninterrupted days to pile on the memories.

I stop mid-lobby and take a breath, watching her bob her foot to the faint calypso music playing in the bar. Sitting cross-legged, straight-backed, she brings her hand to her naturally plump lips and licks the residual wine slowly from the tip of her finger. Has she always been this sexy? Even in her rolled-cuff jean jacket in the thirty-degree heat, she's cool, calm, collected. So sure of herself. So fiercely Fay.

Meanwhile, my heart is racing like a doe in the wild, jittery and disoriented.

Fay.

My Fay.

My best friend Fay.

The same Fay I see every single day back home in Toronto. The one who held my hair just a couple weeks ago as I puked from food poisoning at that nasty little dive bar we go to all the time. Laughing until we cried because, for some very alien reason, my vomit was neon pink, which bore no resemblance to the fish and chips I had eaten earlier that evening. The same Fay who sits on my couch nearly every night in her sweats to help me put my two kids to bed before we watch *Real Housewives* reruns while stuffing our faces with popcorn and Smarties—a little salty, a little sweet—eternally debating which housewife we love to hate the most. The same Fay who has completely rocked my world for the last six months . . .

Never have I ever fussed over curls and outfits like I did this evening, but ever since Fay and I started hooking up, I'm moisturizing parts of my body I forgot I had. Shaving, primping, hell, I bought glitter balm for this trip! It took me thirty minutes and four outfit changes to finally decide on a bright yellow scoop-neck mini dress, with a floor-length patterned orange kaftan robe thrown over, which I am now regretting because the bottom hemline keeps getting stuck under my sandal, forcing me to hold the slit open, making me look more like Jessica Rabbit than sun-kissed Barbie.

Fay's eyes find mine and lock in, drawing me out of the doorway, closer to her. A hot tingle shoots up my spine. Has she always looked at me like this? How had I never noticed? It's like my body is finally alive. Even the most innocuous activity, like unpacking our clothes together, has taken on new meaning. The way her hand grazed my shoulder when she passed me my toiletry kit sent a shiver up and down my whole body, which is exactly why I had to send her down to the bar to wait for me. I couldn't get ready without it being loaded with sexual energy; every touch, every look . . . it's all foreplay.

"You look gorgeous," Fay says, walking over to meet me where a single pane of glass separates the lobby from the bar. She takes me by the hand, leading me back to the bar. "Like a Greek goddess."

I giggle nervously as I prop myself up on the stool beside her. "I was going for Barbie, but I'll take goddess."

"Did you just roll your eyes at yourself?" Fay raises a brow, settling back onto her stool. "You're funny when you're nervous." She knows all my tells. She pulls my stool closer to hers, and her bare thigh brushes against mine. The same bare thigh I wrapped in an elastic bandage when she got taken down on the soccer pitch in ninth grade, swollen black and blue, she couldn't finish the game; the same bare thigh I want to slide my hand—*stop!* Slow down, there, tiger. No need to rush.

I'm fairly certain Fay can hear my inner thoughts, because she adds, "I am too, but—" She slides her hand up my leg. "No one here knows us. We have the whole weekend to ourselves."

I pull back slightly. The intensity of it all is more than I thought it would be. She's so in, so sure. Nothing is holding her back.

I wish I could say the same.

Flipping my curls out of my face, I shakily reach for her glass and take a swig of her wine. "I can't believe Jack is proposing to Val tonight," I mumble into the glass as I finish it off. "She hasn't missed a trip in nine years."

"Yeah, but his poor timing—" Fay interrupts.

"And Kiara's last-minute ditch," I ramble on.

"Is why we're here alone," we finish in unison.

Fay leans in for a kiss. Her lips, buttery soft against mine; the absence of stubble chaffing my upper lip like a phantom memory breeding guilt in my mind.

I pull away, but Fay's hand still cups my cheek as her eyes hold my gaze.

"What is it?" she asks, attuned to my hesitation.

"You know we can never tell Adam that the girls didn't end up coming, right?" I blurt out.

I watch as Fay's gaze drops to the ground. I can see by the way she's tracing the maze of veins in the marble floor with her eyes that the sound of my husband's name hit her like an anvil to her heart. The truth hovers between us for a moment, an ominous reminder that this is more than a lovers' getaway, it's a duplicitous affair.

"I just mean, you know, he's okay with my going away because it's the one time a year all four of us are together. I don't think he would've agreed if he knew it was just us." I'm fumbling for words, and I'm making it worse. "Because we're always together," I add but I know I need to shut up. All of a sudden, the overly air-conditioned hotel bar is starting to feel like a teeny, tiny, claustrophobic sauna. *Breathe, Zin.* I slip off my kaftan and place it on the stool beside me before I put my hand on Fay's shoulder. "Fay?" I whisper. I want her to know I don't regret being here, in fact, I'm grateful for these few uninterrupted days together; it's like a gift to us before our inevitable breakup.

Adam's work is relocating us to California. Six months from now, my life in Toronto is over, which means Fay and I will come to a crashing end. She may seem all cool and collected on the outside, but she's as mushy as mashed potatoes on the inside, and if she knew I was moving, she'd fall apart. Which is only partially why I can't tell her. The other part is because I'm barely holding on myself. I don't want to go.

I take a deep breath and shake away thoughts of my future. We're here now. "You know I'm happy we're here, right?"

"Yup, sure do." Fay says curtly. She flicks a finger up to grab the bartender's attention. "Another for me. And an añejo, twist of lime, filled to the top with tonic water," she says to him while looking at me. She winks at me with feigned confidence, but I can read through her avoidant tactics. It doesn't take a master's degree in Fay to know I've hurt her feelings.

"Thanks," I whisper.

A mosquito lands on her hand. I swat it away, replacing my hand on hers. With the sweat forming in my palm, she almost manages to slide away, but I squeeze tight, and she releases into me.

The bartender sets my tequila on a napkin in front of me and tops Fay up. In perfect synch, we grab for our drinks and clink glasses. With each sip, the tension dissipates. I set my glass down and lean into Fay. She responds by slipping her fingers up my temple and brushing a curl behind my ear.

"I know he exists." She lets out a breath and her lips curl upward. "But for now," she tilts her head like she's asking a question, "it's just us."

"Just us," I confirm, palms sweating way more than they should. We've done this before. We've done this and then some. I need to quell these California nerves or I'll ruin our weekend.

Cupping my face, Fay gently lays her lips on mine, softly parting them with her tongue. The slow release of her apricot vanilla perfume is intoxicating.

Melting ever so slightly into her, my shoulders relax. That's the power Fay has over me; she can dispel my nervous energy with the lightest touch. It's these moments, these micro-moments, that exemplify how viscerally connected we are.

I press my lips to hers, matching her rhythm.

"I didn't mean to bring him up like that," I start as I gently pull away. "I'm sorry."

"Can we not talk about it?" She takes my hand in hers and closes the little distance I've created, bringing her face to mine again. She kisses my lips. "We can talk back home." She kisses me again. "But here, we can just be together, right?" Kiss. "At dinner, later. Lounging by the pool tomorrow." Kiss. "Spa on Saturday." Kiss. "Paddleboarding on Sunday." Kiss, kiss. "No picking kids up from school, no ballet class, no homework, and certainly no Adam or friends to hide from . . ." Kiss. "Just us." Fay's hand slides down to my gold chain necklace. Hovering over my collarbone, she caresses my skin all the way to my shoulder, sliding the spaghetti strap ever so slightly so that it threatens to fall onto my arm.

I'm so acutely aware of my skin, an electric current feels like it's coursing through my blood with every stroke of her hand. Her fingertips glide down my arm, and when she reaches my hand, she laces her fingers through mine. Holy hell, this feels so, so consuming. I lick my lips and with my free hand I pull Fay in by the neck.

I'm sure everyone in this bar is watching us right now, but I give into the moment. My mouth slightly open, I press my lips against hers and feel her hot tongue push against mine.

Adam would never be caught engaged in PDA, even in the anonymity of an island resort. He'd say "get a room," which is exactly what I'm thinking right now as each kiss draws me closer to Fay.

I shake the image of Adam away, letting any guilt I'm holding onto fall to the wayside, nerves slowly slipping away.

Weaving my fingers through her thick brown hair as our mouths open and close, my attention moves to Fay's other hand, which is slowly finding its way beneath my dress and up my inner thigh.

Just then, my phone lights up on the bar between us, vibrating to the tune of "Pretty Woman." Valentina's face flashes on the screen.

"Oh! This is them!" I push Fay away harder than intended. She adjusts the collar on her jean jacket and frowns, unimpressed by the interruption. "Come on, be a little happy that our best friend just got engaged!" I nudge as I hold up my phone and swipe to answer. "Congratula—" I scream but stop short when I see Val's eyes are puffy with tears. "Why are you crying?"

"We broke up." Valentina whispers between sobs. I'm suddenly very aware of how loud the music is in the bar. I can hardly hear her. Shaking her head, she continues, "No estoy buena, chicas. It was horrible." She wipes her tears away, sweeping her hand methodically under each eye to remove the running green liner.

I watch as her fingers move back and forth, matching the movement of Fay's hand that has found its way back to my leg and is now stroking my inner thigh. I squeeze my legs together in an attempt to have Fay park it for a minute so I can focus.

"But the good news is," Val continues. I bring the screen closer to my face so I can hear her better. "I'm coming now!" She turns the camera to show me a half-packed suitcase sitting open on her bed. "I'm making Kiara come too. First flight tomorrow morning." Fay pulls her hand from my leg and lets it dangle like a wet rag between us. Val goes on, unaware of Fay's off-camera disappointment. "I can't bear to sit here alone all weekend. And—" she pauses for dramatic effect "—now the two of you won't be bored out there without us!"

I feign the biggest smile I can to mirror the one now plastered on Val's face. "We're so excited!" I turn the screen to Fay so she can chime in, but the expression on her face is closer to a kid who just found out her birthday party got cancelled. I kick her leg under the counter.

"Yeah, we're excited," she mumbles. "Well, not that you broke up. That you're coming."

Valentina hardly notices Fay's less-than-stellar performance and goes on, "I'll tell you every sordid detail when we get there. Love you both!" She blows a kiss and ends the call.

"Wow," I mouth as I put my phone face down on the bar. "What do you think happened?" I'm already conjuring up theories on what could've possibly gone wrong. Could it be that the rock wasn't big enough? No. Val wouldn't care about the size of the diamond. The shape, maybe, but not the size. Perhaps she finally realized marriage is a black hole that sucks you in only to spit out a half-formed self that, despite any attempt to claw your way back to full shape, the real you is gone forever . . . wait, that's me.

"I know Val's never been one for white-dress weddings, or whatever, but she loves Jack." I can't wrap my brain around what might have happened. Val and Jack have been together forever; there was no scenario in my mind where she'd say no. When Kiara told me Jack was proposing, I immediately started mentally preparing for all the festivities that would forcibly take me back to Montreal. Engagement party, bridal shower, bachelorette, wedding. "Something else is going on here for sure. Hello? Earth to Fay?" I wave a hand in front of her face, but she's glazed over, downtrodden, already projecting how our blissful getaway has been downgraded into stolen kisses, hidden glances, sneaking around like we have been for the last six months.

"Wanna call it a night?" She downs her wine, slams the glass on the bar, and swivels off her stool. "I don't feel like dinner anymore."

"Please don't be like that." I pull her back by the wrist.

"Like what?" She shrugs, defeated. The expression on her face is equal parts disgruntled and forlorn. It hurts to watch the hope flicker and fade so palpably.

"It's fine, let's just go to the room." She brushes the whole thing away. For someone who runs from her feelings, she sure does wear them on her sleeve.

"Is that an invitation?" I raise my brow in an attempt to change the mood but she doesn't take the bait.

"You know I love Val, but I just don't want to pass my whole night conjecturing her love life." She takes in a big inhale. I watch as her chest puffs out and deflates.

"Spend," I say, caressing the nape of her neck.

"What?" She looks at me, shaking her head ever so slightly.

"*Spend* your whole night." I grin. "Not *pass*."

"Are you correcting my English?" She cracks a smile.

Fay and I left Montreal at the same age, but unlike me, Fay grew up speaking French and every once in a while, she says things like *take* a decision instead of *make* a decision. It's one of the many things I love about her, and it solidifies exactly who she is: perfectly imperfect.

"You know I think you're the cutest when you speak *franglais*." I lean in and kiss her softly. "Now about that invitation," I say as I pull away. "Is it still open?"

Fay lets out a chuckle and reaches into her back pocket. She pulls out our room key and holds it up between us. "Always."

Valentina

MONTREAL

"I NEED YOU RIGHT NOW," I SCREAM TO KIARA FROM ACROSS THE room, phone propped up against my jewellery box as I scramble to find my summer clothes in the depths of this dumping ground I once dared call a bedroom. Packing at the same time as convincing my best friend that she has no excuse big enough in the world right now to not be here for me in my time of need feels like a waste of scattered energy. But that's Kiara lately. Checked out and oblivious.

"Can you stop running around the room for a second? I can hardly hear you," she barks at me.

On her command, I throw a fistful of mismatched bikinis into my suitcase and walk over to my dresser. "There," I say as I remove her from speaker. "Better?" Balancing the phone between my ear and shoulder, I wrap my computer charger cord around my fingers then place it in my oversized Louis Neverfull. "I just flipped my whole life upside down. Do you even get that?"

"Yeah, got it. And I'm here for you. But also," Kiara's voice is raspier than usual, "I can't uncancel my trip. Plus, I wasn't kidding when I said I'm not feeling great."

Bleh. She's gonna leave me out to pasture with Fay and Zin, Zin and Fay. It's like Tweedledee and Tweedledum with those two. It's annoying being around people whose inside jokes have inside jokes.

Way less annoying when Kiara's there. Then it's okay, because our schtick has schtick and all's right with the world. Balance restored.

Our group has always been two equal best friendships that come together in a foursome that I think would be best captured by an eight-part HBO series, but I'm biased. Either way, a weekend away alone with the two of them is not my idea of a soft, cushiony fall after my major breakup blow. I need my person.

"Please, Kiara . . ." I'm not above begging at this moment in time. "How sick is sick?" I ask, but before she can answer, I add, "I haven't told you the whole story." I draw out *whole* to spark intrigue. "I sort of did something stupid."

"What did you do?" she howls. I can imagine her eyes bulging out like a cartoon character's.

"I need you to tell me I didn't completely ruin my life." I stop rummaging through my bag and pause. I flash back to a couple of hours ago, sitting across from Jack at our favourite restaurant, L'Express. Under false pretenses, of course. I thought he was taking me for dinner to honour my last day at work. But no. Instead, he marked the occasion with a proposal, and I was left with only one option: to lie.

"Hello? Can you focus?" Kiara's voice jolts me back to my bedroom. "What did you do?" She clears her throat. "Actually, start at the beginning."

I stop to scan my room for everything I have to remember while trying to balance my phone on my shoulder: jean shorts, cover-up, Tom Ford sunnies—both pairs—espadrilles, and my overpriced Le Prunier Plumscreen. I can't put a price on protecting my Casper-white skin. If I don't douse myself in hundred-dollar fifty SPF, I risk looking like a tomato on fire. On our girls trip to Peru a couple years ago, between the altitude at Machu Picchu and the scorching sun, my Canadian blood proved to be stronger than my Venezuelan blood, and I had a bucket of burnt skin that peeled off to prove it. "Let's just talk about it when I get to Fort Lauderdale. I checked, and there's still room on our flight."

"Girl, I'm seriously sick." She coughs performatively and then adds, "Also, Wren took the day off work to hang with me tomorrow. I can't just ditch him."

"But you can ditch me?!" I shriek.

"Would you stop that?" Kiara says. She lowers her voice to a whisper. "I am not ditching you."

"Fine, sorry." I roll my eyes. "Gucci slides or Birks?" I hover over both pairs in deep contemplation.

"Neither," she says without hesitation. Her aversion for brand names coming through loud and clear with her fake gags.

"Great: both." I throw the sandals at my luggage. "Please just say you'll come!"

"You don't sound super upset, Val. What's going on? All you've ever talked about was how much you love Jack." Her voice is firm and high-pitched all at once. "So this, like, mini I'm-turning-thirty crisis or whatever needs to chill. Unless this is about Valentina's, in which case, don't punish Jack just because you're having second thoughts about taking over your dad's fashion empire." She stretches out *empire*, and I know she's teasingly shoving my privilege in my face. "Either way, it's time to grow up, Peter Pan. Put on your big-girl panties, call Jack back, and plead temporary insanity, see if he'll take you back."

This is Kiara's way of showing love. She beats it into you. Even though her callous tone has kick-started my anxiety, I have to remind myself that she's not yelling at me, it's just her hot Israeli temper that rears its head whenever she feels super passionate about something. Regardless of the topic—it could be politics or overpriced eggs—when her voice gets firm, there's no angling. In college, she was so finicky about leaving our apartment lights on—wasting electricity and all—that one time, when I'd forgotten to turn them off as we left to go out dancing, she actually made me foot the entire month's rent. Or when I left the fridge door open too long: "Sure, let it beep and beep until the milk sours and cows everywhere just keel over into submission." I've learned not to get in her way when she's on these rants.

I thought age would temper her, but it turns out Wren was the antidote. Unfortunately, it's not because he's the perfect sweet to her spicy, but rather it's his manipulative tactics that have weakened her. At least, that's what I think. That's probably the real reason she's resisting the trip. Kiara walks on eggshells around her fiancé. Last Christmas, they were at my parents' for dinner, and I witnessed him shush her. Like, for real, his-finger-to-her-mouth shush her. I tried to intervene, but she laughed and played along, making it seem like it was some bit they do. I would do anything to break those two up, and if coming on this trip pisses him off, then consider me giddy with hope that with a swift one-two punch, Kiara could be rid of that asshole *and* I could have my best friend, not just for the weekend, but maybe back in Montreal for good.

"First, it's not second thoughts, but we'll get to that later. Second, it's not if I want Jack or if I don't want Jack," I start. "And, yeah, maybe it's a whatever-life crisis, but trust me, after what I told him, he won't take me back." I pause. "Ever."

"What'd you tell him?" Kiara's tone darkens like she's accusing me of murder.

"Is that judgment I hear?" I gasp jokingly, but Kiara is unresponsive.

"I'm coming!" she yells away from the phone, to Wren, I assume. "Gimme a sec, Wren is looking for the Advil."

Oh, is he sick too? I wanna say, but I hold back. The last thing I want to do is push her in the wrong direction by being passive aggressive.

I hit speaker and put the phone down to unzip my skinny jeans and peel them off, tossing them at my laundry basket. I miss, and they land in a pile of dirty clothes. The growing mess confronts me like a blaring metaphor for my life.

I cross the room gathering T-shirts, pajamas, jeans, and whatever else I find along the way, and then dump it all in the laundry basket, bumping into my dresser as I trip over a perfume cap, sending the photo of Jack and me lying on the grassy lower field of McGill floating to the floor.

A photo that captures a time I hold so close to my heart. Back in the day when it was sleepless nights at the library and all-nighters on

Saint-Laurent. The afternoon we took this picture, I was lying out on a blanket, scribbling in a journal, building some metaphor about the denim in *The Sisterhood of the Traveling Pants*, and listening to Jack on his guitar. I remember he played a song I had never heard; *I wrote this one for you*, he'd said. It was about sparks at first sight and how ours was the forever kind of love.

It's barely been a few hours since he dropped me off at our apartment, and I already feel his absence. Who will do Supermarket Sweep with me on the weekends to make grocery shopping less boring? Or eat Milano cookies while hiking, because walking is boring without snacks? Or leave me fridge notes before work—an ode to William Carlos Williams—confessions about gone fruit and other innuendos? I knew when I said no that he'd be gone, but I didn't think it would be this jarring.

A gnawing feeling like a tangled sailor's knot pulls at my stomach. He's my first boyfriend, he's all I've ever known, and I just blew it all up. I can't explain why because I don't think even I fully know yet. When he was on bended knee, I panicked. I saw my whole predictable life staring up at me, and I couldn't find a yes inside me from my existential crisis.

"Hello?" Kiara is back. "Val?"

"Sorry!" I race over to the phone. "So, you coming?" I ask, forcing a little pep into my voice. She's silent, and I know she's had enough of my little song and dance. "Okay, okay. You're not wrong, maybe I am punishing Jack because I have to take over my dad's business. I feel like my life is over." I laugh nervously.

"So, this is about your job?" The recrimination in her voice is palpable.

I try on her accusation for size: it took me years to build my reputation at Jazz. Tagline after tagline, I climbed my way from junior copywriter to head of copywriting in under five years, and if I had been able to stick around, my boss said she saw me moving to the strategy department and working my way to director by year's end. But it was an exercise in futility. Of Sisyphean proportion. Because I don't map my course—I never have. I always knew there was an expiration date to Jazz, and today marked my last day. Plucked from my chosen field of marketing and thrown into the business of fashion. Not that I don't love fashion but, I like writing about it, not selling it. More importantly, I don't want to be Eduardo's daughter-cum-CEO and Jack's wife-to-be all by Monday morning. Is that so wrong?

"I just started to feel suffocated, you know?"

With Kiara's heavy silence on the other end of the line, I take one last good look at the photo before I shove it into the back of my sock drawer.

"Spare me the poor little rich girl sob story." Kiara snickers, punctuating each word with a fake cry. "Come to me when your dad *takes* all of your savings rather than hands them to you on a gold platter." I hate it when she does this. She puts our struggles on a hierarchy and then it's like there's nothing I can say. Like she hasn't witnessed first-hand what my so-called privileged life looks like on the inside—its pressures, its constraints. But I take it, because trying to convince her that having an inheritance doesn't equate to happiness is a losing battle. I'd know, after two decades' worth of trying.

Plus, I've also witnessed *her* struggles first-hand and can see how her opinions on my privileged life feel like fact to her.

"Yes, yes, blah, blah, I know."

"People would kill for your good fortune," she adds. "You know that, right?"

"Are you coming or not?" I ask as I plop down on my bed. "I'll show you what Jack's face looked like when I squashed his dreams. It'll be seared into my memory forever." I contort my face, dropping my jaw to the floor in exaggerated shock, then I realize she can't see me. "It was like the dentist told him to open wide while staring directly into a solar eclipse."

"That bad, huh?" Kiara bursts into laughter. "You're evil."

Only with humour do I know that I can get through to her. It's our love language.

"You get me," I sigh, placing my hand on my heart. "This is why I need you. Please come. Just tell Wren that if you don't come to us, then we'll come to you. That should scare him straight," I laugh. "Oh! Or tell him it's a last-minute bachelorette. He can't say no to that!"

"I'll try, but this better not be some lame attempt to not plan me a real bachelorette," Kiara responds. "Because I want the full nine yards."

If I know Kiara, she's caving.

I roll out of bed at 3 a.m. before my alarm has the chance to accost me. I have about three hours until my flight. Which means a little under seven hours until I meet Kiara at Fort Lauderdale airport—and not too much longer before we're lying on the sandy beach in the Bahamas.

My eyelids are stuck together with sticky unfinished dreams. A sleepless night of tossing and turning in the vast emptiness of my king-size bed. Actually, tossing is an understatement. It was more like flailing around in an epic battle with my duvet—and to be clear, I lost.

I reach for my phone and click into my packing list to make sure I have everything I need. Passport, check. Four undies, check. Three bikinis, check. Sunglasses times two, check. Oh! Meds. Can't forget those. It would suck if I made a last-minute decision to escape my impending new reality and shack up in the Bahamas for a couple months only to have to return because I forgot my meds. I can see the headline now: "Heartbroken Woman's Escape Plan Foiled by Panic Attack!"

Before I head downstairs, I click into my group chat with the girls. Kiara has taken it upon herself to change the chat name every time something notable happens in one of our lives. A couple weeks ago, Zin posted a pic of her most recent speeding ticket in our thread. She had been caught going sixty in a thirty zone. Kiara hit her with a barrage of options, including *Soccer Mom by Day, Speed Racer by Night*. She settled on *The Fast and the Furious: Minivan Mayhem*. Now it is aptly entitled *Dirty Thirty* to honour that we are all turning the big three-oh this year.

On my way to the airport, I text. See you soon. I add an airplane emoji, followed by a kissy face and two hearts. My millennial-use of emojis should give everyone a good laugh when they wake up.

My phone chimes. Zin hearts my message. Then Fay adds a slew of random emojis that mean absolutely nothing. I guess they're still up. I send another smiley face followed by a cocktail emoji, because why not.

Nothing from Kiara.

She better be sleeping and not bailing.

Estoy abajo, my dad texts. I can't keep him waiting, so I pop an extra blister pack into my bag (you never know) and scan my apartment once more to make sure I haven't forgotten anything. Locking the door behind me, I toss my phone into my bag and head down the stairs; the sound of my luggage banging against each step echoes loudly through the empty hallway.

Stepping out into the bitter Montreal cold, I mentally add *escaping winter* to my list of reasons why this trip matters so much.

"Where's Mom?" I ask as I get into my dad's car. "I thought she was coming?"

"She wanted to, but she stayed up late catching up on her telenovelas, so I let her sleep." He tilts his head. "Ximena was about to find out who killed Jorge. It was juicy stuff."

I raise my eyebrow and whisper, "So she saw that it was Diana who killed him?"

"¡Ay, por Dios!" My dad bangs the steering wheel and shoots me a look.

I make an *O* with my mouth and cover it guiltily. "Sorry, sorry!"

"I'm kidding. I knew already, but shh, don't tell Mamá." He winks, and we both giggle.

I put my phone down and bongo the dashboard. "*¡Vámonos!*"

My dad turns on the music and fills the car with the Gipsy Kings. Sweet sounds that transport me to my childhood, memories of my mom swaying as she chops veggies, Papá staring at her from across the room with passion and an unwavering love that feels impossible. They've kept the romance alive for nearly forty years of marriage, and their love burns hotter and brighter with each passing day. My dad's words, not mine.

"Oye, amor. I'm happy you decided to join your friends." My dad looks over at me with wistful eyes as he nudges my feet off the dashboard. Last time I left stains on his dash, I heard about it through spring.

I exhale and smile. "Sí, Papá. I am too. I need this. A fun weekend with my girls is just what the doctor ordered. I don't want to think about anything else right now. Just drink, laugh, and laugh some more." I look at him for confirmation. "Sí?"

"You deserve it." My dad sighs. "It's been a year since the four of you have been all together? The last trip, right?"

I nod. We all used to get together a lot more before fiancés (Kiara), kids (Zinnia), and jobs (three out of four of us). Our busy lives have gotten the best of us, and things aren't quite like they used to be. Thank goodness I had the foresight to put this annual trip in our friendship contract way back before we all parted ways for university, before getting the four of us in one place at the same time was harder than doing neurosurgery in the dark. Last year, I tried to instate a weekly FaceTime, mandatory as per my guidelines, but week after week, only Fay showed up, and that was just to let me know that she couldn't stay on. At least we have our group text, or we'd have become strangers by now.

The mere thought sends a shudder down my spine.

The sound of my dad's voice brings me back to the car. ". . . and then, when you come back, you'll be la reina de Valentina." He taps my knee, smiling from ear to ear. He looks at me with stars in his eyes, staring at me long enough that he swerves into the lane over. "Oops!" He straightens out. "Now, let the music wash over you and the waves move through you, mi'ja." He pulls my face toward him so he can kiss my forehead as we pull up to a red light. "You will be okay, just remember that. Jack will come back to you. He just needs time." There it is. I was wondering why he was taking this breakup so well; he thinks it's temporary. He smiles and pinches my cheeks.

"Sí, Papá, time. And maybe I need to *want* him to come back to me, right?" I add defensively. He shrugs his shoulders and looks at me with furrowed brows. "It's just, can I ask you something?"

"Anything." He smiles, stretching his hand out to tap my thigh.

"Do we really have to take Mr. Filomena out of his office?" I start. "I feel weird making him move for me."

"First, it's Russell," my dad chuckles. "When you're the boss, you'll call the accountant by his first name. Second, don't worry so much about these formalities. Everyone is excited to work with you. They love Valentina's, and they love you."

No, they love Eduardo, I want to say. The man behind Valentina's, not his eponymous daughter. "I know they love me, but look what happened when Eloise started."

"Eloise is a young designer, of course our team was resistant to some of her ideas," he explains. "We've been doing this for three decades. We built this company before fashion houses were called brands." He rolls his eyes at me, and I smile complicitly. "But it's not the same with you. They will accept you with open arms. Trust me, mi vida."

That's what I am to him. I'm his life. So, who am I to contradict him? There's no world in which someone doesn't love his Valentina. If my dad could seal my future with a swirl of a wand, I'd run Valentina's for the next thirty years until Jack and my eldest child took over, and so on and so forth ad infinitum.

I smile, because what else is there to do? He drums his fingers on the steering wheel happily in time to the music. I pull out my phone and open my Notes app, scrolling past my ever-growing grocery list and clicking open the new note I added last night while I was battling my blanket. My Life Without Jack. I stare at the little black letters that fill the white screen and add one more thought: The look on his face, down on his knee, still grips my heart. Why did I panic?

Exhale. I'll find time to explore that later.

I hit the return key and go back to my list entitled blog ideas, and scroll down to *Siempre Valentina*. It's a blog I started working on a few months ago. I had this idea that it would be cool if I wrote about each of our girls trips from over the years, a sort of ode to the good, the hard, and the crazy times in our friendship. The twist is that I'd weave in fashion, because so much of who anyone is gets expressed through their clothes. I haven't told anyone other than Zinnia and Jack about it. They've both always been so supportive of my writing. Fay, on the other hand, thinks it's a waste of time to blog, to which she adds that anything short of traditionally published work is for philistines. (Her words, not mine. Or, more likely, words she inherited from her grandmother.) I'd have told Kiara, but I don't think Wren would approve; Kiara's name shall not appear anywhere without legal contracts. Douchebag. Will Kiara come, or will she bail? The eternal question to our tenth annual girls trips looms as I ponder whether I will ever see the Chloé sunhat I loaned her ever again.

"Ya estamos, mi amor." My dad breaks my thoughts as we pull up to departures.

"Thanks." I point to Air Canada. "I'm right over there."

Dad gets out of the car to help with my bag and walk me to the door. I give him a big hug, and he cups my head at both ears, leaning his forehead on mine. "Everything will work itself out. Promise me that for the next three days you will just live, laugh, and love."

"You sound like a coffee mug." I laugh, and my dad kisses my cheek. "But yeah, I will."

"Give the girls hugs for me." He kisses my other cheek. "Tell them we miss them, and Zin has to send more pictures of those kids of hers. Darla's getting so big. I want to see her in her tutu."

I push my cheek against his and linger for a few extra seconds.

"Just be with your friends. They'll make your heart feel whole." He always knows just what to say.

"*You* make my heart whole, Papá!" I say over my shoulder as I walk through the spinning door. "Tell Mom I love her! Love you to the moon!"

"To the far side, mi amor. Safe flight!" I glance back as I walk to the check-in counter, and he stands waving at me from the glass door. My dad fades from my view with each step I take, but experience tells me he won't move until I'm completely out of sight.

Aboard the plane, I close my eyes and slip into a memory of the trip that started it all: Mexico, nine years ago. We've come a long way since girls trips on a budget, but we've maintained the "no frills, all thrills" policy. Saving money the whole year to spend it all on our one blowout vacation. Every year we say we could never top the last, but I think that with the promise of Kiara's fake bachelorette, we'll set a new standard: we'll have to party harder than ever to have photo evidence that will hold up in Wren's court.

I chuckle to myself as I look out onto the runway, then I reach for my phone to text Kiara again before airplane mode is enforced. She still hasn't replied to my group message, and the thought of her ditching sends a stabbing pain to my gut. Last time I was alone with Fay and Zin was in Toronto in September, and I felt like I was third-wheeling the whole time. There was this weird energy, but when I addressed it, they acted like I was the weird one. I can't with any of that this weekend. Only Kiara will know how to get me out of this mess I've created.

About to take off. Meet you at the gate? Three dots blink back at me. I don't even realize I'm clenching my fist in a silent prayer until her response appears.

Not coming. Don't be pissed.

I feel the air deflate from my chest as the plane leaves the ground.

Kiara

MIAMI

THESE TRIPS JUST AREN'T AS SIMPLE AS THEY USED TO BE.

And they're certainly not worth fighting with Wren over. Three days away and a year to pay, that's what I imagine will be my fate if I tell him I've changed my mind and want to go again. He wouldn't get that my best friend in the whole world needs me right now. All he sees when I say *girls trip* is girls gone wild, dancing topless on bars or whatever he thinks we do when he's not there. His mind is stuck in spring break mode, aka South Beach, right now. It's the reason I didn't mention this impromptu bachelorette to him. That would've made him tweak twelve ways from Sunday.

Speaking of tweaking, if I were to tell Val that Wren is the real reason I'm not coming, she'd get all protective and start planning my return to Montreal. She thinks I don't notice, but I can tell Wren's not her favourite person. When we got engaged last summer, she and Jack came to visit and opted not to stay at our place, which made no sense since we have a two-bedroom condo. Val insisted that staying at the Grand Beach Hotel was about comfort above all else and that they didn't want to intrude on Wren's daughter's space, but Raven sleeps at her mother's every other week, so the truth came in loud and clear: it was about keeping her distance from Wren. What I don't know is why she won't give him a chance.

Either way, between the mountain of work that's been piling up and the money it'll cost me to rebook my trip, it's simpler for everyone if I just hang back.

"Did you tell Val you're still not going?" Wren yells from the bathroom as he flushes the toilet. He walks over to me in the kitchen and wraps his bare arms around me from behind. I nod and put my phone face down on the counter. His hot breath behind my ear sends a shiver down my spine. "You know I don't like to share you." He whips me around and kisses my lips.

"Toothpaste-y." I smile as I wipe my mouth with the back of my hand.

Wren opens his mouth wide and exhales his minty breath right into my face. "You love it." He laughs and kisses my cheek. "But seriously, I'm happy you're staying. I'll have you all to myself all weekend." He lowers himself before me, kneeling as he lifts my pajama top and licks my skin, tracing small kisses around my belly button. "Now go get ready for breakfast. I've got a fun day planned for us."

I cup his cheeks and pull him back up so we're face to face, pushing my forehead against his. His six-feet hovering only two inches taller than my five-ten. "I could cream you in ball this afternoon?" I kiss his lips. We pause there, his arms wrapped around my waist, mine around his neck, as we stare at each other for a moment. "Or we could hit up the new arcade that opened on the beach?" His tousled hair, still undone from sleep, tickles my cheek as it falls over his eyes. He shakes his head back and slicks his hand through his hair.

In one fell swoop, Wren lifts me onto the counter, squeezing himself between my legs. He leans into me, his strong jawline softening and his cheeks dimpling as he smiles. He raises his eyebrows suggestively. "You want to go out there," he nods to our window, "when we have this to ourselves for three whole days?"

"Right." I smile as I look around at our empty condo. Because Wren and his ex share custody, every other weekend is filled with homework or Little League practice. When we don't have Raven, we're too tired from having worked all week that we laze about like sloths. We rarely have enough energy to get groceries, let alone for any physical activity.

But this weekend is filled with possibilities. We both took today off, which means we have three uninterrupted days of Wren and Kiara time.

I toss my braids over my shoulder and tilt my head until they hang behind me. Wren takes his cue and begins to kiss my neck.

"I say we order in," he lifts me off the counter, "and don't leave that bed," he continues to kiss my neck as he carries me over to our room, "until Monday morning." We're halfway to our bedroom when his phone dings. As swiftly as he lifted me onto his hips, he puts me down. "Let me just tell Max to fuck off," he says as he races back to the kitchen to grab his phone.

"I'll just wait for you right here," I say, lowering my panties and looking over my shoulder with a flirtatious grin, but he's already on his phone, walking away.

"Fuck me," he mutters under his breath. "Fuck, fuck, fuck."

"What is it?" I pull up my underwear and turn back to join him in the kitchen. I perch myself back up on the counter beside him and wait until he's done responding to whatever message just came in. He's typing frantically and shaking his head angrily as his thumbs hit the screen.

I know there's no way that it's about me, yet I'm still holding my breath in hope that the anger on Wren's face won't be directed my way.

He looks up at me, still shaking his head, and tightens his lips. "Fucking Max," he says as he slams his phone back on the counter; the whooshing sound of an email sent sits heavy between us.

"So much for playing hooky," he mutters under his breath as he heads over to the kitchen table, where his papers and files are scattered about. "Duty calls." He starts shuffling them into their respective piles. He's *angranizing*—organizing while angry.

"So, no breakfast?" I ask in my softest voice, batting my lashes.

"Obviously," he snipes as he throws his hands up in the air, sending some of his documents to the floor. "Fuck! Are you kidding me?"

"Sorry," I recoil at his outburst as I hop off the counter to help him clean up. "I was just being facetious." I smile nervously.

"No," he states firmly. "Stop." He holds his hand out and waves it in my face.

"It's okay." I begin to crawl under the table to fetch some out-of-reach papers.

"Stop!" he yells, his voice louder this time. "There's an order. You're just making a mess." Before I can react, his hand grips my ankle firmly. He's under the table, stretching my leg out, dragging me toward him, away from his papers. My shoulder knocks the edge of a chair, sending it to the floor, hitting Wren in the head as it falls.

"Ow," he yells, throwing his papers down once again.

"Oh, shit! You okay, baby?" I move closer to him, placing my hand on his shoulder.

"What the hell, Kiara?" he shouts and flinches away from me.

Tears roll out of my eyes, a combination of fear and humiliation. "I'm sorry, I was just trying to help." I rub his head as the tears roll down my cheek and into my mouth.

"Why are *you* crying?" His voice cuts sharply as he pushes himself to standing. He picks up the chair and replaces it at the head of the table, then he continues to straighten out his papers.

I feel like a child who's about to be sent to her room.

"Sorry," I whisper.

"It's fine." He slides his hand through his hair. "I need to be at the office by nine, so if you wouldn't mind." He looks down at me and, although he doesn't say them, the missing words are *get out of my way*.

Our day totally got derailed, but I can't make this about me. Instead, I leave him to tidy up his papers in peace, watching as he meticulously stacks two piles, slowly placing a paper clip to bind one stack and shoving the other pile into a folder.

"Wren?" I start softly. "Do you think you'll make it to dinner tonight?"

If he heard me, he acts like he didn't.

"Should I cancel Cecconi's?" I repeat, against my better judgment.

"Max and I are gonna have to work double time to finish this case," he says as he whips around to face me. "The last thing I'm thinking about is dinner. I'll probably have to work through the weekend."

My heart thuds into my stomach. "What?" I gasp, immediately picturing myself holed up in this condo all weekend alone. I can feel my cheeks flush.

Wren shoots me a look as he stands up. "Don't even. This is work." He walks past me into our bedroom.

"Right, well then," I start as I follow him into our room. I stop in the doorway and watch as he rips around, putting himself together. He changes out of his basketball shorts and tosses them into the laundry basket from across the room. He hurries over to the closet to pull out his suit pants and a collared shirt because *you never know when a client might stop by.*

Meanwhile, I'm standing there in my PJs mourning the loss of not one, but two fun-filled weekend plans.

"You know what? If you're going to be at work, why don't I—" I step into our room slowly and inch toward the bed. "I mean, I could still meet Val in time for our flight," I continue quietly, plopping down and reaching for my laptop that's sitting open on my pillow. I had been doing work earlier this morning to send my substitute lesson plans before school starts. I open my email to my booking reference for the Bahamas, turning the screen around to show Wren. "My seat is still available." I smile.

"You mean, because I have to work, you think you'll just step out all weekend?" He walks over to me, closing my laptop as he kisses my lips. He jumps onto the bed and stretches his arm out to his nightstand for his watch, then kisses my shoulder again before he stands back up.

If Wren had it his way, I'd stay within a one-mile radius of him at all times. He likes me where he can see me, is what he says. I used to think his jealousy was romantic; now it feels overpowering.

"Well, it's silly for me to just hang around if you won't be here?" I fold my arms across my chest. Vive la résistance.

"You'd be a terrible lawyer." He laughs, and I know he means it lovingly, teasingly, but the statement also has a threatening quality to it. He slips his watch onto his wrist, clips it closed, and kisses me again.

"It's just," I start again. "Val broke up with Jack." I watch Wren's face for a reaction. He nods his head. I see his eyes moving, so I know he's thinking something. But he says nothing. I sit and wait in silence for him to respond. Did I appeal to his senses? Or did I just dig my own grave? "She needs me right now," I add quietly, my voice faltering.

"When I get back tonight, I'm gonna wanna see you."

"And what time will that be?" I ask. He shoots me a look, and I know not to press. He hates it when I mention anything about working late. *Billable hours*, he says, which is exactly what my father used to say when my mom nagged him about his work. Although, it's less nagging and more curiosity, but the nuance is lost on men completely.

Moving quietly like he's in a silent movie, he disappears into the bathroom. I cock my head to the side to watch him. He's facing the mirror as he reaches into the vanity to pull out a bottle. I hear a gentle slap—he always smacks his cheeks with aftershave—followed by the sound of running water. I can only see his back from the bed, but I know he's brushing his teeth again.

He shuts off the water and walks back into the bedroom.

The silence is heavy, like a thick wool blanket, only rather than feel comforted by its warmth, I feel suffocated by its weight.

"Are you gonna say something?" I ask, but, again, he doesn't respond.

I watch as he moves to open the cupboard and pull out his shoes. He walks over to the bed, sits beside me, and begins slowly and methodically putting them on. When he's done tying his laces, he pushes himself off the bed and heads for the door. He knocks the archway twice and whips around.

"Go," he says with a smile, and walks away. I stare at the hollow archway and watch as Wren's body reappears and fills the space again. "Or don't go," he states, still smiling. I'm so confused. "It's up to you, Kiara. You're a big girl." I watch as he puts his hands in his pockets and rocks back and forth on his heels. "All I know is that these trips are a desperate attempt to stay young and relevant, and you're above that. Think about what kind of message you're sending Raven when she finds out you're off on some singles trip." He opens his eyes wide and gives a judgmental nod.

I thought he'd pull out wet T-shirt contests, but he played the Raven card. Well done, Wren. He certainly knows what to say to make me doubt my intentions.

Gathering my thoughts, I stare blankly at him and clock his cunning remark as a sly attack, one that flies under the radar. It's his tone more than anything else, something that can't be explained, only experienced. It's why I lose every fight we have, because whenever I try to explain that he hurt my feelings, he twists the script and calls me overly emotional or dramatic.

It's double standards, that's what it is, and I refuse to sit around all weekend while everyone is off busy having a life, and I'm what? Bingeing Netflix and takeout alone? No way.

"You know what," I push myself up to stand. "I think I will go."

"You wanna go so bad, then by all means, don't let me stop you." I follow Wren as he walks calmly to the front door and swings it open. He motions exaggeratedly, showing me the exit.

"I do. I wanna go." I lower my eyes to hide my tears.

"No need for the dramatics," he says as he presses his hands to my head and brings me close for a kiss. "If it means this much to you, I won't stop you." He slaps my butt and closes the door.

"Really?" I tread lightly, tempering my reaction so he doesn't retract the offer. Meanwhile, I'm doing mental somersaults at everything I'd need to pack to make the flight on time.

Wren walks back to the kitchen and shuffles the two piles of papers into his briefcase. I stand by the door and watch as he heads over to the fridge and takes out an apple. He tosses it in the air, catches it, and moves back toward me.

"Okay, well if I go," I stutter, "I'd be back Sunday night." I smile as I lean into him for a kiss.

"Just let me know whatever you decide to do," he says, his lips barely grazing mine as he walks out the front door.

"I will." I wave. "Love you."

He throws his hand up in the air and doesn't look back.

After I check in, I beeline through security. Fort Lauderdale airport is tiny, so it takes all of thirty seconds for me to find Val's arrival time so I can surprise her at the gate. I catch a glimpse of her from afar; she's sitting all scrunched up by the check-in desk, playing on her phone.

"Are you kidding me with this? I'm meant to believe that you just got dumped? I wouldn't look like this if I had Erika Jayne's glam squad on me twenty-four-seven!" I pull my elastic out of my hair and let my braids fall to my waist as I hover over her.

"Kiara! You came!" Val lowers her phone and shoots up out of her seat, beaming with happiness through her perfect teeth and dimpled cheeks. "And Erika Jayne? Really?" She opens her arms wide, hands flexed, ready to envelop me in a hug. She grabs me tightly and holds on longer than normal. I breathe her in, letting my shoulders relax in her arms. All the tension I was holding onto dissipates. I take in the familiar scent of her Paco Rabanne perfume. Same Valentina.

"Man, did I miss you," I say as we pull apart.

"No, me more." She smiles and pulls me in for another hug. "You have no idea what this means to me."

I give her the up and down: grey New Balance running shoes, grey Aritzia leggings with matching grey oversized sweatshirt, perfect long chocolate brown hair with a trendy puffy little grey headband and yesterday's beach waves because, well, Val is just that kind of girl. Halfway between that effortlessly athletic *it* girl and Blair Waldorf on the steps of the Met. Polar opposite of what I look like. Awkwardly tall, pear bottom, and breasts to feed a full daycare. If I had her outfit on, I'd look like I'd been working a yard sale in the hot sun, pit stains and all.

Where Val had this picture-perfect family, I had a dysfunctional one. Shitty dad, nightshift-working mom. While she got straight As in all her classes, I struggled just to pass my modified math program. She was class president; I was her campaign manager.

I always felt like polyester to her cashmere, but that was my own schtick. Val never made me feel like anything less than one-hundred-percent merino wool. By university, all of her accomplishments—

editor-in-chief at the McGill *Tribune*, class valedictorian—were no longer a measure of my failures but rather a testament to our mutual support for one another. We dormed together, worked at the campus bookshop together, and by the grit of my teeth, I graduated top of my class right next to her. I even got the first job I applied for: Plum's Elementary. My own homeroom and everything.

"How come you came?" Val asks, motioning for me to sit in the empty seat next to her. "I mean, I'm all for an airport surprise, but you could've texted. You feeling better?" We both know my illness was a lie, but I appreciate her playing along.

"With this cold going around, I didn't think it would be wise to come, but in the end, Wren insisted I come." Except I still haven't told him I left. He'll only know I decided to go when he gets home tonight and sees the note I left him. Hopefully he'll be too tired to be mad, and I'll be too far away to turn back. Win-win. Sort of.

"You know, you don't have to convince me that he's nice," Val offers, a softness in her eyes. "You love him—that's all that matters."

"Right, well, I do." I shake out my shoulders, attempting to release the crick in my neck that has returned. "You know I met him right here at this gate two years ago?" I point to the ticket counter.

Val nods. "Didn't you tell me he was yelling at a lady in a fit of rage?" She raises an eyebrow.

"Yeah," I reply defensively. "But only because Raven forgot her doll on the plane, and they wouldn't let him back on to grab it." That's probably the quality I love most about Wren; he's an incredible father. He would do anything for Raven, which I think says a lot about his character. He reminds me of Eduardo in that way. So present, doting over his little girl like she's the best thing since sliced bread. Raven looks at Wren the way Val looks at Eduardo, like her dad is a hero. Meanwhile, all I ever did was exist, and that was enough to upset my father. Too fat, too dumb, too slow, too much like my mother. I was a combination of not enough and way too much, and he let me know it every chance he got. When he walked out on us, he made sure to leave no room for doubt—he left because of me.

"Ahh," Val sighs like she's hearing the story for the first time. Folding her arms across her chest, she continues, "So it's okay to chew someone out if it's in the name of a lost Cabbage Patch Kid?"

"American Girl Doll," I start, but my phone begins to buzz in my back pocket, and my mind immediately goes to Wren. I should text him. Let him know my flight number. He won't be mad; he insisted I go.

"Yo." Val waves a hand in front of my face. "I said, should we grab a coffee? I barely slept, and connections are the worst." Val laughs as she rubs her eyes, her waterproof mascara not smudging even a bit. "I might need an IV!"

"Sure," I say as I check my phone. Six missed calls, thirteen text messages. I brace myself for what's to come as I slide open the screen.

you actually left?

I came home to pick up a paper and saw your note

hello?

you kidding me?

what the hell, kiki

answer me

I look up to see if Val can read my messages, but she's rummaging through her bag. "You know what, actually, I'll meet you back here. I just need to call Wren. Will you grab me a chai latte?" I turn to head for the bathroom. "Oh, and do oat milk, please."

"How very basic of you." Val laughs and rolls her eyes.

"You know how I do." I purse my lips, smirk, and strut off.

She pulls out her wallet and adds, "It's on me." Then, she blows me a kiss and heads toward the nearest Starbucks.

I go to the bathroom to splash some water on my face. The cold water hits my skin, but the shock doesn't stop the tears from falling. I dry my cheeks with industrial paper towel and check my phone again, scrolling through the rest of his messages.

oh so you think you can just leave and not answer

all right.

that's how you wanna play it

no problem

have fun but don't think you're coming back home

Val won't be the only single one

peace

we're done

I feel like the walls are closing in on me.

Staring at my phone, I watch the three little dots blink threateningly. I know he'll keep going until I answer him. Paralyzed, I start typing but delete. Nothing I say will cool him off right now. My chest caves in and puffs out as my breathing becomes more and more audible. I squeeze my eyes shut, relax my shoulders, and reply: sorry I left. I really am. I'll miss you. Val really needs me. She says thank you for sharing me with her. I want to add a piece about how he said I should go, or how it's a good thing for Raven to see strong female friendships, but I know it'll only make things worse if I try to build a case around my departure.

I slip my phone into my back pocket. I look at my reflection in the mirror. *You got this, Kiara.*

I clip my braids up into a half ponytail and walk over to the Hudson News & Gifts. A table of bestsellers sits at the centre of the shop, a colourful array of book covers beaming up at me. My eye lands on one in particular: it's got a giant exhaust pipe on the cover with oversized words superimposed across it. *Gaslighting: Is It Me or You?*

I pick it up and leaf through the first few pages. "When in a dynamic where gaslighting is present, one partner might constantly feel the need to manage the other's emotional outbursts. It's important in those events to explore your emotions and not let them fall to the wayside as a way to keep the peace." The words jump off the page at me. Is this what's happening with Wren and me? I read on: "Remember, gaslighting is a form of abuse and manipulation, and so although these coping mechanisms may temporarily diffuse the behaviour, they will not address the underlying issue. In fact, they may work to reinforce the power dynamic, leaving the victim to—"

I slam the book shut. I'm no victim.

Wren isn't abusive. He's not gaslighting me. If anyone has to manage anyone's emotions, it's him. I'm the sensitive one.

I push out three quick breaths and let new energy flow through me. He's just mad because he has to work all weekend. That's all. Plus, he's all bark, no bite. I set the book down and back away from the table, moving closer to the magazine stand. Maybe something trashy to read poolside will lift my mood. A beautiful, or shall I say blushing, bride stares at me from the cover of a bridal magazine. I pull it off the shelf and flip through pages upon pages of happy, smiling brides, summery floral arrangements, and not-horrible-looking bridesmaid dresses.

I feel calmer already.

I walk back to our gate and find Val sitting by the window, playing on her phone, her legs up on her luggage.

"What took you so long?" she asks, putting her phone on her lap.

"Magazines," I say, holding up *Brides* and *Martha Stewart Weddings*. At twelve dollars a pop, I splurged on aspirational weddings I know I can never afford, but a girl can dream. I sit down next to her. "Where's my basic drink?"

"Right next to your basic bag." She points to a small table next to my cotton tote with *World's Greatest Teacher* written across the front, a red apple right under it. "Cute bag. Your students really love you." She smiles.

"How d'you know I didn't buy it for myself?" I wink.

"Imagine?! You wouldn't." We laugh. "Or would you?" She rests her hand on my knee. "I missed you. I could do without the blushing brides staring up at me though." She taps the cover of my magazine.

"Oh shit, sorry." I chuckle. "Amnesia moment."

"No!" She smiles, shaking her head. "Just because *I'm* not getting married doesn't mean I don't wanna hear about your wedding. How's planning going?"

"Fantastic." I smile nervously as I tap my fingers on the cover of *Bride*. "Wren is so involved; you'd think this was his first marriage."

Val smiles, waiting for me to go on, but I let out a heavy breath. The truth is, other than nail down a date, we haven't done much else. I swiftly change the subject. "Tell me what happened with Jack, please. I'll assess if it's reversible. What went wrong?"

Val takes the bait and leans closer to me. "Truth?"

"I'd see through your lies anyway," I say as I pull my right foot onto the chair and hug my leg to my chest.

"Well, Jack didn't." She takes a sip of her coffee and looks up at me from her cup like she's just laid out a clue in life's biggest mystery.

"What's that supposed to mean?"

"It just means that I lied and I regret it. But also, I'm mad at him." She stares at me, waiting for me to prompt her to go on. I take my cue and nod.

"Why?" I ask.

"Well, firstly, because I love him, and if he hadn't proposed, we'd still be together." She stares at me still.

I nod again.

"But also, he *did* propose, which means he wants to move into the next phase of life, and I really don't." She takes a sip, but I can see her chin quivering from behind her coffee cup. "We're in different places. It doesn't matter that he's perfect. He, or *we*, got complacent. I don't know, it all just got so routine. Why get married when we already act like an old married couple? Is it so wrong that I want something that makes my stomach jump or my heart sparkle?"

I'm staring at her, waiting for more to the story. So far, I still can't wrap my head around why she said no. "Well, first of all, heart sparkling is not a thing." I put my hand on her shoulder and wink. "And, no, it's not wrong, but . . ." I pause and take a deep breath, gearing up for what I'm about to say next. I know it's going to ruffle her feathers. "You tend to sabotage the good things in your life, and Jack is a good thing, Val. So, can you just spill already? What lie did you tell him?"

"Can I just tell you how he proposed? It was so—*so*—impersonal, like he read a how-to guide. It could've been for anyone. Fancy dinner, champagne, ring in ice cream, down on one knee." I'm rolling my hands to signal for her to move on with her long-winded story and get to the point, mostly because I know this part already. Jack and I planned it together. In fact, I suggested it based off the fact that there isn't a rom-com Val doesn't love, and so why not trope out with the whole ring-in-the-dessert proposal? Although, from the way she's telling the story, I was way off base. "So, he's looking up at me, and in that moment, I saw my whole life flash before my eyes. I panicked. Instead of saying no, I blurted out—*I cheated*."

"You what?! When? With who?" Her confession jolts me back to the conversation. Val cheated? How is this the first time I'm hearing about this?

"That's the thing . . ." She looks down into her half-empty cup and slides a finger around the rim to catch the foam. She licks her finger and starts again. "Kiara, I didn't cheat." She shakes her head. "Who would I even cheat with? Jack is the one and only person I've ever been with." She holds up one finger for emphasis. "You know that."

"But then why lie?" I've known Jack as long as Val has. He's not just one of the good ones; he's the poster child for golden boys the world over. She'd be hard-pressed to find anyone who would treat her better than Jack does. I'd know. I twirl the ring dangling from my necklace. The one Wren refuses to resize. He insists that if he makes it bigger, it'll lose the original design. He also insists that if I lose a few pounds, it'll slip right on. I let it go and it hits my chest. "He must've been so crushed."

"He was. And I felt horrible when I heard the words tumble out of my mouth; I instantly regretted it. But also, once I said them, I felt free. Is that a sign?" I wonder what my get-out-of-jail-free card would be with Wren? I shake the thought out of my mind. Val finds my eye and locks my gaze. "I just saw myself five years from now flirting with the grocery bagger just to feel a buzz, wondering if my husband really chose me or if I was just the logical next step."

I want to feel bad for her, but she's making that face, the one reserved for making me feel like I didn't *take* the last piece of lasagna, someone just *gave* it to me. She is completely unaware that her face tells the story of how entitled she is: *Look at me. I'm perfect and don't have to work for it.* But to be fair, she's unaware of how beautiful she is, and she really doesn't care. Still, sitting here, her expression doe-eyed and blissfully innocent, stirs in me a bitterness; she's eliciting empathy when in reality she knows she not only deeply hurt Jack but is making an issue where no issue needs to be.

"You're horrible," I state. "I've never been one to say anything other than the hard-pressed truth, and that truth is, you'll never do better than Jack."

"I know, I'm horrible," she drawls, then pauses. "I needed to hear that from you." She bobs her head up and down and then continues, "And also, I need one thing from you." She scrunches up her nose.

"What?" I tilt my head.

"I need you not to tell anyone," she starts, then she waves the idea away. "I mean, the girls know I said no, but they need to think I cheated. In case they speak to Jack. I need him to think it's true. At least until I figure out if this is a sparkle, timing, or Jack thing."

I nod yes, but inside, I'm so confused why Val did this to him. She could've simply said she needed time to think, or even just flat-out said no, but to lie? To make him think she cheated on him? That sort of thing can really screw with a person's sense of trust, make him question their whole relationship. Hell, even *I* am questioning Val right now. No good can come of this. I can feel it in my bones. And from the tears rolling down Val's cheeks, I can tell she feels it too.

"Can we talk about something else?" She wipes her eyes, erasing any proof that she's even mildly sad about the breakup. "Like our tenth annual trip." She raises her coffee cup. "That's a milestone we should celebrate."

"Okay, but we don't need to pretend our real lives don't exist in order to have fun." I place my hand on her knee. "And we can't pretend we're having fun to avoid our problems." I hear the words coming out of my mouth, and they feel sticky, tangled in my own web of lies. But there's just no version of this trip where I bring up my Wren-doubts for everyone to paw at.

"Deep," Val says with a laugh, my hypocrisy flying over her head. She nods to my buzzing phone, the *Kill Bill* theme song drumming in the background.

"It's Wren," I say as I reach into my back pocket to click the side button, sending him to voicemail. "I'll call him back after."

"Okay." She shrugs. If she has theories on why I'm not answering, she lets it slide. "It might be fun to write for one of these." She pulls a magazine off my lap and skims through the first few pages. "Wait. 'How to shed belly fat before your big day'?" she reads and scrunches up her face. "Ugh, I can't believe this shit gets published."

I pull the magazine toward me so I can see. Lemon juice in the morning, ginger tea at night. That seems fairly innocuous. "Those dresses are pretty tight." I squint as I scan the page.

"Stop." Val yanks the magazine away. "You're perfect."

"I never said I wasn't." I laugh.

The *Kill Bill* ring tone starts up again. I pull out my phone and silence it again. "Probably looking for his socks or whatever. It's fine."

Val furrows her brow suspiciously but then takes the opportunity to start on a monologue about all of her blog ideas. I make like I'm listening, but a hot bubble of anxiety is tightening in my stomach. Ignoring Wren's calls is going to turn into a thing, I know it.

My mind flashes back to this past Valentine's when Wren, in what he considered to be a romantic gesture, took me—along with his work friends Max, Sally, and a woman I hadn't ever met—to Cecconi's for dinner. From the moment we sat down, the conversation was consumed by legal jargon and inside jokes. The four of them kept using this word—*stapify*—that I had never heard of. Whatever it meant, it was hilarious, because every time one of them slipped it into dialogue, it would send the table into an uproar. I tried to ask Wren what it meant, but he kept shushing me. "It's not polite to interrupt," he teased in a whiny voice. "Don't you teach your students that?"

The table fell silent. Everyone stared at their plates, clearly uncomfortable. After a beat, Wren added, "Just kidding," punctuated by a chuckle, as if that made it better. The awkward silence gave way to laughter—not mine, of course. I just sat there, cheeks burning, trying to convince myself I had imagined the sting in his words. Sally picked up on my humiliation; she leaned over and clarified, whispering that *stapify* was a word they made up that simply means to staple something. Not funny at all, if you ask me.

So I did what any sane person would do: I pulled out my phone and proceeded to play Word Scramble for the remainder of the evening. When dinner was over, we got in the car, and I told him he really hurt my feelings talking to me like that in front of our friends. He responded by telling me that the only person who should apologize was me for embarrassing him by acting like a teenager playing video games at the dinner table. I tried to explain to him that it was in response to not being included, but my attempt was useless. He shut down the conversation, and we drove home in silence.

Later, when we got home, I went to the bathroom to wash up and get ready for bed. I tried to bite back my tears, but I burst out crying anyway. Wren walked in quietly behind me and wrapped his arms around my waist, holding me tightly against his chest. He whispered into my ear how soft and beautiful I was. I can still hear his words in my ear: "Kiara, if only you knew how incredible you are. Every inch of you is damn near perfection. Even if you do act like a brooding teenager sometimes." He kissed my neck and spun me around. Looking into his eyes, I knew he was mad at himself for yelling at me. This was his way of apologizing. He licked his lips and told me I looked like a lollipop as he hiked up my red skirt. All was forgiven as we made up with sex on the bathroom floor. When I woke up, spooning on the cold tile, I tried replaying the dinner in my head to see where things went wrong, but I couldn't; it was all so blurry. Was I too sensitive? Maybe I *was* acting like a brooding teen.

Val has paused her diatribe, and she's staring at me, waiting for a reaction. "Wow, sounds amazing," I say with enthusiasm, hoping my response matches whatever she was talking about. I reach into my bag to pull out my phone. "I should just check to see if Wren's okay. Maybe Raven's sick now too." Val nods, clocking my lie.

I'm worried about you - can you please answer?

I hold my phone and think of what to respond. What's my reason for ignoring his calls?

Love you babe, I type, fingers trembling. Phone is being fussy. Sorry. I hit send.

OK babe, just make sure to call me when you land.

I let out a deep breath I hadn't realized I was holding. He just wants to ensure I'm okay, that's why he's calling and texting incessantly. Although, the barrage of earlier messages *was* aggressive . . .

"Keeks?" My phone drops to the floor when I feel Val's hand on my shoulder. Live wire. "They're calling our flight. Time to board." She bends down to grab my phone, but I yank it from her before she can see the screen. Just in case. "Tell Wren I'll get you back in one piece and to stop blowing up your phone!"

I toss my phone into my purse and line up with Val to board. When we get installed in our seats, I take out my phone to reply to Wren's last message, but I already have three new ones:

babe?

wtf?

hello?

I open the camera and make a kissy face as I hold up *Bride* magazine. I send it to Wren along with a message that reads Of course I'll text when I land. I love you, babe. Miss you already. Gonna power off for the flight. Xoxo. I take a deep breath and hit the mini airplane icon and toss my phone back in my bag. I pull out my glasses along with a stack of papers to grade as the plane begins to take off.

I rest my head on the window and rehearse what I'll say to Wren when we land. My throat feels constricted, tightening with every line I run: *It's just three days, you'll be at the office the whole time, you said yourself I should go* . . . I watch as a single tear hits the stack of tests on my lap.

Val taps my thigh and starts softly. "Hey, Keeks? A wise woman once told me we don't need to pretend our real lives don't exist in order to have fun." She nods her head to my purse, as though Wren were stowed away inside it.

I shake my head and wipe my cheek dry with the back of my hand. "Whoever said that sounds boring," I say with a laugh.

"Okay, well, you can talk to me if you want to." She leans her head on my shoulder. "I'm happy you decided to come."

"You think I'd leave you alone with ol' Betty and Veronica?" I laugh again, adjusting my glasses, tapping my purple pen against the top page. "You know what?" I say as I bend over to reach for my purse. I shove my work into the back pocket and zip up my bag. "Two Caesars, please," I say as I wave over the flight attendant who's just begun her aisle service. I plaster a toothy smile on my face and wink at Val. "Let's leave real life on the ground, shall we?"

Fay

NASSAU

EVER HEARD RADIO SILENCE? TUMBLEWEEDS? CRICKETS?

That's been our morning. An awkward waiting game for Val and Kiara to arrive. Rules are: no talking, no eye contact, and, certainly, no touching. At least that's what it feels like.

We've been sitting in the lobby, on what can only be described as the world's most uncomfortable couch—oversized seat, firm cushions, low backs, and wait for it, yes, leather—eyes fixed on the automatic sliding doors. Well, Zin is watching the doors. I'm staring at Zin. A far cry from how we were last night.

"You know, we still have at least twenty minutes before they arrive?" I state matter-of-factly. I reach over to push a curl behind her ear, but she flinches. "Or not," I mumble to myself.

"What's that supposed to mean?" Zin turns to face me.

"Nothing," I respond defensively. "Just that you're hot one second and cold the next. I'm just trying to take your temperature, that's all."

Zin bites her top lip and leans back. She rubs her hands together, and I can tell she's more than nervous—she's freaking out.

"I'm sorry, it's just that—" I start but stop myself when I notice she's picking dead skin off her fingernails. If I don't change the subject, she'll make herself bleed. I place my hand on top of hers and lower them into her lap. "I'm surprised Wren let Kiara come," I offer.

Zin furrows her brows and turns to me. "Let?"

"Yeah *let*," I scoff. "Wren runs that show." I push myself off the couch, peeling my thighs off the leather, leaving a puddle of sweat where I was sitting. "Remember I told you about Christmas dinner with Val's parents? He was such a dick, but it was subtle. You know? Like, small things. Serving himself first, making comments about what Kiara should eat, constantly interrupting her." I roll my eyes and lean back. A small drip of the complimentary juice I'm holding sloshes its way out of the glass and onto Zin's arm. "Sorry," I giggle.

She lifts her arm up and wipes off the droplet. "I've never seen him do that. I find him charming." Zin shrugs. "He's always so polite, and he's cute with my kids, at least that's how it seems whenever I've chatted with them on FaceTime."

"Well, not everyone is how they seem." I raise my brow. "Let's just leave it at that."

"True," she responds, setting her empty glass down on the table beside her. "People assume Adam is amazing just because he does a few drop-offs at school. Meanwhile, no one sees that I do the bulk of the parenting."

"You wouldn't have it any other way." I smile teasingly. I want to say more, like how Adam is hardly anything like Wren; he's actually a good guy and not as bad a dad as Zin makes him out to be. I could also add that, to the outside world, she seems like a happily married woman, but I don't want to stoke that fire, nor do I really care to talk about Adam. I lean over to kiss Zin, but she flinches.

"Did I say something wrong?" I ask, sitting back down beside her. Zin's body clams up and ices off.

"No," she responds, shrugging like I'm crazy for asking. "Why?"

Oh, no reason. Maybe because every time we get one step closer to solidifying things between us, you take a giant leap back and confuse the crap out of me.

"Nothing. Never mind." I lower my eyes and take a deep breath. "Is this how it's going to be when the girls get here?" I check my phone for the time. We have about ten minutes before our alone time is plucked from us. "Look, I'm not saying we need to announce it to them, like, 'Hey! We're together,' but—" I stop. "I'm just saying, they'd be happy for us. Maybe we don't need to hide it either. Wasn't it nice kissing out in the open like that last night?" I lean into her again and she flinches . . . again. I'm not even sure she notices she's doing it. It's instinctual, which is worse.

I tug at my jean shorts again, adjusting them from riding completely up my crotch. The sound of my sticky thighs peeling off the couch echoes awkwardly between us.

"I've told you already, I'm not ready to tell anyone," Zin states, leaving no room for misinterpretation.

"Val and Keeks are hardly *anyone*," I start, my heart in my stomach from the firmness of her tone. It's a last-ditch effort, and I feel pathetic for begging, but there you have it. I'm desperate for her to show me that she's as committed as I am. That this is real. "They're our best friends." I take her hand in mine, and this time she doesn't pull away. "They'll take one look at us and know we're up to something. Especially you. You can't keep a secret to save your life. Remember Val's *surprise* quinceañera?" I raise a brow. "You told her the precise time and location of her party because the anxiety of keeping a secret from her was giving you acid reflux." I smile, but her face stays stoic.

"Exactly. So you know how difficult this is for me. If you haven't noticed, I've been keeping this," she motions between us, "very secret, leading a double life for months, and it's killing me." She stops and slows her breath and then adds, "I hope you can understand."

Understand? I could write the book on understanding. Putting Zin first. All her worries, her concerns, her marriage, her kids. The list is never-ending. All I do is understand. But this is hard for me too. And who is there to understand me? Being someone's dirty secret feels fifty shades of shitty, and not being able to talk to our friends about it, well, that's beyond lonely.

"Remember when we first met?" I start, and Zin's face softens. "I was the new girl at school who brought brown paper bag lunches filled with canned corn. I sat at that cafeteria table every day all by myself.

For weeks, I'd eat lunch alone, get picked last—if at all—for partner work, and never ever did I get invited to a party." I let out a sigh. Zin nods, travelling back to Mount West High with me. She could tell this story better than I can. She was so angry when she learned that my mom switched me out of my private French school after losing her job. She couldn't afford tuition, what with all the alcohol she was spending money on. She was down to her last dollar and had to choose: school or booze. Off to public school I went.

"Where's this going, Fay?" Zin asks.

"Remember what you said the first time we spoke?" I pause.

Zin stares at me knowingly. "*I like your jacket?*" She smiles, her nose scrunched up.

I nod. Zinnia was such a beautiful kid. Never went through that awkward phase. I was sitting in the cafeteria, hunger pangs pulling at my belly, when Zin walked up to me. Feline-like, her footsteps were light yet articulate. The kind of cadence only a dancer could pull off. I'd seen her in class before, but I'd never looked at her that closely. At her milky white skin, blue almond-shaped eyes, tight blond curls, and the softest petal pink smile. The sight of her caught my breath. "I like your jacket," she whispered. I could immediately tell from the shakiness in her voice how shy she was, how bold and foreign this move was. They were simple words, but it was her way of looking out for me. Ensuring I wouldn't be all alone at lunch anymore. I returned the compliment by awkwardly blurting out that I liked her face, and she giggled and her eyes lit up with even more tenderness. It was love at first sight. For me at least.

"After that, you said, *Come sit with me and my friends*. Then you pointed to Val and Kiara and added, *I have some extra pizza in my lunch*." Zin smiles as I fill in the memory for her. "It took thirty seconds for you to change my life. It was the nicest thing anyone had ever done for me."

"Fay, you were eating canned corn." She waves me away. "What normal human watches that and doesn't intervene?"

"Either way, I promised you then and I promise you now—" I take her hand in mine "—I will never do anything that could hurt you. If this is too much," I bring her hand to my heart, "just be honest." My heart would break into a million pieces, but that's neither here nor there. I hold my face steady, hoping she can't see through my valiant attempt to put her needs before mine.

Because that's what Zinnia means to me. She gave me friendship; she showed me that there is good in this world at a time when I was at my lowest. What I love most about her is that she does it all without realizing how altruistic she truly is.

That day in the cafeteria, when I sat with the three of them, I remember thinking: *This could change everything*, followed by, *Don't fuck this up*.

The four of us did everything together: coloured our hair, spent endless afternoons at the mall, stayed up late for *SNL* with buckets of ice cream. But while we've always been a foursome, Zin and I had our own side friendship. We experimented with drugs, skydiving, after-hours parties, all-nighters where we'd end up at Moe's eating junk food at four in the morning, sharing everything from grilled cheese and fries to secrets and dreams. Even though I was in the proverbial closet, she knew I was gay. I never had to say it out loud; it's like she knew by osmosis. Still, I never risked announcing it for fear that my declaration was a sure-fire way to confirm I was in love with her and lose everything that meant anything to me.

After high school, when it came time to apply to universities, Val and Kiara opted to stay local and go to McGill, but Zin and I wanted to get the hell of out Montreal. We aspired to move to New York City together for school. The perfect city for me to study visual arts and her, dance. But the big city meant big money, and obviously my mother couldn't afford to put me through university—never mind an American one—so I applied to a few backups. I tried appealing to my grandmother to help me so I could live out my Parsons dream, but she said no real artist needs to study art. I never knew if she was against formal education or if she was telling me I wasn't a real artist.

Either way, Zinnia got a full scholarship to Juilliard, and I got into Emily Carr University in Vancouver, full scholarship too, which wasn't something I could turn down, especially when I didn't even get waitlisted at Parsons. I thought the distance would ruin our friendship, but we stayed close through emails, texts, phone calls between classes. We even sent each other postcards, which I still have tucked away in my desk at the gallery.

Both my mother and grandmother passed away the year I graduated from university. Mom from alcohol poisoning, my grandmother from old age. Alongside the grief of losing the only family I had left in the world, I also felt a new kind of freedom made possible due to the inheritance my grandmother left me (apparently, she could have put me through school and then some). I made plans to move to New York the day after that diploma hit my hand. Zin and I had said we'd get an apartment together. She was every choreographer's top pick, so we knew she'd get hired straight out of school. I had an internship at a little gallery lined up. We were all set. Life together in NYC. But life had different plans for Zin.

She had met Adam (which I had known about), gotten pregnant (which I hadn't known about), dropped out of school, and moved to Toronto all in the span of three months. I couldn't be mad that she chose Adam and the family they were creating. So I accepted it and that was that.

But she hadn't even told me she moved.

Our versions of the story vary slightly. Hers was something along the lines of *of course I told you*, while my version was too pathetic to admit. I lived with breath bated for three years, and when I graduated, I moved to New York to be reunited with my best friend, but she had already left months prior without so much as a text message or a forwarding address. Cut to me at Penn Station, luggage in hand, like a lovesick fool.

Here we are again, ten years later. Heart in my hand like a fool, because I know deep down that when the time comes, she's gonna choose Adam again.

"You know how I feel about you, right?" She stares at me with her ice blue eyes and perfect porcelain skin, her soft hand on mine as she interlaces our fingers. "Please, Fay. Understand the position I'm in. We can't tell our friends. We can't tell anyone. I have everything to lose."

I think about how much I've lost. How I gave up on our New York dream and packed it in to follow her to Toronto without so much as a hiccup. How I spent my grandmother's entire inheritance—less the money I wasted getting to NYC—investing in my own gallery in Toronto. No experience, no network, yet I made it work . . . until now. I've had my gallery for nearly seven successful years and it's finally on its last leg. If I don't find an artist that will sell, I'll have to close my doors.

I feel so detached from my life ever since I hopped back into the closet with Zin. It's so hard to be in love with someone who's half-in, half-out at all times. The sentiment has trickled into my professional life.

"What about what we stand to win?" I tuck a ringlet of blond hair behind her ear. This time, I feel the gentle pressure of her head resting into the palm of my hand. "Happiness, connection, true love. Don't you want this?"

I trace her skin with the back of my hand and finally rest my fingers on her face, calming my heartbeat to synch with hers. My happy place. Never in my wildest imagination would I have believed that we'd be doing this. Never would I have imagined that one night, six months ago, sitting on my gallery stoop, Zin would be crying into my shoulder about how unhappy she was at home. How everything felt wrong. How Adam wasn't right for her. Over the years, we'd talked about their mismatch, but that night, it was less about the marathon of motherhood and her passionless marriage and more about how something felt different inside her. I didn't catch onto what she was insinuating until she held my chin and gazed into my eyes, holding me there with intensity. There was a heaviness and a lightness in the air, and it made my head spin. My heart nearly jumped out of my chest with excitement, terror, hope, fear . . . had this always been meant to be? I remember thinking, *If I blink, will I make it go away?* She held my gaze, looking deep into me, and as though she could read my heart, her face came closer to mine. I could feel her breath, hot on my face, as she closed the space between us. I let my eyes close, in what I can only describe as a free-fall from ten thousand feet in the air. The culmination of a love finally finding its source. When she kissed me, we lit aflame.

"Just promise me that you feel this too," I say, leaning forward to kiss her lips. "This is real, right?"

Zin kisses me back lightly, squeezing my hand in hers. "Of course it is. You have to know that." She sighs, fighting back the tears that are pooling in her eyes. "I wouldn't have started this if I wasn't sure about you. I just can't—"

Through a mirage of flooding sunlight and a parting sea of spring-breakers, Val and Kiara appear through the sliding doors like a vision on some reality TV set. They are strutting toward us, wind-swept hair and cascading sun framing their silhouettes. Zin snaps her hand away from mine as though I were a burning stove.

Even from afar, I can make out Kiara's ski-slope nose and high cheekbones perfectly contoured with her down-to-there braids. She's bejewelled a few strands with purple beads, and they bounce on her striped crochet tank top with each step. Her long legs, barely covered in cut-offs, nearly reach Val's waist. They're laughing as they make their way to the couch.

"Ladies!" Val sings, throwing her arms up in the air, her voice echoing throughout the lobby. "We're here!" She pulls Zin in for a hug first.

"Yeah, luckily this one said no." Kiara motions sloppily to Val. Speaking way louder than publicly appropriate, Kiara stumbles over like a Muppet from *Fraggle Rock*, fighting with her luggage. She yanks the handle and pops the suitcase over the curb, wheeling it behind her like it's a wailing toddler. I make my way to stand and reach out to Kiara for a hug. The alcohol on her breath sails between us.

"Wow!" I exclaim, waving one hand in front of my face and using the other to block my nose. "You good?"

Staring at me with exaggerated confusion, Kiara responds, "Yeah!" She stumbles. "Why wouldn't I be?"

Maybe because you're fall-on-your-face-drunk and it's barely afternoon, I think.

"Oh my god, Zin!" Kiara pushes me aside and grabs Zinnia's hand to twirl her around. "You look amazing! Are you kidding me with that hair, that bod!" She holds up Zin's button-down shirt. "Goals! I bet after I have kids, I'll be stuffing my sagging belly into a high-waisted bikini and trying to pass it off as the latest trend."

If there's one thing Kiara is good at, it's self-deprecation. I used to think she was fishing for compliments. Then I moved on to my theory that she was insecure. Now I think—or actually, now I know—she does it as a form of self-protection.

"Relax, Kiara, you're gorgeous." Zin goes in for a hug and holds Kiara up to keep her from falling onto the couch. "Whoa there, you okay?"

Val pantomimes a drink and rolls her eyes like she's drunk. *Yeah, we noticed.* One boozy flight, two drunk friends, and this trip is already a far cry from what I had in mind. Not to mention that Zin and I didn't get to finish our conversation.

"Well, I, for one, am so excited to see you two!" Zinnia claps her hands. "Texting just isn't as good as flesh and bone." She pinches Kiara's arm and then motions to the bar. "Shall we?"

"Añejo for you, añejo for me, añejo for everybodyyyy!" Kiara cries out, fist pumping in the air.

"Wait, wait, wait! I'm dripping sweat." Val pumps her sweatshirt away from her body. "If we're gonna start drinking, can I at least change first?"

"You mean, *continue* drinking?" I raise a brow and point to Kiara. She burps, and the sound echoes through the lobby.

"What's your glitch?" Kiara speaks slowly, drawing out every syllable. "We're in vacation mode." She taps the tip of my nose playfully. I look over at Val, but she just shrugs and laughs it off.

Zinnia shoots me a look telling me to play nice, but the lingering frustration of our romantic-getaway-turned-spring-break-debauch-fest has me thrown. I need a minute to wrap my brain around the tornado that just blew in. I swat Kiara's hand out of my face and grab her suitcase.

"Check-in is at four, so why don't you guys go change in our room?" I glance at Zin. I need a small sign that she is as annoyed with this disruption as I am. But she gives me a thumbs-up and quickly looks away. I clap my hands and add, "Okay, go get dressed, I'll order us enough drinks to catch up to Kiara." A little fun in the sun is exactly what I need to get the edge off.

"Wait, first, lean in for a pic, ladies. Hashtag Bahama Mama!" Kiara pulls out her phone and holds it high so we all fit in the frame. As she clicks, she loses her footing and stumbles, tripping on my sandal and falling onto the couch. Her phone hits the ground, and she erupts into laughter.

I help her up and straighten her out. We hover close enough to snap our pic before Kiara almost falls over again.

"Zin, how about you head upstairs with Val while I babysit Kiara. I'll help her change in the bathroom here and then grab us some pool chairs." I smile and wink, hoping she'll reciprocate. I mean, she can for sure agree that we don't have to worry about Kiara picking up on a vibe; if she keeps going at this pace, she'll be too blitzed to notice up from down.

"Good plan," Zin says, walking toward the elevator. She presses the up button and stands back, one hand on her hip, the other sliding through her hair. She turns back toward me before she steps onto the elevator and gives me a half-nervous, half-flirtatious smile. The sign I've been waiting for. I feel my shoulders release as I smile. I resolve that I need to trust she wants this as much as I do. She feels what I feel.

This is real.

Zinnia

"I HAVE TO WARN YOU, OUR ROOM IS A MESS," I TELL VAL AS WE HEAD down the hallway. "We danced at the tiki bar until like three a.m." I lie.

Last night already feels like a far-distant memory. Whatever comforts we indulged in when we had the resort to ourselves have become abruptly compromised now that Val and Kiara are here. But I can't think about that now, because I'm about to open the door to a living shrine of last night's intimate adventures. Not to mention that I woke up this morning to little notes Fay had left all over the room: *you're beautiful*, read a little one on the night table, *I can't believe this is happening* written on the to-go cup of coffee, *let's sneak some kisses on the beach later* said a note tacked with gum to our bathroom mirror, and if Val catches a glimpse of any of it . . .

"Why are you running?" Val yells as I swing open the door.

"I really gotta pee," I call out over my shoulder as I open the latch to prop the door open for her. She's only a few paces behind, which gives me about twenty seconds to get rid of all the evidence.

"I'll just be a sec," I yell over my shoulder when I hear the room door shut. I'm in the bathroom pulling at the glob of gum on the mirror that stubbornly won't budge.

"It's freakin' hot here," Val says as I re-enter the room, closing the bathroom door behind me, gum still very much stuck on the mirror.

She's standing at the foot of the bed, suitcase laid open in front of her, nose deep in her clothes, searching for a bathing suit.

She slips off her sweater and proceeds to exaggeratedly fan the air in front of her to create a breeze. "Why aren't you pumping the AC?" She walks over to the thermostat, clicks a button, and the air comes on. "Ahh, that's better." She pulls out a bikini top and heads to the bathroom. "I'll be just a sec. Pool first, right? Hey, you okay?" She finally stops what she's doing and looks at me.

"Yeah, why?" I laugh nervously.

"Because you're staring at me like you've seen a ghost, that's why." She laughs and walks into the bathroom, leaving the door open for conversation.

Fay's right. I can't keep a secret to save my life. In my mind, Val is going to look at the mirror, see that white glob of gum, and start asking questions. I need to breathe and act natural, otherwise Val will figure it all out and that's the last thing I need.

"Why is there gum on the mirror?" Val laughs as she walks out of the bathroom. I'm scanning my brain for a response or funny joke but I'm drawing a blank. "You should probably call down to have them clean the room." She walks over to me and hands me the strings of her bikini. "Could you tie this?" I grab the two ends and tie a double knot. "My dad sends his love to you and the kids. Wants pics of Darla in her tutu." She smiles.

"Eduardo's the best." I grab my phone and thank my lucky stars for the change in topic, looking for a cute photo to send. "There." I smile and plop down on the bed. "You know, Adam's alone with the kids for, like, the first time ever. When the sitter bailed last minute, he said he could handle it. Between Saul's daycare schedule and Darla's homework and dance, I was this close," I bring my fingers together, "to cancelling too. Looks like fate brought us together."

"Fate." Val rolls her eyes. "*And* Adam is their father. It's not like he doesn't know what he's doing." She rummages through her bag and pulls out her bikini bottoms.

"Let's just say he's no Eduardo," I say as I start folding her sweater.

"Well, at the very least," Val tugs the sweater away from me, balls it up, and tosses it back into her luggage, "they'll all be alive when you get back." She laughs as she peels off her leggings and walks back to the bathroom to switch into her bikini bottom. "No harm, no foul, right?" She calls out.

Right. The worst thing Adam can do this weekend is forget Darla's ballet slippers. That doesn't make him a bad dad. I, on the other hand, am ruining our marriage. I guess that's perspective for me.

I shake out my shoulders and stretch my arms. "You ready to tell me what happened with Jack?"

"I will, just gimme a sec," Val says over her shoulder, walking over to the toilet. Shutting the glass door behind her, she yells, "There's a phone in the bathroom!" Her best *Pretty Woman* impersonation.

"Don't answer it," I respond on cue.

"Do you have a tampon? I got my period on the car ride over here. I tried to get the cab driver to stop, but Kiara looked like she was gonna barf."

"I actually do. I'm expecting my period any day now." My mind goes back to last night at the bar, as Fay's fingers were sliding down my stomach toward the heat between my legs. "It *is* warm in here, right?" I'm heating up just thinking about Fay. How am I gonna do this? I walk over to the thermostat and see it's set at sixty-eight. "'Kay, I'm not gonna lower it or we'll die of frostbite. Here," I say as I slip Val a tampon through the door. "Let me know if you want me to put it in for you."

At that, I giggle, reminding Val of the time Kiara got sick in Colorado.

"Remember how profusely she was sweating during the steam?" Val laughs, flushing the toilet. "No! It was the sauna!" she corrects herself and joins me on the bed.

"Right." I laugh. "Sweating like a beer bottle in the desert sun? We walked out of the hot room, and she dropped to the floor. For real, something could've been wrong with her. We were such idiots!"

"Whatever, it was only half scary. The other half was hilarious." Val waves her hands in front of her, and continues laughing.

"You're right, it was full-on hilarious. We legit had to carry all five-foot-ten of her up to her room." Val covers her mouth and laughs like she's gasping for air. "You were holding her head, I had her hips, and Fay was holding her feet, directing us. She was all *pivot*!" She imitates Fay imitating Ross, and I lose it. It's like we're twenty-six again, riding the elevator, holding Kiara's body like a corpse, hoping she wasn't dying of heat stroke. "And that's when I plopped her onto her bed, and my hands were full of blood!" Val's face scrunches up with disgust. Not the saving-a-life kind of blood; it was the that-came-out-of-where kind of blood. I mean, no woman wants to touch a handful of her own menstrual fluid, let alone a friend's. "If I had known she had her period, I totally would've opted for her head or feet!" she adds.

"Oh my god! Remember when she came to?" I let out a burst of laughter.

"What did she say again?" Val says between breaths. "She opened her eyes, she looked up at me, and she whispered: *Thank god I'm not pregnant. Can you put a tampon in for me?* And then she passed out!"

Convulsing with laughter, we barely make it through the story. "I was the one," I catch my breath, "elected to tend to her. I felt like I was being voted off the island!"

"Come on, you loved it," Val smiles, nudging my shoulder. "You're in your element when you get to take care of people." She stands up and slides on her jean shorts. "Okay, pool?"

I wipe the tears from my eyes and hold my hand out to take hers.

"Ugh, I needed this," I say. "I'm happy you came."

"Me too." Val throws on a cover up over her bikini top. "Ready!"

These resorts are designed to immerse you in rest from the moment you arrive, not a single iota of energy expended to even open the door. Everything is automatic, drinks available at every countertop, staff waiting on you hand and foot, and a murmur of waves crashing in the background like a white noise meditation soundtrack washing out the sound of your own thoughts. Even the beige tones of the common areas of the hotel set against the sandy beach they look onto is soothing to the eyes, everything seamlessly connected like an infinity pool of interior architecture. It's a welcome escape from my reality.

If I weren't here right now, I'd be knee deep in a week's worth of laundry, dropping Darla off at ballet, rushing her to speech therapy, and hauling Saul around with me against his will. It's like I live the life of a single mom, which is the ultimate paradox since I'm far from single. But that's the silent arrangement we have. Adam works out of the house; I work in the house. I never thought my life would look so much like exhaustion, wrapped in resentment, dipped in identity loss. Yet here I am.

I should be happier. Grateful, even. Adam has given me what I always wanted: a family. Along with Adam came a whole slew of Rappaports: brothers, sisters, nieces, nephews, father, *and* mother. His parents even have two dogs they bring with them everywhere, because they're family and family sticks together. Because of Adam, I've gotten holiday dinners, football Sundays, family vacations . . . it's everything I never had growing up, and everything I'd always yearned for. It's so me to finally get what I want and it not be enough. But how was I supposed to know that it would consume me entirely? The worst part is, I don't think Adam notices how unhappy I am, and the honest truth is that I haven't told him otherwise. But it's like he doesn't seem to notice that the Zinnia he had once known—fallen in love with—has been completely erased.

Then there's Fay. Whispering in my ear that I should take time for myself. Pushing me to take photography more seriously or get back into dance classes. She's well intentioned, only it has the reverse effect. When she sends me links to photography classes, rather than make me feel inspired, I am reminded how little time I have for myself. She thinks I'm making excuses and says that finding time for myself is a choice.

Choice. A concept that feels like an empty promise because there's no future where Fay and I work. No version of my life where I stay in

Toronto rather than move to California with Adam come September. What choice do I have? I can't split my family up.

"Hey, Val," I say as I take her by the wrist, holding her back from stepping onto the pool deck. I look out and notice Fay and Kiara on a daybed facing the lobby. Fay is sitting up, slathering herself in suntan lotion, and Kiara is sipping a cocktail. "Is Kiara okay?"

"Yeah, why do you ask?"

"I don't know, something Fay said earlier." I push my hand through my curls and toss them anxiously. "It's fine, never mind."

Val simply shrugs and we walk over to join Fay and Kiara. We catch the tail end of their conversation. Kiara is slurring her words as she goes on and on about how hard it is to be a stepmother.

Fay shifts over on her daybed to make space for me but I unfold my beach towel and lay it out on the daybed beside Kiara.

"It's like they have this unbreakable bond," she says, sipping the last bit of her pink drink. "And I know Raven loves me." She holds up her phone and turns it around so we can all see a cute picture of her and Raven at the waterslides. A picture of Wren and Kiara kissing takes over the screen to the *Kill Bill* theme music. Kiara hits the red circle, declining the call. "Anyway." Kiara laughs nervously and leans back in her chair. Maybe Fay wasn't entirely wrong about Wren—maybe there's something about him I'm missing. I shoot Val a look but she just smiles. "It's just hard to find my place with her, you know?"

"Of course it is. Maybe she's resisting you a little because she doesn't understand the whole two moms thing. But with time, she'll figure out who she wants you to be to her," I say, validating Kiara's very real worry about her role. She's nodding along as I pull off my oversized button-down and sprawl out onto my towel. "Pass the lotion," I say, holding my hand out toward Fay, who is staring at me with a confused look on her face. "What?"

"What do you mean *two moms* thing?" Fay asks.

Shit. I hadn't thought about how my comment would land in Fay's ears. I close my eyes and take a breath.

"It changes a family dynamic when new people are introduced," Kiara swoops in, unknowingly saving me from having to explain that my kids know Fay as Auntie Fay and that I don't know that I want it any other way. I'm their mom.

I pretend to be struggling with the Sun Bum cap to buy myself some time, even though Fay's eyes are piercing through my skin.

"I don't know," Fay starts. "I think Raven is lucky to have more people who love her."

"Blah, blah." Val gets between us and asks, "Pool volleyball, anyone?" She points to a few guys who are splashing around mid-game.

Kiara grins, assessing the situation: four guys, boisterous, grunting with each toss. "Nah. Too intense for me right now."

"Come on . . . for fun?" Val begs. She's standing at the foot of Kiara's daybed, making puppy dog eyes, but Kiara ignores her as she continues to sip at her now empty daiquiri glass, shaking her head.

"*For fun?* That's what losers always say." Fay laughs, and winks at me as she pops up off the daybed and dives into the pool. Val whips around and jumps in after her. I follow next.

"I'll get us more drinks." Kiara waves her hand in the air to no one in particular. "Another wine cooler, Fay?"

"I'm all good. One and done," Fay asserts, plunging underwater. Her leg grazes my skin as she swims away. It's almost as though she's doing it on purpose so we get caught.

"Bor-ing," Kiara sings. When she realizes no one is coming to take her order, she stands up, adjusts her one-piece, and walks toward the cabana bar.

We swim over to the group of guys huddled around the volleyball net.

"Mind if we join you?" Fay asks.

"Sure," one guy replies and tosses her the ball, which she instinctively volleys back. Just like that, the game is on.

We play for the better part of an hour, and between shots, I glance over to Kiara, waving her over in an attempt to have her join us, but she continues to ignore me and sits there sipping away, watching us lose.

"We could really use your help over here." I finally say after about fifteen minutes. "We're dying."

"Fine, I'll play, but points for shots," Kiara says, showing me her drink before she puts it down and jumps into the pool.

Val and I exchange a glance.

One guy comes closer to the net and says, "You sure you ladies can handle that?"

I know exactly what must be going through these guys' minds. They've watched Kiara kick back drink after drink, and they're thinking there's no way our sloshed friend is going to bring anything to our team. Points for shots in their minds mean when they get points, we take shots. Little do they know that Kiara was not only our high school volleyball team captain, she also played for the McGill basketball team *and* led them to win the championship every year she played. No, she didn't just win. That undercuts how she dominated; she set records that I believe still haven't been broken.

Even wasted, Kiara will blow these guys out of the pool. I almost feel sorry for them.

The four of us nod sheepishly, exchanging smiles.

"Game on," one guy says with a laugh, and serves the ball.

It feels good to be in the pool like this, the four of us letting loose.

We barely finish our first set before Kiara has scored ten points in a row and two of the guys have tapped out.

"You really gave them a run for their money." Fay high-fives Kiara.

"Ohhhh." Kiara shakes out her shoulders. "We should've played for money!"

"You," I bow down to Kiara, laughing, "are my queen."

I climb out of the pool and dry myself off. "Who wants to take a walk on the beach?"

Fay jumps out of the pool just as Val raises her hand straight up in the air like a good student waiting to be picked. I look between them and point to Val. "Okay, Val, why don't you come with me?" I smile.

She claps her hands playfully and swims over to the ladder.

"Catch you guys later," Kiara calls out and then looks back to Fay and the remaining guys. "Two on two?" she offers, spinning the ball on her finger. Fay dives back into the pool.

By the time we reach the shoreline, Val is halfway through her story about what happened with Jack. Her voice fades into the background as I focus on my footsteps gently pressing into the wet sand. A bird on the horizon catches my eye. It's soaring above the water; it's so far away yet its outline is perfectly crisp in contrast against the blue sky. I take out my phone to capture the movement of flight, like a ballerina leaping across the stage.

"That's when I told him I cheated," Val says with a sigh, tucking her windblown hair behind her ear. She's staring at me, waiting for a reaction. "It's just that I don't think of myself as a cheater, you know? Hello?"

"Sorry, yes, I know." I squint as I focus my camera. "Just one sec, sorry. It's just that bird way out at sea, nothing but sky and water all around. It's pure tranquility. Isn't that beautiful?" I snap the shot.

As though a tape were playing back in my head, I hear what she just confessed and blurt out, "Wait! You cheated?"

She nods. "I knew you weren't listening!"

I look at Val guiltily as I slip my phone into my pocket. "Sorry! Start over. Who? What?"

"Right." Val takes a deep breath. She starts walking ahead quickly, and I pick up my pace to keep up with her. "Don't look at me like that, please," she continues, her face pained as she searches for words. "It was the biggest mistake of my life. Cheating is the most horrendous thing. I fucked everything up for a one-night stand."

I feel like a rock the size of an avocado pit is lodged in my throat.

"You're judging me." She turns to look at me.

"Absolutely not! Why would I judge you?" All I want to say is *you're not alone, I cheated too!* But two cheaters aren't better than one. At least mine isn't a one-night stand, but whatever, that's splitting hairs in the good-people-do-horrible-things club.

"Who was he? Someone from work?" I ask, trying to picture Val with anyone other than Jack, which is impossible—he was her first and only boyfriend.

"I don't want to get into it. He wasn't anyone special." She lowers her eyes, avoiding my gaze. "I feel wracked with guilt every time I picture Jack's face when I told him. He never saw it coming."

Why would he? Val's story just doesn't seem plausible. She's not a one-night stand kind of girl. Something's not adding up. Aside from the fact that this mystery man has no name and totally came out of nowhere, I'd say the question's not *if* she's lying, but *why*. Even the way she recounted the proposal feels overproduced, rehearsed in some way.

"But I'm confused. Why did you cheat?" I press. "A one-night stand seems reckless. Did you have feelings for this guy? Do you regret it?" Maybe she can give me some insight as to how she sleeps at night with all the guilt.

"Regret which part? Cheating or destroying my relationship?" she asks bluntly.

"Both, I guess," I reply.

She runs her hand through her hair and sweeps it to one side. "Think about it: What if Adam cheated on you? One night, and bam!" A boxer's punch to the heart. "Everything is different. Not to mention that you have two kids . . . at least in my case it's just Jack." Val smiles and gives me jazz hands.

I feign a smile back, appreciating her attempt to lighten the mood with a *Will & Grace* reference. "I don't know, I think there's more to it, like *why* did you cheat?" I shrug, turning my face away so I can collect my thoughts. Doesn't intention matter? "Ugh, when did we become adults?" I turn back and hold my hand up to shield my eyes from the sun.

"Chica, you've been an adult since the day you saw those two pink lines." She laughs. "All I know is that this stays between us. If Fay finds out, she'll be all 'How dare you break Jack's heart for some flaccid one-night stand? Don't you know better than to lead with your libido?'" She's about to flip from Fay's line to her own in her imaginary script, but just then the wind picks up, whipping her hair across her face. "Ugh, I got sand in my teeth," she laughs, pushing her hair away and twisting it into a bun at the back of her head. Without an elastic, she pulls a few strands through, and the bun remains in place. "Anyway, what was I saying? Right, my libido ruined my life."

That makes two of us.

I hold my arm out and pull her in, holding her close to me as we walk together.

She leans her head onto me and doesn't say anything. She seems sullen. Maybe she did cheat on Jack. Maybe it was her cry for help. Maybe she's just as confused about how to get through life as I am, and this was a cry for help, or maybe I'm projecting.

"You know, you should tell Fay," I suggest. "Perhaps she'll have something interesting to say about the morality of cheating." *And I want to hear it*, I think. Val contorts her face into a question mark, her eyebrows working overtime. I put my hands up and laugh. "Fine, she'll probably take Jack's side, but she wouldn't judge you—she'd be there for you, and you know it."

"Ha! I swear if I'd have given her a gavel back in the lobby, she would've judged Kiara's ass all the way into sobriety!"

If you knew the whole story, I think, *you'd know it wasn't judgment, it was concern.*

"She just wants what's best for you. For all of us," I say.

We continue to walk silently along the shoreline. Shoulder-to-shoulder, I follow Val's cadence, letting the water glisten over my feet.

"Talk to me about you," Val starts again. "How's Adam? The kids?"

"Well, for Christmas he bought me a Chanel purse." I nudge her shoulder. "Something about a 'classic Boy bag'?"

Val opens her mouth so wide I could fit said Boy bag inside it. I put my hand under her chin and close her mouth.

"You've arrived," she says and shakes her shoulders in a little happy dance, smiling from ear to ear.

"Shut up." I shove her shoulder playfully. "It sounds like the best gift ever, but I don't know. Call me ungrateful, but it's just not me. I don't really like all the luxurious gifts he buys me. Never have. They're more symbols of his status than symbols of our love, you know?"

"Well, what would you have wanted?" Val asks, and I'm stumped. I hadn't thought further than how the purse was a metaphor for Adam not really knowing me.

I exhale. "I don't know."

"Adam's one of the good ones, Zin. I'm sure if you told him you preferred, I don't know, a blender, he'd gladly get you one." Val laughs. She knows that a blender is the furthest thing from what I would want, but the absurdity of her suggestion is yet another reminder of how lost I am.

"He's sort of like my dad in a way." Val pulls out her phone. "You know, I've been writing a whole ton recently, and I have this one journal I keep about him." She turns her phone to me so I can see her notes. "Like all the things he's taught me about life, and friendship, and love." She scrolls, and the list seems infinite.

Eduardo certainly is a brilliant man. So is Val's mom, Paula. They were my surrogate parents growing up. Even though Val could never totally understand my parentless woes—my mother, who skipped out on me at fourteen, and my father, who gave up on me a few years later—she still opened her home to me and took me in like a sister. I owe a lot to the de la Vegas. Well, we all do, actually. Late nights in her kitchen, hunched over Baskin-Robbins World Class Chocolate ice cream, crying over my parents or bad boyfriends. I remember one night, Eduardo pulled up a stool, grabbed a spoon, and fed us advice about life. *It hurts because it matters*, he'd say, never letting me pretend I wasn't in pain. *Feel it, and let it guide you.*

"Val," I pull her phone closer to me, "these aren't notes, this is a full-blown book."

"I have a few more like this." She clicks out and shows me an endless list of blog ideas. "One about our trips too." She smiles.

"Well, you'll publish them all one day." I hold my hands up like I'm framing a marquee. "*Siempre Valentina.* That's what you used to call your journal, right?"

"How do you remember that?" She stares off, and I can imagine she's already envisioning herself giving book tours and signing movie deals. That's her lot in life: she has it all, and it all comes easily.

"You'll have one reader for sure." I wink at her and purse my lips to blow her a kiss. "Truth is, anything you do will be amazing. Siempre. *Always*, right?"

Val throws her arm around my shoulder and tugs me close to her. "Thank you for always being there, Zin," she says. "Just being able to talk and let it all out feels like I've lifted a ten-ton elephant from my chest." Val exhales and rolls her eyes. "Even though, come Monday, that elephant will find its way right back here." She thumps her chest. "Can you believe I have to run a whole goddamn company?"

"Have to?" Val's words ring with privilege. "I wish I could have an opportunity like that just handed to me. Plus, I love Valentina's."

"I know you do. I just mean, I know what I want to be doing." She waves her phone at me. "And I don't get to do it." I raise my brow, unimpressed. "Come on! Would you want to be Mr. Filomena's boss? Valentina's is an office of eight sixty-year-olds designing dresses for other sixty-year-olds. And that was ten years ago!"

I let out a laugh. "Okay, okay, I get it."

I let the warm water wash over my sandy feet as Val dives into a monologue on her CEO anxiety. Her floral cover up flutters behind her in the breeze like she's in a photo shoot. I look down at my button-up and mangled pedicure. The contrast of her glamour against my ordinariness is a reminder that though the de la Vegas may have taken me in, privilege only runs blood deep.

I wish I could tell her about Fay. Her insight and advice are usually spot on. When she's not in Val-Val Land, like she is right now, it's usually her I call to figure out a problem. A close second to Fay, actually, depending on the subject matter. For example, when I need help sorting out a friend problem, I'll call Val. When I need life advice or insight into my marital woes, it's usually Fay. Except now, since she's the one I'm fucking up my marriage with.

As though on cue, I feel my back pocket buzz. Adam on FaceTime.

"I have to answer this, Saul is probably tantruming about eating lunch. Gimme a sec," I say, holding up a finger. "Hey, Adam," I say with a trill. "Let me just find somewhere shady so I can see you better." I push against the sand as I make my way over to an umbrella and pop a squat on a beach chair.

"How's the trip, babe?" he asks. I can see the kids on the couch behind him watching TV.

"Beautiful." I turn the phone around to give him a panoramic view. "Just what the doctor ordered. You? What's up?"

"I mean, not much since we spoke this morning, just, um, Saul refuses to eat the turkey burgers you left for us . . . I thought maybe, I mean, I know I fed him mac and cheese last night, but honestly, he loves it. Do you care?"

"Mac and cheese is fine." What I really want to say is, *You know I care—I prefer the kids don't eat boxed food*, but whatever. "Do what's easiest. And thank you again. It's so stunning here." I feel the guilt rise in my chest. "Maybe we'll bring the kids for Christmas next year?"

"I think we'll have plenty of beach time in California." I feel my breath catch as Val approaches and, clearly, by the change of expression on her face, hears the news. "Okay, well I just wanted to check in, say hi, see your pretty face." He turns the phone around and points it to the kids. "Say hi to Mom!"

Neither of them budge. They're zombies watching the *Minions* movie.

I whisper *love you* and hit the red dot before he has time to return the sentiment. I slip my phone into my back pocket and cup my face in my hands, taking a moment to breathe as I drown out the sound of Val's questions.

"Does Fay know yet?" Fay's name snaps my attention. "Or you gonna pull a New-York-Toronto-gate two-point-oh?"

In through the nose, out through the mouth.

"Hello? Did you tell Fay?"

"Tell me what?" Fay appears out of nowhere.

Valentina

THE LOOK ON ZIN'S FACE SAYS IT ALL. FAY HAS NO CLUE.

"Tell me what?" Fay repeats.

"That Zin wants a blender," I say, and Zin cracks a smile, grateful that I sensed the tension that has formed around us. I watch as her chest visibly deflates.

"Weird." Fay laughs, shaking her head. "Whatever, Kiara fell asleep by the pool, and I'm going up to our room to finish some work, so here are your things." She plops down our beach bags in the sand by Zin's feet. "Also, it's four already, so you can check in," she directs at me.

"Oh, good idea," I say as I rub Zin's shoulder. I give her a quick wink and nod my head so she knows her secret is safe with me. "You coming?"

"I'm gonna stay here for a bit." Zin lies back on the chair, crossing her feet at the ankles.

"'Kay, love you." I bend over to kiss her cheek. "Ready," I say to Fay as I stand up and hoist my beach bag onto my shoulder.

"Meet downstairs at six," Fay calls out to me as I roll my suitcase out of her room after checking in.

When I finally get up to my own room, I tap my card over my door handle and let out a heavy sigh. Alone at last.

I feel charged and reconnected, but I also need some me-time to unpack and shower, maybe slip in a power nap if I'm gonna last past eight.

I've never felt more my age more than I do right now. Every bone in my body wants to crawl into bed and nap, but I can't imagine wasting a single second sleeping when the sea is right there beyond my balcony.

After my shower, I head over to the glass door, laptop in hand, and slide it open. Soaking in the smell of fresh saltwater wafting through the air, I look out and totally understand why so many authors write by the water. The steady crash of waves washes out all distractions, blurring the line between reality and imagination. The perfect backdrop for self-exploration.

I open my laptop and click into a new document. I start typing, and the words flow through me like the tide. Pulling me in deeper with each sentence, my thoughts rise and fall one by one. I feel lucid and free, unconstrained by creative briefs and client asks. I work everything out on the page, the one place I can always be honest.

Blogging is my version form of journaling. I discovered it at Jazz. Between short-form, long-form, campaigns, pitches, and taglines, blogging feels like the most natural format for me to express myself. Its conversational, journal style is so authentic to my voice. It feels intimate and personal in a way that no other writing has felt for me. Not to mention that when I was blogging for brands, the weekly publishing schedule that allowed me to get instant feedback and engage with the audience in real time.

I feel like I still have so much left to discover at Jazz. Not just about marketing, but about myself. I'm not ready to take over Valentina's. I'm not ready to give up my dream and settle into my career. Or should I say, my father's career. I never planned to work in fashion, and even though I always knew I would have to one day, I thought I'd have a plan on how to wiggle my way out once the day came.

Zin's words on the beach triggered an avalanche of thoughts I didn't feel equipped to defend at the time. Because the honest truth is that she's right. I am privileged to have this opportunity. But isn't opportunity subjective? What they call privilege, I call pressure.

I know it's my dad's way of showing love, securing my future. Ensuring I never have to know what it feels like to live hand-to-mouth.

I remember when I was applying to universities, the dozens of brochures from the best journalism and creative writing programs in North America were all spread out on my desk. I dreamed of the days I would chase a story, riding the high of seeing people holding the paper, my words in their hands. Cut to my dad saying business school was the only option. He wasn't a tyrant about it. He let me work for the school paper, but that was the extent of journalism I was allowed to pursue. He didn't risk everything when he fled Venezuela for me to throw it away. His worst nightmare was not knowing if my paycheque would cover my rent.

Every birthday, every dinner, every chance he got, my dad would raise a glass and say, *I built all this for you mi'ja. From nothing we come, and now I have the good fortune to give you a future.* My dad doesn't seem to think my lack of knowledge or experience is an issue; he says all I need is three months under his tutelage and I'll be fine. So fine, in fact, that he plans to retire and let me steer the ship alone. It's been his plan all along, and he's never wavered from it.

It feels especially shitty knowing that everyone is thinking the same thing: I didn't earn this. I know I'd be thinking that if I were, oh, I don't know, say, Ricardo, my father's right-hand man. Of course, he's going to smile and congratulate me Monday morning, but what he'll really be doing is waiting for me to prove I can't hack it . . . a likely outcome.

Ugh. Why didn't I just say yes to Jack? Maybe *he* could've run Valentina's. Papá would've totally been okay with that.

Enough. I need to snap out of this negative downward spiral.

I'm not gonna waste a single second more on that which I cannot change.

I continue to type away, weaving *Siempre Valentina* through metaphors about daiquiris and volleyball courts and every inside joke that got us through bikini mishaps and poolside laughs.

Just as I'm punctuating my last sentence on the intricate colour palette of the Bahamian landscape, how the blues blur into each other as naturally as Kiara's thoughts intertwine with mine, how Fay's and my appetites synch up, or how Zin always knows my mind, my phone rings.

"Hola, Val," my dad sings on the other end of the line, salsa music blaring in the background. "How are you?"

"Hi, Papá, everything's fine. Just in my room getting some work done before dinner." I finally look up from my screen and think about how Jack would love it here. He'd probably look out from the balcony and say something smart like how the beach loungers look like splotches in an impressionist painting. He'd love the downtime between activities, lazing around in the room, playing guitar on the balcony unbound by the schedules of daily life. A sadness swells in the pit of my stomach. I draw in a shaky breath to fight the tears from falling.

"Ay, Valentina, shh," my dad whispers, and I can feel him hug me through the phone. "Cariña, are you crying? What's going on? Tell me."

I lick a rolling tear. Tastes like the sea.

"Amor, why are you sitting alone in your room when you are with your friends? Have you shared the news about Jack?"

"Yes, a little." I follow his lead. "They're just as torn up as I am," I lie. Again. Just hearing my dad's voice is a moral reminder that even though I may not actually be a cheater, I am a liar. And my lies are piling up.

"¡Dile que la extraño!" I hear my mom screaming in the background.

"I miss her too." I smile.

"She hears you. She misses you," my dad repeats, calling out to my mom. "Mi'ja, not all is lost. You have a ton to celebrate. Your friends must be excited for you. I'm sure they can't wait to toast your reign at Valentina's." He pronounces every syllable with a thick accent, emphasizing the Spanish *B* in *Valentina*. His pride is palpable.

Well, he's right about that at least. My friends will want to drink tonight, and hopefully I'll get inebriated past the point of any intellectualizing so I can stop overthinking my big, messy life. I place my laptop down on the lounger and step inside my room, the AC hitting me in the face. I adjust the thermostat and go over to my beach bag for my meds.

"Amor mía," my dad continues, "are you okay? Is there something else going on?"

I squeeze my eyes shut and let a tear roll down my cheek.

"I know there are a lot of changes. But it's only over with Jack if you want it to be." I shake my head, thankful he can't see me. Of course he thinks I'm crying about Jack, and maybe I am a little. But for the first time in my life, my tears are because of my father. I could never tell him that I don't want Valentina's. That it's his dream and not mine. It would crush him. "Cry, mi'ja, it's okay. That's what these tears are about. If you knew what to do, you would do it. The tears are the tension." At that, my tears turn to sobs. "And they blur your vision to remind you that things are still unclear. When your heart is sure, the tears will go away, and you will know what to do." Maybe this clarity my dad speaks of will make an appearance and he'll come to his senses and make Ricardo his CEO. There's an idea. Lord knows Ricardo is way more equipped for the title than I'll ever be.

"Thank you, Papá," I whisper, wiping away my tears. If he knew that he is the one obstructing my path, he'd be heartbroken. "I love you," I say with a heavy sigh.

"Let me in!" Kiara's voice echoes in the hallway. She knocks like a heavy metal drummer. "Come on, chica, open up!"

"Coming!" I yell. "Papá? Tell Mom I love her and I'll call you guys later. Ciao, ciao!" I hang up as I swing open the door. "I was just about to get dressed!" Kiara rolls her eyes at me. I'm getting so good at telling lies, they just roll off my tongue at this point. I head to my closet and sift through my outfit options. My hair is still in a towel on my head, which is a dead giveaway that I'm far from ready, but I pull off the towel and brush it out, twisting it into a quick top knot. "See?" I smile at Kiara, who is staring at me with the look of death. "Halfway done."

The clock on the nightstand says 6:03, and I realize that between writing and chatting with my dad, I'm already late to dinner. "All of my outfits are planned, so it'll take me two secs." I grit my teeth in an overperformed smile.

"Blah, blah, blah." Kiara quacks her hands at me and rolls her eyes. "Just hurry up, I'm famished, and I don't want to upset Zin and Fay." She plops onto my bed and flicks on the TV.

My long navy ba&sh Paris midi dress hangs in the closet next to a pair of black scalloped shorts and white cami that I was planning to wear if we took a city tour. "Which one?" I hold up both options for Kiara to choose.

"Honestly couldn't care less." She narrows her eyes. "The dress." She rolls her hands, motioning for me to hurry up.

"Chill out, we're on vacation, no need to stress." I slip on my dress, apply a layer of clear lip gloss, check for my key card, and wave Kiara to the door. "Good? Quick enough?" I say as we leave my room and head for the elevator.

"You look *noiice*," Kiara says as she looks me up and down.

"Thanks. It's not too, I don't know, fancy?"

"Val, relax. It's dinner. You look perfect," she snaps.

"Hungry?" I ask.

"Hangry, if you must know."

"I couldn't tell." I roll my eyes and give a chuckle.

We step off the elevator, and Zinnia and Fay are waiting for us in the lobby.

"Sorry, sorry, we're late!" Kiara says.

"Not late at all!" Zinnia beams. "Drink?" She hands me and Kiara a flute of champagne. "You guys look hot."

"Back atcha," I reply.

"Shall we?" Fay inches closer to Zinnia and puts her glass in the air. We all raise our glasses to meet hers.

"To us!" Zinnia exclaims.

"To us," we echo.

Kiara

"WHO'S IN FOR TRUTH OR DARE?" VAL SAYS AS SHE MOUNTS A BARstool. A juicy grin crawls across her face like she's already got her twelve truths lined up.

I curl my lip at the idea. I don't have the emotional bandwidth for a deep night of sip-slow-and-dish, and the last thing I need is to be dared to dance with some stranger. I pull a stool out from under the bar next to Val and swivel it as I sit down.

Val notices my reluctance and tries again. "Movie trivia?" She raises an eyebrow.

"No, but I'll do alphabets," I offer.

"Oh alphabets! Yes!" Zin claps wildly. "We haven't played that since Mexico!"

Fay pats Zin's head like she's a child who needs to be reminded to calm down. "Right, because we were like twenty years old, and some of us," she meets Zin's gaze, "could handle our alcohol back then."

"I could handle my alcohol," Zin defends. "I just got a little too drunk that one time, come on!"

"Yes," I chime in. "It's called *shitfaced*, but I'm not judging."

We all laugh. "Only you can rewrite the narrative on that night because you don't remember most of it." I tap Zin's back, wind myself up on the barstool, and then launch myself to swivel around two full times.

"I don't think any of us forget the sight of Zinnia ransacking the hotel store for gum to spit into her glass so she could find a drink that started with the letter *X*. Like xylitol-infused yuzu vodka shots are even a thing." Val laughs. "But you made it work." She tilts her head to Zinnia in reverence.

"Right," Fay starts. "If you hadn't projectile vomited—"

"Twice!" Val holds up two fingers and smiles.

"Um," Fay starts, "we probably would've had to go to the hospital to have your stomach pumped. So, play at your peril, ladies. I'm out."

"Come on, you guys," Zin pleads. "I promise I'll stop if it's too much." She raises her hand, three fingers up, as if to say *Scout's honour*. "Promise! I don't care to win—it'll just be fun!"

"Ha!" Val laughs. "Like you didn't care to win when you sent that volleyball flying at that guy's face earlier."

"Bring it." Zin pulls her shoulders back and puffs her chest, doing her best cheerleader impression.

"Oh, it's already been broughten," Val snaps back.

"It's just twenty-seven drinks." Zinnia pouts her lips and puts her hands in prayer. "Say yes."

"Okay, first of all, it's twenty-six," Fay scoffs and puts her arm around Zinnia's shoulder. "And I'm fine if you guys play, I just don't wanna drink."

Fay leans in and whispers something into Zin's ear, running her hand up her spine. Zinnia nods, and Fay lets her hand linger for a moment before Zin breaks away. If I didn't know better, I'd say the two of them are up to something. I can't put my finger on what it is exactly, but they've been whispering to each other and exchanging glances all day.

"I'll go first!" Zinnia exclaims, her hand high in the air like she's in my grade five class. "Three apple martinis, please," she asks the bartender.

The rules of the game are simple: order drinks that start with each letter of the alphabet in a round robin. First one to screw up the order, quit drinking, or vomit, loses.

"Are you kidding me?" Val pushes Zin out of the way. "Scratch that. She looks directly at Fay and adds, "You can at least have one drink with us." She winks. "Can we have four shots of your Casamigos añejo, please?" She winks at me like we're in on some secret that the all-inclusive comes with free drinks.

"And chase it with four shots of bourbon," I add, and wink back. "Pappy Van Winkle." We're going top-shelf tonight, baby.

"No, make it three," Fay says firmly, rolling up the sleeves of her shirt. "I told you I'm not playing, and I'm serious. I'm too old for this shit."

Buzzkill.

"Maybe you can join in at *W*?" Zin asks, holding Fay's stare. "You'll have some wine, right?" She nudges Fay, and the expression on Fay's face softens.

What the hell is up with these two?

The bartender lines up six shots in front of us. We reach for our glasses and hold them up. "¡Pa' arriba, pa' abajo, pa' centro, pa' dentro!" Clinking our drinks together, we shoot them down like the competitive imbibers we are.

"What's next?" I ask.

We move on to caipirinhas topped with cherries (Zinnia's request) and dragon-fruit daiquiris (sweeter than I had expected), and my stomach is already turning from the nasty combination of sugar, fruit, and alcohol. I'm about to order us some espresso martinis when Fay leans into Zinnia's shoulder, brushes her hair aside, and whispers something into her ear again.

I don't think it's the alcohol getting the best of me—something is off. My gut is telling me that Zin's hiding something. From the way Fay is doting over her, it seems like maybe she's worried about her. Oh my god! Maybe she's pregnant again!

No. That theory doesn't hold. She's been drinking all day, and she just downed two shots and two drinks more. I stretch my arms and lean back over my stool to see if she faked them, pouring them out onto the ground, but the floor beneath her is bone dry.

Are they mad at me?

I slide off my seat and walk over to stand between them. They are so close to one another; I can barely wedge myself through. "Hello, mate?" I say in my best Australian accent.

"Don't do that." Fay smiles and shakes her head.

"Do what? What were you two talking about?" I continue in my regular voice.

"I was just saying that it's so good to see Zinnia let loose like this." Fay takes a step back, speaking loudly to get her voice over the music. "She needs this time away from her kids. That's all."

Because she's sick? I wonder. "Is that all?" I ask, raising a brow.

"What's that supposed to mean?" Fay defends.

"Whoa," I push back. "Chill out."

"No, you chill, Kiara." Val flashes a smile. "You guys, she's hangry. She just needs some food in her system if she plans to keep drinking." She slides over a small bowl of almonds. Zin stops them mid-slide and takes a few, popping them in her mouth before she hands the bowl over to me.

I put a handful of almonds in my mouth and feel my saliva gather like a tidal wave. When I swallow, I let out a burp and grab a few more. "Good call, but maybe we should order some actual food, like nachos or something."

"Done," Fay says, knocking the bar twice. She puts a hand up and waves the bartender over, orders a plate of wings, nachos, and some fries. "Did you want something else?" She puts her hand on Zin's and Zin flinches away.

"There!" I point. "That! What's that?!" I scream and rush back over to the end of the bar where Val is swaying to the music. "I'm not crazy. You saw that, right?" I ask Val, but she's not paying attention. "Zin, are you sick?"

"Sick?" Zinnia looks at me, offended by the suggestion. "Why? Do I look like shit?"

I turn to Val for some backup, but she's now sidled her way onto the dance floor. Four drinks in, and she's already blasé, wasted, and cha-chaing to the music. Her dress is twirling to the beat. Aside from the old guy with an overgrown moustache grooving alongside her on the checkered floor, she's the only person dancing.

"Yes! This is what I came for!" Zinnia hops off her stool. She throws her arms up and twirls like she's a backup dancer in *Mamma Mia!* as she joins Val on the floor.

I one-two-step over to them. "Will you order the espresso martinis?" I call over my shoulder to Fay. I know she's up to something, but I'm not gonna waste a good buzz trying to figure it out.

The deejay is playing the most perfect throwback playlist. He's covered everything from the Spice Girls and the "Macarena" to Britney and "Backstreet's Back." But when he starts on the slow jams, we all take our cue to head back to the bar. I hop onto my stool and slip my right sandal off to give my aching foot some relief.

"Hmm, what comes after *E*?" Zinnia leans over me, almost toppling us both down to the floor. She's slurring her words already. "*F!*" she yells, a streak of pride spreading across her face at completing the basic task of remembering the alphabet. "Oh! What's the one with fire?!" She puts her hand up for a high-five. I shouldn't leave her hanging, but it's sort of hilarious to see her staggering around like Gumby right now.

"You haven't even had your espresso martini yet!" I laugh. "We can slow down if you need. Lightweight."

"Who you calling a lightweight?" Her head is bobbing around, heavy like a bowling ball, and she can barely keep herself up. "Okay, okay, how about instead of four of each drink," she holds up four fingers, "we all share one." She lowers three fingers and holds one up for emphasis. "That way we can make it through the entire alphabet."

"How about you slow down, and we call it a night," Fay says softly. And there's that look again.

"She can decide for herself," I say. "She's not a child."

Fay gives me that face, the one she reserves for when she's judging people who pretend to care about things like global warming and sustainability but leave the water running while they load the dishwasher or go to Walmart to buy their vitamins and toilet paper because it's "closer" than their local independent grocery store. Basically, Fay's resting judge face. She claims she has zero mal intent—*It's my face, the one I was born with*, she says. But it's the slightest twitch of her upper lip and subtle flare of her nostril that transforms a harmless, seemingly innocuous remark into something obviously holier than thou.

"Guys." Val runs over, her face beet red and her eyes are brimming with laugh tears. "Um, you guys." She taps on Fay's shoulder and nudges my elbow. She points our attention to Zin, who has found her way back to the dance floor and is leaning on Moustache Man for support while she dances, if you can call what she's doing dancing.

"No, I can't. I'm done." Fay slams her hand on the bar and sends our basket of wings crashing to the floor. "G'night." At that, she turns, walks over to the dance floor, yanks Zinnia by the wrist, and drags her out of the bar.

"What the hell is Fay's problem?" I look at Val, but she has already fallen asleep, propped onto her elbow at the bar.

Waking up hungover is not my idea of fun. Add to that the fact that the AC is broken in my room and I'm basically butter in a sauna. My room stinks like a frat house. After drinks and dancing, I came back up and raided the mini bar, one mini bottle at a time. I reach for the hotel phone to call down for coffee to save me from my worsening migraine, when there's a knock at my door.

"Wakey, wakey, I've got lattes," comes Zin's voice from outside my room.

The words of an angel. I roll out of bed, pulling down my T-shirt to cover my ass, and open the door, rubbing the back of my hands over my eyes to save me from the light accosting me from the hallway.

"Rise and shine, it's a beautiful day. Let's go!" Zin sings cheerfully.

"Your energy needs to chill," I grumble, grabbing the white cup from her hand. "Coffee, yes. Beautiful day . . . no. It's only nine a.m., and I'm on vacation. No way I'm headed out this early." I take a sip of coffee and head back into bed, pulling the blanket over my face.

"I'm gonna sleep a bit more. Don't wait for me, I'll meet you guys by the pool later."

"I booked us all for spa treatments. We've got a start time of ten thirty." Zin gently pulls my blanket back. "Just take a quick shower and come have breakfast with us before we go," she says as she scans the room for my clothes. "You can sleep on the massage bed." She pulls the blanket off my face.

"Whoa! Who died and made you queen?" I give Zin my nastiest death stare before I burrito myself in my blanket.

The *Kill Bill* theme song starts to play. My hand wiggles its way blindly to my phone, and I click the silence button on what I know without looking is Wren.

"Sorry, I don't mean to be snippy, but my head is pounding." I pull the blanket down from my face and find Zinnia is now standing over my pillow. From this angle, her vertically challenged frame appears gigantic. Squinting, I muster a half smile and say, "I'll be waiting by the pool with cocktails when you guys are done luxuriating in bath salts and mud masks. Good?"

"Have it your way," Zin caves. "But text the girls to let them know you aren't coming. You know I hate being the bearer of bad news." She leans over and pulls the plug out of my phone. "And call Wren back." She tosses my phone at me.

My phone vibrates again, making the bed buzz. My heart thuds, and I take a deep breath to bring back a steady rhythm.

I wait for the sound of the door to click closed before I emerge from under my blanket. I chug down my latte as I hold my phone up, staring at the screen.

I've been avoiding Wren's calls since I got here. Every time I pick up the phone to call or text him back, something stops me. I keep saying I'll get to it later, but later never comes.

Nine on a Saturday morning. I tap my phone, paralyzed just thinking about what to say to him. Calling him now feels like a bad idea. He's probably on his way to work. Or he had a late night—potentially an all-nighter—and he's calling me on his way home from work. In either scenario, his mood will be shitty. Better if I try him later.

Yeah. After lunch.

I make my way around my room gathering everything I need for the spa. Maybe a little quiet time and a massage aren't a bad idea. I put my bag together—bridal magazines, sunblock, sunglasses, oversized hat—then I pull on my bathing suit and check myself in the mirror.

Meh.

I'm about to throw my phone in my purse when it rings again. It startles me and I accidentally send Wren to voicemail. Fuck. He's going to be so pissed.

I take a deep breath and decide it's time to bite the bullet. I click his number to call him back, but it goes straight to voicemail. He must be trying to call me again.

I open our text thread and write him to say that I'm trying to call him but that my phone's still being fussy. It's the perfect blanket excuse for why I haven't been calling or texting.

My phone lights up with a text.

ok babe. just got back to the office. tried you . . . you good?

Yeah, just calling you back but connection is weird, I reply.

call me around 4. miss your sweet face. He adds a kissy emoji.

Will do - love you.

I don't know why I thought Wren would be mad. He just wanted to say good morning.

Holding my phone in my hand, I turn the camera to face me and snap a selfie. I look like a whale in this bathing suit, but I send the pic anyway.

Hitting the pool. I hit send. Then I add, No filter lol.

babe, I don't have time for chit-chat. at work. call at 4.

There it is. The mood. He wants me to text, so I do, but when I do, he wants me to stop. It's confusing. Plus, I can only imagine what he would say if I said *yo babe, at work, don't have time for this*. In his mind, it doesn't matter if I'm in front of twenty-eight students and explaining long division, I'd be expected to stop and take his call. The hypocrisy kills me.

I don't have the energy for this.

Hangover is killing me. Love you all, will call when I wake up to see where you're at!

I hit send and toss my phone onto the counter.

I slip my beach bag off my shoulder, no longer in a spa mood. My phone buzzes like a firecracker. Two, three, four texts come in at once.

I pick up my phone and slide it open to realize I didn't send my last message to my girls. I sent it to Wren.

you got wasted, really?

faking bathing suit pics?

nice

fucking liar

I walk over to the curtain and pull it shut. I throw my phone at the wall and it lands on the floor with a thud. I crawl into my unmade bed to fall back asleep.

When I wake up, it's a little before three o'clock, and although my headache is gone, my stomach is growling with hunger. I stretch my legs and arms and roll out of bed.

I pick up my phone and see no missed calls and only one message from Fay from a couple hours ago. Guess you're ditching the spa? Call when you wake up.

If she only knew that I had sent exactly that message to her hours earlier—or rather, to Wren, by accident.

The girls are probably back by now, wondering if I died up here. Shoulders sagging, I grab my beach bag and head down to the pool. I feel like a celebrity staving off paparazzi wearing my oversized sunglasses and hat indoors, but I look a wreck without them.

When I get to the pool deck, the blistering sun hits me like a house on fire. A cacophony of children's laughter and splashing water, excited squeals punctuating the joyful atmosphere, triggers my headache and exacerbates my frustration at not finding a single empty pool chair.

I scan the area but don't see my friends. What I do see is a barbecue going, which accounts for the smell of sizzling burgers wafting through the air, stirring my hunger. If I don't get food in me fast, I might keel over.

Holding my stomach, I walk to the far side of the pool where I've located the one available pool chair left to lie down on. I type a message to the girls that I'm by the pool and double-check that I'm in the right chat before I hit send. Then, I order a grilled cheese, fries, and a cocktail.

"Excuse me, ma'am? Your lunch." A voice jolts me awake. I open my eyes and see a pool boy bending over me, blocking the sun as he rests a tray on my side table. I should be more bothered by the service—waking a sleeping guest is probably against some resort rule—but holy hell, it's like the god Adonis himself is standing over me. The sun's rays contour a halo of angelic yellow around his face, and as my eyes adjust, the full vision of him comes into focus. Curly brown hair, full lips, piercing brown eyes, high cheekbones, a jawline so sharp it looks like it was chiselled by a sculptor, and a fitted white polo hugging his olive skin.

"Who are you calling ma'am?" I muse, fluttering my lashes. I inch my body to sit up. Self-consciously, I take off my sunhat to hide my belly. "Thanks for waking me. I probably could've slept the day away."

"No problem," he says as he takes a step back. "Let me know if I can get you anything else."

In the hot romance version of this moment, I'd reply with something flirty and he'd whisk me away right there on the pool deck. We'd then proceed to make love for hours and only come up for air for him to tell me how beautiful I am.

"I'm all good, thanks," I reply, coming back down to earth.

He double-clicks his pen, and I watch as he walks away, tight white chinos hugging his buttocks.

Get a grip.

Reaching to bring the table closer to my chair, I clumsily bump the plate off, which sets off an embarrassingly loud bang. Mojito all over the floor, grilled cheese sopping up alcohol as it sits in a puddle of liquid, and, of course, for added humiliation, french fries scattered everywhere, including inside my bag. If that weren't bad enough, I shriek reflexively, and the entire pool deck stops and stares. I feel like I'm caught in a freeze-frame.

The pool boy comes rushing back. "It's okay, ma'am. I got this." Kneeling by my chair, he begins picking up my spoiled lunch, fry by soggy fry.

I slide off my chair and kneel beside him, picking up the pieces of sandwich. One looks fairly dry, and I consider salvaging it because I'm that hungry, but I swat the thought away.

"Could you please stop calling me ma'am? I'm probably younger than you," I say with a laugh as I grab fries by the fistful and dump them onto his tray.

He catches my eye and half smiles. I notice a scar on his upper lip and feel compelled to reach out and touch it. Locked in a staring contest, I'm wrapped up in the moment and lose all sense of what's normal social behaviour. Gently, I glide my finger over the scar.

"How'd you get this?" I ask, my fingers still on his skin.

He brings his hand to his mouth and our fingers touch. We stay there for a moment and then he lowers our hands slowly, reaches into his little black apron, and pulls out a stack of napkins to soak up my mojito from the pool deck.

"My mom tossed me up in the air to settle me from all my cryin' and when she caught me, I bit my lip." He licks his scar. "When she tells the story, she always adds that I deliberately hurt myself so I could get more hugs." He shrugs, grabbing the soggy slice of grilled cheese out of my hand and tossing it onto his tray.

"I have a scar too," I say, pointing to my shoulder. "I got it when I was in high school. I was out with my girlfriends one night playing frisbee in the park. It got dark, and I didn't see the park bench. I slammed right into it." Once I hear myself tell the story, I'm mortified. First I dump my lunch, then I bang into a bench. He must think I am the biggest klutz. "I mean, I did it on purpose so my friends would hug me."

He laughs. Without breaking eye contact, he finishes cleaning up my mess and holds out a hand to help me up. He towers over me, which puts him at six-five, at least. He smiles, and I'm smitten.

"My name's Kiara, by the way." I keep hold of his hand.

"Frankie," he responds.

A tense, foreboding tone, akin to a quickening heartbeat plays from my purse. The *Kill Bill* theme song interrupts our staring contest. Wren. Shit! What was I thinking?

"Is it four o'clock?" I ask nervously, but the knot in my stomach confirms the answer.

"Let me go check that for you," Frankie replies, pointing to his watchless wrist. "And let me bring you a fresh grilled cheese and fries. It was nice to meet you." He locks my gaze and then adds, "Kiara." My name in his mouth like sweet surrender.

As though in slow motion, I watch Frankie walk away and disappear into the hotel kitchen.

"Hello," I say, phone raised and finger in my ear so I can hear Wren over the music. "Hello?" I repeat softly.

"So now you're *actually* at the pool?" His voice is justifiably upset.

"I'm sorry," I start. "I can explain."

"Whatever Keeks, it's four fifteen. The least you can do is call when you say you'll call." I pull my phone away to verify the time, his voice droning on in the background. Five missed calls. "Hello? You there?" he asks, a bull repeatedly ramming into me.

My voice is blocked.

"You ignoring me now?"

I want to speak but no words come out.

"I don't have time for this shit. Peace out. Don't call me, I won't answer."

I take a few heaving breaths in and close my eyes. I feel the air pass through my lips as I exhale slowly. What just happened?

Staring at the phone in my hand, I watch tear drops land on the screen, tiny puddles of fear.

With trembling fingers, I start texting: I couldn't hear you babe. Told you my phone is fussy here. Bad reception. Love you. Hope you're OK.

oh makes sense - I couldn't hear you. love you babe. go up to the room now to call me back so we can catch up

I take a deep breath as I look up from my phone, contemplating what I should respond. I don't want to go up to my room, but I can't tell him that.

Plus, Frankie will be coming back with my lunch soon and I'm starving. I start writing that I'll call him after I eat, but I delete it all. I can't text him that. It would set off a deluge of angry messages. And, I would deserve each and every one of them.

Ugh, why am I overthinking this? I should go to my room to call Wren back then come back down to eat. Although, I could probably just call him from the lobby since my phone isn't *actually* being fussy.

All I want to do is pull the towel back over my face and sleep until tomorrow. Make everything go away.

Fay

"WHAT HAPPENED HERE?" I ASK, ASSESSING THE SCENE: MINT leaves and lime hang off Kiara's beach bag, and her towel is soaked, emitting a faint smell of rum. Val picks up a drenched fry off the pool deck as evidence in my inquiry. "Wasting no time at all, I see." I plop down beside Zinnia, who is already on the end of Kiara's chair and soaking in the sun.

"Really nice, guys," she hisses. "I'm starving, and I just spilled my whole lunch, so maybe ease up." She adjusts her sunglasses, pushing me over slightly with her foot so she can extend her legs. She tilts her head back exaggeratedly to show me that she is now sunbathing and this conversation is over.

"Right." I bite my lip so as not to react. After the way she was sussing me out last night, the last thing I want to do is poke at her, but she's coming undone. I've never seen her drink this much, which is to say that it can only be one of two things: a cry for help or an escape plan. Either way, I'm not touching it with a ten-foot pole. I've already learned how impossible it is to get between someone and their alcohol. "Val and I are gonna paddleboard. You wanna join?" I say, attempting to cut the tension. I nod to the infinite blue in front of us and glance over at Val, who is conveniently quiet, and then at Zin, who is pretending that suntanning is pulling all her focus.

Kiara shakes her head no and continues to concentrate on suntanning.

"You haven't been to the beach at all," I add, but she pulls her leg away from me. "We said nothing when you ditched the spa, but can you actually be on this girls trip with us?" I mouth *help* to Val, but she gives me a thumbs-up like she's encouraging a toddler to go play with her toys.

"We just really want to spend time together, what do you say?" I add.

"Actually, I was just gonna head back up to my room to make a call." She shoves her hat on her head and stands up.

"Please, Keeks, don't leave. Just talk to us." I look at Val, who mouths *stop*. Her eyes are wide, and she's cutting her throat. "Is everything okay with Wren?" I blurt out, and Val hits her forehead, letting out a grunt.

"I knew you were talking about me last night!" Kiara snaps at me. "Just waiting for the perfect time to come at me. You and Zin at the bar, Statler and Waldorf in your little peanut gallery." She's wagging her fingers at me like I've performed some sort of curse on her.

"Whoa, on s'calme," I respond. "Chill out, I was just asking." I stand to meet her face to face. Val and Zin stand behind me like they're my bodyguards, ready to hold Kiara down if it comes to that.

"It's not like that, Keeks," Val finally chimes in.

"Look who found her voice," I turn to her and roll my eyes. Val hits my head playfully and shushes me.

Kiara hates being confronted. Anything that feels like criticism is taken as a personal affront to her character. Val knows that and avoids it like the plague. Meanwhile, she was the first to suggest I say something. *Just create an opening*, she said, *then we'll step in.*

But I blew it. I came in fast and hard.

"Please don't be mad," Val puts her hands together in prayer position at her chest. "We're just worried about you, that's all."

The look on Val's face is halfway between petrified cat and sad mime. The idea that Kiara could be mad at her is probably making her heart skitz. The only time they've ever gone without talking was science class in grade ten, and that's only if you count passing notes as not talking.

"Worried? Why?" Kiara puts her hands on her hips. Her stance reads *epic fight energy*.

"Because," Zin starts, "you've been drunk since you got here."

"I'm on vacation," she enunciates slowly and clearly.

"And you're avoiding Wren's calls," I continue. "Don't think we haven't noticed."

She rolls her eyes.

"And you're acting different," Val adds softly. "Not yourself."

Kiara takes a step toward us. "Have you ever thought that maybe I'm not the one acting differently and that all three of you have changed?" Her voice is low, like a growl. She's pointing her finger at us, and I can tell she is about to go ballistic. I brace myself for what's to come, but then she does the unexpected. She puts her dukes down and lets out a breath.

"You know what?" she says, sitting down on the side table, shoulders slumped. "These trips used to be a lot simpler. When did we switch out adventures on a dime for lounging around some expensive resort? It's like some desperate attempt to be young and relevant."

The words out of my mouth. I mean, I wouldn't have said it quite like that, but she's not wrong. This trip cost more than any of our other trips, and we've been everywhere from Spain and Costa Rica to Thailand and Peru. Seeing the world, that's what they were about. Not sipping cocktails by the pool.

"I blame Val." I turn and point to Val, who already has her hands up like the Hamburglar.

She winces. "What the—"

"What? You planned this trip," I double down.

"Cool it," Zin interjects. "We all agreed that the Bahamas was a good idea. Don't blame Val. We can snorkel, swim with pigs, kitesurf . . ."

"Exactly." Val sticks out her tongue at me.

Zin walks over to stand beside Kiara and places a hand on her shoulder. She picks up a few braids and gently places them over her shoulder. "But you know what, Keeks?" She lowers down so they are face to face. "They probably wouldn't let you hangglide drunk, so there's that."

Kiara rolls her eyes.

"Your grilled cheese and fries, Kiara," a pool boy holding a tray says, approaching the four of us. Kiara stands up off the side table, making room for him to place the tray down. She swivels around, giggling flirtatiously, and sits on the pool chair beside me.

"Seems like we've found Kiara's definition of adventure," I say, and Kiara whips around to give me the eye. "Oh, it's okay when Zin teases?" I ask.

"Who is that?" Val whispers in my ear.

"Thank you, Frankie," Kiara says to the pool boy softly.

We watch him walk away, and the second he's out of earshot, Kiara turns back to me and snaps, "Why did you say that? That was so embarrassing!" She grabs half of her grilled cheese and walks away.

"*Thank you, Frankie*," I repeat, imitating Kiara. "What was that?" I stretch out on the pool chair and watch as Kiara scampers toward the bar where Frankie is pouring alcoholic slush into plastic cups.

"In this week's episode of *Real Housewives*, Kiara throws herself at resort staff," Val speaks into her invisible microphone. "Stay tuned to witness every last embarrassing moment."

Val and I laugh, but Zinnia shakes her head at us. "You guys, stop. Leave her alone."

We watch as Kiara reaches for a daiquiri, places her other hand on Frankie's shoulder, then laughs at whatever it is he just said. Frankie whispers something into her ear, and I let out a grunt louder than intended. Zin nudges me to stop. I can't help myself; this is ridiculous. Are we all just going to sit here and let her blow up her life?

"If we were good friends, we'd stop her," I state.

"I agree," Zin says, lowering her Ray-Bans onto her face. "But we have to let her play this out. Something is obviously going on, and when she's ready, she'll talk to us."

"Spoken like a true mother." I laugh. If it were up to me, I'd yank her away and force her to face her problems. I wouldn't let her make a mistake this big. Zin may be under the impression that Wren is a good guy, but I know Wren, and this won't end well. "I can't watch this." I push myself off the seat and sit on the newly vacant chair beside us, facing the other direction.

Val sprawls out on her chair and taps for Zin to join her, but Zin stands up and moves two steps closer to the bar.

"I wanna see if I can lip read," Zin says, using her hand to shield her eyes from the sun like a visor.

Val and I look at each other and giggle. In a past life, Zin was a sleuth. All she needs right now is a trench coat and a magnifying glass and she would be in her very own version of Inspector Gadget.

"Life's too complicated to add self-sabotage to the mix, you know what I mean?" I say as I grab the other half of Kiara's grilled cheese and take a bite.

"Do I ever," Val responds with a grin. "Wait, why is your life complicated? The gallery?" She reaches for a fry.

"No, no, my life is the same as usual." I look at Zin to see if she's paying attention, but she's still all eyes on Kiara, who is now pouring another daiquiri and clinking glasses with three spring breakers. "Gallery's comme çi comme ça." I motion my hand to show *so-so*. "Sales have been hard; the art world has really changed. Not sure when people started valuing bargain bin 'art,' but hey, there you have it: they'd prefer a canvas with bubble letters that say *dream*. But I can't teach philistines to appreciate what they can't understand." I shrug.

Zinnia whips her head around to face me. "You have that sculptor you were showing. The one who sold out her entire collection?"

"Such a little multi-tasker." I laugh. "I didn't realize you were listening. But yeah, I have that sculptor, I'll be fine." If she agrees to show her next collection at my gallery, that is. And even with that, I'd have to sell out completely just to tide me over for one more month. Zin has no clue the world of shit I'm in with the gallery, and I don't want her to find out. I need her to know that she can depend on me as a partner and stepmom to Darla and Saul. "It's all good though, really. Nothing to tell." I can't remember, do friends not make secrets or do secrets not make friends?

"I get it," Val says. "Your art gallery is everything to you. It's your passion. I know a little something about that."

No you don't, I think. My gallery is not just my passion, it's my livelihood. I don't have a fallback plan. I don't have a pile of money waiting to cushion me if I fail. I sunk the rest of my grandmother's inheritance into this gallery, and if I don't make some serious sales in the next few months, I won't make rent, and I'll have to close my doors . . . forever.

"No more of this." I shake my hands out as if to wash away the shop talk. I just want to keep things light. Well that and jump Zin. "Bon, should we head for the beach?" I clap my hands.

"You two go ahead, I'm gonna hang back," Zin says. "See if maybe I can get somewhere with Keeks." She motions her head to the bar.

"You sure?" I pat her shoulder, but she flinches.

"Yeah, go." She waves us away.

Val jumps up. "Watch our stuff?"

We walk toward the pebbled path that worms its way to the beach, and I feel the warmth of the sun, smell the coconut scent that wafts through the air. Looking out at the sea, a young couple holding hands as the waves crash at their knees catches my eye. I imagine from the tension in her shoulders that the woman is nervous about something. Maybe she's scared to tell her boyfriend she loves him for the first time, or she needs to come clean about something. I play out the scene in my mind, even though I know she's probably just holding her shoulders by her ears because the water is bitingly cold.

He holds her hand tightly as their feet carry them deeper into the water with every step. She shivers and leans into him, and he kisses her head. He tugs her into the water playfully, her back landing flat against the tide. She yells out with a laugh and swings to punch his arm, but she misses and falls back into the current. I can't help but feel a twist of jealousy.

This could've been Zin and me right now, basking in each other openly, sun-kissed and happy. But instead, we're hiding. And not that well, might I add, since even blitzed Kiara seems to be onto us. Good news is the thought of the two of us being together is so unfathomable that she's guessed illness and pregnancy over a love affair.

We keep walking along the shoreline toward the paddleboard cabana. I take in the huge, expansive sea stretching out in brilliant turquoise. Soft sand beneath my feet, all I should see is the beauty around me as I breathe in the salty air and bask in the warm breeze. Instead, I feel the weight of my secret threatening to burst out of my chest.

I bend over and scoop a handful of wet sand, letting it slip through my fingers as the water curls back. "I have a girlfriend," I blurt out.

There's nothing in the world I've ever kept from Val, and I need her to tell me that what I'm doing is going to work out. That Zin and I are meant to be.

"What?" I can't tell if her question is asked with excitement or if she didn't hear me. She rolls her hands to indicate that I should go on, so I guess she's listening.

"She's married," I continue. "But it's the real deal, she's leaving h—" I stop myself, but Val doesn't seem to notice.

We approach the paddleboards and sign our names on the dangling clipboard. "At least I think it's the real deal," I murmur to myself as I pull on my life vest. "God, I hope I don't end up with a broken heart again."

Val's vacant stare is adding to the intensity of my fear.

I thought I'd feel lighter getting this off my chest, but Val's reaction isn't what I thought it would be.

"Heartbreak is inevitable," Val says indifferently as she thrusts her paddleboard down into the sand. She flings herself onto the board, shoulders sagging by her side.

I regret having said anything.

"Is this about Jack?" I ask, kneeling on her board beside her. I place my hand on her thigh. She takes my hand and looks up at me. "Zin told me everything," I say.

She flinches, dropping my hand. "She told you I cheated?"

"No." I shake my head. "No, I didn't know— Wait, what? You cheated?" I stare at her, waiting for her to respond, but she's wearing a vexed look on her face that clues me in to the fact that I'm not the only one keeping secrets around here.

Zinnia

I'M WATCHING KIARA AS SHE RESTS A HAND ON FRANKIE'S CHEST, full belly laughing. She glances back at me, and I wave her over, but she just tosses her braids over her shoulders and narrows back in on whatever Frankie is saying. I sit back to ponder a strategy on how to get Kiara away from what could be the biggest mistake of her life. She's too drunk and way too flirty to be in her right mind, and she'll live to regret this moment if she lets it get too far. If *I* let it get too far.

My silent pleas for her to return aren't working, so I grab the Sun Bum and march over to the cabana.

"Hey, I need your help," I say, throwing my arm over her shoulder. "I can't reach my back." I smile coyly at Frankie. "Vacation problems!" I laugh as I grab Kiara's wrist and pull her away by force.

"I'll be back!" Kiara waves her fingers at Frankie. "What the hell?" she snaps at me when we get back to our pool chairs.

"I thought it best to drag you away from whatever it was that you were doing over there before someone gets hurt," I say, tossing the Sun Bum into Kiara's bag.

Her face clocks the situation and her expression transforms from annoyed to defensive.

"Oh my god, do you really think I'd cheat on Wren?" She folds her arms across her chest. Then she reaches for her daiquiri, her fourth cocktail, if I'm counting correctly. "My character is my integrity."

The number of times I've heard Kiara say those words; she wears them like a badge of honour. I remember one time, when we were younger, we were at Val's house hanging around, dishing about our love interests. Well, not me. I was silent, having sworn Kiara to secrecy about my crush: Jonah Rolkin. He was head of the theatre club and so cute. He had asked me to go for pizza, but, because we all knew Val liked him too, I turned him down. Kiara knew how much it would hurt Val if she found out. But that night, Val accurately accused me of being silent because of Jonah. Apparently, my secret was public knowledge. Val was heartbroken. I immediately accused Kiara—she was the only person I had told. I was pissed at her for weeks only to find out that it was Jonah who had told Val. I apologized umpteen times for blaming her, but she was so hurt that I could believe she could do something so immoral. *My character is my integrity* was all she kept saying.

"It's a fine line between flirting and . . ." I trail off.

Kiara gazes back toward Frankie and raises her glass, and he nods back at her. She puts the straw to her lips and manages to make the mundane act of sipping a cocktail a sexual provocation. "A little harmless flirting never hurt anyone," she says, and she smiles. "It's healthy. Encouraged, even." She giggles.

Maybe it is innocent. Maybe I'm projecting.

"He's cute," I soften, tilting my head toward the cabana. "Sort of looks like an old Gael García what's-his-face." I snap my fingers.

"Bernal. Mm, yes! That's who it is." Disarmed. "I love that guy!"

I reach for the oil and join Kiara in applying it up and down both legs.

"Want me to get you a drink?" She slurps back the rest of her daiquiri. "It'll give us an excuse to call Gael over," she laughs.

"Nah." I grab her empty glass from her hand. "I think we're done with that."

"Dude, can you just back off? A few drinks won't make me forget my fiancé." Kiara snatches her glass back. "And like I said, I would never cheat on Wren, so stop acting like I'm doing something wrong." She whips her legs around to sit up facing me. "I would never do that to him, or to Raven for that matter."

I shake my head as I search for my words, but nothing comes out. Part of me wants to give Kiara a *hell ya*, a high-five, and move on. But only one of us can honestly sit pretty on the moral high ground, and it isn't me.

I rub my temples and take a deep breath. Letting out a big exhale, I turn my face the other way so Kiara can't see the tears streaming down my cheeks.

"Hey . . . What's going on?" she asks gently.

I take another deep breath and face Kiara. "Can I tell you a secret?"

"You know I'm a vault," she says, cocking her head to the side and raising her brow. "Jonah Rolkin."

"Right." I nod and look away. "But I also know that your moral code is quite high, and that you'll judge me."

"Who's judging who?" She raises her brow and grins. "Judgment suspended," she says with her hands in the air. "Just spill."

"I just need you to tell me I didn't fuck everything up," I add as I pull at my cuticles.

"Would you stop that?" Kiara swats my hands. "Start talking. What did you do?"

I take a deep breath and lean forward, crisscrossing my legs so I'm in butterfly position, and then fold my body over. "I cheated on Adam," I say, my voice muffled.

"You what?" Kiara brings her face closer to mine.

I sit up and look Kiara dead in the eye. "I cheated," I repeat. "On Adam."

Kiara leans back and reaches for her drink. She raises her glass to her mouth and uses her tongue to draw in the straw and take a sip, but there's nothing left. She places her cup on the ground. I watch her intently as I await her reaction. "One-night stand or affair?"

I fling myself back onto my chair and cover my face with my hands. "Does it even matter?"

"Absolutely," Kiara says, getting up and sitting on the edge of my chair. "The distinction is everything. In one case, it's just sex." I think about the difference between Val cheating and my affair. "But a full-blown side thing is a symptom of something missing in your marriage."

"When did you get so wise?" I ask, lowering my hands.

"I'm just saying that you're not a bad person." She rubs my legs. "So, if you cheated, then you should explore why."

Before I know it, I blurt out, "Because I love her." Then I stare at Kiara and wait for her to clock the pronoun.

Like a lightbulb turning on, Kiara's face lights up. "Her?" she shrieks. "Oh, this is juicy. I need another drink." She stands up, but I yank her by the wrist and pull her back down.

"Could you not?" I sigh.

"Fine." She rolls her eyes dramatically, making a show of acquiescing. "So, *love*? Really?" Kiara asks skeptically.

"I've never been this happy in my life," I confirm, and I'm not sure if I'm saying it to persuade her or myself.

She cocks her head. "That's why you look so—" she waves her hand in front of my face and scrunches her nose "—not wound up."

"Right, well," I say. "Then there's that little thing called *my kids*." At the mention of my children, Kiara begins to shake her head. She squints her eyes like she's searching for the answer. I can see the judgment slowly taking over her face. "Can you say something, please? Solve all my problems?" I pick at a piece of skin from my finger.

"Here's what I'll say." She reaches for her beach bag and stands up. "You're moving to California, right?"

"How do you know?" I sit up.

"Val can't keep a secret for shit." Kiara laughs. I roll my eyes and let out a sigh, my lips vibrating as I exhale. "All I'm saying is that unless this chick is moving with you . . ." She stares at me, searching my face for the answer. I lower my eyes. "Right, well then, this relationship has an expiration date. So, what's love gotta do with it, right?"

"Thanks, Keeks." I feign a smile.

"I'm gonna head up and call Wren." Kiara slips her earbuds in one at a time. "Just end it, sooner rather than later. Adam's a good guy. He'll forgive you if you ask nicely."

Right, I think. *What's love gotta do with it* . . .

Kiara bends down and kisses the top of my head. She tells me everything is going to work itself out and then pushes her sunhat back onto her head. "Tell Wren I say hi," I say. She tosses her braids back, and I watch as she sashays her way into the lobby.

Left all alone with my thoughts, I replay our entire conversation in my head. Kiara's drunken insight is too much for me to handle. And hopefully she's drunk enough to forget this conversation ever happened. Do I want Adam to forgive me? I shake my head. No, that's the wrong question. I rewind further: Is Fay just a symptom of a bigger problem? Partly, maybe. But is that wrong? I've been so unhappy with Adam, but no, I love Fay independently of my issues with him—and maybe love has everything to do with it.

The statement feels true, so I repeat it and let it wash over me: I love Fay independently of my issues with Adam. And Fay didn't ruin my marriage. My marriage was already ruined, and Fay saved me. Maybe this relationship doesn't have to have a best-by date. Maybe I should tell Fay about California and see if she'll move with me. Maybe that's been the answer all along.

I walk through the lobby and head to the elevator with a determination I didn't know I had.

When I reach the twenty-fourth floor, I find myself face to face with our hotel door. Instead of using my key, I knock gently and step away, hoping Fay's back from paddleboarding.

"Well, there you are," Fay says, swinging the door open. "If I didn't know any better, I'd say you've been avoiding me." She leans her head out into the hallway and looks both ways before pulling me in.

"Can we talk?" I say as I wiggle out of her hold. I push past her and walk straight for the balcony. She's still wearing her bikini from earlier, her body glistening with sunblock and sweat.

"You look serious," Fay says, following me outside.

I smile and tuck a curl behind my ear. I look around at all the magazines spread across the floor and table. Her laptop is open to a Pinterest mood board filled with images of high-gloss resin finished canvases.

"Sorry, you were working," I start as I leaf through one of the magazines. Fay waves her hand to say it's okay. I go on, "This isn't the sculptor's work. What is all this?"

"One of my other artists, I hope. She's putting together a collection highlighting the tension between fast fashion and sustainability, the environmental impact of consumer waste. I'm looking for inspo on how to show her work. Something less traditional, more in line with her message."

"Like with eco-friendly lighting and nontoxic paints for the walls?" I'm letting myself get sidetracked. Maybe a little small talk will help calm my nerves. They need a sedative; I can legitimately hear my own heartbeat.

"Exactly. I hadn't thought of the lighting, but yes." She closes her laptop and piles the magazines so there's room for us to sit down. "All this eco-stuff, it's gonna cost me a pretty penny."

I clock the comment and add it to the other flippant remarks she's made lately about the gallery. I know the way Fay operates; it's only ever been one artist at a time. But now there's two at once *and* she's working on vacation? Something's going on, but now's not the time—I have a California-sized fish to fry.

"Hey," she knocks my knee playfully, "did Val tell you she cheated on Jack?" She puts her hands by her temples and then makes an explosion.

I nod. "Exactly, it's a little *too* unbelievable if you ask me." I lean back on my hands. *Enough with the small talk*, is what I want to say, but instead I look out over the balcony rail at the human-size chess board, shuffleboards, trapeze-style swings from palm trees, and colourful hammocks spread all around. We are too high for anyone to see us, but still low enough to make out the sounds of children shouting below. Staring off at the pool deck, I take Fay's hand in mine and let out a breath. I twirl her ring between my fingers: a ruby stone she wears on her index finger. A subtle trace of powerful energy and passion.

I don't know where to begin, so I just start talking, hoping something will make sense.

"Fay, the last few months with you have been incredible." I squeeze her clammy hand and keep my eye steady on her ring. "I love being your best friend, and I would never want to lose that. But also, the last six months, when I'm with you, you make me feel something I never knew was possible. It's a love that feels all-consuming. We create an energy that radiates like magic, and I never, ever, not for a moment, want to know what it feels like not to have you right here, right with me, all the time."

I take her hand to my chest and pause to feel her pulse synch with mine. I can feel the heat between us rising. She pushes her forehead against mine, and we both close our eyes. Tears well in my eyes. I thought I had come up here to ask her if she'd consider moving with me, but I could never ask her to choose between me and her work. In a perfect world, this would all work out—Fay would move and we'd have some modern version of a Brady Bunch family out in California—but in the real world, pragmatically, I'm overwhelmed by the mere thought that my family could be torn apart, Fay could lose everything she's worked for, and our love wouldn't be enough to conquer it all.

It's all too much for me. I'm more confused now than I was before. Kiara's words ring in my ear: *what's love gotta do with it* . . .

Fay wipes my tears and lets her hand drop into my lap. Our faces are still so close I can feel her breath on my lips. "It sounds like you're breaking up with me," she starts. "Tell me that's not what you're saying." The expression on her face is resigned, like a lost puppy, but I can see the devastation hovering beneath her controlled gaze.

"I'm saying I feel stuck. I know you want more, and I wholeheartedly want to give you that, but it'll break my home. I can't be a mom who only sees her kids on a part-time basis." The mere thought of shared custody makes me feel like I'm choking. I let out a shaky breath.

"You know I can't do that." I shake my head, feeling the weight of my words pushing my shoulders down, my voice trembling. "But staying with Adam doesn't feel right anymore either." And that's the truth I have yet to explore. Even without Fay, is there still an Adam? "I feel like, no matter what . . ." My voice trails off. Fay reaches out her hand and touches my lip with a finger, a gentle plea for me to stop.

I fold into her lap and let the tears fall. Fay caresses my back, and after a few seconds, she kneels down on the floor in front of my chair and lifts up my head.

"I know all of this, Zin. We've talked about it a dozen times. It's complicated, and there're a lot of moving parts. But we're not pressured for a solution. We have time. I'm sorry I tried to push you to tell Val and Keeks. That was too much too soon. For me, as long as we both still agree that the only thing we know for certain is that we love each other, then we're good." She motions between us. "The rest will work itself out, right? What we're doing here," she says quietly as she cups my face, "I want to keep doing it. One day at a time."

Her voice is shaky, and although she's trying to be strong for me, I can tell that she is more likely trying to convince herself that this will all work out. We're both scared of driving in the dark, but at least she's holding on to hope that our love will guide the way.

I lean into her and reach my hand around the back of her neck. Holding her close, I can feel my shoulders melt as we stay locked there for a moment; all the tension I've been carrying slips away.

I want to make the most of our time together.

Slowly, I untie the top of her bikini and watch as the tiny piece of material slips down between her thighs. Tracing the lines of her collarbone, I can feel my heart begin to race. We lock our gaze, and I know there's no stopping what's about to happen.

Fay's eyes follow mine as I make my way to standing, slowly pulling down my shorts, letting them pool at my ankles. Stepping out, I gently push her back up against the rattan lounge chair and climb on top of her. Skin sticky from the sun, our bodies meld together with traces of salt from the sea mingled with oil and sweat.

"I want you," I whisper into her ear, my breath warm against her skin. "Do you want this?"

Fay licks my lips and opens my mouth with her tongue. Her touch sends shivers down my spine as she slides her fingers down my stomach, slipping into my bikini where I'm waiting for her with a pulsing heat. I mimic her as I push aside her bikini bottom and slip my fingers into her with equal intensity.

We move together with a slow, unhurried rhythm. Even though the map of her body is burned into my memory, each touch and caress is still a discovery sending a pulsing energy between my legs. My straddle tightens as she sits up, cups my breast, and wraps her other arm under my butt to hoist me up off the lounger and onto the concrete floor. Her lips never leave mine.

Legs intertwined, we twirl our fingers around and let mutual moans guide us, harder, deeper, faster. The sounds of shared pleasure fill the air, until we are both breathlessly *oh*-ing in unison. A sensation that had gone dormant years ago that Fay has reawakened. My body shakes in tandem with hers as we both reach sheer ecstasy.

We collapse together, spent on the floor of her balcony, lying in the open air, my head on her chest as we overlook the guests lounging by the pool.

"This is what I want, Fay, and I wouldn't want it with anyone but you." I kiss her softly.

"We can be late for dinner, right?" Fay laughs as she swiftly glides her naked body down my torso until she's looking at me from between my thighs. "I think we can go again," she says, and she presses her tongue into me.

I close my eyes and let my real life fade into the distance.

Valentina

KIARA AND I SIT AT A TABLE FOR FOUR, SWATTING WAITERS AWAY from pressuring us into ordering something. Three texts and a few calls, but Fay and Zin are nowhere to be found.

"You know Fay has a girlfriend?" I dish, rubbing my hands together. I wait for Kiara's reaction, but she stares blankly ahead. "What's up? Why are you glaring at that old couple over there."

"I'm not." She shakes a thought out of her head and looks at me. "I just had an annoying conversation with Wren, that's all."

There it is: my opening. I knew she'd come around eventually. "Wanna talk about it?" I extend my hand across the table.

"No." She purses her lips. "I'm on vacation. I want to drink." Just then, Kiara's phone vibrates. She hits ignore and flips it over.

At least Wren cares enough to keep calling. Jack hasn't reached out once since our dinner.

Although, neither have I. I did attempt an email earlier. After paddleboarding, I went up to my room and wrote him a whole letter telling him the truth. There was no cheating, just lying about cheating. But as I was typing, I found myself incapable of explaining why I did it. Why I blurted out some cockamamie lie when he was down on bended knee. I kept thinking about how Zin said *the why does matter*. I saved the email to drafts; I need time to explore the why before I rope Jack back in. He deserves that, at the very least.

Kiara's phone dings again, and she clicks to ignore it without looking.

"What if it's Fay or Zin?" I ask.

"It's not," she replies firmly and takes a sip of water. We both know I know who it is. I'm just playing her game.

"Tonight should be fun," I mutter sarcastically under my breath. But Kiara doesn't hear me—she's too busy trying to catch the waiter's attention.

Just then, Fay and Zin walk into the restaurant. Like a blast from the past, I'm immediately struck by how Zinnia looks. Wearing this striped button-down dress that is part bohemian, part chic. Exactly her. Eclectic but not too loud. Her style has always said so much about who she is—even though she's been wearing sweats and a top knot for the better part of a decade—she's always been that boho deep down, and tonight, that effervescent hippie vibe is out in spades. Her shoulder-length curls reveal a long neckline filled with turquoise and gold jewellery.

I beam at her. "You look absolutely stunning!"

"It's vintage Valentina's." She twirls. "Your dad gave it to me that summer we interned there."

"'Kay, but only you could pull it off and make it look young." Zinnia has always had an eye for fashion. Not to mention that in our one summer interning, she learned how to sew, make patterns, stitch hems, and all that stuff. Meanwhile, I spent the summer hiding in the supply closets, trying to avoid learning about profit margins, distribution, and warehousing.

"So, how's everyone doing?" Fay asks as she sits down, smiling ear-to-ear. She passes out the menus, which Zin and I take, but Kiara waves away.

"Starved, actually." Kiara motions again for the waiter and finally gets his attention. She probably would've thrown her napkin at him if he walked past her one more time. "You two are super late."

"I'm sorry," Zin says and lowers her head. She lets out a giggle and covers her mouth.

"Good evening, ladies," the waiter starts, pen in hand, ready to take our order. "Does everyone know what they want?"

Fay opens her menu and scans quickly. "Wanna share oysters?" she asks Zin. "Or maybe, do we all want oysters?" She looks at all of us to see who's down for sharing. I nod. Zin shakes her head and buries her face in her menu.

"Maybe you need a moment?" The waiter smiles politely.

"Yeah, sorry," Fay replies in a sorry-not-sorry way.

"Can we hear the specials?" I ask as I close my menu.

Kiara rolls her eyes and taps her fingers on the table as she listens impatiently to the waiter rattle off dish after dish. "I'll do the steak and potatoes, please." She hands him the menu when he's finally done describing the chocolate soufflé.

"Mmm, good choice. I'll do the chicken parm, please, light on the tomato sauce. Oh, and I'll share the oysters with you if you're having them." I point to Fay as I hand my menu shut and hand it to the waiter.

"You know what, let's do the surf 'n' turf platter instead, no?" Fay nods at Zin.

"Okay, I'll do that with you guys?" I ask. "Instead of the parm . . . Is that fine, or is it not enough?"

"Oh my god, will you guys just order!" Kiara blurts out.

"Sorry," Fay says to the waiter, rolling her eyes. "We'll take the large surf 'n' turf, enough for three of us. And you," she points a finger at Kiara, "mind your manners."

Kiara ignores Fay's comment and looks at the waiter. "Can we also get a bottle of champagne, please, a martini, extra dry, and a couple of shots of tequila?" She looks around the table. "You guys want something else?"

"Maybe tonight we don't drink?" Fay says, lifting her eyebrows.

"I'm on vacation," Kiara whines, drawing out each syllable to make her point loud and clear. By now, the words *on vacation* have been thrown around so often, they're beginning to lose their meaning.

"Right, gotcha," Fay says and tightens her lips.

"Will that be all?" the waiter asks, still awkwardly hovering at the corner of our table.

"Water for me, please." Fay hands her menu to the waiter. "Sparkling." Relieved to be dismissed, the waiter takes the menus and hurries away from our table. "Why don't you just come out with it and tell us what's really going on?" Fay pushes. "You've literally spent the last two days tanked." Fay looks at Zin and me for backup, but I look away. "Just tell me it's for fun and not a cry for help, and I'll back off." She looks at me and Zin again, only now we are both staring at Kiara, waiting to hear what she'll say. Fay and Kiara both have their arms folded across their chests like they're in a standoff. We're in our very own *West Side Story*, Bahamas Edition.

Fay pushes Kiara's phone toward her, which, as though on cue, starts to buzz again. Kiara pushes in the side button to make it stop.

"Just answer it," I say softly.

"Leave me alone." Kiara snatches her phone off the table and places it in her lap.

This night is going to fall to shit if I don't turn things around fast.

As though reading my mind, Zinnia offers, "Okay, can we just put all this aside?" I can always count on her to get on board my let's-pretend-nothing-is-wrong train.

"Agreed. It's just a couple of drinks. We're on vacation," I say, and smile. Kiara shoots me a glance to see if I'm mocking her or saving her. I wink at her so she knows I'm on her side, then I add, "A few cocktails never hurt anyone, right?" I look at Fay in hopes that she'll soften.

"Except my mother," she states firmly.

Her words hit me in the face, and it all makes sense now. No wonder Kiara's drinking has had her on edge all weekend.

I extend my hand and place it on Fay's. "I'm so sorry," I say, hoping she can forgive my memory lapse.

"Fuck, I'm sorry too." Kiara locks eyes with Fay. "I can't believe I didn't put two and two together."

Fay huffs and pulls her hand away. "It's fine." She leans forward and reaches for her glass of water, but it's empty. Kiara slides hers over, like a proverbial olive branch, and Fay takes it.

"Your dress really is pretty." I smile at Zinnia, trying to smoothly change the topic. "If Valentina's made a line for our age, I might be more into this job."

"I thought you didn't want the job because you wanted to write," Kiara starts. "If the dresses were prettier, you'd be fine with the career change?"

"That's not what I meant," I defend.

"I know what you meant," Zin chimes in. "You want to bring Valentina's into the twenty-first century. Younger vibe, maybe get some socials going. I get that."

"Yes!" I smile at Zin, thankful for the save. "But also," I look at Kiara, trying to gather my thoughts, "the issue isn't the dresses, and you know that. It's about not having a choice." I sit back and look around the table at all three of my friends staring at me. Not one of them is nodding or agreeing with me. "Plus," I continue to build my argument, clearly needing one, "you know my dad—there's no way he'll let me modernize the company. He still operates in the Stone Age. He doesn't own a laptop, and the only desktop he has sits unused *behind* his desk!" I motion behind me to highlight the absurdity, but still, no reaction. "Whatever." I let out a sigh. No one seems to think my problems matter. "It's my fate. Who am I to fight it?"

"Give me a break," Fay says, finally cutting the silence. Not exactly how I'd hoped, but at least I'm not talking to myself anymore. Fay leans back and nearly collides with the waiter, who is right behind her, carrying our drinks.

Kiara grabs the martini off the tray and swigs it back in one gulp. "This is gonna get ugly," she whispers to Zin, who picks up the glass of champagne the waiter set down in front of her.

"Spare me the poor-little-rich-girl antics," Fay says and rolls her eyes. "Listen, your life isn't over just because you're changing careers. Talk to me when your fate brings you face to face with survival. Your problems are first-world at worst, especially since Eduardo would move mountains to make you happy. Just tell him you want to write, and he'll buy you a publishing house." At that, she pushes her chair back and stands up. "I need to use the bathroom. Excuse me."

Anger flaring in my chest, I feel my cheeks turn red. "No, you excuse me. What the hell was that?" I point to her chair like she's still sitting in it, berating me. "We all know how you could afford that gallery of yours. Same shit, okay, Fay? I know my problems aren't as big as your motherless woes," I look at Zin and Fay, "or whatever the hell you're doing with Wren." I look at Kiara and lean over to her. "You're being reckless, by the way." I straighten out. "But money isn't the answer to everything. You'd know that if you'd listen to me instead of running away from this conversation, pretending you need to use the bathroom." I let out a deep breath. "Friends are supposed to be there for each other. Open hearts open hearts, right?" I repeat my dad's favourite advice. I look at my girls, each one staring back at me, guilty as charged. "Now come on, sit down," I say to Fay with a pouty bottom lip. "Please."

I've made a huge scene, and every person in the restaurant is now openly staring. I wouldn't be surprised if footage of this got turned into a meme.

"Please," I repeat as I sit down.

Fay returns to her seat and slides her chair back under the table. We sit there quietly for a moment and listen as Kiara's phone rings again. Ritualistically, she silences it and pretends nothing happened.

"Good friends aren't just there for you," Fay starts, reaching for her sparkling water. "They also show you a mirror. Tell you the hard truths." She takes a big sip.

"Okay, well, if we're being honest then," I clear my throat and straighten my back, "you're a homewrecker, and that's not okay."

Water sprays out of Fay's mouth. She shoots a look at Zin and then back at me. "I told you not to say anything," Fay hisses.

"Apparently all my friends are cheaters," Kiara says with a smile, lifting her champagne flute to her mouth. "And cuckolds." She winks at Fay.

"What did you tell her exactly?" Zin says, looking more upset by the reveal than I expected.

"Wait, I'm confused. Why are *you* mad?" Kiara leans in.

"I told you Fay has a girlfriend," I remind Kiara.

Kiara nods, remembering the secret I divulged. "Right, she trusted you with a secret, and now you're using it against her. That's exactly why I don't tell you guys diddly squat." She downs her champagne. "All your lies are gonna catch up with you."

"Right, how's your cough, by the way?" I shoot a look at Kiara.

"I didn't lie," Kiara defends. "I *was* sick." But then she rolls her eyes and smiles. The jig is up. She knows there's no use in lying anymore.

"What did you tell them exactly?" Zin whispers into Fay's ear loud enough for me to hear.

"What are you two whispering about?" Kiara asks as she refills her drink. "You know what, actually?" She stops mid-pour. "I teach my students that secrets don't make friends and friends don't make secrets. That's a lesson that's lost on this group." Her phone buzzes again. This time she holds it up for all of us to see. "I have better things to do. I'm out."

"Kiara don't go," Fay calls out as Kiara begins to walk away. "You're being dramatic."

Kiara whips around and stalks forward. My heart begins to pump out of my chest. Something about the anger on her face tells me there's about to be a showdown.

She comes threateningly close to Fay and shoves her face directly in front of her. "What did you call me?"

I look at Zin, both of us holding our breath with anticipation. Fay and Kiara have only fought once in their whole lives, and it was really ugly. It was the summer before we all left for university. Fay was testing the limits of her own life, to put it nicely. One night, she decided it would be a good idea to take a friend's motorcycle for a spin, even though she didn't have a motorcycle license *and* she was high on acid. Kiara lost her mind and fought Fay for the keys. They rolled around for a good ten minutes before Kiara came up for breath, victorious, keys in hand. Fay wouldn't talk to her for weeks, even though it is safe to say, Kiara saved Fay's life.

Unlike what she looks like she'll do now, which is kill her.

"You're. Being. Dra-ma-tic," Fay repeats slowly, pushing her seat back and standing up.

The two of them stand nose to nose, like they're challenging each other to a duel.

"Apologize." Kiara steps even closer, pushing Fay into the table.

"Can you two stop?" Zinnia slams the table with her hands, toppling over our very full champagne flutes.

I push my seat back and scramble with napkins in an attempt to soak up the spill around us. Zinnia and I are both kneeling on the floor, and neither Kiara nor Fay seems to notice the mess. They just keep at each other.

"No, I won't stop, and you know what? You two can take your whispering and your high horse and your fake concern for my life and fuck all the way off," Kiara hisses. "And you know what else?" Kiara turns to me with a seething look in her eyes I've never seen before. "Fay's not wrong. Your problems aren't real problems. Blow up your perfect life with your fake cheating or whatever, but maybe if you take a step back, you'd realize that the only one making your life way more complicated than it has to be is you. Put on your big girl panties and figure your shit out." With that, she grabs her phone and storms out of the restaurant.

The weight of Kiara's words sends a blow to my chest. Echoing Fay's words, I'm beginning to think none of my friends think my pain matters.

I slump back down into my chair and let out a heaving breath. A crew of waiters and busboys scurry about our table, cleaning up the mess we've made.

"At least I talk about my problems rather than silence them." I point to my phone and let out a laugh, trying to hold back my tears, but they come flowing out anyway.

"Kiara's just being Kiara. Hurt people hurt people, right?" Zin repeats my dad's adage in hopes it'll provide welcome solace, but it just makes me cry more. "Oh, sweetie," she puts her hand on mine.

"Well then, Kiara must be *reallllly* hurt. Like, two broken arms away from a full-body cast, if you ask me." Fay snorts and rubs Zinnia's shoulder.

Our waiter sets down a ginormous platter of surf 'n' turf, big enough for a family of eight.

"What was Kiara talking about, *fake cheating*?" Fay leans over and grabs a lobster tail. She cracks it in half and starts to fork out the meat.

"Nothing," I assert. "I've lost my appetite."

When I get to my room, I plop onto my bed. Zinnia insisted that I take some of our meal to go, but I'm just not hungry. My belly is filled with knots, and my mind full of scattered thoughts.

Maybe there's some truth to what my friends are saying about me. Maybe I *am* overcomplicating things. Maybe if I tell my dad I don't want to run Valentina's, he won't flip out and keel over. Maybe, like a really small maybe, he will be happy for me.

At the very least, my friends are right that he won't be *mad* at me. Never in my entire life has my father ever been mad at me. I don't know why I'm so scared to tell him.

Decidedly, I reach for my phone to call him. It's time I put on my big girl panties, as Kiara so kindly put it, and tell my dad to find another CEO. I take a deep breath and click the screen to unlock my phone. There're two missed calls from my mom and a text that reads: call me back, es urgente.

With one fell swoop, my whole world flashes before my eyes. My stomach goes instantly hot, and my mind begins to race. I sit up, shaking as I click my mom's face to place the call.

She picks up after one ring. "Hola, Val?" Her voice is breaking. "Papá tuvo un infarto."

A heart attack? I saw my dad just yesterday morning, bongo-ing away on the dashboard to the Gipsy Kings. He was totally fine.

"Ya está en el hospital—"

I cut my mother off. "Mom, is he okay? Is Dad alive?" If he's at the hospital already, it's a good sign, right? This can't be.

"Sí, sí, he's awake, but come home, mi amor." Chills up and down my spine, I jump off the bed. In my mind I'm already packed, on a plane, and by my father's side, but shock keeps my feet glued to the sky-blue hotel carpet.

I snap to and reach for my computer. "Let me check flights. I'll be on the first one out," I say, opening a browser and keying in a new search: Nassau to Montreal, February 27, one way. I'll pay whatever I have to pay, just get me home so I can see my dad.

The next flight out is in two hours. I purchase it and start throwing all my stuff in my bag. No time for folding. There's zero-to-no-chance I'll make it, but lord knows I'm gonna try. I call down to the lobby to order a car to the airport as I quickly change into leggings and a sweater.

In the elevator, I watch as the numbers slowly descend one by one. The ride down twenty-four floors never felt so long.

I pull out my phone and type a group message. My dad had a heart attack. I'll call from the airport if I can. I'm about to click send but decide to delete Kiara and Fay from the thread. Hurt people may hurt people, but that doesn't excuse either of their behaviour. My problems are real. *This* is real.

By the time I'm in the cab, my anxiety is off the charts. I reach for my meds and pop two. They feel dry, caught in my throat. I swallow as I play out every possible scenario in my mind. What if he dies and I'm not there to tell him how much I love him? What if I don't make it for his last breath? What will happen if . . .

I close my eyes and make a silent prayer. I picture my father dancing in our living room, blasting Spanish ballads as he shakes and shimmies his hips. I imagine him as he spins my mother around and laughs at

Jack, teasing him for his Canadian rhythm, or lack thereof. *That's mi'ja*, he would say with a smile at me as I swung and dipped myself. *Even though Jack should be leading, you know exactly where you're going, with or without him.*

I don't know where I'm going, is what I want to tell him. *I still need you, Papá. Don't die. Please don't die.*

When the cab pulls up to the airport a short time later, I boot it as fast as humanly possible through the terminal. I hear a woman's voice announce the first leg of my flight on the loudspeaker: "This is your final boarding call for flight 2890 to Miami."

Kiara

SIX MISSED PHONE CALLS. THREE SHITTY FRIENDS. AND THE WORST vacation of my life. Sitting on the empty pool deck, faint sound of music overhead, my stomach growls with hunger pains. I wish we had eaten before the fight, then I'd be able to separate this gnawing in my stomach from the pain in my heart.

Try as I might, I can't shake Val's voice out of my head. She's right. I *am* being reckless. I can only keep avoiding Wren for so long before it all piles up, and when it does, it'll hit me in the face.

I swipe Wren's name to FaceTime.

He answers without even saying hello. "I'm out with Max now. Can't talk. But," he pauses, "why d'you look so sad? Not havin' fun with your girls?" He raises a brow, and I immediately feel caught, like if I tell him the truth about what just happened, he'll lord it against me, *I told you so* and all that, but if I lie and say I'm having a good time, he might rage with jealousy.

I take a deep breath and shoot for the middle. "It's been okay. I'd rather be with you in SoBe though." At least that's true. I'd rather be anywhere than here right now.

"Well, if you were, you couldn't wear that." He cackles and turns the phone so Max's face is onscreen. I look down self-consciously at my dress. A lingerie-style, pinstriped cami dress. Sequins, lace. I thought it was cute. I'm about to ask what's wrong with my outfit, but Wren continues. "Yo, let me call you back when we're done here. Gimme an hour tops." Music blares in the background, and Wren's arm goes up, pounding a fist to the beat. A close-up of his face fills the screen as he puckers and kisses the air.

"Okay, I will," I respond, but he's already hung up. A message pops up on my screen: answer when I call you.

I take a deep breath and slip my phone into my skirt pocket. I gaze out at the still water in the pool, a serene setting of a misty light, shining from below, trickling up the palm trees, blending into a dark blue sky. In the cabana, there are a few silhouettes of people standing around, bobbing to muffled music. I feel a gentle tap on my shoulder.

"Hey beautiful." I turn around, and Frankie is standing an inch away from my face. He smiles.

Tucking a loose braid behind my ear, I smile back and let out a sigh. He doesn't say anything. He just gazes at me softly until I feel my chest deflate and my heartbeat slow down, calibrating to his soft, sweet energy.

How is it that I know this man no more than a day and he already has this effect on me? I feel so at ease around him.

Meanwhile, my own fiancé has me teasing out my every word, measuring my actions and reactions. The words from that book flash before my eyes. *It's important in those events to explore your emotions and not let them fall to the wayside as a way to keep the peace.*

"Want to go for a walk?" He grabs my hand, and I'm brought back to the pool deck. Frankie pulls me toward the beach. I don't even feign resistance, letting him whisk me away.

We walk side by side onto the rocky path toward the private beach and the soothing sound of waves rolling calmly onto the shore, like a paint-by-numbers romantic stroll. I let Frankie wrap his arm around me, and I'm acutely aware of how soft his skin feels against mine, two velvety brown arms intertwined like a pretzel. No tension, no power play. Just an easy fit.

"At night, when my shift is over, I stay here and just stare at the sea. My place is more inland, and I don't feel the same energy there. Something about the water synchs with my body. It's like meditating." I could listen to him talk forever. "You know what I mean? You feel it too?"

"I'm no good at meditating," I admit, feeling self-conscious. "I've tried it a few times, but I just end up thinking about everything I need to get done, like a list of things I should be doing instead of sitting around breathing." I pause. I sound like a mumbling idiot. I'm rambling about to-do lists while he's on a spiritual plane. Hoping to steer the conversation back in the right direction, I add, "I don't mind meditation with music playing. It gives me something to focus on."

Not entirely untrue. The only time I ever liked meditating was during a sound bath in San Francisco with the girls last year. I had just moved to Miami the month before. Long distance wasn't working for Wren; with Raven every other week and long work hours, he couldn't handle the back and forth. So, I either moved to Miami or we would break up. He decided it would be easiest to simply sponsor me on spousal conditions, which was only made legally true when we got engaged last summer. I wasn't allowed to leave the States until my documents were official, so we spent our girls weekend in San Fran, which meant spirituality was the theme of the trip. We did float therapy and the Japanese tea garden, and of course meditation and sound baths. Turns out I sort of like some of that stuff, even if I'm not good at it.

"There's no good or bad when it comes to meditating," Frankie says. "We could try it together now. I can guide us if you'd like." He stops walking and stands in front of me, taking my hands in his and placing my palms on his chest. "You can keep pace with my breath, and we can let our minds travel somewhere together—what do you think?"

I think there is nothing sexier than this man asking me to travel with him. Somewhere far away from this vacation, I hope.

I nod.

"Come, let's sit here." He leads me to a nearby spot on the sand. I bend down to take off my sandals, and my phone falls out of my pocket.

My screensaver lights up: the photo of me kissing Wren's cheek. I turn my phone face down before Frankie sees it, and I slide it into my sandals. Finding a comfortable position, I sit crisscross applesauce, like I do with my students. Frankie sits opposite me, our knees touching. He places his hands on my lap and signals that I should place my hands in his.

"Just trust me," he says.

Looking at a tiki torch flickering in the night sky, I focus on the fire and watch as the smoke rises from the heat. Tiny sparkles burst above before they fizzle out. Frankie's voice is a constant hum in the background, cuing me to close my eyes and picture my happy place. I don't think I have one. I shake away the negativity and try to ease into his trance-like script. "Try not to resist your thoughts. Instead, explore anything that comes up, and then gently come back to my voice and your breath."

He takes me on a trip where I am meant to focus on a colour and visualize objects that take on that hue. I close my eyes and see red, bringing me back to a couple weeks ago on Valentine's Day.

Frankie's moved on to white, and I'm jolted out of my memory back to the present. I'm so bad at this. He guides me to orange, and I see a pumpkin, which reminds me of Halloween. I love Halloween. Probably my favourite holiday. More costumes and a chance to play make-believe. Walk through a haunted house, stuff your face with exorbitant amounts of candy, and get spooked by gory, one-eyed monsters—way less scary than the shit that happens in real life.

This past Halloween, Wren didn't want to go to a party or even open the door for trick-or-treaters, so I went full speed with my grade five class. I created a lesson plan around *Glee* and went as Sue Sylvester. We analyzed a bunch of her insults and talked about how her bullying was cloaked in humour and that even though she made us laugh, she was being mean. It was all about bystander intervention. It's easier to laugh along with a bully than it is to stand up to one. I guess that lesson's lost on me. My kids loved it though. Especially the part when I told them to ask their parents if they could watch an episode for homework. Wren thought the whole idea was unwise. His words were *you're basically teaching them how to be jerks*.

Frankie's voice gently guides me away from orange into yellow. I don't think I'm doing this right, because by the time I summon sunshine, we're already on green. Grass. There, that was easy. An image of McGill's lower field comes to mind. So many memories there. I'm not sure I'm supposed to think of memories, maybe just focus on the colour. Ugh, I'm so bad at meditating. Except I could get used to the sound of Frankie's voice. So raspy and deep. I could focus on that.

"Now imagine blue," Frankie continues. "Let the colour wash over you like the blue in the sea and the sky."

Blue. The colour of Wren's eyes. Deep, penetrating . . . my mind races back to that night on the bathroom floor . . . did I forget to take my little blue pill?

"Kiara?" The sound of Frankie's voice snaps me back to the beach. "You okay? You must've gone deep into a state." He hands me my phone, lit up with Wren's face. "Your phone's been ringing."

"I'm engaged," I blurt out.

Frankie drops my phone into my hand, his face blank. My words hover between us like a helicopter chopping up whatever connection we were creating.

"Figured as much when I saw the photo." He points to my hand. "But you're not wearing a ring."

"I wear it here." I pick up the ring dangling from my necklace. "I like to wear it close to my heart," I lie.

"That's sweet. Closer to your heart." He fakes a smile.

I let out a chuckle as I wipe away a tear. "I'm sorry, please don't look at me."

"I can't stop looking at you," he says. "You're breathtaking." Our eyes lock. I shouldn't have told him. I should've let him kiss me. Just to see what it would feel like to have his lips press against mine. To let my hands run through his hair. I need to get out of here.

"Truth is, sometimes this ring feels like it's choking me." I don't know if it's the meditation or how Frankie makes me feel so safe, but I want to be honest with him, to say things I haven't been able to share with my friends. My hand travels back to my neck. "He makes me happy, but also, sometimes, he doesn't. When things are going well, they're great, but we see the world differently, I think, and sometimes that leads him to be a little, I don't know . . ." Possessive? Condescending? "He can get a little mean. He doesn't, like, hurt me or anything, he kinda makes fun of me or whatever, but it's always meant as a joke. He's really funny." I wish I could stop talking because the pity on Frankie's face is making me feel pathetic. "He's a lawyer, you know?" Ugh, why'd I say that? Who cares that he's a lawyer?! "I just mean, he's a really good guy and who cares if I can never pick the movie, right? That's not a big deal. Or is it? My friend Val doesn't really like him. Actually, I don't think any of my friends are too fond of him. They've never really out and said it, but they don't have to. I can tell. I should break up with him. Maybe I will. I'm rambling. I'll stop. I can't believe I just told you all this. I'm sorry."

"Kiara, stop." He takes my hand. "Don't be sorry. You don't need to make excuses or diminish how he makes you feel. You can hide your feelings inside to keep the peace, but eventually, they'll find their way out. So whatever you're feeling, it's worth exploring."

Keep the peace. There are those words again.

"I feel like there was a reason we met," I start, looking into his eyes. "Do you believe in that sort of thing?"

He nods and smiles softly. "I would love to know you more. But I guess the stars aren't aligned in my favour. Maybe in another life."

His white linen shirt blows in the wind, and the scent of his sweat hits me. We sit staring at each other, and I can feel myself leaning closer to him, inching toward his face, his breath, his lips.

My phone rings again. Wren's name scrolls across my screen. "I should answer this." I stare down at my phone, avoiding eye contact.

"Of course," he mutters and moves back.

As I lift the phone to my face, I watch as Frankie slowly stands and walks toward the hotel.

"Hey babe!" I force a peppy tone. Wren's voice vibrates in my ear, but all I can hear is the sound of Frankie's footsteps pressing firmly against the pebble path, and I can't help but question if I just let the man of my dreams walk out of my life.

Fay

MY BREAKFAST PLATE HAS NEVER SEEN THIS MANY CARBS. IT FEELS like I'm eating for four I'm so starved, which is no different from my regular appetite. But this morning, I'm more ravenous than usual. After last night's dinner, Zin and I went back to our room and picked up where we left off before dinner, but not before I reassured her that I did not expose my girlfriend's identity when I divulged my relationship to Val.

After a night tangled up in each other in bed, we watched the sunrise on the beach.

Now, sitting beside me at the lobby café, shovelling food into her mouth, it feels like we're a regular couple sharing breakfast before our flight home. I'm scrolling the *Toronto Canvas* and Zin is editing the photos she took at the beach.

"I grabbed one of these from the bed stand last night." I wave a pen at Zin and then slip it into my purse. I've been collecting pens from every trip we've taken together. I have upward of twenty pens between hotels, restaurants, and museums.

"Sweet, maybe you can turn it into an art exhibit or something," she says.

"You laugh, but I bet it would show well." I lean in to kiss her, but she flinches away at the sight of Kiara walking toward us, navigating the crowded tables, dragging her carry-on behind her.

She pulls out a heavy chair, slumping down beside me.

"You're joining us?" I ask, not even trying to hide that I'm surprised she's talking to us after what transpired last night.

She gazes at her empty plate, meticulously rearranging the fork and knife on and off her napkin. "Why? Am I not invited?" Ahh, that makes more sense. Still on the defensive. She pours water into her glass and reaches for a slice of lemon from Zin's plate. "Do you mind?"

"No, no." Zin throws me a steely look while she pats Kiara's hand. "Take it, and of course you're invited. Here." She hands her a menu, "I'll get the waiter?"

Our table goes quiet. Kiara scans the menu, Zinnia fidgets with her napkin, folding it and unfolding it nervously, and I continue to eat my French toast, pouring more maple syrup onto my strawberries. The clinking of cutlery and chatter all around provides a welcome soundtrack to our otherwise ominous silence.

I feel a pang of remorse for last night. Watching Kiara's body language this morning, she's drawn inward, more reserved than how she's been the past two days. Her movements are smaller, more deliberate, more careful. Maybe last night affected her more than I realize.

My intention wasn't to quell her spunky energy, it was just to make her more conscious of it.

The last thing I want to do right now is apologize, especially since I was right, but I think she needs it, at least to lower her defences. I want her to know that my intentions were good even if my delivery wasn't. I didn't mean for things to go the way they did. It all just got so out of hand.

"I'm—" I start.

"Where's—" Kiara starts at the same time.

We both let out an awkward sigh. "You first," I say.

"I was just gonna ask where Val is." She looks at the empty chair at our table of four.

"Eduardo had a heart attack. Val left last night," Zin announces, lowering her eyes and pinching her lips together.

"How do you know that?" Kiara snaps.

"She texted me," Zin responds.

Kiara's face contorts into what can only be described as a combo of offended and disappointed. "Cool, we were supposed to leave in like an hour. Good thing she let me know she left." She takes a sip of water.

"Are you serious?" I snap back, glad I didn't get that apology out. She's totally fucking deluded. "Like Eduardo's heart attack was a planned way for Val to get out of flying home with you? You've totally lost touch with reality, Keeks." I'm glaring at her, but Kiara seems content with pretending she doesn't hear me. Zin and I exchange a confused look when Kiara, unfazed, waves the waiter over and orders an omelet and black coffee. She reaches for her napkin, places it back on her lap and says, "I'm starving."

"You've changed," I state firmly, knocking the table as I stand.

"Back atcha," Kiara spits out.

"You know what? We're gonna be late for our flight. Let's get out of here."

"Wait!" Zin tugs at my sleeve. Leaning into Kiara, she asks, "Is there anything at all you wanna talk about? 'Cause you know we're here, right?"

I pull my arm free as Zinnia pulls Kiara in for a hug. She holds her head in her hands like she would if it were Darla or Saul. "And call Val," she whispers, then she follows me out of the restaurant.

"You're too nice," I say to Zin as we walk to the lobby. I glance back at Kiara sitting at the table, and she looks so alone, so lost. "If she wants to push us away, then so be it." I say it, but I know I don't mean it.

"Should we be worried about Keeks? I mean, you said it before, she's really not acting like herself," Zin says, exhaling a puff of hot breath onto her phone. She pulls out the bottom of her tank top to wipe the screen clean.

"I mean, I'm more worried about Eduardo at this point." I look down at my own phone. "Should I be hurt that she deliberately omitted me from the message? It *is* weird that she only texted you."

"We talked about this already. She's hurt. This isn't about you."

I scratch my head. "I just can't believe Eduardo is in the hospital."

"I know," Zin says as we step outside. "He'll pull through. He's young and otherwise perfectly healthy." Even as she says it, I can tell she's not entirely convinced it's true. I don't know the stats on heart attacks. But what if he doesn't make it? Eduardo is like a dad to me. To all of us.

We find a seat in a shady spot at the side of the hotel to wait for our cab, trying to avoid the hot sun poking out behind tall buildings across the street. I pull Zin close to me, and she leans her head on my shoulder. "At least I have you," I whisper in her ear. "And maybe this time next year, everyone will know about us so we can hold hands like this for the world to see." I slide my hand into hers.

I lean down to kiss her on the mouth and exhale a fresh breath of happiness. Zin nestles her face into my neck, and it's proof of how real this is.

This is really happening.

Zinnia

THIS CAN'T BE HAPPENING.

I don't have the heart or will to pull away from her. All the magic, the visceral magnetism, the carnal passion, our very true and profound connection—a love that far eclipses anything I've ever imagined possible. To be felt and seen the way I am with Fay, well it's a far cry from anything I've ever felt with Adam.

Sitting at our gate, ready to board our plane, I'm caught between this dream-like bubble I've created with Fay and the pin that'll burst it all when our flight lands.

Adam. Darla. Saul. My family. My world.

Fay's legs dangling over my lap, she's rustling her fingers through my hair, breathing into my neck, kissing me behind my ear. I'm so envious of how fully present she is, mostly because I've spared her the weight of my very real either/or situation.

In the cab ride over, Fay asked what the plan was for when we get back home. She kept repeating *no pressure, but maybe we can find a way for a sleepover this week*. She's under the impression that I'm untethered, all-in, certain, that this weekend was a giant leap forward and that we'll be able to keep it going when we get home.

She kept whispering *I love you* into my neck, and it's like something flipped inside of me. I relished in the sound of those words all weekend, and all of a sudden, they feel suffocating.

And now, in the harsh light of this tiny terminal, I'm acutely aware that whatever steps she thinks we've taken forward the last few days will have amounted to nothing by the time we hit the ground in four hours.

I'm a horrible person.

"How are we gonna keep this magic going when we get back?" Fay asks with a smile, interlacing her hands with mine as though she's read my mind. "Hello? Zin? Where'd you go?" Fay snaps a finger in my face. She's been talking, and I must've zoned out. "I can tell you're somewhere else. Wanna talk about it?"

It's ironic that my biggest issue with Adam is how my mind can be somewhere else and he would never know it. He's so in his own world sometimes that he wouldn't notice if my eyes were red and puffy from crying for a week. Meanwhile, my mind wanders for all of ten seconds, and Fay catches me before I have a chance to fake focus. It's both comforting and confronting. Nowhere to hide. I want to tell her that "all-in" for me still means one day at a time. I'm not ready to drastically upend my life, regardless of how incredible this weekend was. But it's like the only way to make her happy is if I promise to walk back into my house and announce to Adam that I'm leaving him.

Instead, I say, "I want to talk to you, Fay, but I don't want to hurt you."

"When a conversation starts like that, I know I'm about to get hurt. What's up, Zin? What's been going on with you?" She pushes away from me and places her knee up on the bench. Her body language and her face say *hurt me and I'll kill you.*

"I love you, Fay, you know I do. Last night was magical. Every night this weekend has been magical. I've never felt lifted so high above ground. It feels like I'm floating." I pause. "You are everything I've always wanted, everything that's always been missing."

"But . . . ?" she drawls.

"*But*," I start, "my kids." I feel the tears that've been forming in my eyes finally pop and roll out onto my cheeks.

"I don't know why you keep bringing up your kids. We've talked about this a million times." Fay puts her hand to her face and rubs her eyes. I can tell I've hit a nerve. She lowers her hand and takes mine in hers. "I love your kids. I mean, if I'm good enough to be Darla's godmother, aren't I good enough to be her step—"

"Don't." I pull my hand back and place it on my lap. I knew that *two moms* comment would come back to haunt me. Fay is staring at me intently, waiting for me to speak. I take a deep breath and start, "I'd run away with you tomorrow if I could. I hope you know that. But what about the rest of my life? If I throw this at Adam out of nowhere, it would do more than just hurt him. It could potentially turn my children into collateral damage, start a custody war that would turn their lives upside down. Aside from the fact that I don't have a penny to my name to actually afford my life without Adam, I can't put my children through what I experienced as a kid. I spent my childhood wondering what I did to make my mother not want to see me. My children are everything to me. Just thinking that they might feel even an iota of what I felt . . ." My voice trails off as the tears roll down my cheek.

"You are not your mother." Fay cups my face. "You are an incredible mom. So present and loving. Divorce doesn't mean walking out on your children."

"Doesn't it, though?" I say quietly. My only other reference is Kiara's dad, and the day he left was the last day she ever saw him. I know divorce is more common these days, but I don't want to be on that side of the statistic.

"Hey." Fay extends her hand to touch my cheek. I look at her, and we stay locked like that for a moment. "This," she says, waving her hand back and forth at us, "this is not just a passing fling. This isn't you running out on your kids. This is real love. They'll still have you and Adam, and they'll have me too."

Never one for vulnerability, I can tell she's trying to be strong for the both of us, but I can hear the fear in her voice; she's shutting down, retreating into her shell.

If I don't figure this out, I could lose the love of my life *and* my best friend. What would I do without Fay?

Tears burst out of my eyes, and I can't stop myself. I bury my face into my hands and let out a wail. Fay folds over me and leans her head on my back, stroking my hair.

"I can't uproot my life, and I can't make these huge life changes—" The hypocrisy in my words stops me in my tracks. California. "Look, I'm just not ready to make that—I'm just not ready. I need more time. One day at a time, remember? That's what we said."

She kneels on the floor and looks up at me from between my knees in what looks like she's about to pop the question in a massive display of public affection. Our entire gate is now watching because apparently we make dramatic scenes everywhere we go. I bring my face closer to hers so she quiets her voice.

"From the way you're talking now, it doesn't sound like one day at a time, Zin. I think you know you're not leaving Adam, and you're just stringing me along. I don't deserve that."

No you don't, I think, but I choke on my words.

"You're not ready to be with me, like *really* be with me. Not now, not ever. The worst part is, I know you're not being honest about why. Instead, you're using your kids as an excuse to hold you back from doing what you really want. Just like you do with everything else in your life."

"What the hell is that supposed to mean?" I pull back, offended at the low blow. "Did you have that dagger ready in your pocket?"

"You're saying you don't put shit off?" She's challenging me with raised brows. "Why haven't you submitted your work to that magazine I told you about? You think you're an amateur, but honestly, you have the eye, and I would know it. A class or two and you could take this photography 'hobby' to the next level, but every time I bring it up, your excuse is that you're too busy with homework or researching summer camps. I mean come on. They have their own lives, why can't you have one too! God forbid you do one thing for yourself. You blame your children, you make motherhood look like you're in prison with a life sentence, but the only person holding you hostage is yourself. Plenty of moms work. Hell, plenty of parents get divorced!" She pushes herself off her seat and starts to pace. "You keep saying you feel lost, like Zin doesn't exist, well here is an opportunity to stand up and be someone, and you're finding excuses. Finally an opportunity to be seen out in the open, and you're finding the first hole to crawl into. Classic Zin."

I feel like I've been hit by a two-ton truck. "Wow! You know, once you say shit, you can't take it back."

"Right, like that time you said, 'Hey let's move to New York together, just kidding, I'm in Toronto but forgot to tell you.'" She's doing her best Zin voice, and it's making my skin itchy.

I let out a puff of air. "Oh my god, Fay, that was like eight years ago!" I stand up and stop her mid-stride, turning her shoulders so she looks at me. "Do you honestly think I hate being a mom and I blame everyone else for my pathetic, unfulfilled housewife life?"

She shrugs her shoulders and purses her lips.

"And do you really think being an artist is what will make me happy? Because you're just living it up in that gallery of yours."

Her eyes widen, and I can tell I hit a nerve.

"I'm just saying, it's not like taking pictures and running away with you will solve everything, and you know it."

She shrugs again and shakes her head. I let out a sigh and slump back into my chair.

All the things we've never said until now sit thick as fog between us.

We stare at each other for a few seconds as we let the dust settle. A voice comes over the loudspeaker announcing that our flight is boarding.

"I'm sorry, Zin. I am. But you have a choice, and if you choose me, we can make it work." Fay takes a seat on the chair beside me. "I love you. And I love your kids."

"Let's board. We'll finish this on the plane." I stand and hold out my hand, but she flinches away. "Fay? Whatever it is, we'll work it out. Come on," I motion to the lounge that has quickly emptied out, "we'll miss our flight." The voice comes on again, reminding us that our zone is boarding.

Fay crosses her arms and lifts her head. She stares me dead in the eye and says, "I need you to answer me before I get on that plane. I need to know that when we land, you aren't going to transform back into Zin, my friend, a married woman who kisses me in a closet. I can't go back to the way things were, Zin. I need to feel like we're moving forward. I need to know that you plan to tell Adam at some point in the future. I want to know we're creating something real here."

"Don't do this, please. I can't promise you anything right now. All I can promise is that I do love you." As the words come out, I feel more certain than anything that they're true. "I love you so much," I whisper again. "What I feel for you is real. That's the best I can do right now." My chin quivers as I rub my arm across my face to wipe away the tears. "I'm sorry."

She takes hold of her carry-on handle and lifts it up. "If time is what you want, then I'll give you time . . . and space. I'm going to Montreal. I'll stay with Val. She'll need the support, and I can use some time away to get my mind off all this."

"So, this is it? It's not going exactly how you want at the pace you want, so you're bailing? Talk about classic. Here's classic Fay, everybody." I point to Fay and raise my voice. "Fay the rolling stone. Fay the bailer. Avoid-pain-at-all-costs Fay."

"Screw you, Zinnia."

PART 2

The Space Between

Valentina

MONTREAL, FEBRUARY

THE FRAGILITY OF LIFE FEELS AS SLIPPERY AS THE ICE BENEATH THE wheels of our plane, threatening to shatter under the weight of what awaits me. It is a cruel joke that my dad is lying in a bed right now fighting for his life while I'm stuck on the tarmac listening to the passenger next to me chew her gum like a cow. Doesn't she know it's not polite to be so blissfully unaware while my whole life is falling apart?

I made the flight from the Bahamas to Miami just in the nick of time, which I took as a good sign, but then I proceeded to wait *hours* for my connection to Montreal, and my anxiety kicked back in full swing. When I finally boarded the plane, I popped more anxiety meds and was able to get through half a movie before I dozed for a bit, telling myself that all I had to do was get home. Yet here we are, in Montreal—one step closer to the hospital and the distance couldn't feel greater—stuck on the tarmac for nearly an hour. I'm going to lose my mind. Why won't they just *let me out*?

Every minute is a minute stolen from being with my dad, my rock, my papá . . . the very thought of losing him sends shockwaves through me.

To think I was going to call him and tell him I didn't want to take over Valentina's. Crush his dreams. It's inconceivable now, with his life hanging in the balance, that I tempted fate. All those doubts, all those declarations, I would take them all back if I knew that this is how it would end up.

When they finally announce that we can deboard, I race my way through the airport and thank my lucky stars that there's no line at customs. Carry-on in tow, I bolt through the exit and pull out my phone to tell my mom I'm finally out of the airport when a text pops up.

Jack.

I'm parked at terminal C waiting for you, just let me know when you land and I'll swing around.

No *hi*, no, *do you want me to come grab you*, just *I'm here*, because that's Jack. A sense of relief washes over me. I look up and see his car across the way. I write him back: I see you. Coming.

Jack is standing in front of his car in the brown Canada Goose jacket I bought him two winters ago, shoulders hunched to his ears, cold air puffing out like clouds of smoke from his mouth. He's got a five o'clock shadow, just the way I like him.

His presence at a time like this speaks volumes to his character. My friends on the other hand, well, their silence says it all.

I step out into the shark-grey, bitter cold and snap my jacket against the gust of wind attacking my skin. Walking toward him, I can tell that, even though he's here right now, all is not forgiven. Even from across the street, he's avoiding my gaze. I slow my pace as I draw near. All of me wants to bury my face into his chest, let him catch me as I collapse into his arms. But there's something cold and standoffish about his posture. This Jack is stoic. He mechanically reaches for my suitcase, barely making eye contact as he throws it into the trunk and walks back around to swing my car door open.

"Your dad is going to be fine," he assures me before I even have a chance to say hello. "Get in."

I nod silently. This isn't my Jack at all.

I don't think I truly knew the depth of my love for him until right now. Looking at him reminds me how hurt he is—the way his eyes are vacant, his cheeks deflated, dimples drained of their joy. What was I thinking?

Over the last three days, I've gone back and forth about why I said I cheated. I thought about how maybe I was subconsciously sabotaging our relationship, or maybe it was my instinctual way of saving myself from yet another predetermined moment in my life masquerading as a choice. I even thought maybe he didn't really love me, he just proposed because it was the logical next step. But, looking at him sitting in the car next to me—silent, estranged, distant—I see how wrong all my theories are. I wonder if he could forgive me; what thoughts are coursing through his head now?

Maybe, in a magical world, my dad is faking a heart attack to get me and Jack back together. A hopeful smile tugs at my lips as I hold my phone close to my chest. I close my eyes, take a deep breath, and wipe away my tears. *Please be okay, Papá.*

With tears rolling down my face, I glance over to see through blurry vision how tightly Jack is gripping the steering wheel. Two firm-fisted hands. He may be physically here, but his heart isn't.

It's absurd to even hope that any part of him would be at this airport for me. He's here for my dad.

Throughout our relationship, Jack has become a son to my parents. They've bonded over soccer, chess, and Latin American culture, from the food and the music to the politics and the literature. He's attended every holiday dinner and family vacation and has never missed a birthday or anniversary. He even planned to play doubles with my dad in a tennis fundraiser this summer, an event they were so looking forward to. Summer. That's four months away.

The thought of him not being there, not making it . . . I blink back tears and shake the thought from my head. I can't let myself go there.

There are no redeeming qualities to snow. Not unless I'm looking at it from a warm house, curled up on a couch, drinking hot chocolate by a fire. I've never been partial to winter sports either. None of it—skiing, tubing, skating—could persuade me to hang out in below-zero weather under the pretense that it's "fun." My dad, on the other hand, gets giddy whenever there's a snowstorm. He loves Montreal's erratic and extreme seasons.

Like clockwork, during the first snowfall of the year, Dad breaks out the story of when he and Mom moved here. "Your mother would still be in Venezuela if she had it her way," he always starts as snowflakes fall from the sky. His soft dimples pinch his cheeks as he smiles lovingly at her. "She would have stayed there forever, but I saw our future being corrupted by the ideas of the government, and I couldn't let that get in the way of my family and our future. It was 1983, and oil prices had just collapsed. So many professionals were fleeing the country but mostly scattering around Latin America. I knew we needed to leave, but we had to go farther than the country next door. I opened a map and pointed to the farthest big city in North America: Montreal." He always stops there for effect. So much pride in his voice, as though he discovered Canada. "I always wanted to see the snow. We packed up our lives into one luggage and a dream of greener pastures. Well, there was no green that day. Only white as far as the eye could see. From the tiny airplane window, all we saw was a blanket of snow. It was just beautiful. Like a sparkling, icy white ocean covering the whole city. But when we got our luggage and walked through those airport doors, the freezing wind was unlike anything we'd ever felt before. We only had T-shirts and sandals on! We turned right back around and slept in terminal two for three nights!" I can hear his voice in my heart, pulling the tears, one by one out of my eyes. "But I would do it all over again, mi'ja," he cups my chin every time, "because this city has been kind to us. And we did this all for you, for a better future. And one day, all I built will be yours." I close my eyes, and I can feel his hand on my face. "Winter," he always says, "comes and goes, but like the trees, we will survive the cold and make it to spring. We just need to weather the storm."

I take in a huge inhale and push the boulder that's sitting on my chest down into my belly; an audible sigh leaves my mouth in the phantom shape of stale, grey air.

"He'll be okay," Jack asserts, but I can hear it in his voice—he's worried too.

"How do you know?" I say quietly, staring out the window as we finally approach the hospital. "I keep trying my mom, but she's not picking up. Have you spoken to her?"

"I spoke to her just before I came to get you," he says. "No updates from the doctor yet."

We pull up to emergency, and before the car comes to a stop, I open my door to jump out. I look back at Jack, but before I speak, he says, "Go, go. I'll find a spot and meet you."

I slam the door and make a break for it. I run through the automatic doors with conviction, but as they close behind me, I feel my weight shift and my gait slow.

Hospital lights. The smell of stale coffee. I feel disoriented as heat courses through my shivering body. My knees feel weak. My head light from holding my breath, I'm now panting with anxiety, and the walls feel like they're closing in on me.

I see my mom standing in the waiting room, talking to a doctor. She's wearing the wool blanket she keeps at the foot of her bed. There's not a winter day that goes by that she isn't wrapped in it, regardless of whether she's cooking empanadas or watching her telenovelas. I beeline toward her, but her focus doesn't break. She's hanging onto every word the doctor says and doesn't seem to notice that I've arrived.

"Mamá, how is he?" I tug at her shoulder. She's watching the doctor walk away. "Mamá?" I ask again. This time, she notices me.

"Ay, Cariña. You're here." She collapses into my arms and begins to wail. "Mi vida, por Dios, mi vida." She's swaying back and forth in prayer. Sobbing on my shoulder amidst dozens of other forlorn faces in the waiting room. I rub her back steadily until we both calm down enough to talk.

"Mamá, is Dad okay?" I pull her away so I can see her face. "What did the doctor just say?"

My mom shakes her head and pulls me into the empty chair next to her and starts telling me what happened. I listen as she explains, in her fragmented way, that my dad was fine one minute and on the floor the next. Like every Saturday night for as long as I can remember, they were on a date. When they got home and she was done changing into her pajamas, he wasn't waiting for her in bed. She called out his name, but he didn't answer, so she went downstairs and found him on the living room floor, gripping his chest.

"Mamá," I stop her. I don't want the details of how it happened, I just need to know that he's okay now. "Please, what did the doctor just say?" I repeat my question.

"Is cardi—arres, y ahora, he have surgery." Despite how long she's been in Montreal, her English still sounds like she's speaking Spanish but with English words. It's never impeded me from understanding what she's saying, except for right now. Surgery? So, he's alive? "Now we wait, mi amor. We wait for mi Eduardo to wake up."

Wait?

I can't sit back and wait. I tell my mom not to move while I find the doctor so I can grill her for more answers. It's unlikely that my mom got any real information out of her, or at least nothing she was able to understand.

Just then, Jack appears through the door.

"Did you see him yet? How is he?" He's panting, out of breath. He looks exactly how I must've looked five minutes ago. He removes his jacket and sets it down next to my mother, who takes that as an invitation to stand up and collapse into his arms. As though she were in an instant replay, she begins to sob into Jack's shoulder the way she did with me. "Mi'jo." I'm walking away as I hear her cry and start telling the whole story again.

The doctor who was talking to my mom is standing by the triage desk. "Excuse me, doctor. Can you tell me how Mr. de la Vega is doing? I'm Valentina." I put my hand on my chest. "His daughter."

"Oh, hi dear. Yes, as I just told your mother, your father is still in surgery. We have no news as of now." She looks down and signs a paper, then shoves it into the folder she's holding and turns back to me. "But rest assured, it's all fairly routine. I'll keep you posted when I know more." She barely finishes her sentence before she turns to walk away. Where do these doctors learn their bedside manner?

I pull her elbow to turn her toward me. She gives me a look like she might call security.

"I'm sorry, I—just—" I take a breath. "What kind of surgery? Will he live?"

"Ms. de la Vega, like I told your mother, it's too early to know anything. I'll update you when I have more information." She pulls her arm from my grip, turns on her heel, and walks through the doors.

Time can warp when it's measured in milliseconds. My mother, Jack, and I sit in the waiting room like the living dead for what feels like hours, uncertain if we will ever exhale again. The three of us, silent, staring at the emergency doors opening and closing every few seconds, waiting for someone, anyone, to walk through them, toward us, with news about my father.

Staring off into space is sucking me into a black hole of dark thoughts. But just as I decide to find a vending machine, the doctor I practically accosted earlier walks toward us.

"Is he okay?" I blurt out without giving her a chance to speak. Jack takes my hand in his, and I grip back with all my might.

"He's just waking up now." She claps her hands together and then lets them fall by her hips.

Exhale.

"But not ready for visitors," she continues in anticipation of our next request. "When he's ready, we'll move him to his room." She places a soft hand on my mother's shoulder. "You should go home and get some rest, Mrs. de la Vega. Come back during visiting hours."

The doctor turns to leave, and my mother follows her.

"I go with you," she says.

It's as though the doctor already knows my mom won't take no for an answer. She simply nods in agreement, and I watch as she escorts her through the sliding doors.

My eyes well up, and I fall back onto my chair, cupping my face into my hands and heaving a heavy cry of relief. All the fears of *what if*, all the breath-holding, all the silent praying, it worked. He's alive.

"Why can't I stop crying?" I bury my head into Jack's chest as he hugs me tightly, the familiar scent of Cool Water cologne enveloping me. "He's fine, right? That's what she said. Oh, Jack, what would've happened if—" I feel the gentle rise and fall of Jack's chest crying in rhythm with me.

"He's fine now, Val. Just breathe." He caresses my back. "It's all going to be okay."

I pull away and scan the crowded waiting room. Anxious faces and restless bodies. Each person here is wrapped in their own silent narrative, a story of worry and hope intertwined. How many of them, like me, are clinging to the fragile promise of good news, and how many are on the precipice of a life-altering moment, their worlds about to change inalterably in the four walls of this oppressive, harshly lit room?

I'm one of the lucky ones, blessed with the assurance that my dad is alive to see another day.

This was just a minor blip. Everything will go back to normal, which is exactly what I need in this moment: the familiar comfort of home, of Jack, of my old life. The person I was before any of this happened.

I pull Jack in closer for another hug, another moment to share relief, but he pulls back. His walls are back up, his body tense. He's finally reached the limit on the amount of compassion he can show the woman who broke his heart. Without so much as a smile, he reaches past me for his jacket and starts to walk away.

A heaviness settles in my heart; nothing about my life will ever be the same again.

"Come on, I'll take you home."

Like a choreographed waltz, I silently pull on my coat and follow Jack back out into the cold.

When we get back to my place, Jack keeps the car idling on the street while he helps me bring my things upstairs. He places my bag at my door as I rummage through my purse to find my keys.

"I still have mine," he says as he dangles his keychain in front of me and slides his key into the door.

"Thanks for everything," I whisper, looking up at him expectantly.

He doesn't look at me, just opens the door and wheels my luggage into the entryway.

"It's weird, you know," I start, taking my coat off and hanging it up on the coat rack by the entrance, then I walk toward the kitchen. "The one clear thought that came through the complete fog of my mind when the doctor said that my dad is okay was that my mom won't have to live alone. The two of them are like one being, you know?" I'm standing in the kitchen, pouring myself a glass of juice, talking to Jack as I usually would, as if we both just got back from work and now we're exchanging stories, catching up on our days. Only, when I look up, I notice Jack still standing on the threshold.

"You can come in, you know?" I hold out the glass I poured for him. "We can grab some breakfast or, um, lunch, whatever time it is." I check my watch and then glance back up at Jack, who is fiddling with something in his coat pockets. He looks uncomfortable. "Is four o'clock an acceptable time for linner?" I make an attempt at combining *lunch* and *dinner* in hopes of making him laugh, but he doesn't flinch. "Or not." I set the glass down. "Maybe I'll just pour myself a bowl of cereal and head back to the hospital."

He stands statue-still, staring at me. He wants to leave, but I can tell he's waiting for me to release him, let him know it's okay to go.

"Thank you, Jack." I walk over to him and rest my hand on his shoulder.

I want to tell him that I made an incredible mistake. That I can see clearly now. That my mind is made up. I want to throw my arms around him and tell him that I love him, I can make it better if he'll give me a second chance. I'm about to open my mouth when he breaks away.

"Just call me whenever you're ready for me to come back and get you," Jack says, avoiding my eyes. I can tell how hard this is for him. Like he's tucking away all of his pain just to be there for my dad.

"You can st—" I start, but he turns away and leaves, shutting down any chance I had of love-vomiting all over him.

The instant he shuts the door I feel the tears well up in my eyes all over again. My dad was wrong. The crying doesn't stop when you have clarity, it comes on stronger. Because I finally know without a doubt in my mind that I want Jack back, that I do choose him, yet the tears keep falling.

I walk over to my bedroom and slowly peel off my clothes. I step into the shower, and as the hot water hits my back, I replay all of my interactions with Jack, from the moment I saw his text on my phone at the airport to the way he closed the door when he just said goodbye.

I know he's shut down and hurt, but I also know I'm not imagining there was something forgiving in his eye when he said *come back to get you*. I know there was. At least I have to believe there was.

For now, I'll hold on to the hope that I'm not filling in negative space with wishful thinking. And if I am, so be it. At least it'll get me through a nap without tears.

I throw on my PJs and lay my head on my pillow. Just a little rest before I head back to the hospital.

My phone wakes me with the sound of birds chirping. It must be 6 p.m. already—just about visiting hours. I reach onto my nightstand to silence the alarm when I notice a slew of messages from Fay.

Is your dad ok?

Hello?

I'm coming to mtl

I arrive around eight pm

can I stay with you?

I rub my eyes and check my messages again to be sure I read them correctly. Fay's on her way to Montreal? A small smile creeps onto my face. I shouldn't have doubted that she would be there for me when it counts.

I sit up and swipe through to check my other messages: Two from Zinnia sending me love and telling me to stay strong. Radio silence from Kiara.

I go back to Fay's message to let her know that I'm leaving for the hospital now-ish and that I don't know where I'll be when she lands, but to call me.

My phone is at 17 percent, so I plug it in to charge and then walk over to my dresser to start getting ready. I want to be back at the hospital as soon as possible.

My brain still hasn't fully computed that my father has had a heart attack, survived surgery, and is now in intensive care. It's all a blur. Almost twelve hours of travel, a sleepless night, a full day staring at hospital walls . . .

It's all too much to handle. I head over to the front entrance where my luggage and purse are sitting, and I pull out my anxiety pills. I have no clue how many I've had today or how many are even allowed, but I pop one anyway; I need this anxiety to subside. I take a swig of the orange juice I poured earlier and feel my heart thud again.

Jack.

Deep breath in as I walk back to my room to finish getting ready . . . but I can't. I can't go on with the mundane task of putting clothes on, and instead I let the air fill my lungs as I slide down my dresser and hug my knees to my chest. I lower my head onto my arms, and only when I let out that first cry do I realize I had been holding my breath. I stay there for a moment and let my mind go blank. I empty it of all the preoccupation and trivialities that have consumed me the past few days. Secrets, fighting with friends, problems that, like Kiara said, are not real problems. Because for the first time in my life, I know the difference.

My phone chirps again, so I peel myself off the floor and unplug it from the wall. Battery at 45 percent, I head over to the bathroom to brush my teeth while I call my mom back. She informs me that my dad is awake and that I should come back as soon as I'm ready.

Then she sends me a list of things she wants me to pick up from their house. I dial Jack's number and put it on speaker while I finish getting dressed.

"Hey," I say softly when he picks up. I clear my throat and start again, "Hey, um, I'm ready if you are."

"Yeah, I was just about to tell you I spoke to your mom. I'm already on my way to come get you." Perfectly reliable, amazing Jack.

When he arrives, I jump in the car and decidedly avoid looking at him. Instead, I stare straight ahead and lean into the awkward silence, which, incidentally, seems to be his game plan as well.

First, we swing by my parents' and quickly check everything off my mom's list. I rummage through sock drawers and toiletries, making sure I get all of my dad's favourite items. Then, we hit the bagel shop and pick up a few snacks.

Once we are on our way back to the hospital, Jack finally breaks the awkward silence and asks how my trip was. I catch him up on the broad strokes, trying to keep things light. I don't mention Zin's affair or Fay's girlfriend and certainly don't mention my theory on Wren and Kiara's situation. I briefly gloss over the fight at dinner last night, leaving out all details about my Jack-nundrum, which is what I'm now referring to our breakup as.

"It sounds like it was an okay trip until last night," he says. I know he's making a show of caring about the banalities of our social dynamics when the only real question he must want to ask is: What did they have to say about us? Do they know you cheated? Jack's hands grip the steering wheel as he avoids a snowbank while turning the corner.

"I mean, yes, at some points it was okay, but overall, not our best."

More awkward silence.

"Fay's actually on her way to Montreal. She should be here soon," I say, checking my phone. It's almost eight o'clock, but she hasn't messaged yet, so she probably hasn't landed. "I was sort of pretty horrible to her." I stretch my lips back, baring my teeth in a guilty-as-charged grimace.

"Horrible how?" Jack gives me a quick glance before returning his focus to the road.

"I may or may not have forgotten her mother was an alcoholic," I say.

"Ooh," Jack lets out a puff of air.

"And then I may have spilled her secret to everyone at dinner last night."

"Eesh," Jack doubles down on the *it's-not-looking-good* reaction.

"That's why I'm surprised she's coming. I mean, I know she loves my dad, but Fay's not the bring-you soup-in-bed-when-you're-sick type, she's more the stop-crying-you'll-get-wrinkles type, you know? Like, not the first person I call in a crisis, but whatever." It'll be good to have her here. She'll keep me from drowning in complete sorrow. "I'm grateful that she's willing to put everything that happened behind us to be here for me." I glance at Jack and gauge his reaction. "For my dad," I add. "I'm sorry, we don't need to talk about this," I say. The awkward, heavy silence returns, filling the space between us for the rest of the drive.

When we walk into the hospital entrance, Jack pauses and runs his fingers through his hair, sending snowflakes into the air. Then, he pushes back a strand that's hanging over his eyes. I love it when it grows a little too long and looks tousled and rugged.

The memory of sweeping it behind his ear tugs at my fingers.

"Ready?" he says.

"I hate this place," I say, a chill running up my spine.

Jack puts his arm around my shoulder. "He's fine."

We go up to the ICU and walk down the long hall to my dad's room. Before we enter, I stop.

I take a moment to breathe so that I can be strong for my dad.

"You got this, Val." Jack caresses my arms and looks me in the eye. I try to look away, but he grabs my chin. "He's fine."

"I don't think you can say that enough." I laugh nervously.

I knock lightly before I push the door open. When I see my dad asleep in the tiny hospital bed, tubes in his face and in his arms, my chest tightens. It's so jarring to see my larger-than-life father lying there, so small, so helpless, so mortal. I try to hold back my tears. The last thing he needs right now is to see me fall apart. I walk over to his side and take his hand in mine, and he opens his eyes. We look at each other for a quiet minute before he notices Jack. He lifts a brow and looks back at me, a small smile growing across his face.

"You scared me, Papá." I lower my head into his neck and hug him. I don't know why I even tried to put on a brave face. I bury my head into his shoulder and wrap my arms around him tighter, letting the tears flow like a river. He caresses my back.

"No llores." His voice is dry and crackly. "Don't cry," he repeats. "Ay, mi amor. I'm okay." His hands pull me in tight, but I can feel that it's taking all his strength to hold me. "So," he clears his throat, "Jack. Are you back?" His eyebrow lifts ever so slightly, and he chuckles. He always thinks he's a poet when he rhymes.

A nurse comes in, and Jack is saved from having to tell my father that his visit is strictly platonic.

"Okay, Mr. de la Vega, let's check those vitals." She clicks her pen and writes something down on her clipboard. "How're you feeling?"

"Fantastic," my dad replies.

We all let out a tense laugh.

The nurse checks his IV bag and heart rate monitor, and then she gives a little speech about what we can expect. Discomfort, try not to get up, call if you need anything.

"Pregúntale." My mom nudges me to ask her question.

"My mom wants to know how long he has to stay here?" I ask.

"Oh, a week at least. But recovery is about three months," she explains. Then she looks at my dad. "I'll explain everything over the next few days. But for now, just try to rest. You have a lot of people here who love you. That's good, you'll need the support."

She slips the clipboard into a pocket at the foot of my dad's bed and turns to go.

"So, tell me, Jack." Without skipping a beat, my dad picks up exactly where he left off. "Are you back?"

"Dad!" I nudge his arm lightly. "I'm sorry, Jack. Please excuse my dad. He recently had a heart attack and apparently lost all sense of normal human interaction." I smile nervously.

"You should answer that," Jack says.

"What?" I stare at him confusedly.

"Isn't that your phone?" Jack asks, pointing to my buzzing phone.

"Oh, sorry." I pull my phone out of my purse and turn the screen to show my dad the photo. "It's Fay. I'll be out in the hall." I swipe to answer, but before I say hello, I shoot a look at my dad and say, "Leave Jack alone."

"Jack's there?" I hear Fay ask as I put the phone to my ear, closing the door behind me.

"Yeah." I smile and lean on the wall right outside my dad's room.

"That's big of him," she states. "Did you call him, or was he just there?"

"I'm at the hospital," I shut down her line of questioning. "He's here to see my dad. What's up?" I exhale into the phone.

"Okay, that's good. I'm on my way. How's Eduardo?" I can hear her getting into a car and closing the door. Her voice sounds muffled against her chin. "Shit, I forgot how cold Montreal is."

"Yeah, it's cold but actually quite nice for the end of February. My dad's awake and doing well."

"Ugh, that's good to hear because I really need you right about now."

"What?" I respond. My head does a complete one-eighty, trying to make sense of her comment. "You need *me*?"

Her voice is muffled through the speaker, and I can hear her giving directions to the cab driver. She hasn't lived in this city in over ten years, yet she still thinks she knows how to navigate her way to the hospital better than a guy who literally drives for a living.

"How long will you stay at the hospital?" she asks. "Should I just go straight to your place? I've had a day."

Anger swells in my chest as her voice drones on. It's starting to sound like fingernails on a chalkboard.

I can't believe she had the audacity of accusing me of fabricating problems when here she is so wrapped up in herself that she can't see past the borders of her own hypocrisy.

"Wait," I cut her off, still trying to make sense of what she means. "So, you're here because you need *me*?"

"Come on, Val," she sighs annoyedly. "Don't act like that."

"Like what? Dramatic?" I state accusingly.

"Well, sort of," she says.

Not knowing how to respond, I consider my options. Option A, I could cuss her out and unleash all my pent-up anxiety on her. Or B, I could let this slide and save my energy for more important things.

"You know what, my father is lying in a hospital bed, and I don't have time to go back and forth fighting like teenagers. I'm sorry you wasted your time, but you shouldn't have come," I say as I remove the phone from my ear and click *End*. A well-intended metaphor for our friendship right now.

Jack pokes his head out into the hall. "What was that about?" He reaches his arm out and rests it on my shoulder.

"No bueno." I sigh as I shake my head. "I was thinking maybe a couple more minutes in there, and then I should go home and get some rest. It's gonna be a long week."

"Agreed." He smiles, but there's a flicker of disappointment in his voice. I know I'm not imagining it this time. "But I'll be here with you. I'll take long breaks from work, leave early, go late, all of it. You're not alone."

"That's amazing, thank you." Standing face to face, I summon the strength I need to say what I'm gonna say next. "But I've decided," I take a deep breath. "Well, I'm going to be at work too."

"Work?" Jack takes a step back and scratches his head. "Oh!" It clicks. "Work!" he belts out. His reaction is a testament to how well he knows me. He knows as well as I do that I could *not* go to work tomorrow. Everyone would understand since my father is in the hospital. In fact, I'm sure no one is expecting me to show up, not even my dad. But I need to do this for him. He'll be able to focus on recovering if he knows that I'm at the office running his company.

So tomorrow, I take the reins of Valentina's.

"With my dad in there," I point to the hospital room, "this is the best support I can give him."

"You're a good daughter, Valentina." Jack takes a step toward me and rests a hand on my shoulder.

"Thanks," I say, tucking a strand of hair behind my ear.

My phone lights up. A text from Fay. I swipe it away without opening it. Delete.

"You're doing the right thing." Jack takes another step closer to me. I look up from my phone, and my screensaver lights up the tiny space between us. A close-up of us at the lookout.

"You know, Kiara said something on our trip that really made me think." I look up at Jack and inch closer. "She said that maybe we've changed." I pause. "I think she's right. I have perspective now," I say, tucking my phone into my back pocket, then I place one hand on his arm. "I've realized what I want." I step closer to him, closing the gap between us.

I slip my fingers up along his chest, behind his shoulders, and lock my hands behind his neck.

"Why did I think I could tinker with fate? With what I was meant to do, who I was meant to be with? I know it sounds silly, but part of me feels like everything happens for a reason, and maybe I tried to glitch the system and that's why my dad ended up in a hospital, but it was all a way to lead me back to what was right in front of me all along." The space between our bodies is gone as I lift up onto my toes to reach his lips.

"Don't," he says as he pulls away from me. Like a boxing glove to the chest, all the air is knocked out of my body.

"Oh," I sighed. "I thought—"

"I know what you thought. You thought because I'm here that all is forgotten. You thought that you've changed or had an epiphany, or whatever, and so I forgive you. But I don't. Nothing forgives the fact that you cheated on me."

Oh yeah, *that*.

He takes a giant step back. "I'm not ready to forgive you. You're just questioning everything because your dad is in there." He points to the hospital room, quieting his voice. "But you can't just flip a switch and think I'll come running." He's shaking his head. "I can't do this right now."

"Please, I'm sorry. I know what I did was wrong. But the more I think about it, the more I think I did it to shake things up. Make you jealous, or fight for me . . . I don't know, make things sparkle or something. I don't expect you to forgive me, but—"

"Sparkle?" He raises his eyebrow and lets out a puff of air. "Sparkle? Is that what your excuse is? You cheated because there's no sparkle?" He waves his hand between us back and forth.

"Jack?" I whimper. I want to yell that I lied. I never cheated. But the twistedness of having lied about cheating somehow feels even more hurtful than if I had cheated in the first place. I'm so frustrated. I move closer and place my hand on his cheek. He lets me caress my thumb through his day-old stubble. I move closer and place my lips on his. His lips are warm against mine for all of a moment before he pulls away.

"Stop, Val," he says firmly. "It's over." He pushes me away lightly but with enough assertion that there's zero room for misinterpretation.

I look into his eyes, and I can see that I'm hurting him. Every time he has to reject me is as hard for him as it is for me. The hurt, it's choking him.

There is no two ways to interpret his words. *It's over, it's over, it's over.*

Kiara

MIAMI, MARCH

MIAMI IS FILLED WITH TOURISTS HALF THE YEAR, BUT BY THE END of March, the city starts to feel slightly more local. With the snowbirds packing up and heading back north, it's easier to get a reservation, there are no more lines in the stores, and traffic lightens up, which makes it easier for me now as I run around the city picking up everything we need for dinner.

My and Wren's schedules have been so busy—what with keeping Raven the last few weeks because her mom's been travelling and with Wren's work that comes home with him each night—that we haven't had a single minute alone since before my trip. Hard to believe, but tonight is our first date night *sans* Raven since, oh my god, I don't even know how long. Maybe Valentine's Day.

When I left the Bahamas, I was scared to return to Miami, nervous that Wren would blast me for my "fussy" phone antic. I own that I was basically ghosting my own fiancé. Something hit me when I found out Eduardo had a heart attack and Val didn't bother texting me. Fay and Zin have each other in Toronto. Val has Jack, whether she wants to believe it or not, and me? Without Wren, who do I have? Alone all of Sunday sitting at the airport waiting for my delayed flight, I had plenty of time to ponder my relationship. The only thing that kept pressing against my mind was that I do keep the peace. I hadn't been ghosting

Wren; I had become a ghost. I decided then and there that I would break up with him the instant I landed in Fort Lauderdale.

I decided alone would be better than power dynamics. No more anxiety over Wren's reactions. No more keeping the peace. I was done.

But when I stepped out of the airport, my plans changed. There was Wren, waiting for me with Raven, flowers in hand. The smiles on their faces were so big, so genuinely happy to welcome me home . . . it made me rethink everything. Raven, my sweet little Raven. I was so consumed by my own fear that I hadn't even considered what calling off the wedding might do to her. I decided to give it a week before making any rash decisions, which I'm glad I did because Wren has completely flipped the script. Although these last three weeks have been busier than ever, something has clicked, and we feel like a family. Wren has been incredibly doting over both me and Raven. No jabs or jokes at my expense, no side comments on my outfits. In fact, it's been the polar opposite: compliments, sweet exchanges, and last weekend, he made the three of us breakfast in bed. We watched *Curly Sue* and Raven learn how to lick each finger, one pop at a time.

I'd be lying if I said I wasn't worried about Wren's reaction when I told him how the girls treated me on our trip—leaving out the excessive drinking part, of course. But he said exactly what I was thinking: some friendships aren't meant to last forever. When I mentioned Eduardo's heart attack, he said I should only call Val if I want to fix it, not call if I want to nix it.

Seemed simple enough at the time.

Truth is, at the time, it felt easier to nix it. Toggling between the two worlds is complicated. Being caught in the middle of my friends and my fiancé is impossible. It's worse than being stuck in quicksand.

So, this works. Ish. Except that I miss my friends every day.

Just thinking about all this causes tension in my neck. I don't want to bring that energy home with me. I want to be light and clear-headed for Wren.

When I pull up to the next stoplight, I lower my hands off the steering wheel and exhale, releasing the muscles in my upper body, pushing my shoulders away from my ears. I close my eyes and focus on the smell of the sea air. I think about blue. Blue water as far as the eye can see. Blue like the lining on our wedding invitations. Blue like the night sky that blanketed Frankie and me that last night in the Bahamas. I travel back to that night, sitting cross-legged in front of Frankie, his gentle voice guiding me to steady my breath, telling me how breathing can transport me anywhere in the world, even in the twenty seconds a red light offers. It's amazing how this breathing thing works. Why spend money on a therapist when all I needed was to learn how to breathe?

Honk!

The car behind me jolts me back to Biscayne. I hit the gas pedal and start driving. I'm three minutes away from home, but with the traffic, Waze says fifteen.

Honk, honk, honnnnk. The man lowers his window as he passes me, finger in the air, letting his road rage flare. "Idiot! Move out the way!"

I dial Wren to let him know I'll be a little later than anticipated. We promised each other to meet at five sharp to make the most of the night. We love being in the kitchen together, him by the stove grilling the meat as I dice the veggies, Bruno Mars in the background.

"Hey babe," he sings when he picks up. "I'm almost home. You there yet?"

"Yeah, I'm like a minute away." I lie as I hit the gas.

"Did you get extra lamb chops?" he asks.

"I got six, why?" I thought three each would be enough. But his tone makes me think otherwise. "Should I have gotten more?"

I look over at the grocery bags on the passenger seat and start mentally checking off everything I got. Half a pound of Brussels sprouts and three cobs of corn from the market right next to our apartment in Sunny Isles, six lamb chops from all the way in Wynwood because Wren likes the way the butcher cuts the meat there, and Wren's favourite dessert from a little bakery in Bal Harbour, chocolate Danish laced with strawberry jam. I thought that would be plenty for our dinner and leftovers.

"Yeah. That's not gonna be enough," he says. "Max is joining. Go back?"

I suppress my immediate reaction, which is to tell him Max absolutely cannot join date night. I'd rather invite Road Rage Guy than Max. Douchebag número uno.

I exhale gently, letting all my expectations go. *Maybe it won't be so bad*, I think.

"Hello?" Wren's voice is growing agitated.

"If I go back, I'll be hours with this traffic," I say softly, trying not to sound whiny.

"And if you don't go back, Max has nothing to eat," he pushes.

"You know what?" I know this isn't going to end well if I don't come up with a solution. "I wasn't really in the mood for meat tonight. I'll make extra veggies or whatever, and Max can have my chops." There. I relinquished my portion of meat in a display of martyrdom. That should throw a *oh you're the best* my way and end this.

But instead, silence.

A pervading silence I know all too well.

It's in the silence that my mind goes in a million directions, playing out every possible scenario. It's in the silence that I regret what I've said and start thinking of all the things I could've or should've said and what I can say next to turn this back around. It's in the silence that I know I did something wrong.

"Wren?" I ask softly. "You there?"

"Yeah," he says crisply. "Three each is still not enough. I'll just go myself."

I'm about to reply when the tone on the other end lets me know he's hung up on me.

I feel winded. Belly hot, throat constricted.

Fuck.

I drive on, gripping the wheel tightly with anxiety until I finally reach our garage. I don't know if it's safe to go home or if I should turn around. I pull into my spot and key the butcher's address into Waze to see how long it would realistically take me to go back, but by the time it loads, my anxiety has inflamed to the point where my fingers are trembling. I turn my car off. I need to catch my breath.

I lower my head onto my steering wheel and breathe, letting the sound of Rihanna's voice come through my speakers. I picture her, running, fists fighting with fire, begging for love. *No matter what I do, I'm no good without you.* I'm tired of being played, I'm tired of being hurt, I'm just tired. Why do I keep going back for more? What kind of person am I to keep letting this happen? Every time he talks to me like this, I say, *This is the last time.* But then in the next breath, I also think about how I don't want him to stop loving me. *And I can't get enough . . .*

I don't know what's worse, that I was actually looking forward to date night and obviously he wasn't or that I believed he'd never make me feel this way again.

I feel stupid.

Deep breath in and hold, two, three. Something white. My white jeans shorts, the tote, our grocery bags beside me packed with our uncooked dinner, the car parked in front of me. My future wedding dress. I feel queasy.

"Hey baby, need help?" I jump at the sight of Wren approaching my car and opening the door for me.

"Oh, you scared me. I thought you were going to get the chops," I say, stepping out slowly. I lean back in across the driver's seat to grab the two grocery bags.

"Nah, you're right. Too much traffic." He grabs the bags from my hand. "Let Max starve." He laughs. I scan his face for anger, disappointment, irritation, but there's nothing. "I'd much rather have a little alone time with you before he gets here." He slams the door and leans in for a kiss. He's genuinely happy to see me. I smile and let out the breath I hadn't realized I was holding.

We head over to the elevator, Wren walking behind me carrying the groceries and my tote. When he reaches for the up button, he leans over to kiss me again. I kiss him back but feel the bitter taste of acid come up in my mouth.

"I told Max seven, cool?"

I stare straight ahead.

"Enough time for us to *get to it* if you know what I mean?" He sets the bags down in the elevator and pulls me in toward him, squeezing my butt as he open-mouth kisses me. *Must be love on the brain* continues to float through my mind as he slides his lips to my neck, hot breath warm behind my ear and alleviating all of my fear the old Wren is back. "We could pull this knob and do it right here if you want?" He points to the emergency button and raises his eyebrow. His hand hovers over the button, and I shake my head, pulling his arm back. "Don't!" I smile. He pulls me closer and pushes into me. My shoulders drop, and the tension I've been holding melts further away.

I interlace my fingers behind his neck, pushing my lips hard into his. He shoves me against the mirrored wall, and we make out like sloppy teenagers until we get to the forty-second floor. The elevator doors open, and our neighbour, Old Lady Juarez, is standing in the hallway and staring at us like she just witnessed a crime scene, Wren's tongue still deep down my throat. Nothing she hasn't seen before. Wren and I giggle as we exit the elevator.

"Good evening." Wren nods in greeting as we walk past her toward our door. She doesn't respond.

"I'll start on dinner. Will you help me unpack?" I say over my shoulder as I head into the kitchen.

"No. Come here," he calls out to me from the bedroom, his pants already off.

"Wren, we have like two hours before Max gets here, and nothing is ready." He's not listening, just curling a finger at me, and I can't help but giggle. "Fine, but a quickie," I say as I walk toward him, pulling off my jean shorts as I enter the room. I slip the straps of my tank top off my shoulders, and I climb on top of him.

"Mmm, you feel nice," he moans.

It doesn't take much for us to get right into it, picking up where we left off in the elevator. My hips move back and forth, undulating like a wave, slowly, then quickly, then slowly again. Hands gripping his bare chest, I'm leaning over him, my braids spilling onto his face. I move forward, then back. Wren's holding me at the hips, pushing me as we grind. He licks his fingers, then slips them between the space where our bodies meet. One hand on my clitoris, the other pinching my nipple, he bites his lip and groans. "I'm almost there," he whispers. "Come with me, baby."

I let my head fall back as I rise and fall on top of him, my body bouncing faster than I can control. His fingers circle faster and faster as he grabs my waist with his other hand and cinches me tight. I can feel him finish as he pushes deeper inside of me. I moan out as he grunts loudly, his nose scrunched up to his eyes, mouth wide open.

We rest there a moment, panting together.

"Fast enough?" He winks as he pushes me off of him. "Okay, let's prep dinner." He slaps my butt. I roll over onto my side of the bed and grab a tissue to clean myself up, wiping away all excess leakage before I put my undies back on.

"Let's do this," I pop off the bed and clap my hands.

"Gimme a sec, I'll meet you in there." He rolls over and closes his eyes, his body limp on our bed.

Nothing like a good romp to tire my Wren out. He's out like a light in five seconds flat, so I head over to the kitchen to start on dinner alone. Time to wash the veggies, set the table, season the meat, and pour the red into the decanter.

I toss the potatoes into the sink to soak them in water and start husking the corn. Its bright yellow colour prompts me back to that night on the beach with Frankie. There was only one night about a week ago when I let my curiosity get the better of me. I hid in the bathroom to stalk Frankie on socials while Wren was asleep. His pictures are so hot, but his captions are even hotter. One photo of a beach tiki torch had the caption *In the whispers of the night's sea, the eternal dance of still.* I wanted to comment *Okay Whitman*, but I held back.

Frankie's old soul is a stark contrast to Wren. This is Wren's first go at life, that's for sure. Even at Christmas dinner, Eduardo mentioned that Wren seemed like a young soul. When I asked what he meant, he said *no wisdom behind his eyes*, which is a truth I haven't been able to unhear ever since. I mean, Wren's understanding of anything emotional or spiritual is lower than that of any of my fifth-graders. Not that I'm much better. But, I don't know, around Frankie I felt like maybe I was capable of something deeper. He unlocked something in me that night on the beach. Like maybe I have layers that haven't been peeled back yet. Maybe I'm reaching. I guess I'd just like to believe that there's more to me than what's on the surface, like there's more to tap into.

One night meditating, and all of a sudden you're Deepak Chopra, I imagine Wren saying to me. I wouldn't dare tell Wren that I've been doing visualization exercises. He puts meditation and yoga in the same category as sorcery and psychics.

Lost in thought, I don't notice the water overflowing, sending the potatoes floating over the top of the sink. "Fuck!" I yell. "Fuck, fuck, fuck!"

I look over to our bedroom to see if my screaming woke Wren up. He's still conked. Phew. I reach to close the faucet and start wiping up the water that has now pooled all over the kitchen floor.

"What the hell? What's going on?" Wren rushes over and comes to a stop, standing over me. "Are you kidding me? What's wrong with you?" He storms over to the linen closet to grab the mop.

"Sorry, I was thinking about—"

"You mean you *weren't* thinking, that's the problem." He grabs the cloth from my hand and tosses it onto the counter, mopping up the water. "I got it, just go change for dinner. I'll salt the chops and finish the potatoes."

"I'm sorry," I say in a small voice.

When Max arrives, we pour the wine and sit down to dinner. The first twenty minutes aren't too bad. Max and Wren talk about a case they're working on, and I listen quietly as I dig into my Brussels sprouts. I have my mouth full when Max finally addresses a question to me.

"You decide on a venue yet?" he asks, forking a piece of meat into his mouth.

"Set a venue?" Wren scoffs. "She can't make a single decision to save her life." He places a hand on mine. "First it's grilled cheese for midnight snacks, then it's no midnight snack." Wren caresses my hand while directing his comments at Max.

"Midnight snacks for sure, but I'd want a good burger. Ohh! Make them sliders!" Max's voice is one of those really irritating, throaty male voices that sound like he's choking at all times. Anything and everything he says makes me want to smack the goofy grin off his face.

"Yes, now that's helpful. See, hun, all you have to think about is your dress. Max and I could plan everything else in under a minute."

I don't want this doorknob anywhere near my wedding planning.

"I mean, we'll let you decide on your hairdo and makeup, but we've got the rest." Max belts out a laugh, and the two of them high-five across the table.

Watching them laugh at my expense is too much for me to handle, especially since it hasn't been hard for me to decide the menu, nor has it been a challenge to make our guest list, choose my dress, select a venue, pick an invitation, and decide on floral arrangements. It's Wren who keeps pushing back on every decision I make, but he's not telling that version of the story.

"Sliders are a great idea, thanks Max," I say quietly as I play out a version of this moment where I stand up and reach over the table to grab him by his shirt collar and drag him out of our apartment, all feral, like the fountain scene at the mall in *Mean Girls*. But alas, I just breathe and smile.

"Good girl." Wren laughs again, this time patting my head. "Keep making those quick decisions, and we'll be married by the time Raven is ten!"

"You know, when Raven's ten, I'll be her teacher." I smile at Wren, changing the subject swiftly, trying to segue out of this sorry display of brotherhood. "I'll make her my special helper. She can plan my lessons with me at home and then sit next to me in class." I laugh and nudge his shoulder. That would be so cute.

"Very nice, Keeks. Nepotism." Wren stares at me with a lamb chop in his mouth, juice oozing onto his chin. I can't tell if he's being sarcastic. "Aren't you the one who's always on about how Val has a red carpet rolled out for her, and it makes you hate her?" He pulls the bone away, and his mouth is greasy, filled with flesh. "You want the other kids to hate my little girl?"

"'Kay, first, I don't hate Val. Second, I was only kidding, Wren." I roll my eyes. "I would never set Raven up like that." Not that being my helper would set her up to get bullied. Every teacher has their helpers; it's typical classroom management stuff. "I just meant I can't wait to spend more time with her."

"You can't turn her into your little doll, Keeks," he says to me in all seriousness. "She's gotta learn hard work."

"But you could bump up those grades." Max winks at me and fist-bumps Wren.

Right, because that's not nepotism. I clear my throat as I reach for the potatoes and serve myself a small spoonful. "She'll love the media literacy module. My students love it because I make them watch TV for homework and then we chat in class about all the subtext, you know, like what's being said, what's not being said, who is being represented, what it all means in a more cultural sort of way. It's super cool. Kids are smarter than we give them credit for." I mash down the potatoes with my fork, creating a tic-tac-toe board as I speak. I get carried away whenever I talk about my work. There's no place in the world that makes me happier than my classroom.

"Relax, Kiara, it's grade five," Wren says with a condescending smirk on his face. "From the way you're talking, it's like you think watching *Dora* is raising the consciousness of an entire generation."

Wren and Max burst into laughter.

"First of all, *Dora* is for toddlers," I say, biting back tears. "And second, you're being a jerk." I toss my napkin onto my plate and push my chair out to stand.

"Wait, wait, wait. Hold up." Max puts his hand in the air. I raise my eyebrow and wait for him to speak. "You're still going to work by the time Raven's in grade five?" Max scoffs, looking at Wren like he holds the key to my professional future. The room goes silent. I turn to face Wren and wait for him to answer. We've actually never talked about this, I'm curious what he'll say.

"Come on, Max, enough," he says, reaching his hand over mine. He stands up and puts his arms around me. He might make a few harmless jokes here and there, but he's my fierce protector when it counts. He leans over to kiss my neck. "You know my woman won't work anymore." I whip around and pull my face back. "She'll be too busy taking care of all this." He motions to our apartment. "And this." He motions to himself.

I'm speechless. I'm searching for the words, but I'm so flabbergasted by this display of chauvinism that I just shake my head instead.

"Plus, in order to keep you in the States, I'll have to transfer your work permit to the firm. Your K-1 status is almost up, and we still aren't married, so . . . You can start on some odd job with us probably in a couple months, filing or some shit. It'll just be simpler for citizenship."

Is that even true?

"Is this for real?" I finally spit out. I love my job; those kids are everything to me. I worked my butt off to get my own homeroom, and I'm not gonna give that up just because Wren lives in the nineteenth century. "I can't keep my class because we're not getting married fast enough? Isn't there something else we can do?"

"No, babe. Not unless we get married, like, tomorrow, which we aren't doing. You know I have more to do than think about your little media hobby or whatever it is they pay you for at that school." At that, he sits back down and pulls me onto his lap. "When you make real money, then maybe we'll talk."

"Yeah, and you can't be working when all the little babies start coming," Max adds, raising his brow like he's helping to prove Wren's case.

"Nah, I've got my hands full with Raven. One and done." Wren leans over me and reaches for his glass of wine, oblivious to the shocked look on my face.

I can hardly pick my mouth up off the floor. It's wide open like I'm catching flies. Wren has our whole lives planned out and never thought to tell me I'd be barefoot in the kitchen and, what, maybe filing papers for him every other afternoon? I swallow the knot that has lodged in my throat. What the actual fuck?

I push myself off Wren's lap and slowly start to stack the dinner plates. "I'll start on cleanup," I say quietly.

I walk over to the kitchen, and a wave of nausea comes over me. I try to lay the plates down gently, but they tumble to the floor, shattering.

"You okay over there?" Wren calls out to me.

"Yeah, I'm fine, I just feel a little sick all of a sudden." After hearing what my future looks like, I feel a lot more than a little sick. My mind is going a million ways from sideways, trying to figure out an exit plan. I didn't know this was what I signed up for.

It's one thing when it's jokes about my weight or how I always shrink his T-shirts in the laundry. I'm used to that level of condescension. Been dealing with men like him my whole life. But even my own father didn't treat me like this. It's like I'm a second-class citizen in this relationship.

Does he really expect me to give up everything for him? No work, no kids, nothing . . .

When do I say enough is enough?

"You coming back, babe?" Wren yells from the table.

"Yes, yes, I'm just cutting the Danish. Gimme a minute." Perched over the kitchen island, I try to gather myself. *Keep the peace, or get out of here?*

I take a few deep breaths and feel the food climbing up my throat. I run to the bathroom and barely make it in time to watch my dinner come back up.

"What the hell, Keeks?! You okay in there? Trying to poison us?" I can hear them chuckling over the gurgling sounds of my vomit hitting the toilet.

"No seriously, you all right in there?" Wren asks, now making his way over to me. He places his hand on my back, lowering himself over me to gather my hair and hold it back. "It's okay, baby, let it out."

I wipe the spit that's dangling from my mouth with my wrist. Looking up at him, his face soft and his eyes worried, I smile. "Yeah, I'm okay. I don't know what came over me. Been feeling queasy all day."

He helps me up off the floor and wets a towel. Dabbing my face to bring me back to life, he smooths the hair on my forehead. "I got you, boo." He kisses my lips. "You still taste good, even after puking."

"You're gross." I laugh self-consciously.

That's the confusing thing about Wren: I know if I'm ever in pain, he'll be there for me. "Thank you," I whisper as I move away from the toilet. He grips my face and kisses me again.

I hate that I love him. I hate that even when I'm sweaty and post-vomit, he thinks I'm sexy, making me forget that not just five minutes ago I was contemplating packing my bags.

"Yo, Max, you should go!" Wren yells out from the bathroom. "Kiara's not feeling too hot."

Wren ushers Max out and insists I get into bed. He pours me a glass of water and lowers the lights as he tucks me in.

"I'll clean up dinner. Just rest." He kisses my cheek. I can feel him standing over me, staring at me, worried about me, as I slowly drift off to sleep.

A sudden wave of nausea jolts me awake a short time later. My stomach churning, I scramble out of bed, but my steps are unsteady. I barely reach the sink in time before retching into it.

What the hell has come over me? This can't be food poisoning; I didn't eat any of the chops, and I'm fairly certain you can't get sick from poorly cooked corn—or can you? I groggily reach for my phone, intending to google whether undercooked corn can cause intense vomiting. As I unlock the screen, my gaze falls on the date: March 20. That's when it hits me—I'm a week late. With a sinking feeling,

I open my period tracker app and confirm it: March 13 was my last expected period.

I barf again, but this time from the knots and nerves that are tangling up in my stomach. I rummage through our bathroom vanity, looking for a pregnancy test. I know I bought a box with two sticks last year when we had a little scare. I hid it behind my makeup in a bag of sanitary pads so Raven wouldn't find it. I reach behind my Tarte mascara and open the purple box of ultra-thin pads, pulling out the test. How could I let this happen? A faint memory after Valentine's at Cecconi's crystallizes in my mind.

Walking over to the toilet, I catch a glimpse of myself in the mirror. This is bad. Very, very bad. I wish I could remember if I took my pill that day . . . Is it even possible to get pregnant that easily? It can't be.

One and done, his voice echoes in my mind.

All the air feels like it's been sucked out of the bathroom.

Wren will kill me if I'm pregnant.

I take a deep breath and try to calm down as I take a seat on the toilet, but nothing comes out. I try to relax so I can go. I imagine yellow: daffodils, sunshine, flowing, tinkling. *Please don't be pregnant*, my inner voice gnaws in my head.

Somehow this will all be my fault. *One and done.* He's going to be so mad.

Pretty please, don't be pregnant. A slow trickle releases, and I quickly place the stick between my legs.

What will I do if this test says I'm pregnant?

I should start planning my exit strategy now. Get out of here before he finds out and sends me back to Canada. Or worse, makes me—

I don't even want to go there. I walk over to the door to check that Wren isn't looking for me. I open it slightly, careful not to let the bathroom light spill out into our bedroom. The coast is clear. I click the door shut carefully and walk back over to sit on the ledge of the bathtub.

Please don't be pregnant.

I can't be pregnant.

I wish I could call Val right now. She'd check the test for me, and no matter what it said, she'd tell me we'll figure it out together. But she probably won't answer now. Calling Fay is out of the question. Which leaves Zinnia. I could try texting her—she would know what to say.

I reach for my phone and scroll to her name. I click open a text box and start typing a message, but everything I write feels stupid. We haven't spoken in weeks; I can't just open with *Hey hope your affair's going well. Oh, and I might be pregnant and I'm freaking out.* Letter by letter, I delete the H-E-L-P I typed and shut my phone.

Please don't be pregnant.

I stand up and inch closer to the test that's balanced ever-so-innocently on the ledge of the sink. A perched stick holding my fate in a tiny window.

I reach for the test and feel the weight of it in my hand as I close my eyes and make my last silent prayer: *Please don't be pregnant.*

Two pink lines.

Pregnant.

Fay

TORONTO, APRIL

I LOVE THE SMELL OF EARLY SPRING IN TORONTO. THE CRISP MORNING air, blooming flowers, and the hot sun that grows warmer by the hour. As I stand in front of my closet, trying to choose what to wear, I'm torn between a light sweater and a leather jacket. April is all about layering, so I opt for my Janis Joplin graphic tee, light grey knit sweater, and distressed jean jacket. That way, throughout the day, as the sun shows its shiny face, I can peel back piece by piece.

People linger on their porches, coffee mugs in hand, and the streets are a landscape of flowers flourishing, colours radiant and bold, trees unfurling their leaves. Like an O'Keeffe come to life, which is exactly how I feel: alive again.

I'm three hours away from meeting Zin for the first time since we left each other that dreadful morning in the Bahamas. With some time to reflect, what with Val basically ejecting me from Montreal, I realized I had been at fault in that airport terminal. I should never have given Zin an ultimatum. I knew the pressure would push her away, and I was right, it did.

I tried to own up to all of it, but I have over a hundred failed apology texts and at least three dozen unanswered phone calls that prove she was not ready to hear from me. And then, the other day, I sent a simple three-word text: I miss you. I wasn't expecting a response, but she wrote back that she missed me too and was ready to meet under a few conditions: Nothing alone, somewhere public, and I've got a ton of stuff to get done. She suggested I meet her at Holt Renfrew, something about returning a pair of sandals Adam bought her.

The rebirth of Fay and Zin 2.0: Just Friends Edition, because I'm not stupid enough to hope for anything more.

As I walk down the street, I see young couples draped all over each other on park benches and in cafés, clasping hands and getting in those extra kisses at street corners and over lattes. Parks overflowing with kids running around, sweaters tied at their waists, as they chase soccer balls or play tag. Terraces at full capacity, friends laughing, sharing secrets, gossiping about the goings-on of the previous night. I remember the last time the girls came for a visit. It was about three years ago; Saul was about two years old. Zinnia pushed his stroller to Bradley's Bistro for brunch, and the four of us sat there for over five hours, catching up and reminiscing. We stayed so long that the waiter asked us if he should set us up for dinner.

I wish we could go back to simpler times. Before the Bahamas, before Zin and I kissed, before my life turned to shit. I want those days back when not a single thing could happen in one of our lives without all of us knowing within a group chat in seconds.

Instead, I'm friendless. Girlfriendless. Lonely AF. And one show away from going bust. If this is adulting, unsubscribe, please.

I'm just hoping that we can put our "illicit affair"—or whatever she called it when we finally spoke—behind us so we can make the world right. I'm okay with tucking my love away and holding a torch for her for the rest of my days if it means I can have her back in my life. Because, honestly, life without Zin is just not an option. It's like a garden without flowers: lifeless, monotone, and, well, for lack of a better metaphor, just fucking shitty.

But today, everything is coming up roses.

Before I head downtown, I need to prepare the gallery for tomorrow. I'm stoked to finally show an artist who might actually see some real sales after my sculptor fell through. If she sells well, it would be a huge win for the gallery. And by win, I mean I'd get to keep the place open another couple months.

The artist, Sara Millard, is new to the scene; it's her first show, but her work is sensational. There's one piece I could picture sitting above Zinnia's fireplace—the auburn strokes giving off more heat than the fire below, almost as though the frame itself were on fire. The texture of Millard's canvas lends itself to an intensity, an intimacy where we could get lost in our own little world. I can imagine sitting with Zinnia on the couch, gazing at the painting together, her head in my lap, endless hours debating whether art imitates life or life imitates art.

I shake the thought out of my head before I let myself go too far.

When I get to the gallery, I hang about twelve pieces and install the lights. I repainted the walls yesterday to create a warmer ambiance to show her work. I won't have time to finish all the prep now. I underestimated how long it would take, and I have just under an hour to get downtown to meet Zin. I want to get there a little early, prepare myself. I pop in my earbuds and hit play on my podcast. Nothing like *WTF with Marc Maron* and a long walk to clear my head so I'm not all amped up when I see her.

I practise my speech as I head into Holts, zigzagging through the makeup counters and athleisure-dressed soccer moms. *You're worth more to me than you know . . . I shouldn't have made you choose . . . let's go back to how things were . . . whatever you need is fine with me.*

Just then I spot her, and my mind goes blank.

Across the Nars makeup counter, bright lights shine above her, blonde curls contouring her face gently and accentuating her cheekbones. Only she can make the intense yellow department store lighting work. In her brown woven mules, distressed low-waisted jeans hanging low on her hips, and a cropped white T-shirt just short enough to leave a small ribbon of skin peeking through, she is simple, effortless, totally Zin.

I've only ever loved one other person in my life: Aiyla. She was my girlfriend before Zin and I started up. We had a love-hate relationship that saw me through seven of the most tumultuous years of my romantic life. It was immature love evidenced by the fact that we broke up more times than I can count on two hands. It was discovery, experimentation, lust. It wasn't depth and attraction and stomach-saults and my best friendship all rolled into one.

Zinnia is all those things, only amplified to another degree. It's the kind of love poets write about.

She walks slowly, carefully scanning the lipstick display.

Gosh, she's beautiful. I don't think I realized I'd feel like this just at the sight of her. My heart is jumping out of my chest, and my hands are clamming up.

I study her as she transforms the simple act of reaching for the rouge into a stage performance, and she's the prima ballerina. Extend, pluck, twist, and glide. She leans into the mirror and puckers her lips. First, she purses her lips together, then she pulls out a tissue from the box next to her and wipes it all off.

"I think it looked nice," I whisper shyly as I walk up to her from behind. She whips around, startled.

"Oh my god, you scared me." She pulls me in for a hug and then pushes back. "Did you cut your hair?"

"Yeah." I forgot I chopped it off last month. I run my fingers through my shaggy, square cut and look away, starting to feel self-conscious she won't like it. "It's already grown out."

"I like it," she states, as though she read my mind. "Suits you. And is that a—" she brings her face closer to mine, inspecting the side of my neck "—a feather?"

"Yup!" I giggle nervously, covering the space right below my ear. "I got a tattoo."

"Mmm," she mumbles. I can tell she's hurt. She was supposed to come with me to get my first tattoo, and now this feather sits like a symbol on my body of a moment we lost. "It's pretty." She traces the thin lines and lingers her finger at the base of the feather. I try not to read into it but the hair at the back of my neck stands up. I think she notices because she pulls her hand away from my skin and quickly shuffles toward the eyeshadow.

"So how've you been?" I ask.

"I've been good. You?"

"Yeah, good." This is painful.

She snaps a Laura Mercier eye compact shut and places it back on the Limited Edition showcase.

"Okay, well since you're here, let's head up to the shoe section?" Zin holds her bag up to show me the pair she brought to exchange. "The sandals Adam got me are too big. I want to see if they maybe have my size."

"Yeah, sure," I reply. I can tell she's trying to act natural, but each word she says is punctuated with awkwardness. I knew it would feel weird, but this is worse than weird. This is bad.

Uncomfortable.

It's not us.

"Okay, great." She starts for the escalators. "Unless you wanted to buy something down here first?" We both take a step at the same time and bump into each other.

"Sorry," I say.

"No, it's me, sorry."

I shrug off the cringe-worthy clumsiness and remind myself it's Zin. It's me and Zin. I got this. "I have an exhibit tomorrow. Maybe I'll find some shoes too. Let's shop, shall we?" As if I had even one extra dollar to spare on new shoes, I motion to the escalator and let her take the first step toward the women's shoe department.

We float our way up to the second floor, Zin one step above me. We both reach for the rubber rail, and when our skin makes contact, my stomach tightens. I know she feels me there because goose pimples have formed up and down her arm.

We both pull away. Me, instinctively. Her, deliberately.

I follow her off the escalator onto the floor and turn my attention to the shoe displays, pretending we came here to shop and not address the reason I asked her to meet.

Browsing the shelves, we move around each other like two people instructed to remain at a choreographed two feet apart. Never coming too close, brushing past each other but never quite making contact. If someone were watching us, they'd think we were perfect strangers.

I follow her to the nearest cash and stand a foot behind her while she explains to the clerk that while the gift is lovely, the size won't work. The salesperson explains that she'll keep the shoes at the cash so Zin can browse freely.

"You speak to Kiara lately?" Zin asks, stepping away from the cash.

Small talk it is.

"Nope. Not Kiara, and not Val, either, actually. I didn't see her even once while I was in Montreal. Not Eduardo either."

"That's weird. Was it family only?" She reaches for a pump, inspects it, and then replaces it on its stand.

"Something like that." I sigh, leaving out the fact that I cooped myself up in the airport hotel overnight and took the train home the next day.

"I haven't spoken to anyone, either, if that makes you feel any better." Her voice trails off as she moves toward a floating display at the centre of the floor. "Bahamas feels like a blip in the ether."

I scan her face to see if she meant just the trip or our relationship too.

She turns away and grabs a pair of Valentino slides. "Hey, these are nice," she calls out, dangling a stud-crusted slip-on in her hand.

"Yeah, if you're planning to beat someone with a sandal." We laugh. "Who needs that many studs on a shoe?!" I take one from her and pretend to hit her with it. "And three hundred dollars! What are these made of? Pure gold?"

"I know." She laughs and places the sandal back on its stand. "But Adam insists on buying me expensive shit." She points to another pair of studded shoes. "So would you please help me find something wearable?"

Zin continues to pick up shoe after shoe, inspecting each one with the precision of a cobbler. Every time she reaches for a shoe on the higher shelves, her T-shirt rides up and more skin is revealed. I make my way over to her and grab a pair of Stella McCartney platforms, and my arm brushes along hers. Electricity sparks, and I can see her chest rise with her breath. "I can see you in these," I say.

"Just these?" she asks as she slips one sandal out of my hand.

Is she flirting with me? I instantly have an image of her wearing nothing but these white platforms.

We stand there, motionless, both holding a single shoe. I know that what I say in this moment matters. All my senses are heightened right now. "You smell like a citrus drink," I blurt out. "Like a creamsicle." I smile.

She smiles back and tosses her hair from side to side so the scent of her shampoo showers us in sweet vanilla orange notes. She's definitely flirting with me.

I drop the shoe, and it lands between us. "Shit." I laugh nervously. I bend to pick it up, and my head knocks into hers as she does the same. "Fuck, sorry!" I say, reaching for her face. "You okay?"

She rubs her forehead. "Yeah, I'm fine." She smiles, and we lock eyes. I move my hand from her cheek to her neck, bringing my face closer to hers. I take a deep breath and let the hot air release through my mouth behind her ear. She quivers.

"Is this okay?" I ask. Nodding ever so slightly, I can feel her feet firmly planted, holding still to make the moment last. "How about this?" I slip my hand around her waist and tease her with the faintest touch of my hand against her braless back.

I can't help myself. I'm intoxicated by everything about her, her very essence makes me feel like I can't breathe. I'm stupid to think a platonic friendship between us is possible. She's the love of my life. Always has been. Always will be. Nothing could ever change that.

"Shoes," she says with a nod, pushing me away.

"Right," I say. "Shoes."

"Never mind, I can't do this." She exhales sharply and throws the shoe she was holding onto a display table. "Fucking elevator, I never know where it is. Like they hide it on purpose!" She's walking frantically and turning in circles, searching for the elusive elevator that's right in front of her.

"Zinnia, wait!" I say, grabbing her wrist to swing her around so she's facing me. "I'm sorry. I shouldn't have touched you like that. I way overstepped." Here's the moment when I'm supposed to say all the things about how I'm totally not in love with her. How we can be just friends, and how I'll restrain myself. I won't caress her back. Or picture her naked in nothing but sandals. Or hope that she'll accidentally brush her skin against mine. Fuck!

I know what I'm supposed to say, but it's as though my mouth has a mind of its own because the words just start falling out.

"Please don't leave, Zin," I beg, extending my hand to take hers. "Tell me what to say, what to do, what to feel. I'll do it, just please—" I stop myself. "Please just be honest with yourself, Zin. Tell me you didn't feel that back there. Tell me you weren't flirting, and I'll back off."

She's staring at me. Eyes locked on mine.

Waiting.

I'm waiting for her to put me out of my misery. She's waiting for me to, what? Give her an out?

After a short pause that feels like an eternity wrapped in forever enveloped in the infinite expanse of silence, she cups the side of my face. I have no idea what she's thinking or what I can say to rewind time and take it back. I'm about to tell her to forget it. That I don't want to push her. My intention is not to pressure her, not today, not ever. I start, "Zin—"

"Stop," she says, holding one of her hands up in front of my face. "Follow me."

Zin takes me by the hand and drags me through the shoe department into ladies' eveningwear. She pulls me into a changing room, and before I know what's happening, she's locked the door. In one fell swoop, her T-shirt is on the floor beside us.

I can't believe what I'm looking at . . . what's happening?

I'm sure I look like an idiot staring at her, but I don't know what to do. I feel like one false move and all this could go away. I swallow the pebble lodged in my throat as Zin takes a step closer to me. She pushes me down onto the bench and lowers herself onto her knees, unbuttoning my pants. One button at a time, she looks up at me from between my legs, and I can feel heat and desire swell with every second. She strokes my leg slowly as she pulls off my pants, and then she glides her hands up my thighs. Throbbing with excitement, I'm wet before her fingers reach me, her tongue a warm and welcome pressure. She licks my skin all the way up to my breasts, fingers deep inside of me. It doesn't take long for me to push her down onto the floor and climb on top of her. I move my hands slowly up her hips and lean carefully, deliberately toward her breasts.

With quiet moans, I swirl my tongue lightly on her nipples and then kiss every inch of her body, moving slowly toward her hips, kiss by kiss. I unbutton her jeans and pull them down along with her underwear and feel a penetrating heat emanating from between her legs. I slide down and start to swirl my tongue up and down, harder and harder, quicker and quicker, until she's gasping. I slink back up to her mouth, and our lips meet.

"This." She breathes into me and grazes her lips on mine. "Is. Everything." She pushes my lips apart with her tongue.

"I love you." It tumbles out of my mouth, and I instantly regret it.

She pulls back a bit and looks me in the eye, then tilts her head slowly, and I watch as the sides of her mouth curl up into a smile. She presses her lips against mine softly, and I follow her lead, ignoring the whirlwind of emotions twisting inside of me. I want to interpret her kisses, but I'm unclear what they mean. She didn't say it back. Stretched beyond the point where I can form intellectual thought, I push away my propensity to overthink—we're here now, that's what matters, right? I swat away any doubt or thought that might detract from this moment of visceral bliss and let my entire body melt against the pressure of her fingers finding their way back inside me. I push my fingers into her and match her rhythm. She moans loudly, and for a millisecond, I'm reminded that we are in a changing room and place a hand over her mouth. I can feel her whole body quivering, her chest moving up and down as she tries to catch her breath.

When we're both done, we collapse side-by-side on the tiny fitting room floor.

"I should've called back, but—" she finally whispers between breaths.

"Don't, I shouldn't have pushed." I rest my head on her chest.

"I was scared." She kisses my head. "You have no idea how many times I picked up the phone to text or call, but I just couldn't bring myself to."

I lift my eyes to look at hers. "It's fi—"

"Fay, I love you," she says. She lowers her eyes, and I can tell by the strained expression on her face that she feels bad for how we left things. This must've weighed on her just like it did me.

"I love you too." I say, caressing the small mound of her breast.

"We should probably get out of here," Zin giggles.

She kisses me and the bolts to a stand. When we're both finally dressed, we swing open the fitting room door, and there's a lineup of women waiting to try on their clothes, all of whom know exactly what was going on just three feet away from them. It only makes me feel closer to Zin. More jokes that belong just to us. We laugh, holding hands as we walk as close to each other as humanly possible, no way of telling where she ends and I begin. I could stay like this forever.

We make our way outside without saying a word to one another, but this time, our silence is one of shared joy, not awkward disconnect.

"Will you come to the opening tomorrow?" I ask, putting on my sunglasses.

"No, no, no!" She hits her forehead and turns around.

"What is it?" I ask. Despite her declaration of love, I instantly worry that this might have been a one-time thing.

"I left my shoes at the cash!" She slumps her shoulders in exaggerated annoyance. "I have to go back in." She turns back toward the door, and I'm left wondering what happens next. I need to let Zin's actions speak for themselves. She wouldn't reel me back in if she wasn't sure.

She whips back around and plants a kiss on my lips. "But yeah," she brushes her fingers through my hair, "I'll be there for sure." She smiles and walks back toward the store.

All of my worries and questions fade away. I know everything I need to know. She's chosen me.

Zinnia

TORONTO, MAY

"WELCOME BACK!" ADAM SINGS OVER HIS SHOULDER. I HEAR HIM turn off the faucet, and within a split-second, he's rushing over to meet me at the front entrance. He reaches to grab my overnight bag as I slip off my Birks. "How was it?" He leans into me, pecks my cheek, and throws my bag over his shoulder, leaving it by the foot of the stairs. "How did Fay take the news? Did she cry? She for sure cried." Going a mile a minute, he's back at the kitchen sink finishing up the dishes, and I can barely get a word in.

After a spa weekend in cottage country, Adam's energy is akin to a bunny on speed. I can't blame him though—he hasn't had adult conversation in two full days.

"Being in nature always makes for a smoother landing," he says as he dries his hands. "Tell me I wasn't right?" He turns around and leans back onto the sink; I'm perched over the island. "Create a good headspace so that when you hit her with *we're moving to California*, she at least has a lake to jump into. Brilliant."

So brilliant, in fact, that he's the one who found us the place—the same cottage we rented when we went last summer with our kids—and footed the bill.

"Yes." I nod and wink exaggeratedly. "You're a genius."

Except for one tiny little detail . . .

I didn't tell her.

It wasn't the right time. Which, if I told Adam, would prompt him to rattle off all the other "not right times." Morning yoga? Too many people around. A ride-along to pick the kids up from school? Not enough time to process. While helping her at the gallery? Very unprofessional. And finally, evening walks once the kids are asleep? Why ruin a perfectly good stroll with soul-crushing news?

I walk over to the sink, run the tap, and reach to fill the kettle. "Should I make us some tea?"

Adam wraps his arms around my waist. He kisses my neck lightly and stays there for a while, swaying back and forth to the music: Marvin Gaye's voice singing to us from our Sonos speakers.

"I missed you," he says softly, sweeping my hair away from my neck, tracing a line from my ear to my collarbone with his finger. "I still can't believe you got this." He tickles my feather tattoo, the one I got to match Fay's. I can feel him smiling behind me as he traces the contour of the stem.

I squeeze my eyes shut to stop the tears from forming, but that feeling in the pit of my stomach is back. I'm a horrible person.

"Me neither." I clear my throat. "You know what?" I whip around and push him away slightly. "I think I'll shower before dinner if you don't mind."

"What about the tea? Want chamomile or green?" Adam calls after me as I race up the stairs.

"Sure!" I yell.

Before I head into a shower, I walk to the end of the hallway to Saul's room. I creak open the door and slip through quietly. He's sound asleep. I gently kiss him good night and then cross the hall to do the same with Darla. I had hoped to get back early enough to put them to bed, but our two-hour drive ended up taking us nearly four and a half with traffic.

Whenever I'm away from home, I feel an ache, an absence in my heart. Like something is missing. Ironically, I get that same yearning when I'm apart from Fay. It's that old saying *home is where the heart is*. Except my heart is being split between two homes. This one with my children and the one Fay and I have created. Home is no longer a heart-containing metaphor; instead it's a fractured space, one that pulls me in two different directions, never fully whole.

I walk over to the shower and turn the faucet on to burning. I wait until the steam builds before stepping in. As the water beats down my back, I can't help but feel like I'm washing away the shame. What makes me feel worse is that Adam doesn't even know to look for it. Why would he? It's Fay. Why should there be anything suspicious about a weekend away with Fay? It's the easiest affair to get away with.

I let out a deep breath and step out of the shower, pulling a towel around my body. The mirror's all foggy from the hot water; I clear a section and look at my reflection.

I'm such a jerk.

I head into our room and lie across our duvet. Large white and dark-purple flowers woven on green stems against a grey backdrop. I remember when I brought it home, Adam expressed actual hatred toward it. He said it was too *feminine* and *delicate* and that no man should be made to sleep in what could only be described as a botanical garden. To make himself feel better, when we get into bed, he lets out a growl and flexes his muscles to make a big show of being a man. It's sweet that he didn't ask me to return the duvet, and his little performance always makes me laugh.

I reach for a plush pillow and fold it under my head, closing my eyes and letting images of last night float through my mind. Fay's soft, buttery skin against mine, our legs intertwined as we explored parts of each other under the open sky. Waking up next to the woman I love, holding hands as we hiked through the woods, bathing together. And the sex, oh, the sex. I take a deep breath and can still smell her citrus floral perfume on my sweater.

Every moment was perfect, from the midnight tarot readings and vision boards to the early morning hot tub and skinny dipping in the lake. All those cliché romantic moments that I could never imagine having with Adam.

I'm just not in love with him. And now that I know what true love feels like, I can honestly say I don't think I ever really was.

How did Fay take the news? Adam's question replays in my mind, boiling my guilt over like a storm coming ashore.

"Hey Zin? You out of the shower yet?" Adam calls from outside our door. "Saul woke up and is crying. Says he wants to say goodnight to you before he goes back to bed." I hear him meltdown in the background. "I told him he could come kiss you when you got out of the shower." I fluff up my pillow and sit up as the door swings open. "Go on," he encourages as he releases our son from his arms, and he runs toward me. I squeeze my little munchkin in a tight hug.

"Oh, Mummy missed you, sweetheart." I rock him back and forth, secretly happy he woke up. I close my eyes and breathe him in. "Bad dream?" I ask, and he nods, resting his head on my chest.

"So, you're killing me!" Adam places a teacup on my nightstand and then moves to join Saul and me on the bed. "How'd she take it?" He's staring at me with laser focus.

"Oh, um, yeah, not well. I mean, I started to tell her, but she has a lot going on right now, with the gallery and tax season, you know, and, um, the leaky pipe." I snap my fingers and nod my head. "It's a whole thing," I add, fumbling over my lies. Adam is staring at me with a facial expression that reads *bullshit*.

"Leaky pipes?" he asks. "Tax season? That doesn't even make sense."

I run my fingers through Saul's curls and resign to just tell him the truth. "I decided in the end not to tell her yet." I pause and lower my hand, reflexively pulling at my cuticle. "I think I'll tell her when we finalize the house. I can show her pictures so she can imagine herself visiting." I look at our son and smile. "Right, Saul?" I deflect. "Does Mummy have a good idea?" I bring my nose to his and bunny kiss him. He giggles in agreement.

Maybe that's the real reason I haven't told Fay: because I can't picture myself in California. Until it happens, it's not real, and honestly, a part of me hopes that between now and then, I'll come up with a plan.

Or, at the very least, if I close my eyes hard enough, I can pretend it isn't happening.

"Well that was a waste of a trip," Adam says, propping himself up on his elbows. "Tell her to come over for dinner this week; we'll tell her together." The thought of Adam breaking the news to Fay makes my stomach somersault.

Saul wiggles out of my arms and begins to jump on the bed. Adam grabs his ankles, sweeping him down onto his back. He then proceeds to tickle him until he's laughing so hard he's crying. "Stop!" he begs between laughs. Adam pulls his hands away, hovering them high above and wiggles them around, threatening to squeeze his sides again until he screams. It's in these moments, these tiny glimpses of sheer joy, that I know I should be here, with my family. But I can't be sure because I'm overwhelmed with sadness.

That's the problem with being split in two, you can't be present because you're nowhere.

"Hello? Zin?" Adam waves his hands in front of my face. "You there?"

"Oh, sorry. Just tired. He should really get back to bed." I pull Saul toward me. "It's time to go dodo, sweetie." I bring him close, gently pressing his cheek to mine. "I'll put him back to bed and be down soon. Maybe you and I can order dinner?"

"I ordered Chinese last night; I could just warm up the leftovers?"

"Perfect," I say, slowly making my way to the door.

When I get downstairs, Adam's parked on the couch, watching basketball, two big bowls of noodles and chicken sitting in front of him on the coffee table.

"Hey babe," he says when I sit down beside him. He nods toward a bowl and adds, "That one's yours." We eat silently while watching sweaty men run up and down a court dribbling a ball.

Adam yells at the TV, and I stare at the ceiling.

When we're done, I collect our bowls and carry them over to the sink, the dishes heavy with the weight of routine. Before tackling the kitchen, I check the family schedule pinned on the fridge to make sure the kids' stuff is prepped and ready for the morning rush. I pour their water bottles and start to assemble the sandwiches for lunch.

No cheese. Great.

Darla's reading log is empty. And Saul's bag is covered in yogurt, all crusty and emitting a foul odour.

"Hey Adam?" I call over the announcement of some unprecedented, never-before-seen three-pointer, but he doesn't hear me over the TV. "Adam?" I repeat as I walk over to him. "Did you do the kids' homework with them?" I turn down the volume, but he doesn't seem to notice.

"Damn it!" He erupts at the TV. "What d'you need?" he asks, eyes still fixed on the screen.

"Did Saul pick something for show and tell?" I ask. "Darla's reading log? Did you do any homework at all this weekend?"

"Shoot the ball!" He stands up, pumping his fists at the game, cheering as a player takes a shot. The player misses, and Adam slumps back onto the couch. "It's fine, I'll just write their teachers and explain they didn't have time to do their homework on account of being kids."

"Adam!" I roll my eyes and exhale sharply, angry that he leaves all the real parenting to me, but then I remember I have no moral ground to stand on. "Never mind."

"What?" He looks at me, waiting for my usual lecture on pulling his weight. "They're in elementary school, not Harvard."

"You're right, it's fine." *Perspective*, I remind myself. I rub my temple and move toward the stairs. "I'm gonna go to bed. You coming?"

"Nah, I'm gonna catch the end of the Lakers game." He turns around and smiles. "Gonna be our home team soon."

"Right," I say.

Home.

In bed, I pick up my phone and scroll through my camera to replay the weekend's highlights picture after picture. There's one of us kissing in our pajamas, eating leftover spaghetti in bed before we went on to spend most of the morning in the hot tub—steaming more from the sex than the water temperature. I swipe and zoom in on one of a fallen log on the path to the water where Fay and I sat and meditated together earlier this morning.

I text it to her: Love this photo . . . a fallen log that lifted us up.

What dreams are made of, Fay replies with a winky face. My kinda girls trip.

You should post that pic, it's a beauty, she adds.

I go back to the photo to inspect what Fay sees in it. She's right, it does have a serene quality to it. Amidst the calm promise of budding trees, you sense the chaos of what winter had left behind—whatever natural force took down the tree. I used to be suspicious of her belief in my photography—everyone snaps photos on their phone they think are incredible, why would mine be different?—but I know a good photo when I see one, and this one is good.

Fay and I talked about how taking pictures isn't just my way of capturing a moment to savour it. It's the story behind a photo that breeds enduring energy: what's there, what's been left out, the significance of how the objects have been framed. Each photo has a past, a present, and an unknown future, holding the memory of the countless people who will come in contact with it. In that way, the photo itself becomes its own story.

I post it to socials and caption it: *every tree has a story*.

I scroll for a while until I land on one of Kiara's photos: a pic of the cast from *Modern Family* with a caption about how her students loved learning about stereotyping and discrimination in the form of humour and sarcasm. I click over to her feed to see what else is new in her life. A ton of posts about her media literacy program, even some links to download lesson plans. She's always been so good at her job; I love that she's using social media to spread knowledge. I keep scrolling until I get to February. The picture of the four of us from the Bahamas when she and Val arrived. The promise of an amazing trip ahead.

I can't believe we haven't spoken since then. For the life of me, I can't remember why. In part, I think I conflated Fay and Kiara's drama with my own. In reality, their fight had nothing to do with me. I don't think it had anything to do with them, either, if I'm being honest, but every time I've tried to bring it up with Fay, she just tells me she's not ready to talk about it. I don't push. Instead, I take the path of least resistance, which is exactly what I did by not reaching out to Kiara. Val, on the other hand, is a whole other story. I texted her a few times after Eduardo's heart attack, but she never replied, and I tried again over the last couple weeks to no avail. Radio silence. And there's no world where she can say she didn't see them because she has read receipts on.

Nervous energy knots up in my stomach as I stare at our four faces, happy and smiling.

I key in *miss you* under the post. A small gesture, but it's a good first step to mend what's broken. I'm about to swipe out of her feed when I see a heart go red. Kiara liked it. She's online.

White flags waving, I click out of socials and try her on video chat. She answers after one ring.

"Hi!" I beam. I shock even myself with how surprised I sound that she picked up. I clear my throat and settle my excitement before I try again. "Hi, how are you?"

Kiara's face fills the screen. It looks fuller than usual, younger, cheeks flushed. She looks happy.

"Yeah, it's been a while. How are you?" She flips the question back.

"Good, kids are great," I respond.

"And how are *you*?" she asks again.

"Good, good." I toss my hair to one side. "So, what's been going on?" I ask, not sure where to start.

She stares at the ceiling beyond the frame of the phone, and a huge smile grows on her face.

"What? What is it?!" I insist.

"Well, speaking of kids . . ." She pauses, and I immediately think of Raven. I hope everything's okay. I mean, she's smiling so it can't be bad news. Maybe she's—

"I'm pregnant!" Kiara pulls the phone back and stands to the side so I can see her tiny belly. She pulls up her T-shirt, but I can barely make out a bump.

"Oh my god, Kiara! Congratulations!" That explains the plump cheeks. I can't believe we haven't spoken in a long enough time for her to have new life growing inside of her. A pang of sadness pulls at my heart. "How far along are you?"

"Just thirteen weeks, but holy fuck, pregnancy is no joke. My morning sickness has been so intense and lasts way past morning." She props the phone up and sits back. "I meant to text you when I found out. Been dying to tell you, actually." Her expression changes, and I can see the sadness behind her eyes. "I regret that I didn't. I'm sorry."

"Are you kidding?" I shake my head. "I'm the one who's sorry!"

"'Kay, stop." She waves me away. "I can't do sappy, I'll cry. I cry for everything now, by the way."

Kiara dives into a list of all the first trimester symptoms: exhaustion (she's fallen asleep while giving her students a test), nausea (she's barfed everywhere from Target to the corner of Lincoln and Collins), and cravings (ice cream topped with Doritos and sriracha).

"Whatever happened to pickles?" I laugh, fake-vomiting at the idea of cheesy, spicy ice cream.

I never got to do this when I was having my kids. We were so young when I was pregnant, none of my girls understood what I was going through, how life-changing it all was. They'd ask how I was doing but had zero concept of how all-consuming it can be. From the stretch marks and weight gain to the breastfeeding and potty training, I went through it alone. I mean, Fay was always there in her way, but only as much as someone can be who hasn't experienced it herself.

"I'm sorry I haven't been around."

"Don't be like that. It's fine." She brushes the air with her hands, waving away her tears and my guilt. "But seriously, I've been eating like a mad woman." She stands up off her stool and moves away from the camera. She lifts her tank top again and turns to let me see every angle like she's in a 360 camera booth. "Did I gain a lot of weight?" She scrunches up her face and holds up a hand to hide her face. "Be honest."

"Kiara, you're pregnant, you're supposed to gain weight." She winces. "And you look amazing."

"I don't know." She sighs. "With two trimesters left to go, maybe I should slow down on the junk food. At least that's what Wren says."

Well, Wren needs to shut his mouth and not comment on your body, I think. If he's going to say something about every pound she gains, it's going to be a long nine months. Not to mention post-birth. It took me months to shed the baby weight, which didn't bother me as much as I know it'll bother Kiara. For as long as I've known her, she's struggled with her body image. So the last thing she needs is Wren chiming in on the scale.

"Doesn't he know you're eating for two?" I raise my brow.

"No, it's not like that." Her defences shoot up. "He's been amazing, really." A tear falls onto her cheek.

I have so much compassion for Kiara in this moment. I remember all the ups and downs of those years when I was pregnant with my kids, body on loan, acting like anything but myself. Never mind the fact that my body kept changing, my eating habits fluctuated, my mood swung back and forth.

"Well, speaking of Wren," I start. "How's he feeling about all this?"

"I didn't tell him right away." She shakes her head. "He had told me he didn't want more kids, so I was sort of scared about how he'd react. But I was even more scared about how he'd feel when he found out I'd kept it from him."

"The whole damned if you do, damned if you don't," I say. "I get it." More than you know.

"Yeah, well, turns out I was scared for nothing because when I told him, he was over the moon. Like, talking to my belly and everything."

"What would you have done if he was mad?" I press. I've always been the only one to defend Wren, but right now he's giving me the ick.

She flips her braids and leans onto her elbows, propping the phone against something so I can see from her shoulders up. "I thought about that a lot the first weeks. I even considered packing up and moving back to Montreal. Never telling him. Raising my baby alone. But—" She lets out a heavy sigh. "I couldn't do that to Raven." Her belly is out of frame, but I can see her hand move toward it as she continues. "This is her baby brother, you know?"

I nod. "Wait," I clock her words. "It's a boy?"

Kiara's smile grows, showing every single one of her teeth. She has that pregnant glow. I take a screenshot to show Fay later.

"Well, maybe." She laughs. "We don't know yet. But Wren is convinced. All he wants is a son. A younger brother for his Raven. He even bought little baby Air Force Ones. He says even if it's a girl, she'll be into basketball, being my baby and all."

We're catching up on lost time, but in some ways, it feels like we're picking up exactly where we left off. Slipping right back into our friendship.

"Have you told Val?" I ask, curious if they've spoken at all these last few months or if Val's giving her the same silent treatment she's been giving me.

"No." She shakes her head, lowering her eyes. "I haven't spoken to her since . . ." her voice trails off.

"Me neither," I sigh. "She won't return my texts."

I don't even ask if she's reconciled with Fay. I already know the answer.

We sit staring at each other for a moment, and I can tell she's thinking what I'm thinking: *everything's changed.*

"Enough about that." She wipes another tear from her face. "When's the big move? California, right?"

"You know, for someone who was fall-on-your-face-frat-girl drunk the entire time, you certainly have a sharp memory."

She nods proudly. "If I remember correctly, there was an affair with a certain *her* as well?"

Right.

"Well, to answer both your questions, I move in September and that's when my affair will end." I turn over onto my side, adjusting my blanket so it can prop up my phone. Unless in some unexpected twist of fate Adam gets fired or told that we can stay in Toronto. One can hope.

"Ohhh the plot thickens." She rubs her hands together. "Who is this mystery woman anyway? Does she have a name?"

"I can't get into that now," *because if I told you it was Fay, it would unfurl a whole host of questions I'm not ready to answer*. "Can I tell you something though?" I steady myself onto my elbow, head in my hand.

Kiara nods, waiting for me to go on.

"I really don't want to move. I'm happy here, you know? I have everything I need within walking distance. I love the little bubble I've created, and my kids love their school. I don't know anyone there, and Adam will be at work all the time. What will I do?"

That's the real question I've been scared to face. I don't want to uproot my whole life so we can move Adam closer to his dream while I move farther from my newfound happiness.

But also, I can't stay in Toronto just for Fay. How would that be different from going to California for Adam?

"Tell me about it," Kiara says, biting the inside of her cheek.

"What do you mean?"

"Wren wants me to quit working." She takes in a deep breath and nods like she knows exactly how that sounds.

"He what?" I scoff. The idea of Kiara not teaching is like asking a dolphin not to swim. It's who she is.

"I don't want to get into it. I'll figure it out." She's crying again and it reminds me that there's just something about growing a baby that both fills you with life and sucks it right out of you. "Listen, if I were you, I'd think about what makes me happy and go from there. And you know, if you don't want to move, you should tell Adam. He's not gonna make you do something you don't want to do. What does Fay think about all this?"

"I don't know." I shake my head. "I just wanna do what's best for my kids and my family," I say, sidestepping the Fay-bomb as I slump back down onto my pillow.

"And what about what's best for Zin?" She tilts her head to the side. "This is your life too. You have a say."

I bite the inside of my cheeks nervously as I think about why I hadn't ever considered telling Adam I didn't want to go. It wasn't even a conversation. He came home one day and announced his work was relocating him. I simply agreed, and that was that.

"I don't know what to think anymore." Now I'm crying.

"The real question is—" she pauses "—are you taking your girlfriend with you?"

"Yeah, shoving her into Darla's carry-on." I stick out my tongue.

"You laugh, but stranger things have happened."

I hear Adam's footsteps in the hall, and then the bedroom door opens slowly.

"Oh, you're up?" he asks surprised.

"I gotta go." I whip the phone around so Kiara can see Adam. They exchange a wave. "But I love you." I smile at my best friend. "Talk tomorrow?"

"Okay." Kiara smiles. "We'll be here." She lowers the phone for a moment. I giggle and wave to her belly. She blows me a kiss and then fades to black.

"Kiara's pregnant?" Adam asks as he climbs into bed. I nod tentatively, uncertain how much of our conversation he overheard. "Gonna be a tall baby."

I laugh as I wipe away my tears, part lingering emotion, part relief.

"Why're you crying?" He laughs, reaching over to hand me a tissue from his nightstand.

"A lot on my mind, I guess." I wipe my face. "I guess I've been thinking about what I'll do in California?" The inflection in my voice makes it sound like a question, hoping maybe he has the answer.

"Same thing you do here," he responds unflinchingly as he leans over to hit the light. "Take care of the kids, you know? You'll find ways to fill your days."

Right. I lay my head back onto my pillow as I stare into the dark. Adam lets out a low growl and pulls the blanket up to his face.

"Happy you're home," he says softly, turning over, blissfully unaware of my fractured heart.

Valentina

MONTREAL, JUNE

STARING OUT THE WINDOW OF BIJOU CAFÉ ONTO NOTRE-DAME Street, I take in the scene: people lazing about perched on shop windows, sidewalks crowded with lineups for Sunday brunch. We only get a few hot months to hang outdoors, and the people in this city make it their mission to take in every sun-soaked minute. True Montrealers shed their jackets and don their shorts by April despite the fact that there's usually still snow on the ground. Come June, forget it. The sun beats down so hard, there's no escaping the thick, balmy heat. Today is one of those truly sticky, humid days, the kind where people are ducking into shops pretending to be interested in overpriced antique lamps just to get two minutes of free air conditioning.

Beaming through the café window, the sun warms my bare arms and heats the oak bench where I'm installed, latte in hand, hacking away at budgets for the upcoming fall campaign photo shoot alongside Eloise, Valentina's senior dress designer. It's become a sort of ritual to have Sunday meetings, but she doesn't mind as long as she gets to pick the brunch spot and I foot the bill.

"These should be illegal," Eloise says, shoving a forkful of ricotta pancakes drenched with maple syrup into her mouth.

"Yeah, my avo toast isn't half bad," I say as I take a small bite. "Mmm, okay, so you think we could pull off the Lachine Canal as a backdrop?"

"Listen, it could end up looking slightly industrial, but you said young, right? And nothing says young like a floral gown frivolously worn in a field by the water," she replies, wiping a drop of syrup off her chin.

Frivolous isn't the intention—I don't want people to think our dresses aren't worth anything. But if we want to hit a younger demographic, it can't just be about the clothes, it's about who's wearing them and where, how they're styled, and how they're talked about. Four major points I brought up with my dad last week at our board meeting. He disagreed. No, he more than disagreed, he vetoed. "Our target market is sixty-plus, mi'ja. Older women want elegance, they want opulence, and they want to walk into a store and be treated to high-end service," he said firmly. His words came in loud and clear: no social media, no lifestyle blog, and certainly no influencer models.

Regardless of my title, my dad is still very much calling the shots. Only, from behind the kitchen table rather than his office desk. I love him, but nightly meetings masked as family dinners? You can take the man out of the office . . .

Truth is, my father has a clear vision for Valentina's, it's just not mine. If I'm going to run this company, then I want to create a culture and not just sell clothes. He, on the other hand, has an unfavourable opinion about fashion houses turning into a "brand." He uses air quotes and a sour-lemon face to emphasize that he sees brands as trend-driven, buzzworthy, and vapid. The gap between us is too wide to bridge; he doesn't even want to understand the power of fashion influencers and what they can do to expand our markets. *Valentina's is about tradition and family values, mi'ja. I don't want to become synonymous with fast fashion.*

Our fabrics are the finest Italian silks, French velvets, and Portuguese linens; everything is handcrafted and screams high-end. We couldn't be further from fast fashion.

"I'm a little hesitant about what my father will think about the canal." I pull a face as I flip through our lookbook. "These are amazing. You've made our dresses feel more *of* our time and less *stuck* in time. I could totally see these blowing up on socials."

"Steady, young grasshopper," Eloise says. She shoves another bite of pancakes into her mouth. "You're doing a great job, just master one thing at a time."

"Couldn't have said it better myself," I sigh. "You know, even though the place basically runs itself, I still managed to approve a shipment of last season's dresses to buyers for the summer launch. Now, they've got racks of velvet and long sleeves instead of florals and silks. Yup," I scoff. "Cost us a pretty penny to fix that mess. I wish I could stick to things like campaigns and photo shoots and leave all the business stuff to someone else."

"Go easy on yourself." Eloise smiles. "You'll find your footing. And as for the photo shoot," she says as she taps the lookbook, "I say we stick to the Basilica for now. You'll make the changes you want eventually."

She would know. When she first started, which was only a couple of months before I did, Mr. Filomena wouldn't so much as look at her. He kept referring to her as Elsa as a way of proving there was no space in our small company of eight for her and her new ideas.

"You're right, let's do the Basilica as planned," I say as I clip a photo of the monument to the lookbook and shut it, sliding it away from me. "Slow and steady."

"Good choice, boss," she says, making note of the location on her laptop.

"Couldn't be further from true," I say, and I furrow my brow.

I peek over at her screen and see a mood board she has for next season's designs. A collection slightly more modern than this one but enough to keep pushing the dial younger, moving away from the stuffy and pretentious dresses we usually make where models look like the First Lady, complete with pearl necklace.

"I love these," I say, tapping on the loosely fitted silk dresses. I could totally see Zinnia wearing these.

"We start small, right?" Eloise's thick Italian accent is enhanced by her exaggerated hand gestures. "Like these dresses, capisce?" She nods while patting the lookbook.

Slumping my shoulders, I stick my fork into a piece of pancake that floated to the edge of her plate. "You mind?"

"All yours." She slides her plate closer to me. "I gotta go."

"I just have to finish up here, then see that apartment down the street I told you about."

"Right, your Jo-nundrum?" she tilts her head.

"Jack. Jack-nundrum." I wave my hand. "Whatever, um, yeah, but we're still on for tonight, right?" I ask as I lick my fork. "Thea's in the Old Port?" She nods. "I'll drop you a pin," I say. I take out my phone and search for Thea's address to share with Eloise as she hovers by the side of the table. "There," I say self-consciously.

Rather than wonder if I'll ever speak to my friends again, I've decided it was time to make new ones. Eloise is an easy fit. She's been so welcoming, and she doesn't judge my love-hate relationship with Valentina's. If anything, she sees what it's been like for me trying to make a place for myself in my father's shadow and is really supportive about it. The only thing is, aside from work, we don't really have much else to talk about, which is why I insisted we grab drinks together tonight. I want to move this friendship to the next level and get to know her outside of work, especially since we leave for our first buying trip together to Milan soon. Plus, it beats sitting at home, poring over budgets and Excel sheets all by my lonesome.

Eloise bends over to kiss goodbye, both cheeks. She throws on her sunglasses and heads for the door. As she pulls the door open, a crowd of hipsters catch my eye. A mosaic of style that never ceases to amaze me.

Observing the group hanging right outside on the Bijou terrace—skinny shorts and tube socks, moustachioed and greasy—there's one girl in a scarf and floral midi dress who passes a joint to the woman on her left. She reminds me of Zin, bohemian chic yet timelessly in style. Right beside the group, there are two women strolling along, window shopping, peeking into the antique furniture store across the street. They look like they just stepped off the set of a forties movie scene: curly bobs and swing dresses, kitten heels, and one of them is even wearing a fascinator. I take out my phone to snap a pic. This is the kind of stuff I've been blogging about on *Siempre Valentina*—the kind of stuff that just breathes youth and the eccentric street culture of Montreal.

My generation wants more than clothing, we want to feel connected to the people behind the brand in a very personal and real way, which is why Kiara, Fay, and Zin are the main characters of every piece. I feature capsule collections, daily looks, and the stories that inspire trends. Hopefully my dad will see the value in blogging rather than vilify it as another "brand" tactic and let me post to Valentina's website.

Slow and steady.

It might be double the work to run a company and blog on the side, but the daily grind doesn't fill my soul the way writing does, so there's that. I drop the photo to my desktop and open a fresh document. I begin typing away.

An Eclectic Culture of a New Gen Aesthetic.

The paradox of fashion is that clothing conceals us while simultaneously showing the world who we are. But even more paradoxical is looking at a group of friends who, stylewise, make no sense together.

Like what's Fay—a classic rocker, always bold and out there—doing with a fade-into-the-background, simple yet timeless friend like me? Fay's clothes make a statement, even if that statement is to be understated. She's a T-shirt and jeans kind of girl, and each tee she wears tells you all about the summer she spent touring like a fangirl with the Dave Matthews Band. The look is pedestrian, like you'd miss her in a lineup, except for the fact that she radiates cool. I'd like to say I ooze the same confidence, but I'm more subdued. I keep on top of trends, as the job demands, but I never forsake who I am to trend out with a choker or a miniskirt. Neither would Kiara. She's always dressed ready for a pickup game. White jean shorts, muscle tank, and runners—minimalist gold accessories from anklets to hair clips, because style can never forsake function.

A fact not lost on Zinnia. Effortless and free, her style transports you back to an era when your clothes told the world what you stood for. Activism through florals, cropped vests, and corduroy. Except when she pulls a look, it feels totally revamped and refreshed.

Apart, we each stay true to ourselves. Together, we look like a mishmash of a century's worth of styles.

That's where the definition of style and friendship collide with the eclecticism of our generation: it's in our togetherness that we become even more ourselves.

I hit save and sign off *Siempre Valentina*. With three minutes to spare, I'll be just on time to meet the realtor at the new apartment. I glance outside to see if my bike is still there—not that anyone would steal it in this city—and from the corner of my eye, a couple on a motorcycle catches my attention. They're backing into a spot right across from the café, the passenger hugging the driver tightly. He gets off the bike and holds out his hand to help her down. The driver kicks the stand and peels off his helmet—

Jack. I gasp. On a motorcycle?

With some girl?

I can already tell she's beautiful by the way she moves, but when she lifts off her helmet, she releases her long, flowy hair, and it cascades past her shoulders down her mid-back, and the extent of said beauty is confirmed.

My stomach burns with trapped heat. Frantically, I shut my laptop and throw it into my backpack, but not before I spill my coffee all over the fall lookbook. In a perfect world, I wouldn't have called attention to myself, but my world is far from perfect. I grab a stack of napkins from the table beside and pat myself down. No amount of dabbing is going to dry the coffee that's now imprinted like a Rorschach inkblot across my chest. I attempt to air dry my papers, but the exercise proves futile. Instead, I shove the wet pages into my bag and bolt to the back patio for refuge. I have to catch my breath, make an exit plan.

Fuck! He's really moved on.

After my dad left the hospital, Jack stopped coming around. I tried reaching out to him a few times. I tried to explain why I kissed him in the hospital that day, that it wasn't a reaction to my dad's heart attack. I wrote him long messages apologizing about how everything went down and how saying no was the biggest mistakes of my life, but he eventually asked me to stop calling. I hoped that he'd find a way to forgive me, or that I'd stop loving him, but no. None of that happened, which is why I'm so unprepared for this moment. I never in a million years thought he might actually have a girlfriend.

Especially not Gisele fucking Bündchen.

I wonder how long they've been together.

Is it serious?

It feels too soon.

Ugh, this is so embarrassing. I don't need this right now. *Gorgeous new girlfriend, meet my ex. She's still learning how to drink without spilling all over herself.*

I hope they take their brunch to go.

Maybe I should cancel my appointment and move in here. They've got coffee and sustenance, and their seating isn't too bad.

I'm being silly. I should just walk out, head high, and if I run into him, I'll just smile, I'll give him the highlights on work, skipping over the very real facts that I'm lonely, I miss him desperately, and now I'm also heartbroken that he has a girlfriend.

I want to scream.

I peer through the window to see if they've walked in yet. The coast is clear. I don't see them anywhere. Maybe they went to October Pizza across the street instead.

Just in case, I wait a few more minutes, hovering behind the door before I make a break for it. I block my face with my purse as I beeline for the exit. Turning left, I slam right into her.

Overpuckered, overplumped red lips, Blondie T-shirt and Levi's jean shorts that sit snugly on her butt like they were painted on. She's freaking perfect.

"Sorry," I say, keeping my head lowered as I walk quickly toward the door, hoping Jack doesn't notice.

"Val?" Jack says loudly to confirm that it's me. "How strange is this?"

"Not that strange. Small city." I'm so nervous that I let out an awkward giggle.

Deep breath in. You got this.

"Hi, I'm Val." I put out my hand.

"Poppy. Nice to meet you." Like the seed? She's so friendly. I hate her already.

"Nice to meet you too." I pull my top knot down and let my hair fall onto my back, hoping it has the same effect hers did a moment ago. Jack used to love my hair when it was down and wild. I throw a glance his way.

"You're wearing your hair wavy," he states, but it sounds like a question.

"Yeah, just trying some new stuff." He took the bait. "Beautiful day, eh?"

"Yeah. Been a crazy nice couple of weeks. We're lucky."

"Cool. I was just, um, writing over there." I point to where I was sitting. A large puddle of coffee with half a dozen napkins on top is visible on the floor under the table. I point to my top, "Small accident," I laugh.

"Best coffee in the city," Jack says to Poppy, ignoring my attempt at covering up my embarrassment. She smiles and inches closer to hold his hand. I need to get out of here.

I point past them toward the door. "Okay, so, um, enjoy," I say, and I take off before either of them has a chance to say goodbye. But as I'm running off, I hear Jack explain who I am. The word *ex* cuts like a knife.

Despite my mishap, I arrive right on time to meet the realtor outside of a charming four-storey walk-up in Saint-Henri. It'll be a welcome change to move out of the apartment I lived in with Jack. It's too big for just one person. But despite its vastness, the walls feel like they're closing in. Every corner reminds me of him. Even the simple act of opening the cabinet above the sink reminds me of mornings getting ready together for work or evenings brushing our teeth, singing the alphabet to make sure we brushed the full two minutes. *Oral hygiene*, we would both say with exaggerated smiles, spitting excess toothpaste out on the count of three.

I decided a couple weeks ago that it was time to get out of there. And that was before I knew Poppy existed.

Saint-Henri will be a welcome change. It's closer to the office, it's a two-bedroom yet still more affordable for one, and the neighbourhood is more my age.

When I walk in, I'm immediately struck by how quaint the place is. The floors creak, which I love. The walls are papered with large floral patterns—also love. The windows are floor-to-ceiling, and there's a balcony. Love, love, love! Even though the bathroom is the size of a coffin, it has wainscotting and a rain shower, which is so my style. I walk toward the primary bedroom—a stone's throw from the kitchen—and I first notice the up-lighting on either side of the bed. Then, my eye moves to the moss-green curtains. In two corners of the room, there are huge Monstera deliciosa plants. The second bedroom is equally cute, with damask wallpaper, floating shelves, and a bright yellow canopy. I could easily turn it into an at-home office or keep it as a guest room with a fold-out couch. I could see myself living here. Moving on.

Just then my phone buzzes.

You look good.

Jack. My heart stops.

Aren't you with your new girlfriend? I write back.

Just a second date. Where were you off to in such a hurry?

New apartment. Our lease is up. I wait for a reply, but nothing comes in. I reread my message and edit it: My lease.

Time slows to a glacial pace as I stare at my screen, watching absolutely nothing happen, no three dots. Is he still on his date with Poppy? Is that why he stopped responding? I shake my head, trying to dispel my thoughts. Why would he message me mid-date if he wasn't planning to respond? Doesn't he realize I'm dying right now, waiting for him to write back?

And then his message pops up: I hope you find what you're looking for.

As a writer, I know when a conversation is over. Unless I start a whole new subject, we're done here. I close our thread and slip my phone into my backpack. Why would he write me out of nowhere just to stop writing me? Should I not have told him about the apartment?

I look up and see the realtor waiting for me to get off my phone and make a decision. I scan the room one more time. "Can I keep the furniture?" I ask, eyeing the hanging hammock in the living room. "Or, at least this," I say as I walk over and take a seat on an auburn velvet armchair. "I love everything in here." I don't want to bring a single thing from my Jack-partment.

"I'm sure we can work something out," she responds.

"So, you said it's available September first, right?"

She nods.

"Okay, well, I love it. I'll take it."

Maybe it's wrong to shake hands before ironing out the details, but I don't want to live in my place one second more than I have to, and this place is giving me I-could-be-happy-here vibes.

I hop onto my bike and start heading east. As I pedal, I sink into despair about how no one will ever love me like Jack loved me. Luckily the ride is long enough for me to overthink my way from utter desperation to anger to sadness to frustration, finally collapsing into complete confusion.

Why would he write me while he was on a date? Did it not go well? Why would he text me just to stop texting me?

I convince myself that he wouldn't have written if he didn't want to keep the conversation going. All I need now is to think of what I could write him to show him I want to keep talking.

Dripping sweat after my ride home, I hop into the shower and start thinking up all kinds of openers to send Jack. *When did you get a hog?* Oh my god, that's so lame. Who says *hog*?

If I get ready quickly, I could get to Old Montreal early and snap a pic outside the Big Top, a pretty backdrop for a selfie I could send to Jack. I haven't worked out the text portion yet, but a photo of me outside the place he took me for our anniversary is the perfect conversation starter.

I hurry out of the shower and dry myself off before I pull on a wraparound floral midi dress with a pair of ballerina slippers. I leave my hair loose and wavy (because he just said he liked that) and apply a deep shade of red lipstick to match the petunias on my dress. One last look in the mirror before I throw on my Chloe backpack and head out the door.

I park my bike closer to Thea's and then skip down to the water to make my detour to the Big Top. I snap a selfie and send it to Jack, captionless.

I have about thirty minutes to kill before I meet Eloise, so I head back up the cobblestone road, phone in hand, anxiously awaiting his reply. With all the tourists filling the streets, there's enough to look at to keep my mind busy.

By the time I get to Thea's, I'm a few minutes late, but I'm apparently earlier than Eloise. I prop myself up at the bar to wait for her and place my phone face up beside me.

Still no reply from Jack.

The bartender leans onto his elbows across from me and asks if I know what I want.

"I'll have a glass of rosé," I say.

Maybe Jack's phone died. Or he dropped it while driving and rolled over it with his motorcycle.

"Will someone be joining you?" The bartender breaks my thought, pouring me a generous glass of wine.

"Yes, my friend should be on her way." My phone lights up, and I grab it faster than a kid grabbing the last piece of candy from a piñata. *Please be Jack*, I think.

Eloise.

Not gonna make it. I wanna finish up some stuff before we leave for Milan.

Bummer. I needed some girl time. Eloise might not be my best friend—or friend, really, for that matter—but I thought tonight would be a great opportunity to set that ship in motion. Plus, I could really use someone to talk to right now, maybe tell me my selfie wasn't cringe. I can't really get mad that she's prioritizing work though. I mean, I am her boss.

I text her back: Gonna be such a great trip! See you at work tmrw.

Eloise gives my message a thumbs-up. Great, two rejections in one night. Lay it on me.

"Never mind," I say to the bartender, reaching for my glass and taking a big sip.

"Who would stand you up?" He raises his brow and shoots me a half smile. I bite my bottom lip and stare at him for a good thirty seconds too long.

"Cheers," I say, because I don't know how else to respond. I raise my glass in the air toward him, and he reaches below the bar to pull out his drink.

"Cheers," he says.

He goes back to prepping his bar, slicing lemons, and pulling mint leaves off their stems. "You from Montreal?" he asks.

"Born and raised. How about you?" I ask.

"I'm from Alberta. Moved here last year for work."

"To work here?" I motion to the restaurant.

"No, not to work here," he teases. "I'm a graphic designer. I'm working freelance for now, but I'm hoping to start at an agency if a job opens up."

"Oh yeah? Which agency d'you have your eyes on? Maybe I can hook you up."

"Jazz is my top pick, but I'll take anything, really."

"Well, today might be your lucky day. I mean of all the bars, in all of Montreal, I walked into yours." I smile flirtatiously. He looks at me like he has no idea what I'm talking about and that I might be slightly crazy. I clear my throat. "You're sitting across from a former Jazz employee." He doesn't need to know that I now run a fashion empire.

The mystery feels sexier. "But I still know everyone there. I mostly worked on the content side, but I know the whole creative team."

"No kidding. Yeah, I mean, that would be awesome if you could, like, send me a contact or whatever." His green eyes pierce through me. Shaved head, hoarse voice, tight T-shirt, he's the epitome of cliché, but in a hot way. All he needs is a cigarette dangling from his mouth and he'd be the poster child of the quintessential bartender.

"You any good?" I ask, immediately realizing I need to clarify my question. "I mean, at graphic design."

"I think I'm pretty good." He winks at me. "Always room to learn more though."

Oh my god, oh my god. Did I just come onto him? Is *he* coming onto me?

Do I like it?

Abandoning his citrus, he walks over to where I'm sitting and leans his elbows on the bar. "Would you want to teach me?"

Bold move.

I immediately feel a tingle between my legs. I want to reciprocate his flirtation, but I haven't done this in a while—or ever, really. Only Jack. I feel my chest move up and down as my breath gets more intense. I bite my lip and stare into his eyes, speechless.

He stays there, staring at me, waiting for me to make my move. But I have no clue what to say or do.

"How about you give me your number and I call you when I'm off work?" he says. He's done this before.

"You kicking me out?"

"Nope, just securing you for later." He tops off my drink.

My mind is a blur. I can't think straight, and I know it's not because of the wine. I check my phone. Still no reply.

I down my drink and hold out my hand. "Pass me your phone," I say. He slides his phone over to me, and I type in my number and name my contact *Rosé*. I send myself a text that reads Bar Guy.

I hand him back his phone, and he smiles as he looks at the screen. "Expect my call around midnight."

At that, I swirl off my seat, wink at him, and tell him I'll be waiting. Then I dart out of there. I've never done something like that in my life. I feel utterly exhilarated and petrified all at once.

I run across the street to Place d'Youville to catch my breath and reorient myself. I find a bench to sit on and look out onto the square. There's a group of people playing bongos, dancing around, and one of them is the spitting image of Zinnia. I squint my eyes to be sure it's not actually her.

"Zin?" I call out, but when a few of the dancers turn in my direction, I instantly see that I was mistaken. "Sorry." I wave my hand. "I thought you were my friend."

Undisturbed, they go back to banging their bongos and hopping around to the beat.

I've been seeing Zinnia everywhere. It started after she sent me that text a few weeks ago, and it's been happening more and more frequently. The other day, I chased a woman down the cereal aisle because I would have sworn on my life that it was Zin.

I pull out my phone and scroll through my favourites until I reach her contact. A picture of Zin and me from our trip to Costa Rica a few years ago. I love this picture because it's right before I promised her I would try the zip line if she went first—only to totally ditch her once I saw the height we were at. She's got her helmet on, strapped to a cord, and I've got my thumbs up like a dweeb right behind her. It's so us.

I look up at her doppelgänger and decide that the universe is conspiring to tell me it's time to forgive and forget. I move onto a bench a little farther away from the music and click on Zin's contact to FaceTime her. It barely rings once, and her face appears on my screen.

"Forgive me. I suck. I love you. Please be my friend again?" she says all in one breath like she was waiting for my call.

I chuckle as I let out a huge sigh. "That's exactly why I called." I'm so happy to be looking at Zin's face right now. "You're forgiven." I flip the screen around. "Mostly because I'm seeing you everywhere."

"That tiny blond girl hopping about like she's got a broken leg?" Zin's voice comes through loud and clear: she's offended. "Well, if that's what it takes . . . I'm just happy you called, because I really want to tell you how sorry I am."

"Like I said, I forgive you." I pause. "But, I think I'd just like to understand why. Why haven't you reached out, like *really* reach out?"

"I have! I texted you a whole bunch of times," Zin responds.

"It was virtue signalling at best, and you know it. You didn't even call my dad." I sigh. "I'm more confused than anything. What did I do to deserve the silent treatment? Especially considering my dad . . . I mean, I know Fay and Kiara had a lot of nasty things to say about me, but I didn't think that transferred to you."

"No! It doesn't. I hate that you think that." Zin props herself up against her headboard. "I have no excuse or explanation other than I suck. I would take it back if I could." The screen shakes a little as Zinnia reaches for a tissue.

"The person you owe the biggest apology to is my father." I start to cry too. "You're like a daughter to him."

"I'm gonna call." She rubs her eye with the tissue, leaving a KISS streak of mascara under her eyes.

"You look like Starchild, by the way." I smile. She brings the phone closer to her face to use her camera as a mirror. I watch as she swipes away her tears. "My turn to apologize."

"You have nothing to apologize for," she replies, shaking her head.

"Not true." I stand up and start strolling toward the water. "As my dad always says, a true friend sees their reflection in the reactions of others, and so I reflected, and here's what I came up with: I spent a little bit too much time on our trip talking about everything that was going on in my life and not enough time listening to what was going on in yours. For that, I'm sorry."

I was really in a bad spot when I left for that trip, and I had this hope that my friends would rally around me to make me feel better about my life. The problem is that I expected them to suspend whatever was happening in their lives to be there for me. That's not the kind of friend I want to be. Not to Zin, at least.

I might make Kiara and Fay work a little harder, show me how sorry they really are.

"Apology accepted," Zinnia says as she does a one-handed nose blow. "It's like almost nine at night, why are you—" she squints and brings the phone closer to her face "—is that de la Commune?" She pronounces it like a real anglophone.

"My my, how we've lost our French," I joke.

"'Kay, but seriously, why are you out alone all dressed up?"

I fill her in on the last couple months, from Jack picking me up from the hospital to severing contact completely to bumping into him today at Bijou with Poppy, our text exchange, my selfie, and hot Bar Guy.

Zin's jaw drops lower and lower with each morsel of information I feed her.

"I know, right? It's a lot," I say with a sigh.

"BACK. UP."

"Did I come on too strong? I feel like such an idiot."

"Which part? The selfie or putting your number in some rando's phone?" She laughs. "Because both are a little out of character." She raises her brow.

I am such an idiot. What was I thinking? Jack is probably mocking my selfie with Poppy right about now.

"Well, if I can advise one thing," she starts, and I bring the screen closer so I don't miss a thing. I need all the advice I can get right now. "Whatever happens tonight, cover up so you don't end up preggo like our dear old Keeks."

I feel like I just got punched in the stomach.

I lower the phone and slump down onto the sidewalk.

Kiara's pregnant?

"You there?" Zin's voice chimes through the phone.

I raise it back so I can see her again. "Yeah, I'm here." Even though it feels like my soul has lifted out of my body.

"You didn't know?" she asks, a puzzled look flickering on her face.

"We haven't spoken," I whisper. She's my person and she's pregnant, and I wasn't her first phone call.

"Oh, I thought for sure she would've by now." She looks stumped. "I'm sorry, I shouldn't have said anything."

"It's fine." I shake my head. "Well, it's not fine, but it is what it is, right?"

A group of skateboarders roll by boisterously, distracting me from the deep, dark rabbit hole I'm falling into.

I didn't think Kiara could hurt me more than she did on that trip. The name calling, the judgment, and then not caring whether my father lived or died. It was all so horrible. But I would have forgiven her.

This is worse somehow.

Because now I know she doesn't want to be forgiven. She's etched me out of her life completely.

I'm such an idiot for thinking that she was probably just as sad as I've been. I thought she was over there racking her brain, trying to figure out how to make it up to me. A part of me, like a huge part of me, believed it was only a matter of time until she reached out. I never stopped to think she was done with me.

That's what this is.

News this big . . .

There is nothing that has ever happened in my life that I didn't want to tell Kiara about. She's my first phone call.

She's my person.

Was my person.

"I think I'm gonna get on my bike and head home," I say dejectedly. I need to be in my cozy sweats, on my couch, pulling a Bridget Jones with a bottle of wine and a tub of Ben & Jerry's. "I love you. Thanks for the chat."

"I love you too," she says. I'm about to hang up when Zin calls out, "Oh, wait! One last question."

"The answer is no, you should never wear that head wrap in public." I giggle.

Zin quirks an eyebrow, adjusting her terry cloth headband. "What I was gonna ask is, any chance you'll come visit before I move?"

"That would be amazing, maybe end of summer?" I ask.

Zin nods ecstatically. "I guess that's a yes." We both let out a laugh.

"Sure is!"

She blows me a kiss. "Call me tomorrow with all the juice."

When I get home, I do exactly as planned. I change into PJs, clean off my makeup, and hunker down in front of the TV, wine and ice cream at hand.

I've also imagined several scenarios to explain why Kiara wouldn't have called me to tell me she's pregnant. A) She's a bitch.

Actually, that's as far as I got. But I also concocted a plan for if she ever does reach out. I would tell her where to shove it.

I shovel a spoonful of Half Baked into my mouth and let the freezing cold numb my tongue.

Tonight sucks.

The cherry on top of my ice cream is that it's past midnight and Bar Guy hasn't texted yet, which is probably for the best. It was a stupid idea to give him my number in the first place. Although, why'd he take it if he wasn't going to use it?

Why do I feel so rejected?

It's coming from all ends, that's why.

Maybe I should just go to sleep and forget this whole thing. One-night stands aren't really my style anyway.

My phone buzzes. Bar Guy. I move to decline.

Not tonight: bad idea. I know this won't end well.

With the way I'm feeling, I'll end up turning his booty call into Crychella.

Super sexy.

I bet Poppy would never cry during sex.

Bleh.

Second date, my ass.

I picture her climbing off Jack's bike, gripping him around the waist. Holding hands on the street. I bet if Poppy sent him a picture, he'd respond.

My phone buzzes again. Bar Guy.

Fuck it!

Before I know what I'm doing, I'm sliding to answer, giving him my apartment code.

I rush to the bathroom to freshen up, wash my face, brush my teeth, and go to change my underwear. I can do better than granny panties. I open my top drawer and move the piles of cotton around until I find my one and only silky thong. I tug it gently, but it's caught on something. I pull harder, and as it comes loose, it brings something with it that practically hits me in the face: the picture of me and Jack that I hid in here months ago. *Not now*, I think. I shove it in the drawer, deeper this time, all the way to the back.

I go back to my living room to clean up all evidence of my pathetic pity party, throwing the empty ice cream tub into the garbage and transferring my wine from my *Decaf? No thanks, I'm not a quitter* mug into a proper long-stem glass. I leave the door slightly ajar and grab a book off my shelf to flip through while I sit down to wait.

He'll let himself into my apartment and find me sitting here like, "Oh, de Beauvoir, yeah no big deal."

I hear footsteps in the hall and then a tap at the door.

"Hello?" he sings.

Not wanting to seem eager, I count to ten Mississippis in my head, and then I set my book and glass down to greet him by the door.

The second he enters my apartment, he has me up against the wall, and we start to kiss. He leads me to the couch, and we fall onto it kissing, petting, touching, thrusting. I don't even know this guy's name, and he's pushing himself inside of me. Is this what one-night stands are like? I've really been missing out.

When round one is done on the couch, we move into the bedroom, then the shower, then the kitchen counter, and then back to bed again.

The next morning, I wake up to an apartment that looks like a tornado hit it. I turn over and see Bar Guy asleep in my bed and remember a tornado *did* come through here.

I feel his leg slide up mine, his knee pushing between my legs. I check my clock. Six. We've barely been asleep an hour, and he's already moving his fingers into me, deeper and deeper. He kisses my neck and whispers, "Good morning." I can barely respond as he's giving me what will be my ninety-seventh orgasm.

I cover my face with a pillow and muffle a scream of sheer ecstasy. I flip him over and mount him. Pulling him into me, slowly and then all at once, we go one more round, and then I tap out.

"That was amazing," I say, catching my breath. "I don't think I can go anymore."

"Yeah, I should head home." He searches the floor, but no pants are to be found.

"I think they're on the couch." I smile shyly.

He heads for his pants, and I follow him, throwing on a bathrobe as I walk through my living room.

A gentle knock sounds at the door. "Are you expecting someone?" he asks.

"No, not that I remember." I walk over to answer it. "Can you put your pants on maybe?" I gesture to his naked body, and he gives me a wink. He's staring at me like he wants to fuck me again, and I'm starting to think that maybe that's just his face. "Faster, please." I roll my hands.

He moves to put on his pants, and I head for the door.

"Who is it?" I ask, holding the knob ready to answer. Who would be here this early in the morning?

"Jack. Can we talk?" comes the answer from the other side of the door.

Shit, shit, shit!

I slam my body up against the wall so he can't see me. Not that he can see through the door, but I'm not thinking straight.

"Val? Are you gonna let me in?"

I don't know what to do.

I don't know how to answer the door without Jack seeing—fuck, what is this guy's name?!

"Do you think you could hide in my room?" I whisper to Bar Guy, who is now in my kitchen, serving himself a tall glass of water. Bar Guy gives me a thumbs-up but continues to stand in my kitchen bare-chested as he chugs his water . . . slowly.

"Val? If you want me to go, just say the word," Jack says. "But I came here to say something, so I'll say it out here in the hall if you don't let me in." Jack pauses. "Try as I might, I can't stop thinking about you. I spent all night trying to think about how to reply to your message, but nothing was good enough. Instead, I found myself unconsciously driving here instead of the gym. I can't get you out of my head. I miss you. I just, it's not, it's, I mean, can you answer the door? This would be much easier if I could see your face."

Once Bar Guy is safely in my bedroom, door shut, I swing the front door open.

"I love you too," I blurt out. I take a beat and realize Jack never said that he loves me, only that he misses me. I exhale. "And I miss you." I slow down and take a deep breath as I inch toward him, running one hand through his hair as the other wraps around his waist. I want to jump into his arms and hold his face close to mine, feel his breath, his lips against mine . . .

Jack smiles and inches toward me. He takes a step forward, leans in and kisses me. Softly. Slowly. My shoulders melt as our tongues move around with familiarity and newfound passion. The moment is usurped by the pang of guilt that twists my stomach in a knot. My mind flashes to the impending chaos behind door number two.

I push my thoughts aside as Jack pulls away, locking his eyes on mine with the sweetest smile. Gently, he swipes my hair back and brushes his lips against mine again, only this time he's holding my body closer and closer to his as he moves us toward my bedroom.

My mind is spinning. I need to think fast.

"Want to grab a bite before I head into the office?" I say, sliding away from him.

Jack doesn't pick up on the panic that's taken my face hostage. "It's six a.m., nothing is open." He takes another step closer to my bedroom. "Plus, I'd rather be here—" he kisses me "—with you."

My stomach turns. Stay calm. Stay focused. Handle with care.

I pin Jack against the wall beside my room, shoving myself against him. I need time to think.

"Oh! Sweetie's is open early. Let's go there." I pull him off the wall and start walking toward the front door.

"Val, you're in a bathrobe," he says, letting go of my hand. "What's going on here?"

"Nothing, I'm starving." I smile and let out a nervous giggle. "I'll just get dressed so we can go."

A *thud* comes from my room.

"You know what? I can go like this."

"Val?" Jack furrows his brow. "Is there someone in there?" He moves closer to the bedroom, placing his hand on the doorknob as I rush to wedge myself between him and the door.

"I can explain," I try to speak calmly, but the high-pitched tone only leaves more room for suspicion. He moves me aside gently. "Jack, don't go in there," I plead.

It's too late. He opens the door and is faced with Bar Guy sitting half-naked on my bed, playing Candy Crush on his phone.

Puta de madre! I think. How long does it take to get dressed and hide in a closet?

Without saying a word, Jack turns around, walks to the front door, and reaches for the knob. He takes one last scan of the apartment like he's finally seeing what he's walked into: the messed-up blankets, the clothes on the floor, the glasses of wine on my kitchen counter. The pain in his face tells me all I need to know.

This time we're done for good.

"You're a real bitch," he says, and he slams the door behind him.

Kiara

MIAMI, JULY

I TURN UP THE RADIO AND SING ALONG TO DRAKE LIKE I'M A BACKUP vocalist on tour: loud and dramatic. I'm driving down Collins on my way home from picking up our gender results from my OB/GYN. Technically, I could have waited until tomorrow, since I have my weekly, but I couldn't wait a whole twenty-four hours to find out if we're having a boy or girl. I ripped that envelope so fast and my falling tears nearly blurred out the word *boy*. I am so beyond happy to announce to Wren that we are giving Raven a baby brother. His desire to spawn a male heir has been so strong, I think my body knew not to get it wrong.

Up and down the road, there are beachgoers carrying their folding chairs and coolers, joggers running past on the sidewalk, and moms walking in pairs as they push their babies in strollers. I always imagined that when I got pregnant, I'd time it with Val so we could do everything from picking out paint swatches for our baby's rooms together to having a joint shower. But that's a wasted daydream; I'm twenty weeks in, and there's no Val in sight.

She doesn't even know I'm pregnant.

I place my hand on my belly and think about how sad it'll be that my baby won't ever know Aunt Val . . . I let out a sigh and then flick the thought away. No sadness allowed. Things may not be exactly how I pictured them, but I'm grateful that I get to be a mother. The mere thought of holding this baby in my arms in a few months brings deep joy to my heart.

What probably consumes my thoughts the most—when I'm not busy googling every symptom from acid reflux to varicose veins—is the natural phenomenon that is the human body. How from one day to the next, I went from one body to two. Pregnancy is mind-blowing. There is a tiny being, a whole human, growing inside of me. I don't think I ever quite grasped just how transcendent pregnancy is. That my body can grow another person as I go about my ordinary life—sleep, eat, cook, grow a baby . . . Like, how are more people not baffled by this?

There's nothing like it. Smiling, arms flailing out of the sunroof, volume up, I'm shimmying in my seat to the beat as the chorus kicks in.

I stop by Mama Bear on the way home from the doctor's to buy matching father-son outfits. Wren's T-shirt says *The Original*, Baby Boy's says *The Remix*. Then, I go home to get started on the fish soup, the one my grandma makes whenever there's a celebration. All the tastes of my childhood that Wren has come to love. A healthy combination of Jamaican spices mixed with Israeli cuisine. It seems like an unlikely pair, but the tang and salt blend beautifully.

As I'm pouring in the pimento, my phone buzzes in my pocket.

"Hey baby," I sing as I stir the soup. Mmm, smells so good.

Wren speaks loudly into the speakerphone from his office. "Not sure I'm gonna make it home until late. Killer case, and I'm all alone here tonight." I can always tell when he's doing ten things at once: his voice sounds like it's a hundred miles away, and the thwack of drawers closing and papers rustling add depth to the distance. "Sorry, babe. Maybe we could order an anchovy and pineapple pizza just to make it easier?" he suggests, because he knows I can't say no to anchovies right now. Damn cravings.

"But I told you, I'm making us fish soup." My stomach does a gurgling thing, cramping on my side. A physical reaction to the thought of celebrating alone. "Remember, I just picked up our gender results?" I try not to sound too disappointed.

"If you're making fish soup then let me guess, it's a boy?" he states. His matter-of-fact tone squeezes out any joy this fish soup was bringing me.

"Sure is!" I say half-heartedly, trying to stay as upbeat as possible. I switch off the stove, throwing the wooden spoon onto the counter. Who am I kidding? This night is as good as over. I walk over to the living room and pick up the remote. "Well, should I at least wait for you to start the movie? *Two Weeks Notice* is on Netflix. We could have pizza in bed?"

"Nah, I don't want to watch that shit. You know what? Watch what you want, I'll hit Bally after work. Don't wait up."

We hang up, and I walk over to our bed, where I had set out the matching outfits encircled in blue confetti. I pick up the itty-bitty newborn onesie and hold it to my belly.

"You're gonna look so cute in this, little man," I smile, looking down at my Remix.

A tear rolls down my cheek. There's that pang of sadness again.

I try to flick it away, but it presses heavily on my chest.

Whatever burst of sweetness Wren displayed in the first few weeks, doting over me, making sure I had everything I needed, holding my hair back when I vomited, it has all faded back to black. It was small comments here and there at first. Then, one night he told me that if I gained too much weight, he would stop finding me attractive.

When I cried, he told me I was being too sensitive. "I hope our baby has my sense of humour," he added.

I certainly hope he doesn't, I thought, but didn't dare say it out loud.

We've stopped being intimate. He barely kisses me. Not like we ever see each other anymore.

It's like he doesn't care that I exist at all. He's worked late every night for three weeks straight, he never asks how I'm feeling, and never, not once, has he come to a doctor's appointment with me.

My skin is quite thick—I can handle a lot. I choke it back, let it roll off my shoulders like my mother taught me when my father left us. *No use crying, baby*, she told me, *tears are for things that matter, things we can control*. She built me with the strength she lacked.

She's right. I can't control the fact that he's the father of my baby. Although you wouldn't know it by the way he acts.

Then there's the worst of all. He made me quit my job, and I know no one can make you quit anything, but he just kept coming at me with the comments about how minimal my salary is and how my job is a joke and how if he's the top earner then he decides on childcare and he wants his baby home until kindergarten because that's what he did with Raven and this child should get nothing less than what she had.

But Raven's mother *wanted* to be a stay-at-home mother. I love my job. Lov*ed.*

No use complaining if you aren't gonna do anything about it, right?

So that's exactly what I've been doing.

Between summer break and mat leave, the timing made sense to give my notice. But I haven't stopped working. I've been channelling all of this negative energy and transforming it into a positive. I've been spending my days developing a body-positive curriculum that I can hopefully bring to the school board and help implement in their K-through-twelve programs when I return to work one day. I've struggled my whole life with feeling uncomfortable in my body, and I don't want a single other girl out there to feel how I felt. I'm taking my experience—all the comments, the weight fluctuation, judgment, and ill-fitting clothes—and turning it into something constructive. The curriculum primarily focuses on body image, with discussions on self-esteem and beauty ideals throughout history, and then there's a section on how to foster a healthy relationship with our bodies.

I'm so scared Wren will find out that I've been working on this that I haven't shared it with anyone, I only ever work from coffee shops, *and* I keep a secret file on my laptop entitled *Hormone Stuff*, so if he ever uses my computer, he won't click in and stumble upon my research. He'll mock me, or worse, make me quit that too.

All I know is that I finally understand Zinnia after all these years; motherhood is lonely . . . and I'm not even a mom yet. Flick the sadness. Flick, flick it away.

I fold the onesie and T-shirt and place them in my dresser, then lie down on my bed and turn on the TV. I get to the Netflix home page and angle my phone in front of the movie menu. I take a shot and post it to socials with the caption *What should I watch tonight?* Within seconds, I get a direct message.

Maybe Wren changed his mind.

I swipe out of my feed and see Frankie's name at the top of my messages. My stomach flips. I haven't thought about him in months. I click to open his message. I'd want you to pick the movie. And then a couple seconds later, he adds: As long as I could see you again.

I close the message box and set my phone down so fast, you'd think I was holding hot coal. I can't believe he remembers me *and* he wants to see me again.

I take a deep breath and pick up my phone to reply. Or should I just ignore his message and move on with my life?

I set my phone down by my side and take a deep breath. I'm pregnant. With Wren's baby. I shouldn't reply.

But I'd be lying if I said I'm not intrigued. Maybe I could just . . . I pick up my phone and open the message box. I wouldn't want to be rude.

My pick is Two Weeks Notice. Thoughts?

I love Sandra and Hugh. Let's do it.

Lol. You do? I mean, I do too. It's my go-to for when I need a good pick-me-up.

I love a good rom com - and Sandy's a badass in that movie.

Yeah she's a bad bitch. Nerdy but hot as hell.

My kind of woman. She can glass harp with the best of em.

LMAO—That's Miss Congeniality but I'm impressed with your nineties knowledge.

Early aughts, but who's keeping track?

There's a long pause as I think about what to say next. This is Frankie. Hot Frankie. And I'd be lying if I said the attention didn't feel good . . .

What must only be seconds borders on feeling like an awkward eternity. Enough time to feel the pang of guilt cramping in my stomach. This isn't just some innocent conversation on socials.

I gotta go. Nice chatting, I write and swipe out before Frankie has a chance to respond.

What was I thinking?

My mind races with all sorts of scenarios: What if Wren finds these DMs, accuses me of cheating, and leaves me without waiting for an explanation? He would fight me for full custody and win. He's a fucking lawyer.

I open the conversation and meticulously delete each and every message. I've lived with Wren long enough to know how to stay out of trouble.

The next morning, I'm in the kitchen with Wren getting ready for my OB/GYN appointment. Since my mother had gestational diabetes, I have to test a little earlier than most to ensure I don't have it too. I pack an apple (I wonder if there's too much sugar in a green apple?) and oat bar (the protein kind, sugar-free) to eat after I take the test and get weighed in. I've spent a lifetime avoiding the scale, and regardless of how hard I'm working on body positivity, it's still very much a work in progress. There's no woman on Earth who enjoys having their weight tracked like cattle week after week.

"I don't know," I say to Wren as he mixes his protein powder into his shake. He drinks a vat of that stuff every morning, and the smell of it makes me want to regurgitate. "He's been kicking for a couple weeks but this feels different. Sharper. More painful."

"That's my boy," Wren smiles proudly. "All the men in my family are natural-born soccer players." He turns on the blender.

"But what if it's not?" I yell over the noise.

"What?" Wren yells back and then puts a finger up for me to hold my thought for the next twenty seconds until his shake is done blending.

When the noise stops, I start again. "I said, I don't know." I put a hand on my belly. "These kicks are really strong. What if it's something else?"

Wren walks over to the sink and pours his shake into his Thermos. Then he walks over to the kitchen table and grabs his briefcase. "Don't put those negative thoughts out there. Baby Boy can hear you."

"I'll call you after the appointment," I call out as he opens the front door. "Let you know how it goes."

"Cool." He waves his hand as he leaves.

As I pull up to the doctor's office, I feel a sharp cramp on the side of my belly. Instinctively, I place my hand on my stomach and close my eyes. I leave my hand there for a moment and think positive thoughts: maybe our boy *will* be a soccer player.

I walk into the elevator and hit the button for the fifth floor when I feel the cramp again, except this time it's more like a hockey puck to my ribs. I double over from the shock and grab my side. I take a deep inhale, hold my breath, and count to five to make the pain go away, but it lingers.

I catch a nurse walking by as the elevator doors slide open. "Excuse me, do you think I can get a urine cup right away? I really need to go to the bathroom." Maybe that's all this is. Soccer kicks and emergency pee.

She turns to a cart, grabs a cup, and says, "Why don't you give me your health insurance card, and I'll check you in while you're in there?"

"Yes, thank you." I pull my hand away from my side to retrieve my medical card, but then the kicking starts again. The pain is getting worse. I yelp again.

"You all right?" She bends over and places her arm on my back. She must feel me sweating because she's flapping a stack of papers up and down at my face.

"Yeah." I let out a deep breath. "Actually, do you know if it's normal that the baby is kicking this hard?"

The nurse helps me stand and hands me the cup that I dropped on the floor. "Try to take deep breaths, dear. I'll let the doctor know you're here. She'll check you right away."

I make my way to the bathroom and steady myself as I hover, holding the cup between my legs. As I watch the stream fill the cup, I notice a little blood. That can't be normal. Why am I bleeding?

My heart quickens as the sweat starts to form again on the back of my neck. In my panic, I stop focusing on the cup and pee all over my hand. Gross.

Once I've cleaned up and wrapped the cup in starchy industrial brown paper towel, I reach for the doorknob but double over in pain again. I yelp, and the echo of my fear-filled cry reverberates in the bathroom, making the walls feel like they're caving in on me.

Something feels dangerously wrong.

The cramping is getting more and more intense, like a dull pain wrapping around the lower part of my back. I rush out of the bathroom to try to find the same nurse who helped me earlier.

"Something's happening." I gasp in pain, holding my belly. "There was blood and—"

"Follow me," the nurse commands as she leads me to the nearest room.

"Take everything off, please, and put this on." She lays a gown on the table. "Just breathe." Yeah, like that's possible. "I'll go get the doctor. Don't worry, everything will be okay," she says, shutting the door.

Then why are you rushing off to get the doctor?

I undress and put on a gown. Propping myself up onto the exam bed, I lay my head back and feel tears well in my eyes. I squeeze them shut, and a stream gently rolls down my cheek.

It's all going to be okay, I repeat in my head. My baby is strong and healthy, and we are going to be okay.

It has to be okay.

"You hear that, Baby Boy? You have to be okay. Mama will take care of you," I say to my belly. Wren's right, they can hear everything. Positive thoughts. "I love you," I whisper.

The doctor walks in and looks at me with an expression I can't discern. Is it bad news? Is it worry? Is it pity?

"Kiara, how are you doing today?" she asks. She's holding a clipboard and checks off some boxes, then dips a stick into my urine sample. "So, twenty weeks, huh? Nurse tells me there's a little blood in your urine, and you said you've been feeling cramps? How long has that been going on?"

"He's been kicking for a while, but today, I guess, it felt a lot more pronounced. Like, kicking but also cramping, I think. I read in the forums that it could be normal because of how he's sitting in there or the position of the placenta . . ." I say nervously pointing to my belly. "But then there was blood when I peed. Is this bad?" I try to hold back the tears. "Is my baby okay?" I push myself up the paper-lined table, and it crumples as I sit up.

"Let's not jump to conclusions." She smiles and rolls her chair over to the bed. "Why don't we take a listen and see what's going on? I've ordered an hCG test, so that'll give us more information." She presses into the four corners of my belly quite firmly. The pressure makes me wince. When she's done, she takes out her stethoscope and lifts my gown. I wince again as the cold metal touches my skin. She presses down to locate my baby boy.

Please be okay, please be okay, please be okay.

She feels around silently. I say nothing and hold my breath so that she can hear him loud and clear. She clears her throat and retracts the stethoscope. Wrapping it around her neck, she reaches for the doppler and squirts some blue gel onto my stomach. Like a pantomime, she is wordless, going through the motions of a routine checkup. Only this time, the routine checkup feels like a horror movie. I close my eyes and let my head rest gently against the blue padding.

Please be okay, please be okay, oh god, please be okay.

"Can you show me where you feel the kicking?"

I motion to my lower left pelvis.

She smiles, but I can't tell if she's placating me. "And the bleeding started today as well?"

Why is she asking me again? I told her all this already.

Too scared my voice will fail me, I nod.

Just tell me what's wrong with my baby. My heart is pounding, and tears are falling out of my eyes like a waterfall. I close them and pray . . . *Please be okay, please be okay.*

The doctor pulls out a tissue and wipes the gel from my belly.

"Ow!" I cry out from the pressure.

Pushing the monitor back, she swivels her chair toward my feet. "Why don't I give you a quick internal to get a closer look?" She looks up at me from between my legs. "Can you scooch down for me, please?"

"Did you see something on the ultrasound?" I ask as I open my legs. I know she knows something; I can feel it. *Just tell me.*

"Did you hear his heartbeat before?" I ask again, but she's not answering me.

"Hmm." She looks up at me from between my legs. "There's blood here. More than I'd like to see. You said the bleeding just started today?" She holds up her blood-stained hands and pushes her chair away from me. *Yes today!* I scream in my head. Why is she asking me that again?

I nod my head vigorously, fear coursing through me. I know this part of the movie. This is the part when she says he's not going to make it. My eyes continue to well up with tears, and I shake my head. I don't want to hear it. *Please be okay, please be okay, please be okay.*

"Did you hear his heartbeat?" I repeat. "Is my baby okay?" One last desperate plea that he's okay. Maybe if I pray hard enough . . .

She pulls her gloves off and rests a hand on my knee. Her face looks worn with sadness. She lowers her eyes and nods and then looks directly at me and says, "Kiara, I can't confirm until your hCG results are back, but . . ." She shakes her head and closes her eyes.

No!

"I was unable to detect a heartbeat, and with the amount of blood . . ." She pauses.

No!

"Would you like to call your partner so he can be here?"

No!

"Um, he's in court," I lie. "I'm fine alone." Because that's what I am. Alone.

They wheel me into another room to wait for my results, the same room where I heard a heartbeat for the first time. It wasn't but two months ago that I lay here, listening to the drumming sound of our baby, the life growing inside of me. The posters of breastfeeding instructions, doula information, and a growth chart of what your baby looks like every week. Today, at twenty weeks, the size of a banana, my baby should be a fully formed little boy.

Please be okay. I repeat to my baby boy. Maybe when the results come back they'll realize they made a mistake you're fine. Doctors make mistakes.

I visualize myself holding my baby, tightly wrapped in a sky-blue blanket, blue to match his *Remix* onesie I just bought him. *You're gonna be okay. Please be okay.*

Just then, the cramping starts again, and I scream out in pain. A cramp so intense it feels like my insides are ripping me in half, trying to claw their way out.

All of a sudden, it feels like I'm in a kaleidoscope: The room is spinning, and I can't tell up from down. I'm vomiting from the pain, and there's a nice lady holding an ice chip to my mouth between heaves. I hear people talking, but the only word I make out is *oxytocin*, and I know nothing good can come from that. That's the drug they give you to induce labour. Or in my case, to perform a D&C.

Everything moves around me like a blur. The only thing I feel is immense pain and then complete numbness.

One minute I'm two, then all of a sudden, I'm one again. But this time, one feels like none.

My baby's gone.

The room goes dark.

When I wake up, it's late afternoon, and I'm alone in a small hospital room. They said they'll keep me for a few hours to monitor me, make sure everything is okay and give the meds and painkillers time to wear off before they discharge me. Lying in the bed, all by myself, I weep. Fragments of sorrow pierce my skin like shards from a shattered mirror.

I'm shaking and sobbing.

A nurse comes in. "I heard you crying from the hallway. Can I get you something, sweetie?" she asks, caressing my knee.

"I'm fine," I mutter and turn over on my side.

"Is there someone you could call? Maybe the baby's father?"

I nod yes and point to my purse. Every part of me wants to avoid telling him, but I have to let him know. I told him I'd call him when my appointment was done, which was hours ago at this point.

When the nurse leaves, I pull out my phone and see I have three missed calls from Wren and one text.

Yo, how'd it go?

I call him, but he doesn't pick up.

In a meeting. All good?

I reply, No.

I wait a minute, then two, then three. He doesn't respond. I call him again, but he doesn't answer.

Gimme a sec, wrapping up.

Wren, I lost the baby. I know it's not something I should send in a text, but I won't be able to say the words out loud; it feels safer this way. I hit send and stare at the screen, waiting for him to call me.

Seven minutes later, Wren calls. "What happened?" he asks. "Did you fall down or something?"

"No," I mumble. "The kicking this morning was—" I can't finish my sentence. My stomach tightens, and the tears spill out again.

Gone. Our baby is gone.

"She couldn't find a heartbeat, and then I was bleeding— I—" I cry loudly into the phone and just keep repeating *sorry, I'm so sorry, I'm so sorry.*

"Would you just tell me what happened? You're blubbering." He sounds angry. "Should I come get you right now? How long do you have to stay?"

Should he come? I should know the answer to that. I should want my fiancé here, the father of my . . . "Yes," I whisper. "Please come. I don't know how long they'll keep me, but they said I can't drive myself home."

"Okay. I'm on my way."

Less than twenty minutes later, the door swings open. Wren barges in like a man on fire. He blazes toward me, panting and out of breath. "I came as fast as I could, but parking around here is impossible. How you doing?"

I shake my head to say *not good*, but before I get the words out, he buries my face into his chest and holds me like that while I cry.

"Baby, don't worry. It's gonna be okay. You're gonna be okay." He's patting my head, stroking me softly. I wish I had called him earlier; I wish he had been here when I found out. My Wren, he always comes through in these moments. I don't know why I doubt him.

I concentrate on his face to stop myself from crying, but my chin is quivering, and my body is shaking. I'm freezing and sweating at the same time.

"Hey, listen, it's okay. This is completely normal. We'll just try again." He's patting my head. "This wasn't our baby. Think how much fun we'll have making the next one."

Any comfort I felt in his presence slips away as he goes on and on about how this is all part of the process and how this happens all the time. He's not angry at all, he's indifferent.

None of what he's saying is what I want to hear. All I keep playing in my head are the words *not our baby*. Blaring like a siren in my mind and yanking at my heart. *Not our baby.* How could he say it wasn't our baby when my little boy was in *my* body? It was *my* baby. The only baby I almost had. And now he's gone, and I'll never get to hold him or hug him or even meet him. *Not our baby.* I want to yell, but instead I nod and rest my head back onto my pillow, clenching my jaw to release the agony. There's no point in contradicting him. No point in telling him *this* was our baby. I don't want to try again. I want *this* baby. My baby.

I place my hand on my empty belly and turn over to face the wall. I wish Val were here.

It's been two weeks since I lost the baby—that's what they like to call it, *lost*, like I misplaced him, let him wander off at a mall or something, like it's all my fault—and I haven't been able to leave my bed. I stare at the ceiling, the weight of grief pressing down on me. Wren's dismissive words replaying in my mind.

I cry myself to sleep most nights. But I try as hard as possible not to show my sadness because it only annoys him. Tonight, he's at work, so I cry openly. Loudly. Desperately. I fill the emptiness with my grief.

It was just twenty weeks. Get over it. This shit always happens.

My first son. I don't care what Wren says, he will always be my baby. I may not be able to find him, but he wasn't lost to me. Every second of every day, he is right there, in my mind, ever-present in my heart.

Lost the baby. Because *miscarriage* sounds too clinical. Who cares what you call it? He's gone. One day he's safe and sound in my belly, and the next he's not. Nowhere to be found. Gone from the world forever.

He was my whole world. Every decision I made was for him, every meal I ate was for him, every dream I had, he was in it.

Not our baby.

I hate Wren. I hate him, and my hatred is all I can hold on to because it feels better to hate than to feel the pain that consumes me.

The sting of loss and grief feels too great to bear alone. With trembling fingers, I pick up my phone and start texting the one person I need right now.

I relive every moment as I type out my story. From the anxiety I felt when I first learned I was pregnant to the joy of picking out onesies for my baby boy, from fearing Wren and convincing myself that he loved me and that he was a good guy to quitting my job to the cramps and the blood and the—

My breath catches in my throat as I see the words appear before me: I lost the baby in bold black and white. I sob as I continue to type out my text through blurry vision: Please forgive me, I've been a terrible friend. I understand if you never want to talk to me again. I was such a jerk in every possible way and I'll spend the rest of my days making it up to you. I'm so sorry, you didn't deserve it. I don't know who I've become. I know you never liked Wren and you were right. Why didn't I see that he was a total asshole . . . I don't know what to do but I can't do this alone. My life is falling apart and I need you. I love you.

I don't even read it over. I just hit send, and only then do I realize it's two in the morning and she's probably asleep.

But it takes less than a minute for Val to respond. I'll be on the first flight out in the morning. I love you too.

Fay

TORONTO, AUGUST

"BREATHE IN, AHHH, AND BREATHE OUT, OHHH," THE YOGA INSTRUCtor says as she guides us through the last down dog. "Let your breath guide you, and with this last exhale, open your mouth wide and push the air out of your body, ahhh."

"Ahhh," I push out among a chorus of women.

Yoga Mondays at Zin's has become my favourite day of the week. I used to love it solely for the purpose of post-yoga, once all the other moms leave and Zin and I have the house to ourselves for a couple hours. But I've actually grown to *like it* like it. Despite what my thin frame may convey, it's all metabolism, not exercise—my lifestyle is an unhealthy combo of cerebral and sedentary. So, weekly yoga it's been for me.

Zin's been into yoga for the longest time. She discovered it in high school. It's the reason she was voted most likely to move to Asia and become a Buddhist, abandoning the North American lifestyle, opting for a slower pace. She's always been the flowy skirt, floral scarf type, but where our classmates were wrong is that, while she may be a hippie at heart, she's a city girl through and through. I can't imagine her living anywhere else but right here amidst the hustle of a busy city.

"When you're ready, come into your final resting pose," she continues as she slowly weaves through the labyrinth of our mats. "Shavasana, everyone. Legs stretched long, and palms facing upward. Close your eyes."

My body tingles with new energy and a sensation of calmness, like I'm floating in warm water, too rooted to drown, suspended in air. That doesn't even make sense, but as I lie here with my eyes closed, that's how I imagine my body: weightless.

I open my eyes slightly to look over at Zinnia, who is lying nymph-like beside me. She has a lot to do with how I've been feeling lately. Probably more than the yoga. We've been riding a love wave the last few months; I could live in this feeling forever.

"Thank you for practising with me today," the teacher says, bringing her hands to her chest.

I shut my eyes and continue to lie totally still, partly to stretch out this meditative state, partly to avoid the post-yoga mingle. If I lie here long enough, I can skip saying goodbye to the other ladies.

"Why don't I just bring Betsy to rehearsal Sunday? Darla loves carpooling," Zin says to a woman standing by the door.

"You sure you don't mind?" her friend responds, hand to chest to show her undying gratitude.

"Of course, it's my pleasure." Zin proceeds to give each of her friends a one-armed hug as they leave and then shuts the door behind her.

I open my eyes slowly. Lifting myself off my mat, I sigh heavily. "Ahhh. Alone at last."

Zin smiles as she walks past me into the kitchen. "Convenient resting pose you had there," she laughs.

I reach for the mat spray. I get a whiff of the eucalyptus and tea tree as I rhythmically spritz big circles. "This stuff smells amazing," I call out as I move on to clean Zin's mat.

When I'm done, I head into the kitchen to find Zin already making us matcha lattes. "Hell-ooo?" I sing to get her attention.

She's staring blankly out of the window by the sink.

"I'm going to miss this," she finally says softly.

"Miss what? Me cleaning up after you? Yeah, don't get too used to it. It'll only happen this once." She looks back at me, but I can tell her mind is somewhere else. "Zin? You there?" I break her daze, and she lets out a sigh.

"You're so spaced out," I tease. "Yoga might be making you *too* zen, if that's possible." I press my hand onto her lower back and kiss the nape of her neck.

"Should we take these to go and head out for a walk? It's stunning outside," Zin says as she pours our lattes into travel mugs, ignoring my comment.

"Can I change first?" I look down at my bike shorts and giggle. "I can't go to work like this after."

Zinnia nods and grabs our drinks. "I'll wait by the door," she says, slipping on her Birks.

When I'm done changing into more appropriate attire, the two of us head out, lattes in hand. I take my first sip and pull a face.

"I don't think I can ever get used to this taste, bleh." I gag slightly, and Zin laughs at me, wiping the little bit of green I have moustachioed over my lip. "What? I don't like it. Tastes like cardboard. I'm surprised you like it."

"That's good, right? Still stuff we can discover about each other." She bumps my shoulder and smiles. She takes a sip and wrinkles her nose. "Ugh, you're right. Maybe I burnt the milk or something. This doesn't taste right."

We continue to walk, holding our not-to-be-consumed lattes in the blissful silence only two people who are extremely comfortable with each other can share.

"You ever think this city is too fast-paced for you, like you want to hit a button and make everyone just slow down?" Zin finally breaks the silence. Eyes glazed over, she's staring off again, somewhere far ahead.

"I don't know what you mean. I mean, I know what you mean. Toronto can feel all hustle and grind, but it's nothing like New York. Toronto is in slow motion in comparison. Plus, you and I have a groove here. We know how to find our pace and relax." I nudge her. "Park?" I point down the street. We turn west and walk toward the park path. "We could hit up a nice terrace after or the market. I only need to be at work by noon." I slip my fingers through hers, and we walk hand in hand. Normally, Zin and I don't make public displays of affection. Too risky.

But it never stops me from trying. Some days, I get away with a stolen peck in an alley, others I'm lucky to get in a quick ten-second handhold. Here I am, caressing her hand for the better part of three city blocks, and she hasn't moved away. It's a testament to the progress we've made.

I feel a lot more confident about our relationship ever since we got back together. After our foray into cottage country right before summer, Zin made it undeniably clear through her actions that she chooses me. At least, that's how I feel, totally secure in our love every single day.

"I guess I just meant, like, do you see yourself living here forever?"

"One thousand percent. Till we're old and grey." I wink and peck her cheek. "Swinging together on our porch, the kids visiting us with their kids, we'll be grandmas together . . . we have our whole lives ahead of us, and that life is right here." I pull her hand close to my heart as we walk in step. "Zin, you feel that?"

"What?"

"My heart."

She nods, but the forlorn expression she wears tells me she's lost in thought.

"Hey, where is this line of questioning coming from?" I stop walking so I can look at her. "You okay?"

"Yeah, yeah, I'm fine." She waves me away. She rests her head on my shoulder, and we start walking again until we're on the other side of the park and near a coffee shop.

When the warm, nutty aroma of coffee hits us, we both look at each other, and as though it were scripted, we dump the rest of our matcha lattes out and head straight for the café. Now with two oat milk cappuccinos in hand, we grab a spot on the bench on the terrace.

"So, what are you and Val gonna do when she gets here?" I ask as I take my first sip. "You see, now this—" I take another sip "—this is not cardboard."

"Well, she lands around noon, and she's meeting you at the gallery," she says slowly, but it comes out more like a question, every syllable stretched out as though she's looking for confirmation.

Val's visit is all part of Zin's big plan: after months and months of radio silence, Zin convinced Val to give me a chance to apologize. She arranged for her to stop by the gallery before spending the weekend with Zin and the kids. Adam's out of town, and so Val came to give her a hand with the kids, playing auntie for a few days. Meanwhile, I suggested we all have a slumber party—but Zin wouldn't hear of it; no blurring the boundaries when the kids are home.

"You'll apologize and own your part, right?" She's talking to me like I'm one of her kids. "The trip, Eduardo, Montreal, all of it?" The look on her face doesn't leave any room for me to say no.

I nod. "Yes, all of it." I swallow hard.

"Grovel if you have to." She takes a sip and flutters her lashes. "Yum. I also just got an update on Kiara," Zin starts as though she could hear what I was thinking. The judgment in her eyes says everything that she doesn't say out loud: I'm a jerk for not calling Kiara about the miscarriage, I'm a jerk for not reaching out to Val about her dad, I'm a jerk, jerk, jerk. Now it's time I start making things right.

When it comes to Val, I get it. It's all on me. I was pretty rough with her at that last supper. Kiara, on the other hand—I don't know. She's the one that got up in my face like she was ready to punch me just because I said what everyone was thinking: *You're marrying a jackass and getting shitfaced to avoid your problems*. In my opinion, that is what makes a good friend, and you know what? Turns out I was right, and she left him, so why am I the one who has to apologize?

Because she lost a baby . . . that's why.

That trumps everything.

Maybe my heart is made of stone because, I don't know, I'm still not ready to talk to her.

"I'm gonna call her, I promise," I say to appease Zin. It's not a total lie. I won't let this linger on forever, and it's easier to tell her what she wants to hear now to buy myself some time to work through my feelings.

"I had miscarriage once, you know?" Zin says softly.

"You did?" I move closer to her, resting my hand on her shoulder. "What else don't I know about you?" Zin's right, still so much to discover about one another.

She nods and stares off like she's pulling the memory from her mind. "After Darla. Saul's my rainbow baby. It was only after six weeks. How do you not know?" She looks confused, trying to do mental math on the year.

"If it was right before Saul, I was probably in Istanbul." She looks at me like it all adds up: Aiyla.

"Well, it was early on, so I guess it wasn't as bad as for Keeks. But it was—" she pauses "—it was strange. You know? Feeling like you have no control over what could happen. Like my body was operating of its own accord and I was just there for the ride. It was so awful, but Adam was great." I wince. "He didn't say shit like 'better luck next time,' or whatever garbage Wren was spewing."

"Ugh, let's not get started on Wren. Good riddance." I take Zin's hand in mine and shake my head.

"You were totally right about him, by the way," she says. "I can't believe I never saw it."

"Maybe you didn't want to." I slip a curl behind her ear. "You know, it doesn't matter . . . when you lose a baby, it's still a loss. Six weeks is enough time to form a bond and dream up a life. Pain is pain. You shouldn't compare."

That's probably where I should start when I see Val. Don't compare. It all made sense in my mind back when I was fighting the good fight. I was so annoyed that she was whining over her privilege that I threw it in her face. Sort of hypocritical, as Zin has pointed out many a time, since I used my grandmother's inheritance to purchase the gallery. When I said it was totally different because I worked there for years and earned my way to owner, she said I was splitting hairs. Either way, I wasn't letting Val experience her pain. Instead, I wanted her to own how trivial it was in comparison to others'. That was shitty of me.

"We had names picked out, you know?" Zin pulls away and turns to me. "We didn't use any of them for Saul. It felt wrong, because, contrary to Wren's position, babies aren't replaceable."

"Is that what he's saying? Man, just when you think he's the worst, he goes and does something even more horrible." I wonder if he was saying shit like this to Kiara back in February. I can imagine that if he was whispering this bullying shit in her ear, then she was probably sinking into despair. It doesn't excuse the drinking, but it does explain it. *Hurt people hurt people.* She was calling for help, and none of us answered.

A tear stings behind my eye, and I squeeze it away. "The shit women endure in silence. You're an incredible woman, Zinnia. Have I told you how lucky I am that you're my best friend?"

"Girlfriend!" She shoves me gently and smiles.

I'll never get tired of hearing her say those words.

We finish our coffees on our walk toward my gallery. When we get to the door, we kiss goodbye and make plans to meet at Blime's for dinner with Val.

"Tell Val to leave her suitcase at your gallery. We'll grab it after dinner and take a cab from there. Or maybe she'll want to unpack and change before dinner . . . I'll leave a key under the mat and text to let her know, and then . . ." Zin's voice trails off. She's deep in organization mode.

I laugh. "Oh my god, can you stop planning every minute of everyone's life? Go relax and pick up a kid or something."

"Okay, okay, bye," Zin says. "I have so much to do!" she adds, throwing her arm up to wave. I watch as she sashays down the street. She knows I'm watching because she turns around to blow me a kiss.

I have less than an hour before Val arrives, and I have so much I need to get done before she gets here. Two buyers to call, an artist to prep for next week's show, and three invoices to process. I move quickly, checking items off my list one by one.

I'm playing over what I'll say when Val gets here while I print out the leaflets for the exhibit. I've reconciled with my part in all this. Especially that bozo move of flying to Montreal and asking her to be there for me. I was in such a Zin bubble that I don't think I let the gravity of Eduardo's heart attack really register. Thanks to Zin's wisdom and tireless attempts for me to see the error of my ways, I can own that I may also come off as slightly judgy. *Is it wrong to have high moral standards for the company I keep?* I had asked, not sarcastically. To which she replied that when I stand at a moral distance, it pushes people away. *There's a big difference if you judge from above or standing at eye level. One is condemnation, one is understanding.*

I want Val to know that I regret not checking in on Eduardo. I'm mad at myself for not putting his health above all else. He's like a father to me—to all of us. Maybe there was a synapse in my brain that snapped, I don't know. All I know is that when my mother was in the hospital, I was there every day, and I never saw the end coming. If it weren't for my girls who sat in that room with me, I never would have gotten through it.

Fuck, I really was a jerk.

I see Val through the window, pulling a Louis Vuitton carry-on behind her. She looks like a cut-out from a magazine. High-waisted black jeans, white Converse, and a ribbed one-shoulder tank top.

"Hey, did you change your hair?" She looks me up and down as she swings the door open, letting herself in.

"A while ago." I toss my hair from side to side. It's grown in, but it's still shorter than I usually keep it. "Like it?"

"Love, actually." We stand face to face, staring at each other awkwardly on the threshold. No hug, no *I miss you*, just a standoff that feels like two magnets repelling each other with equal force.

Why can't I get out of my own way? In my mind, I saw this going only one way: I was going to flood her with all my heartfelt apologies. Yet, here she is, standing in my gallery, and I can't even pull her in for a hug hello.

"Mmm." I breathe. "Isn't that air conditioning delicious?"

Val walks to the centre of the room and spins slowly to take in all the art on the walls.

"I'll give you the grand old tour in a minute." I walk over to my desk and staple the last leaflet, then shove it into a drawer.

Val walks slowly toward a large piece on the feature wall—a wildly colourful painting of a horse running on a lake leaving glitter dust in the wind behind it. She stops and stands in front of it. Everyone who has seen it says they can feel the movement. As an observer, we stand motionless but can feel the painting release a burst of energy. It's the biggest piece in the show, and it's framed in metallic gold, which is neither the obvious choice nor the norm, but this artist has a vision and likes to control how her work is hung.

All her pieces have animals in them, but none as marvellous as this one. This one, entitled *The Reckoning*, is my favourite, and I know it won't be easy to sell. I mean, it's ginormous for one, so it won't fit in most homes, but it's also controversial. From afar, it's a running horse, but if you look closely, it's made up of multiple images. It was inspired by the concept of gestalt: the whole is greater than the sum of its parts. In this case, I think the artist achieved more than just a synecdoche of collage. The parts are meant to add layers of meaning that I would argue are individually quite remarkable and collectively empowering.

One image is of a mother breastfeeding her baby surrounded by four men. Three of the men are hiding their eyes while one is staring wantingly at the woman's exposed breast. Another image is of a man taking a woman from behind while another man is spanking her with a willow branch. You have to look closely at the images to see each story, but each is more intense than the next. Most visitors spend at least an hour staring at the piece, but so far, no buyer.

"This painting is insane. Who is the artist?" Val asks.

"You would die if I told you how old she is. She's like Gen Z's Tarana Burke. Guess."

"I don't know, like twelve?" She laughs. "But in Benjamin Button years."

I laugh. "Okay, ready? She's eighteen. First year at Columbia in Political Science, but can you believe how provocative and thoughtful this piece is? It's her best work, hands down."

"Yeah, it's sensational, and I mean that in the purest sense of the word."

She walks toward me and hops up to sit on my desk, legs dangling. "So, should we talk?"

"Do we have to?" I joke. She tilts her head to the side, and I let out a heavy sigh. "Yeah, let's talk."

"I've been meaning to call you," she starts, "but every time I pick up the phone, I realize I'm still mad."

"I know, and I want to apologize, but maybe—" I pause, standing a few feet away from my desk "—why don't you tell me why you're mad?" I want to hear it from her. Is it the trip? Eduardo? Maybe even some Jack stuff I may or may not have been flippant about . . .

"Okay," she says, "let's start at the top." She holds out her hand and pulls back her first finger.

She's got a list.

"First, my heart was broken when I got to the Bahamas. I had just split up with Jack, and I'd had to give up my job. A job that I really cared about. The way you responded to my problems was so—"

"Obnoxious?" I offer.

She exhales sharply. "Dismissive. Like me and my little problems didn't matter. You brushed me off like I was a pest you wanted to get rid of. And then that comment about my father buying me a publishing house. What the hell was that?"

I curl my lips back. "Ugh, I forgot I said that." I pull my chair over and sit down, rolling it toward Val. "Can I just blanket apologize for all of it?"

"No." She folds her arms. "No, because if it's how you feel, then it'll come up again, and I want to know how you really feel about me. Do you really think I'm spoiled?"

I push my chair back and stand up. "Look, trumping all else, can we start by my apologizing for not being there for you when your dad was in the hospital? His health should've been my first and only concern. I know that, and I want you to know I know that."

"Thank you," she mutters through tight lips. "But we'll get to that part later."

"Okay." I let out an exhausted breath as I rub my temples. "I'm sorry. I screwed up, and I shouldn't have said those things. It was wrong to call you names, and I know that you feel like I diminished your feelings by shoving your wealth in your face. I get that. But—"

"But?" she repeats and hops off my desk.

"But a good friend shouldn't just tell you what you want to hear all the time. Val, we aren't teenagers anymore. You're going to have to learn that not everyone will agree with you and your choices, and sometimes a reality check is what a good friend will give you. When we were in the Bahamas, you went on and on about 'should I with Jack, should I not with Jack,' meanwhile, you sabotaged that relationship, cheated on him for who knows what reason, and took no ownership of how that impacted him. Like, there was no world where Jack would forgive you—yet there you were, crying on the beach about how you loved him and wanted him back. Like all you considered was how *you* felt. So, yeah, I guess that's a bit spoiled. I mean, you lit a match and flung it at him and then what? You expected that I'd help you devise a plan on how to get him back? Like I'm some sort of side gig in your Val show? That's not how the world operates. You want me to tell you that I'm gonna change and this won't come up again, but guess what? I will always tell you like it is, that's who I am." Direct, blunt, tell-it-like-it-is, that's the code the Gauthier women lived (and died) by.

The anger is spewing out of my mouth, and I can't stop it. I thought I was going to apologize profusely; instead, I'm screaming at her. My heart is pounding out of my chest, and Val is standing in front of me, floored by my little speech, staring at me in complete and utter dismay.

"You know, if you want to talk to me about what makes a good friend?" she says, crying now and shaking as she steps closer to me. She puts her hand on my shoulder and continues, "A good friend would help me find my way out of the dark, not just turn on the light and blind me with it."

"That's fancy," I say with a grin, hoping to loosen the tension. "You come up with that yourself?"

"Fay, listen to me," she starts, her voice loud and clear like she's about to rip me a new one. "I'm not trying to change you, but what you just said about me, it's like you can only see things from your point of view. I want you to tell me like it is; I love that about you. But I also want you to know that when I left Jazz, I was leaving a piece of myself behind. A part of me that I would never get to explore. Then Jack proposed, and I just saw the rest of my life being stunted. Locked and loaded, done. I tried to explain that to you, and I thought you'd understand. Like, how lucky are you that you get to do what you love every day." She sweeps her arm around, indicating my gallery. "This piece." She points to *The Reckoning*. "This place." She walks to the centre of the room. "I never shoved it in your face that your grandmother basically bought you this ticket. Instead, I revere you for your hard work and see this gallery as a testament to your freedom. I don't have what you have. We both have wealth, Fay; only wealth to me isn't counted in dollars. Wealth is having choices. And mine are limited." She places a hand on her chest, the tears falling out of her eyes onto my floor. "Valentina's is not my freedom. How do you not see that your family money bought you freedom while mine bought me chains."

"I get that," I start. "And in your world, that's your truth. It's on me for not seeing that. I wish you had explained that then."

We sit silently for a moment; a newfound understanding fills the space of all that's gone unspoken. I've envied Val ever since I first met her. Her seemingly perfect life, her loving and beautiful family, her confidence, her wealth, and her ability to do anything she put her mind to were all a gift. It had never occurred to me that her professional destiny felt like a trap tighter than a noose and that having the freedom to choose her own career path, as I did, was all she ever wanted.

"You didn't let me." She walks back to me and puts her hand on my shoulder. "Honestly, I don't think I had the clarity at the time. You know, I have to apologize. I know that you hide behind your beliefs as a way to not show emotion. I may have been focused on my *Val show*, or whatever you called it, but I also saw the look on your face when you mentioned your mother. You hardly ever bring her up, and it's easy to forget sometimes how hard it was losing her to alcohol. Then I said that thing about your motherless woes, and I felt like such a jerk. I didn't mean that." She stops and wipes her face. "Do you have a tissue?" she asks, sniffing back her tears. I reach into my desk and hand her one.

There are so many things I want to say right now, so many things I want to defend or refute, but she's right. I hide behind my morality. That's when it hits me. I have no one to hold a mirror up for me. No one to tell me that what I'm doing is wrong. Zinnia cheating on Adam with me is morally corrupt, even if it is my heaven on earth. I'm here setting up standards on what I expect from my friends, meanwhile I'm no better.

"You're the furthest thing from a jerk," I say through my tears. "Why am I even crying? This is silly. I love you. And again, I'm so sorry. I'm so glad Zinnia arranged for us to talk."

"Me too," Val says.

"Sometimes I feel like if it weren't for her, you'd have left me back in high school," I say. "Like I'm her appendage, and you guys are forced to include me. I feel like Phoebe; I lift right out."

"You," she takes a step forward and pulls me in for a hug, "are like a sister to me, so if you're anyone's appendage, it's mine."

She locks her eyes on mine, and I let out a laugh, breaking all the built-up tension.

"It's hard having feelings, huh?" We both laugh. "No, I mean it, Fay, you're my best friend whether you like it or not." She takes my hand.

I look down at my toes, suddenly feeling like I need to revise my version of our history. We *are* sisters. In fact, my friends are all the family I've got.

"You don't just lift right out," she says. "It doesn't work like that. And if you need me to show you how much you mean to me, then I'll lean into that. Okay? I choose you, every damn day. I love you."

"I love you too." I soften.

Val cups my face and adds, "Make me sound like a narcissist ever again, and I'll wrap these fingers so tight around your little neck."

We both giggle. I pull her in for another hug.

"I'm sorry I was that bad."

"Forgiven," I state. "I'm sorry too. I know I can be harsh at times. I'm working on it." I nudge her lightly and let out a big sigh. "How *is* Eduardo?"

"He's great. You should call him—he'd love to hear from you."

"It's been killing me not calling," I say. "But I had no idea what you'd told him, and I didn't want to—"

"What?"

"Make things worse, I don't know." I sigh. "I'm calling him first thing tomorrow morning. And Jack?"

"Well, I definitively screwed that up." She grimaces. "He'll never take me back, but not for the reason you think. I didn't cheat like I said I did." She pauses and looks up at me coyly.

"Out with it," I urge.

"I want to preface by saying that I love Jack and if I thought I had a shot at getting him back, I'd do whatever I could. But our story doesn't end that way, so instead," she smiles, "let's just say I've been having my fair share of fun."

I gasp. In all my life, I never would have imagined Val out there playing the field, but if she's in her wild-girl era, I'm all for it. "Dish!"

She waves me away. "Can we stop talking about me? How are you? Still with the girl you were seeing in the Bahamas?"

"Actually, yes." I can feel my face turning red. Should I tell her it's Zinnia? I bite the inside of my cheek as I contemplate my options. If I tell her the truth, I'll be forsaking Zinnia's trust. But I'm not about to make up some fake girlfriend, either, that would be a blatant lie. I decide on vague and force a smile. "Going stronger than ever. It's nothing short of a Nora Ephron book, except none of the drama and all of the love."

"¡Ay qué linda! You're in love!" She pushes me, and I fall back onto my chair. "Will I meet her? Is she coming for dinner with us tonight?"

I swivel around and take a breath. "No, she heard you're a narcissist and opted to sit this one out."

"Ah, right, good ol' narcissistic me." She pats her chest and bows exaggeratedly, and we both burst into laughter.

"I almost forgot!" I snap my fingers and reach into my top drawer. "I want to show you something!" I pull out the pen, the one I took from the resort in the Bahamas. "I stole one at breakfast the day we left. The waiter never saw it coming." I wink.

She takes it from my hands. "Petty thief." She winks at me. "If this pen could tell the story of our trip—"

"It would probably punctuate the final stop of our friendship," I say with a grin.

Val stares at me and then shakes off the thought. "I'm writing about all of them and you guys on—"

"*Siempre Valentina?*" I say because I already know. I've read every instalment. "Your writing captures us all so well. You've got such a way with words, chica."

"You've read it?" she asks, surprised.

"Every single post." I sit back in my chair. "They're great—I love how you weave in tales from our trips with fashion and friendship. Quite the sorceress."

"Aw, thanks. Means a lot coming from you." She wraps the ends of her hair around the pen. "High praise from the mighty judge."

I wince.

"Too soon?"

We both let out a laugh.

Val twirls her hair until she's spun it into a bun at the top of her head, looping the ends through so it stays up on its own and then shoves the pen through to keep the bun in place. "Can I tell you something?" she asks. I lean in. "I hate it. I hate running a company. I just feel so stuck." She motions to my empty gallery. "I don't know how you do it."

"I was thinking the same thing of you. I'm not sure how you do it all, run a business and write a weekly blog. I'm exhausted just trying to keep this little place open."

"Still struggling?" she asks.

I nod. "To use your words, no bueno. Unless I sell *The Reckoning*, of course."

"I can ask my rich dad to buy it," Val says with a laugh.

"That would be nice. Just let me know where to send the invoice."

Val plucks another pen out of my desk drawer and says, "Ten years of trips, huh? So, what story does this one tell?"

I inspect the side of the pen as she holds it to my face: *Sol Oasis*. "That one's Morocco."

"Oh my god! Remember our trip to Marrakech? All I wanted to do was see the sites, experience the markets, and visit that fabulous Yves Saint Laurent museum." She waves the pen in my face. "But, no, no, no, you guys wanted to play Bedouin, and we had to drink tea in the desert and ride camels like it's two hundred BC."

I stick out my tongue at her. "You know you loved it."

"It was a once-in-a-lifetime experience," she admits. "I would've never done those things if it weren't for you guys."

"Marrakech is still probably one of my favourite trips to date. That night dancing in the desert being the highlight."

"I think you mean *stuck* in the desert!" We burst out laughing.

"Remember when Zin planned our trip to Ibiza?" I asked, pulling out the pen we stole from the Española Hotel.

"You mean *Elvitha*," she lisps.

"Okay, yeah, *Elvitha*," I respond. "We should've never left her in charge. How stupid were we to let those men pitch us a cheap stay in their homes right after we got off that boat?"

"I know, right? Felt like we were at an auction house right there at the port!"

"It's crazy that we believed Zin when she said that's how it's done there. Like, how would she have even known that?"

"Four twenty-something girls getting into a foreign guy's car because he promised us a nice mountain view of the sea?" Val laughs. "My dad would be so proud!"

"That was by far the stupidest thing we've ever done. We were so unworldly." I sigh. "He literally could've chopped us into pieces and left us to float away at sea."

"Yup." Val laughs. She puts her hands in front of her and holds them out like she's framing a landscape. "But that view!"

"Ahh, that view." I stare off, holding up my hands like hers. "Gotta hand it to Zin. A toddler at home and a baby on the way, and she still planned the perfect trip. And, in the end she was right: no hotel would've lent to the magic like that house did."

"Yeah, she's also the one who planned Vegas." Val grabs the pen from the Bellagio.

"No, that was Keeks," I correct her. "And that trip is top two, up there with Marrakech for sure."

"Really?!" Val asks. "I mean, I loved every minute, but you and Zin were stuck in bed with food poisoning the whole time!"

True. Val had the time of her life in Las Vegas. She and Kiara were gambling the entire time, and between the two of them, they walked away with over two thousand dollars. Meanwhile, Zin and I got food poisoning from the all-you-can-eat lobster buffet. Vomit and cramps aside, holing up in bed watching back-to-back movies with Zin was the perfect trip.

"I'll never go back there," I tease, but I would totally go back. The Fine Art Gallery in our hotel had some serious artwork. Picasso, Warhol, Van Gogh, you name it. "You think we'll keep doing these trips?"

"I don't know." Val tosses my pens into the drawer. She smiles and goes on, "That totally depends on whether you and Kiara ever make up."

The question on everyone's mind.

"I feel so guilty, like we should've done more to help her. She was miserable, and we all knew it." I lower my head.

"Wouldn't have worked. I beat myself up over it all the time, but she was under his spell. But this, this miscarriage, it was the last straw. You should call her." Val bats her lashes at me and then starts to walk along the gallery wall, gliding her finger gently along each frame. "The two of you are so stubborn."

"I'm not being stubborn, Val. I just don't know how to be there for her. I'd call her, but I'd probably say all the wrong things." I pull a face.

"I just yelled at you when all I meant to do was apologize. Luckily, you still forgave me. Kiara's not as forgiving." We walk over to the front door. "Just give me time to figure out what to say." I rest my hand on her shoulder. "Come on, let's go for lunch. We have all afternoon before dinner tonight with Zin."

Val grabs her luggage at the entrance. "You know she's moving back to Montreal?" she offers as I start to key in the alarm.

"What?" I ask as we exit. I shut the door behind us and put the key in the lock.

"I was down there helping Keeks pack up a couple weeks ago. It took less than four hours to gather her belongings and book it back to Montreal. She's staying with her mom for the next two weeks and then moving into my new place with me on September first."

"That's cool," I say, tugging at the door to be sure it's locked. "Well, who knows, maybe we'll make up, and instead of a big trip in February, Zin and I can just come to Montreal. Maybe even for a de la Vega Christmas? What do you think? Could be nice."

"I don't think Zin will fly her entire family from California for Christmas, but okay," she says with a laugh as she starts to walk away. "Maybe she'll miss the snow." She stops and turns around when she realizes I'm not walking with her. I'm standing by my gallery door, completely confused by what I just heard.

"California?" I ask. "Why would Zin be in California?"

"Oh, fuck!" Val slaps her hand on her forehead. "She still hasn't told you?!"

"What didn't she tell me? *Talk faster.*" I feel my face burning. "You just said Zinnia and her family will be in California for Christmas," I speak slowly. "Is she spending the holiday there? Why wouldn't she tell me that? What am I missing?" I feel my heart quicken.

"Ugh, Fay, I don't know why she hasn't told you." She shakes her head and steps closer to me. "Adam's been relocated. They're leaving in a few weeks, so I just assumed—" She pauses. "I'm sorry."

Leaving in a few weeks? For, what, forever?

An image of me standing in Penn station, bag in hand, comes tumbling back and threatens to knock me over. My knees are shaking, and my heart is bursting into a thousand million pieces.

I feel like I've been pushed, face first, down a flight of stairs into a pile of dirt.

I'm so fucking stupid.

"That's why I'm here. To help her pack up her home and do a few last-minute things she needs to get done before they leave." Val's voice fades into the background. "It's horrible that you're finding out like this." She puts a hand on my shoulder and pulls me in for a hug. My feet are glued to the sidewalk. I can't move. I feel her arms wrap around me, but it's surreal, like I'm not here. All the blood has rushed out of my body, and I'm floating above myself, watching my own heart break. Again.

This doesn't make sense. This has to be some sort of practical joke. If Zin's moving to California, why wasn't there a single cardboard box in sight this morning? Why hasn't one of the kids told me? They can't keep a secret this big from their Auntie Fay.

I thought she loved me. Together until we're old and grey. *Do I ever get tired of this city? Would I ever move* . . . I'm such a fucking idiot.

How dumb am I to think that Zinnia could actually love me? I was right in that airport. She doesn't choose me. She never has.

I'm tingling with heat all over. Sadness. Rage. All of it. I'm gonna explode.

"Fay? Speak. What the hell?" Val is waving her hands around now like she's landing a plane.

My whole world is crumbling around me. I need to get out of here.

Half of me wants to run and never look back. The other half wants to ask Zin how she could do this to me. How many times will I let her do this to me?

I have ten million questions, but not a single answer would make this okay. How could she up and move and not tell me? Fuck that, even if she had told me, how could she go? How could she leave me?

How could she tell me she loves me? *We just have to wait until the time is right* . . . All the promises she made. All the patience she asked of me. For what? It's all been bullshit.

"How long has she known?" I ask, tears pooling in my eyes. How long has she been leading me on. Val stares at me, concerned. "You know what? Don't answer that."

The more I think about it, the more I realize I don't, in fact, have a single question; I finally have all the answers.

She's staying with Adam. She chooses him. She loves him.

She doesn't love me. If she loved me, she wouldn't do this to me.

"Fay, come on, let's go to lunch and talk about it." Val takes my hand and tries to pull me along with her, but I don't budge.

"You know what?" I try to take a breath, but it chokes me. I yank my hand back. "I still have a ton to do for the exhibit." I feign the best smile I can.

"Well, why don't I stay and help?"

"No," I blurt out. "No," I say again, softer this time. "You go to Zin's and unpack . . . or pack, or whatever . . . and I'll catch up with you later."

Except I won't.

So much for Nora Ephron.

Zinnia

LOS ANGELES, SEPTEMBER

IT'S BEEN NEARLY TWO WEEKS SINCE WE'VE UNPACKED AND STARTED calling Venice home. But it's been almost five weeks since Fay stopped answering my calls. In that time, I've done a lot of thinking, which has led to a lot of regretting. I should have told her I was moving the second I found out.

It was selfish of me and I handled it all wrong, but in my defence, I couldn't involve her in my decision-making process because if she had known, she would have tried to convince me to stay, and I know I wouldn't have had the heart or energy to be even more caught between worlds. Then again, she would have made it easy because she probably would have folded her life in Toronto to follow me to California, which sounds like a good idea in theory but would have only perpetuated the pain.

I should have never let things get that serious between us, but then I wouldn't have gotten to experience our love. I should have told her so she could have mentally prepared, but then our entire relationship would have been shadowed by an imminent goodbye.

And round and round my mind goes.

I know what I did was wrong. I know I messed up. And I know I'm a coward. I chose the path of least resistance, and I'll regret it forever. But also because it took moving four thousand kilometres away to see things clearly: I did what I did because it was best for my family, and any moment regretting that is a wasted moment.

My kids seem happy here, so I need to find happiness here. That starts with some much-needed time figuring out who I am. In an effort to do just that, I signed up for a photography course. The irony is that the only person I want to tell is Fay.

And round it goes.

I've been sitting on my bed for two hours since I left class, racking my brain on how to tackle my first assignment: a self-portrait.

I've spent the better part of eight years resenting Adam for my choice to leave New York. It was Adam and Darla on one side and me on the other. I chose a family and walked away from my life, my future, my dreams; I did it all without thinking. Like ripping off a Band-Aid, I dropped out of Juilliard, packed up my apartment, and moved to Toronto. I didn't stop for even a second to think because I may have changed my mind. Which is exactly how I felt when California came up, only this time it was Fay on one side and my family on the other.

When I chose motherhood back then, it felt like I was abandoning myself and everything I could be. This time, I promised myself that even though I chose motherhood, it would feel different. Like I can be a mother and become whoever I am going to be. It's what I'm working on, but it still feels like I'm living in the weight of my own absence.

I'm so lost.

So here I am, trying to figure out my entry point to a self-portrait, which by the way is the hardest assignment ever. I should just selfie in the mirror and call it a day because if one thing has become appallingly apparent, it's that I don't know who I am.

In this morning's class, when our teacher assigned this project, she laughed at the irony given the day and age we live in and the advent of smart phones and selfie nation. She went on to clarify that for this project, we need to look at this idea of a self-portrait as an introspective—the story behind our face, the themes of our life, our history, our perspective, what we see and how we're seen. I have no clue where to start, but I've decided that the only place I will find inspiration is if I return to who I was before I was Adam's wife, Darla and Saul's mom, or Fay's ex-girlfriend.

I walk over to my moving boxes, the ones I have yet to unpack, and rummage around until I find the shoebox with old Juilliard photos. A lifetime ago. I find one of me on stage at rehearsal the morning that I found out I was pregnant. When it all began.

It should have been a happy day, and in some ways it truly was. My children have brought meaning to my life that I never knew was possible. I had only ever heard of unconditional love but never had I experienced it myself. Not until the day I held Darla in my arms for the first time.

It's crazy to think about how different my life might have been had I chosen differently. One little pill and back to dance practice. But it wasn't that simple. It was a culmination of everything I'd lived through as a child. Adam was the perfect boyfriend and was such a safe choice. A sure thing. He'd give me family, and that life was mine to lose.

There I was, twenty-two years old, being forced to decide: everything I always wanted or everything I always worked for.

I place the photo aside and pick up another one, but this one is from my first year of university. On stage dancing my first solo in choreography with my dance partner—it was taken around the time when Fay had come to visit. She stayed with me in my dorm for four cramped days. When my roommate told our resident advisor that I had a guest, I almost got kicked out of housing. Her plane was leaving the next morning, so we had decided it was easiest to party until her flight. Have a great night and not worry about where we'd sleep. It was the perfect plan. We went for drinks, drinks led to dancing, dancing led to a house party, which led to a walk in the park until the sun came up and we hit a diner for breakfast. One of those young nights when living takes over. No responsibilities, only possibilities.

Sifting through the memories these photos hold, I feel overwhelmed with sadness. I feel nostalgia for who I was and grief for the person I never became. I had so many dreams back then. Broadway first, then choreography, then eventually director, maybe producer . . . the sky was the limit.

I stand up to look in the mirror. Who am I?

Adam's wife.

Mom of two.

Adulteress.

Fay's ex-girlfriend.

I'm defined by the roles I play.

Saved by the phone. It must be 2:30 already, which means it's half past five in Montreal. On Val's visit to Toronto, we promised we wouldn't let a silly thing like time zones stop us from having our standing weekly. So now, every Wednesday around two, Val, Kiara, and I FaceTime before I pick up the kids. I'm so glad I had the foresight to organize this, because it's exactly the anchor I need right now when so much of me is free-floating.

I click on Val's face, and she appears on my screen.

"Hola mami," she sings. "Say hi to Keeks—she's right here." She pans the phone to Kiara and then swings it back to her. "How's your week, sweet cheeks?"

"Oh, you know, same ol'. Keeping myself busy, still haven't made any friends, but I signed up for a photography class. How about you guys? I see you went with mustard." I nod to the wall behind her with the ivy cascading from the basket perched above her window. "I like it."

"Thanks, yeah, it's warm, right? Also, you know how the previous tenant didn't let me keep their furniture . . ." She widens her eyes. "I got this." She turns the phone to show me a hammock.

"Oh, I love that. Reminds me of that coffee shop in, ugh, where was that coffee shop we used to go to when we were kids? The one with the hammock, duh." I laugh.

"I know which one," Kiara chimes in. "It was on Mount Royal." She snaps her fingers. The name is on the tip of our collective tongue.

Fay would remember the spot. We went there every day after theatre practice in grade ten.

"La Belle Tasse!" They say in unison. The Beautiful Cup.

"Yes!" I beam. "That place brings back memories. Is it still there?"

"Nah." Val sighs. "Closed years ago. You'd know if you ever came home."

"Montreal's not home, Val. You know that. I have nothing there." Val scrunches her nose up at me like Barbara Eden. "I mean, except you guys, of course!" And my dad, who is somewhere in the vicinity. He moved out to a small chalet north of the city when I left my childhood home, and I haven't seen him since. Never met Adam or his grandkids, never reached out. That's what Montreal is to me: a reminder that I had to find my own way in life. It's still an open wound.

"Okay, so, photography class?" Val asks. She pours herself a glass of wine and clinks a cheers with Kiara off-screen.

"Yeah, it just started. Nothing to report, really, but I'll tell you more over the coming weeks. Stay tuned." I don't want to tell them about my self-portrait. I know they'll have a million suggestions on what I can do, and I just want to figure it out on my own. "You doing better this week, Kiara?" I ask. She started seeing a therapist in Montreal, hopeful she'll find some solace from the grief and some answers as to why she endured so much abuse from He Who Shall Not Be Named. From what Val tells me, she's still so depressed she barely gets out of bed most days.

"Yeah, I'm okay. I'm not bleeding anymore, but my clothes still don't fit me. Still carrying some of that not-gonna-have-a-baby weight." Kiara forces a laugh, but it's painful to watch.

I have no words. We've connected so much over this experience; it's opened our relationship to a whole other level. But there's still nothing I can say to make it better; there's nothing I can do to bring her baby back. All I can do is coexist in this moment, in an acknowledgement of her loss.

"You just need time," I finally say. "It won't heal the wound, but with time comes distance, and that space will make the pain more bearable. I promise." That's the plain fact.

"Yeah, I know. I'm working on it, and Val's been my rock. You both have." We exchange a smile, and Val wraps an arm around Kiara's shoulder. I feel a pang of jealousy. Nothing like drinks and hugs with your best friend to make the pain easier to endure. I need some of that right about now.

"You written Fay yet?" Val asks, unaware of the scope of her question. She's been pushing me to reach out and apologize for up and leaving Toronto with no warning, but I can't bring myself to do it.

I've typed out a few drafts, but they all grossly undermine the magnitude of my regret.

First attempt: *Please just hear me out . . . let me explain . . . I would do things differently . . . take it all back if I could . . .* Except I don't know that I would . . .

Second attempt: *I plead temporary insanity. California's great . . . come visit some time!*

Third attempt: *Sorry. I suck. Please forgive me.*

Fourth attempt: *I told you one day at a time . . .*

And the fifth—the last attempt: *I miss you.*

It's a work in progress.

"Not yet," I respond. "I'm not quite sure what I'd say."

"So no one's heard from her?" Val looks back and forth between Kiara and me.

Kiara puts her hand up. "I have," she says softly. I lean into the phone to hear her. "She emailed me the other day. Apologized for how she treated me. But . . ."

"But what?" Val asks, eyes popping out of their sockets. "You don't forgive her?" She sets her glass down and props the phone up so I can see both of them as though I were watching a TV show.

"What she did doesn't need forgiveness." Kiara shakes her head. "I went on that trip, and I brought all my problems with me. Rather than talk about them, I put them on all you guys."

"I told you already, you were crying for help, and we were all too scared to answer." Val looks back to me. I nod in agreement.

"Well, that's what Fay said when I apologized," Kiara says and takes a sip of her wine.

"That's great!" Val shoves her playfully, nearly spilling Kiara's drink. "So, you two made up! Everything is back to normal." She looks at me and tilts her head. "Well, except—"

"Semi–back to normal," Kiara cuts in. "So, we exchanged emails, but there's still so much we have to say to each other. I offered to set up a FaceTime chat, but she said she needs time away from all of us for a while. And . . ." Kiara's face scrunches up like she's about to drop a bomb.

"What is it?" I ask nervously.

"She moved to Istanbul." She winces.

"She what?" Val screeches. "How have you not told me this?!"

Kiara and Val are off on a tangent about why she didn't tell her immediately. Kiara pulls out her phone and is now catching Val up on the specifics of Fay's email.

Meanwhile, I've lifted out of this conversation and travelled to Istanbul to find Fay in my mind. An image of her wrapped in Aiyla's arms is all I see.

Why else would she have gone there if not to reconnect with her ex-girlfriend? I shouldn't be surprised or upset. . . . What did I think? That she would just hang around Toronto, depressed that I left? This is a good thing. I should be happy for her. I chose California, and she chose to not sit around and cry about it. Only she moved on so quickly. I thought we hated Aiyla. Why would she run back to her? Maybe because she could give her what I never could—her whole heart.

I stare numbly at the screen. I hear Val's and Kiara's voices drone on, a hum in the background until I hear the sound of my name from the other side of the screen.

"Zin? Hello?" Val repeats. I catch a glimpse of myself in the camera, and I look like I was stabbed in the stomach.

"Hi, sorry, I'm here." I flap my hands in front of my face to dry my eyes before the tears spill out. The lump in my throat is growing and threatening to unleash a full-on flood.

"What's going on, Zin? Speak," Val whispers. I'm guessing it's written all over my face.

I shake my head from side to side as if to say *nothing's wrong*.

"Bullshit." Kiara calls my bluff. "Something's up."

"I'm fine, I promise. I should go before I—"

"Speak!" Val commands again.

"Just come out with it already," Kiara says and picks up the phone to bring it closer to her face.

"What?" I hear Val ask off-camera. She tugs at the phone and reappears in the frame.

I take a heaving breath and pause before I blurt out, "I was cheating on Adam with Fay."

Val looks at me like she just saw a moose in her kitchen.

"I'm always right!" Kiara yells with a huge smile on her face. "You two were acting so sketch in the Bahamas. I mean, I thought I saw her caressing your back at the bar that night and all those weird looks you guys kept giving each other. Fay made me think I was crazy, but—fuck! I knew it!"

"Wait, back up." Val grabs the phone from her and stares at me dumbfounded. She doesn't say anything though. She just looks at me and then looks away, then looks at me and looks away.

The silence is killing me. I know what she's thinking: Fay took off for Istanbul because of me. Not friend me, but girlfriend me, which makes this ten times worse. Not only did I not tell her I was moving, but I also broke her heart. Because I'm a horrible, selfish person who broke up our friendship and ruined everything. "Can you say something, please?" I urge.

"You're not surprised, are you," Kiara chimes in, nudging Val's shoulder.

"No, I mean, Fay's been in love with you since high school. She may as well have drawn F + Z in hearts all over her schoolbooks," Val says. "I'm still processing *affair*." She air quotes. "I guess I should've caught on when I was in Toronto. The matching feather tattoos . . . Looking back, the signs were there, but—" Val raises her brow and smirks but then stops when she notices my reaction: my hand raised swiftly to the side of my neck, fingers tracing the symbol of forever in the shape of a feather. "Aw, Zin, this must be so hard for you."

"I'm sorry I lied to you guys," I start, and I put the phone down and cup my face in my hands. I don't want my friends to witness my breakdown.

"Forget about us," Kiara says.

"Yeah, this is much bigger than I realized," Val adds.

My buzzer dings, reminding me that it's nearly three. I have half an hour before I gotta get to school for pick up. "I don't want to cut our call short, but I think I'll go for a run before I grab the kids." I've taken up running to clear my head, which I've needed to do a lot since we moved.

"We're here for you," Val says.

"Yeah, girl," Kiara adds, resting her head against Val's. "We love you."

"Back atcha," I say, and I hang up.

As I make my way out past the boardwalk, I wrap my paisley scarf around my head to keep my curls from falling into my eyes. I like to run along the water, savour every drop of the sea, the smell of the salt air, the sound of waves crashing on the shoreline. I run to the rhythmic beat of my feet hitting the sand. Just me and the endless expanse of beach.

As I run, I go back to my self-portrait. I was wrong, I don't need to return to who I was before I was Adam's wife, or Darla and Saul's mom, Fay's ex-girlfriend. Who I am today is not a lost version of who I might've been had I chosen differently.

If I were standing at a fork in the road today, what would be on either side?

I turn up Fleetwood Mac and feel a burst of adrenaline as I push myself to run another mile to Stevie Nicks going on about how thunder only happens when it rains.

With newfound conviction, I pick up speed, fuelled by the energy of what could've been. With every step, I feel the sand kick up behind me and hit my calves. I'm dripping sweat and panting from exhaustion and finally fling myself onto the beach to lie like a starfish on the shore.

Staring up at the sun, I already see things more clearly.

If I'm going to snap a photo to tell the story of who I am today, it might show a half-formed woman in search of her identity. Like a Pirandello play, I imagine a version of myself out there living out the same story, hoping an author will come along and write my ending. Only in my case, it would be an amateur photographer looking for a subject to animate.

I know she's out there somewhere; I just need to keep running toward her.

Valentina

MONTREAL, OCTOBER

SINCE KIARA MOVED IN WITH ME, I'VE SLOWED MY PACE. I SPEND MY days at work and most nights at home writing. No more bed hopping—that didn't bode well for me, not with Bar Guy, Greasy-Hair Guy, I-Only-Kiss-With-My-Eyes-Open Guy, or any of the other guys I took home in the past months. I hated the feeling of a heated night followed by a cold bed in the morning.

Kiara has made strides in her mental health. She's processed a lot of her childhood wounds and what drove her toward Wren. The baby, on the other hand, has been a slower healing journey. Together, we've committed to being more intentional with where we put our energy. I mean, if there's a scale from cool thirty-something unattached women who are in their prime to the lame extreme of staying in, acting like a boring old married couple who reminisce about the good old days, I'd say we're somewhere closer to the latter. We're at my parents' for dinner at least once a week, brunch on Sundays, and sometimes we take in a movie, walk on the mountain, or, at our most social, we grab a bite at a restaurant.

But honestly, there's nothing I'd rather be doing than taking advantage of this time with my best friend and savouring every moment with my parents—you never know when they might be taken away from you.

"Kiara, come over here and tell my dad what you were just telling me earlier," I yell from the living room to Kiara, who is standing in my parents' kitchen.

Kiara grabs an extra slice of chorizo pizza from the counter and walks over to sit next to me on the couch. "Oh, I was telling Val that the Gipsy Kings are coming in December to the Bell Centre. I love them, I saw them on their last tour in Miami." Talking with her mouth full, she adds, "They're incredible in person."

"Mm, Eduardo, deberíamos ir a verles. Pro'lly so nice in live," my mom says as she folds her pizza to take a bite.

"You should pro-*bab*-ly go see them, Mom," I taunt her, and she shoots me the same look she always does when I call attention to her Spanglish, the look that says *if you spoke Spanish half as well I spoke English, then I'd let you correct me.*

"I'd love that, Paulita." Papá shimmy shakes and salsas until he ends up face to face with my mom, holds out his hand, and pulls her off the couch to twirl and dip her in time with the music. When the song is over, he plants a wet one on her cheek and escorts her back to her armchair. "I'll check the computer for tickets."

"Maybe you better not, Papá." I curl my lips. "Should we ask your doctor first?" I know I shouldn't be worried, but a live concert, a crowded room, blaring music? Sounds like the perfect recipe for a relapse. Knowing my parents, they'll be up on their feet dancing the whole time, which only worries me more.

"YOLO," he says.

"What do you know about YOLO, Papá?" I laugh.

"Una vida, mi amor. Life is for the living. Of course we're going." He's squinting at the screen, scrolling through performance dates. "Paulita, two tickets on the floor. Es perfecto." He looks at me. "Want to join us? I can grab four?"

Tempted as I am, the Gipsy Kings really aren't my jam. I'm surprised Kiara cared to see them, although it was probably Wren who wanted to go. I glance over at her, but if this triggered a memory, she doesn't seem bothered by it. Or she's not showing it if she is. "I'm good, Papá, thanks though."

"And you, Kiara? You can come with us and leave the ball and chain at home?" my dad says as he winks at me.

"You're too kind, always including me. I'm okay, though." Kiara pulls me in and wraps an arm around my neck. "I couldn't go without Val anyway." She squeezes a little tighter. "Your daughter is the kindest ball and chain a best friend could ask for."

"Aw, Keeks, you're so sweet." I pull on a strand of her curls and watch as it springs back, hovering a good foot away from her head. She's taken her braids out and is wearing her hair curly these days. She looks fantastic. "I wish I could do more. All I want is to see you happy. If I had a magic wand, I'd wave it around and, alakazoo, I'd make you all better."

She cozies her head onto my shoulder, and I wrap my arm around her.

"You two are lucky you have each other," my dad says and claps his hands together like he's praying. "Los amigos son como las estrellas, aunque no se vean, siempre saben que están ahí," he says, his wise words reminding us that friends are like stars—even though we may not see them in the dark sky, it doesn't mean they're not there. A thought that flutters my heart as I think of Fay. When she ran away from Zin to Istanbul, she ran away from me too. I haven't spoken to her in months. I really miss her.

Kiara gets up and spins around the room, dancing with my dad to "Fuego en la piel," my dad's favourite Gipsy Kings song.

I watch as he counts uno, dos, cha cha cha, leading Kiara, whipping her around the room like a pro. I want to remember every little thing about him. The way his lip curls when he tries to hold back a laugh because Kiara is the worst dancer alive, or the way he makes my mother blush when he winks at her as he dips Kiara, thinking it's making her jealous. Even after all these years together, he still flirts with her. I pull out my phone and hit record. I don't want to rely on my memory for this.

"Go dance tonight en la discoteca justo aquí en la calle—what is called, eh, Eduardo," Mom says, snapping her fingers trying to remember the name of the club down the street. "Aquí nex the coffee place we were jesterday?"

"Saint Denis," he calls over the music.

"Yes, in the street San Denis!" She pronounces the *s* with a huge smile, so excited he remembered, she claps her hands like a kid getting a second piece of cake.

"Oh! I know that place, Le Jasmine, yes! Let's go, Val!" Kiara might not be the best dancer, but that never stopped her from beasting out on the dance floor.

"Really? You really want to go out dancing? We're like dinosaurs. Do they even let thirty-year-olds in clubs anymore?"

"That's one thing I miss about Miami: there's no ageism when it comes to partying. This city is for the young. It's annoying. And I, for one, won't stand for it." She pulls me off the couch. "Let's show 'em how it's done! We're going!"

"What happened to self-care Saturday?" I whine. "I just want to sit here and hang out with you guys. I don't care to see other people and dance." I frown as I curl my bottom lip into my most despairing puppy dog face, but Kiara pulls me into the middle of the living room floor and turns up the music. "Maybe after," I mouth quietly, exaggeratingly raising my eyebrows to remind her that tonight we didn't come just to dance and have pizza with my parents; I have something I need to talk about with my dad.

Valentina's. Before I started, I lamented and resented my fate. I had planned to tell my dad I was out before I even stepped foot in the office. Then, when my father was in the hospital, I decided I would give it a fair shot. Try it out in earnest. Well, it's been six months, and I can now wholeheartedly say with first-hand experience: I hate it.

Running a company is no joke. Not to mention I totally suck at it.

I have a plan that I think will make everyone happy, because what I discovered while I was there is that I actually don't hate it *all*. I just want to focus on a department where my skills and passion make the most sense: marketing.

I've implemented some pretty major changes. Slow and steady, like Eloise advised. But once my dad loosened my leash, I went balls to the wall. Valentina's now has not one but three social media channels; I built out the e-shop so that it's not just a landing page, it's a full-suite experience, complete with virtual dressing rooms and exclusive online capsule collections for a younger demographic. My favourite change is that my dad has let me host *Siempre Valentina* on our site. All to say, doing all that *and* being CEO is more work than I can handle.

I plan to announce that I want to step down. (Well, I'll ask nicely if it's possible.)

Kiara and I have practised my speech a gazillion times. I have everything lined up and ready to go. My plan is that Ricardo will take over, and I'll build out the marketing department and expand the business into pop-ups, experiential events, collaborations, and a whole bunch of other ideas.

I know what my dad will say: he wants to keep Valentina's in the family. But I have an answer prepped for that: Ricardo has been like an uncle to me since I was a baby. He held me when I was baptized. That technically makes him family. Plus, unlike me, Ricardo actually wants this.

"Um, right, let's chat a bit more, and then we'll go." Kiara winks at me and pushes me toward my dad.

"Qué pasó?" My dad looks at us suspiciously as he turns down the music. "What's going on with you two? Is this about Jack?"

God bless him. He's still holding onto hope that Jack will forgive me and we will find our way back to each other.

"No, Papá." I sigh and shake my head. "If we were meant to be, it wouldn't have happened like this, right?" We're out of synch. And like my dad used to say, *Life, like dance, is all about timing. You may think you know where you're going, but it's really the music that's moving you.* I have to believe in my heart that we weren't meant to be and if there's any evidence I can pull, it's that Jack and I never danced like my parents.

"So smart, my Valentina." My dad pinches my cheeks and kisses my forehead. I can feel the love pouring out of his heart.

"Papá?" I start, then cough out the questioning tone from my voice and start again. "Papá," I state clearly as I stand up straight. Nothing like good posture to feign confidence. "I want to talk to you about Valentina's."

"No work on the weekends, mi'ja," he asserts as he reaches for the volume knob to turn the music back up. Ever since I was a kid, it's been a rule that we don't talk about work, even homework, on the weekends.

"No, it's not work stuff, it's just a thing," I mumble. "Can you sit down?"

His face gets serious. He sits on the couch and puts his arm around my mom, pulling her in closer like a magnet. "Go ahead."

Now or never, I think as I take in a huge breath. "Okay." I hold my hands together. "Before I took over Valentina's, I was in marketing, remember?"

"Yes, I remember. It was a few months ago; I have heart problems, not memory problems." He laughs. "Go on." His impatience is making me far more nervous than I anticipated.

"Okay, well, first I want to say that it's been an honour to work at Valentina's."

"To *run* Valentina's," he corrects me.

"Yes, run." I let out a big exhale. "And while I'm still just learning the ropes, I'm not—"

"It's been less than a year," he interrupts. "It took me half a decade to get those ropes rigged and working. You'll be fine. Give it time—it's yours to figure out."

Deep breath. I knew this wasn't going to be easy. "So, that's the thing," I say and let out a sigh. "It's not that I'm not good at it. Although, that's true too. It's that I don't want to be good at it." I walk over to sit down beside my parents, placing my hand on my dad's lap. "Papá, I love that you built this incredible company. It's your legacy." He smiles proudly. "It's just that it's not mine." The smile immediately fades away.

"You're quitting?" His chest deflates; his head hangs low. His reaction is far worse than I predicted: he's not mad, he's disappointed.

"No!" I cry out louder than I wanted to. "I mean, not exactly."

"Just say it, Val," Kiara says in an effort to throw me a lifeline.

"I want to stay on, but running a company isn't my passion, marketing is." Avoiding eye contact with my dad, I keep my head lowered as I continue. "It's the best of both worlds. I love all the strategic thinking I have to put into the channel plans and how our—" I pause and bite back the word *brand*, searching my head frantically for the synonym Kiara and I thought of "—how our story is presented to the world. All the copy I create for store clerks and buyers, I'm telling the story of our family. Of Valentina's."

"And, *Siempre Valentina* . . ." Kiara encourages, nodding proudly.

"Right, I love that I can host my blog there, and I want to be doing more of that, but time isn't on my side when I'm busy running budgets and global projections."

"Her stuff is amazing," Kiara chimes in again, swooping in to really hammer it home. "She recently wrote one about me and my relationship. It made me cry."

"Thanks, Keeks," I say and put my hand on my chest.

"I mean it." She pulls out her phone. "That part about how dynamics are an illusion and—" she puts her finger up, squinting at the screen, "'—we step into them under the pretense of inevitable truth. Only they're masks we wear, lest we forget we chose to put them on in the first place. Take Kiara, for example. While others may see her lipstick as a sign of beauty, desire, or control, she dons her red like war paint—a shade of bravery to power her through the pain. Our masks protect us, but they can also be disorienting. When worn too long, we risk losing sight of the true strength that lies beneath.'"

Hearing my words read back to me is what's disorienting. I'm tearing up as I glance over to catch my dad's reaction. Nothing.

"I know that our current demographic isn't online," I jump in. My last-ditch effort for this obviously lost cause. "So this won't convert to revenue right away, but it will with time. Mr. Filomena, I mean, Russell, helped me run the numbers, and we'll begin to see a serious return within . . ." My dad's blank stare slows my roll. I slump down and feel my shoulders release. There's no point. I think my dad's been online three times in his whole life, and one of those times was tonight to buy concert tickets. "Papá, I really believe my efforts will have a greater impact if . . ." My voice trails off. Great. Now I'm crying. So much for confidence. Where's my power lipstick when I need it?

My parents exchange a look and then look back at me. I wish someone would speak. I know I sound desperate, but I was really hopeful that my dad would see the value in this plan. See that it's not just Valentina's that will suffer under my reign, but my happiness hangs in the balance too.

My dad quietly stands up and bends over to kiss my forehead. He slowly walks over to the music and turns it up.

"Baila, mi amor." He puts out a hand for my mom to join him to dance, dance, dance.

"Papá . . ." I whine. "Are you seriously not even gonna answer me?"

"You are Valentina," he says, pointing to me, like I didn't know my name. "Valentina's cannot succeed without you."

"Why is it that you can be so understanding about everything else in life, but this . . ." I cry. I knew there was no way he'd give in to this plan.

"And, by the way, *Siempre Valentina*—" He spins my mother out and pulls her back. Then salsas over to the table to reach for his drink.

Here it comes . . .

"—is brilliant!" He raises his glass.

"Told you so!" Kiara jumps up and down. She walks over to me and drags me onto the floor to dance with her.

"Brilliant?" I'm floored.

My dad approaches me with a smile. He takes me by the shoulders and says, "Mi'ja, you've given a face and a voice to Valentina's. Ricardo tells me that every item of clothing you feature on the blog sells out within days of posting. I may be retired, but I still know everything that is going on in that company."

I stare at my dad, speechless.

"Except I didn't know how much you hated being the boss. That," he cups my face in his hands, "you should've told me sooner."

"I'm sorry, Papá," I lower my eyes.

"Paso a paso, okay? Ricardo will transition. Not to worry."

"I love you, *so much.*" I do. More than words. I throw my arms around him and cry into his neck. We stay like that for a moment, and I feel my heartbeat steady. Slowing down to beat in time with his.

"Mi amor, promise me one thing. Never feel scared to talk to me," he kisses my cheek and continues, "about anything. Keeping secrets is not good for the soul."

Kiara and I exchange a look. Not good for the soul at all.

"Well looky here!" Kiara sings on top of the music. "Looks like we're gonna hit the town!"

I concede.

"¡Sí, sí!" My mother smiles proudly, dancing in my father's arms again. "Go, mi vida."

"¡En esta vida, cuando ganamos, celebramos!" my dad adds as he swirls her around gaily. When we win, we celebrate.

We head into my old room to see if any of the clothes I left here from yesteryear are club-appropriate. I find an old silver halter top and a pair of distressed black skinny jeans I used to wear in high school. I check my mom's closet for something Kiara can wear and find a leather skirt and white leopard top that'll probably fit.

"Hey Keeks, this good?" I turn around, holding the outfit up.

"Perfect!" She grabs the skirt from my hands. "Good thing I wore my knee boots tonight."

When we get to the bar, there's a mob at the door. People don't line up in Montreal, it's counter to our culture. We just crowd around the bouncer and play on our phones, pretending to be too cool to care whether we get in or not.

"I'm not waiting in this thing," I say to Kiara as we approach the crowd.

"'Kay, me neither. Want to just grab a drink somewhere chill instead? I know that's more your speed anyway. We can *talllkkk*," she says with a roll of her eyes.

"Actually, is that—" I squint "—Lucas!" I wave at the bouncer. "I know him," I whisper to Kiara. "Long wait?" I ask as I step toward the red rope.

"Not for you." He unclips the rope. "How are you, gorgeous?" He leans over and gives me a kiss on both cheeks.

I've known Lucas forever. He works as a freelance videographer, one of the best. I just hired him for our winter digital campaign. He refuses to go full-time, despite my pleas. He says it sucks the creativity right out of you when you work in-house.

"This is my friend Kiara," I introduce them.

"Well, Kiara, friend of Val. It's nineties night, so it's hype in there."

"Yes! And we're perfectly dressed!" I pump my fists like an over-excited grade-schooler.

Kiara looks me up and down, surveying our outfits. "We were toddlers in the nineties, but yeah, this works." She laughs.

"Let me know when you take a break. You can join us for a drink." I give Lucas a hug, and we head inside.

"'Kay, he's hot," Kiara says as we head into the club. I laugh because the side convo just last week amongst all the ladies at the office was about how it was such a waste that Lucas was *behind* the camera. "You gonna hit that?"

"No!" I smack her on the shoulder harder than intended.

Kiara rolls her eyes at me. "Yeah, yeah, whatever."

"You know I'm on a celibacy kick. Come on."

Although, it wouldn't hurt to bank Lucas as a winter cuddle partner. Fall is mating season; we're all out there shopping desperately for someone to keep us warm during the colder months. That's probably why Le Jasmine is packed.

"Should we get a drink before we hit the floor?" Kiara asks. She motions to the bar.

We grab the one empty stool available. She sits, and I hover over her. We order our drinks, two tequilas—añejo, añejo—and a twist of lime and scan the crowd, taking in all the neon, chokers, and lip liner.

"Yo, did I mention Lucas is hot!" she says, fanning herself. "So, no Lucas?" she persists.

"We sort of already . . . if you know what I mean?" I bite my lower lip.

"Damn. You really did paint this town, didn't you?" We high-five. "Wait, was he the one you told me reminded you a lot of—"

I nod and take a swig of my drink.

Jack.

Not a day goes by where I don't think about him.

I'll have the image of his face seared into my memory forever. That look when he muttered *bitch* as he left my apartment.

I broke him.

And I ruined my chances . . . twice.

It took some time, but with a ton of reflection, I understand why I lied about cheating when he proposed, why I let him walk into my apartment while Bar Guy was still there, half-naked, why I pushed away the one sure thing in my life . . . my only wish is that he would talk to me so I can explain that none of it was about him, it was never about a spark; it was only ever an immature and desperate plea at gaining some control over my life: to have active agency over the choices I make and not blindly follow some predetermined path someone else paved out for me.

I only wish I had then the clarity I have now. I *do* choose Jack.

I've been journaling a lot about him and us and what I want. Maybe one day I'll send him the letter I wrote; it's basically a thirty-page testament to my mistakes and how I single-handedly sabotaged my chance at happily-ever-after, neatly wrapped into a short story entitled "My Life Without Jack." He'll most likely toss it aside unread, along with all of my apology texts and the deluge of emails I've sent, but it's worth a shot.

"You'll find your guy." Kiara clinks my drink. "Sometimes it's healthier to just go about living and let life find you."

"Whoa, you just come up with that? That's deep shit." We cheers again. "Amen!" I sip my drink and look around at the crowded dance floor. People grinding, winding, bouncing, and mostly rubbing up against each other. "Do you think he misses me?"

Kiara takes my drink out of my hand. "Hell no. We are not doing that tonight."

"What?!" I yell over the music.

She pulls me onto the dance floor. "We are not spending the entire night talking about Jack and the meaninglessness of life." She drops it low to the floor and winds her hips. "Sometimes, we cry to feel better. Sometimes, we dance." She winds her way back up and rubs her back against mine, pulls my hand and twirls me around. "Tonight, we dance."

Heeding my best friend's sage advice, we dance the night away. Remixes of old classics run for the better part of two hours. Every time I try to take a break, I'm pulled back onto the dance floor for the next *best* song. We grind, jerk, twerk, and dance until we are dripping sweat.

I finally convince Kiara it's time to go home a little past last call, but only on the promise that we'll stop for tacos on the walk back to our place. When we step outside, the fresh cool air hits hard. My skin is sticky with sweat; the breeze sends a cool shiver up my spine.

We walk about forty minutes and grab three tacos from the food truck on Crescent, sit down on a bench to eat, nearly shivering to death.

"I'm beyond impressed with you, by the way. You really sold *Siempre Valentina* to your dad." She bumps my shoulder with hers.

"No, my dear, that was all you." I nudge her back as I take a bite out of my taco. My mouth half full, I continue, "When you pulled out my blog and started to quote me, I mean . . ." I smile.

"But I meant it for real, Val, it takes a brave chick to plunge into something she's passionate about. I kind of want to do the same thing."

"Yeah? You want to start a blog?" I tease. I forget sometimes that Kiara left her job, her students, her entire life back in Miami. We've been so focused on her mental health that I haven't even thought about what she might want to do once she's feeling ready to get back to work. Maybe a blog wouldn't be a bad idea.

"No! Oh my god! Imagine me? A writer? No, no." She wipes a bit of guacamole from my chin and continues. "Getting a job teaching here won't happen since the school year already started. I'll be lucky if I can get on a sub list. I'm referring to my body positivity program. I think I'm ready to start working on it again. Take the plunge and bring it to the school board. Try to make it an official part of the primary curriculum."

"Do it!" I shove her a little too hard, and chunks of chicken spill onto her lap. "Sorry." I laugh.

Kiara's unbothered. "Teaching kids about self-esteem and healthy body image is, like, more important than math, right? I mean I can do math, but I *do* body!" She points to my half-naked body. "Maybe not as much as you, though."

I laugh so hard salsa verde flies out of my mouth. "Fact," I affirm. "Kiara, if I learned anything this year, it's that you gotta follow your dream. Take action when you feel called. And I know you don't want to talk about Jack tonight, but I think I am going send him that—"

"Can I tell you something?" Kiara interrupts me and stands to toss our wrappers in the garbage. She sits back down and puts her hand on my leg. "I bumped into Jack last week." I feel a lump form in my throat. "He's moving in with his girlfriend. Poppy."

My whole world goes dark. I didn't think things were that serious between them. I mean, I know there was a third and then fourth date or whatever. I've heard through the grapevine that they were seen at Bijou, the Canal, and all that. But in my mind it wasn't serious. Not move-in serious. Kiara regards me with compassion as I process the information. I'm such a fool.

I wave the topic away. "You know what?" I take in a deep breath. "You were right. Let's not talk about Jack tonight." I hunch over, cupping my face in my hands. "Love shouldn't hurt this much, right?"

"Tell me about it. That's how I feel about Wren." I sit up. This is the first time she's said his name since the breakup. "I thought he was the one." Tears rolling down her cheeks, she pauses as she reaches into her purse to pull out a tissue. "And I know I should hate him, but is it crazy that somewhere inside I sort of miss him? I had a whole life planned, Val, and then suddenly, it was all gone."

Everything she's kept inside for all these weeks is finally spilling out. Her emotional break. It's finally here.

"Oh, Kiara." I caress her head and hold her close. We sit like that on the bench, in each other's arms, crying until the sun comes up.

Just two best friends out celebrating life's big moments.

Kiara

MONTREAL, NOVEMBER

I PULL THE COVERS OVER MY HEAD TO BLOCK OUT THE MORNING light. Too much sun for such a dark day. I slink down further into the middle of my bed and try to fall back asleep even though I know there's no use trying. I haven't slept all week. I've been anticipating—nope, dreading—this moment since that horrible day in July. I thought if I wished hard enough, this day would never come. Or maybe, in some alternate universe, it would slip by without my noticing.

Val isn't making any chipper attempts at getting me out of bed, nor is she trying to distract me with snacks and movies. She heard me loud and clear when I told her that this is what I need. She's giving me permission to go dark for a while. It's not what my therapist recommended, but she's also giving me a pass, trusting that I'll emerge on the other side. What I know for damned sure is that Wren certainly wouldn't have let me get away with this. He'd call it *wallowing* or whatever. *This wasn't our baby*; I can hear his voice ringing in my head. I could imagine how he'd react to my staying in bed today, pulling the blanket off my face and mocking me for caring so much.

Today was supposed to be the best day of my life. My due date. November 21. Contractions, pain, drugs, pushing, the whole shebang, and at the end of it all, I'd hold my baby. My little boy.

There have been moments over the past months where I've been able to distract my mind and be in the moment. But even in those happy moments, the pain is always there in the background, waiting until I'm alone to trickle back in.

I planned for today though. Equipped with my journal, a fully charged laptop for movies in bed, and an aromatherapy kit infused with lavender so that I can be wafted away to sunny fields . . . anywhere but here.

I wish I could just sleep the day away.

I pull the blanket over my head and attempt to make my wish a reality.

When I wake up, it's barely eleven. Hunger gnaws at my stomach. In all my planning, I forgot to stock up on snacks. Against my better judgment, I get out of bed to brave the outdoors and get something to eat. A bagel, lox, and cream cheese at the coffee shop down the street is calling my name.

It's bitterly cold out, but I keep my jacket open so it hits me harder; it hardly takes three minutes for my fingertips to freeze to the point of numbness. When I enter the café, there's not a soul in sight. I guess most people are at work on a Monday morning. I order my bagel and take it to go so I can get back into bed as fast as possible.

As I walk, I notice the white snow and take a deep breath, inhaling the cold, and then exhaling clouds of condensation from my mouth. Grey like the smoke coming out of apartment building chimneys. Or red like the Five Roses sign atop the Montreal mill. Blaring neon lights set against the blue sky. Blue. The colour of the *Remix* onesie I'd picked out for my baby boy. He'd be wearing it right now.

I can almost feel him, rocking him skin-to-skin in my hospital bed.

Tears trickle down my face and freeze against my cheek. I try to wipe them away with my ungloved hands, but both my face and fingers are so numb I can't feel a thing. I toss my takeout bag into a garbage bin. I've lost my appetite.

I sometimes think about Wren. I think about Raven too. About how I lost more than just my baby, I lost a stepdaughter. We were finally starting to get into our own groove. She was so looking forward to being a big sister. I wonder if Wren gave her the space to explore her grief or if he shut her down like he did me.

Propped up on my pillow, I'm in bed scrolling through socials. I click on Wren's page to see how they're doing. Raven looks older. There's a picture of her holding up a sign that says *I'm in Grade Four* with Wren kneeling beside her, smiling. I wish I had been there to help braid her hair and take pictures of her outside on the first day of school. Another picture of Wren and Max being bros at a club, clinking their glasses with huge smiles plastered across their faces, their white shirts wet and sweaty. He seems to have moved on because there's also a beach pic of Wren and a woman. A younger woman, beautiful, prettier than me.

I click out of his page before the doom-scrolling takes on a life of its own. I may be a glutton for punishment, but that's the sort of pain I don't have the energy for.

I flip onto my homepage and snap a pic of myself. I look like a mess. My hair up in a silk scarf, no makeup on, and puffy eyes for days. But that's what I stand for: being real. I caption it *even when it feels impossible to go on living . . .*

Val sends a heart and a comment that she loves me. Zinnia likes it and comments *I love you Keeks, I'm here for you.* Nothing from Fay, but that's to be expected. She's been a ghost on social, which is probably her way of avoiding updates on Zin. A couple minutes later, Frankie hearts my picture and sends me a direct message.

The Miami heat got you cooped up inside?

Oh my god, oh my god, oh my god. I feel my pulse all the way in my brain. I haven't spoken to Frankie in months. After I deleted all his messages, I stopped all notifications from him and unfollowed, which was my less insulting approach to blocking him.

What do I even say back?

Nope I moved back home to Montreal, I key in, and then I add, Ever been?

No but I'd love to. You inviting me?

Fuck. What do I say to that? And as though he is reading my thoughts, he adds, I'm just kidding. Why impossible to go on living? You sick?

Why? I look that shit? Lol. Real. Be real. Not sick, but sad.

Tell me.

You really want to know?

I already know the answer to that. And of all the people in the world, something tells me he not only wants to know, he'll understand.

I was pregnant. And today was my due date.

Was?

I had a miscarriage in July.

Damn. That's hard. A couple seconds pass, and then he adds, You must be devastated. I'm here for you.

Thank you. That's kind of you to say.

How are you honouring the day?

I look around my bed. Can what I'm doing be considered honouring? I was leaning more toward avoidance.

What do you mean? I answer.

I hold my phone in my hand, waiting for a reply. Two minutes go by, and I'm about to set my phone down. Maybe I was wrong to expect the cute pool boy to pause his entire day to help me with mine. But then, a huge message pops up on my screen.

My mom lost a baby when I was thirteen. I was just a kid, but I'll never forget the day she was supposed to give birth. She bought a plant and told the plant everything she ever wanted my baby sister to know. About how beautiful the world can be even on the hardest days and how much she loved her and would always love her. She wrote a letter to her about everything she had already learned from her: how life can be filled with promise and how painful it was to not only lose her baby girl but to have temporarily lost hope. Then she went to the beach and threw the plant into the water and let the waves carry her away. I wanted to plant it in our yard so she could be with us where we could see her, but Mom said she didn't need a plant in our yard to remember her, she was in her heart forever.

I read his message and then reread it letting the tears swell in my eyes until the screen goes blurry.

You there? Did I say the wrong thing?

No—I mean yes, I'm here, and no, not wrong. Perfect. Thank you.

You don't need to thank me. I should thank you for letting me be there for you.

Just when I think Frankie couldn't be more incredible, he ups the ante and thanks me for sharing my feelings. Where has this guy been all my life?

I'm gonna sign off now but . . . thank you, Frankie. You've helped me more than you will ever know. Not just today but a lot since that night on the beach.

I think about you a lot, Kiara. You left your mark on me too . . . You're an exquisite woman.

Exquisite? Me? I don't think I've ever heard that word used to describe me. Funny, yes, killer athlete, yes, but exquisite feels like a stretch. I blush a little and feel thankful he can't see me.

Hey so I'm gonna watch a movie later—want to join me? I type quickly before I lose my nerve. Maybe I don't want to be alone today.

How we gonna do that?

I dunno, we can start the movie at the same time and chat here?

It's a date. You pick the movie. Then he sends a winky face.

A date! I can't believe I have a date with Frankie!

See you later, I type and close the app.

Before movie night, I have something I want to do.

I pull the blanket off my overheated body and reach for my pants. Fully dressed, I throw on my jacket and head out to the plant store.

I hope that winter hasn't killed off every flower in this city.

When you're living out the remaining months of your pregnancy, there's a timeline that keeps you connected to your baby. But once the due date comes and goes, there's nothing left but the past, a vacant space, a memory of what was supposed to be and never was.

November 22. The day after baby wasn't born.

Because Montreal does not have an ocean to toss flowers into, last night I ceremoniously went to the lookout and threw a beautiful arrangement of white Oriental lily petals from over the mountain. I promised myself that every year on the anniversary of his would've-been birthday, I would commemorate his memory with this ritual.

It feels like a plan I can lean into to both honour his life and to alleviate the grief of his death.

As far as plans go, today is the day that I will actually eat the bagel I buy. I get out of bed at the break of dawn and sit by my window to meditate. I go through a few colours: pink, mustard, and coral. Once I'm done, I knock on Val's door to see if she wants anything from the café before heading to the office.

"Nah, I'm good. But I'll take a hug." She looks up at me from her screen and takes off her blue-light glasses. She walks over to me, arms wide open.

"Thanks, Mom," I joke. "I'm actually feeling better this morning." Which is true.

Last night, Frankie and I watched back-to-back Blassics: *Crooklyn* and *Waiting to Exhale*. Midway through the first movie, our side text conversation was so distracting that we decided to video chat instead. His running commentary was like watching a show with the peanut gallery. We paused so much that two movies took six hours. It was perfect.

"You know what?" Val says, pulling on her coat. "I actually will come with you."

Compared to yesterday, it's a warm pre-winter day. Just two sweaters, a Sherpa-lined coat, hat, scarf, gloves, leg warmers, and Ugg boots. Smarter apparel than yesterday's open-jacket and gloveless walk.

"Remind me why we live here again?" I ask as we step into the cold.

"Oh, it's not that bad," Val replies, shoving her hands in her pockets. "You just need to get used to it. Acclimatize. What was all the noise in your room last night? Who were you talking to?"

"Oh, um," I didn't consider the fact that she may have heard us. A wave of shame washes over me for indulging in a double feature while I was supposed to be grieving.

"Okay, fine. Don't tell me. Just answer me this." She pauses and stares at me with concern. "Was it Wren?"

"Oh my gosh, no!" I let out a big puff of breath, and it hangs in the air like smoke from a cigarette. "It was Frankie."

"Who's Frankie?" She has a puzzled look on her face.

"Remember, the guy from the Bahamas?"

"The pool boy? Oh! My! God! Kiara!" She punctuates each word with a clap. "As I live and breathe! He was so hot!" She keeps clapping like a teenager. "Good for you." She hits my arm. "Looks like our set for the *Real Housewives* wasn't so bad after all. Maybe we should go back there for our next girls trip?"

Kiara gives me the side-eye. "Honestly, I don't think I'll be joining any more girls trips."

She stops dead in her tracks. "You're kidding, right?"

"Do I look like I'm kidding?" I make an extra-serious face. "Girl, I'm in no place to be taking trips right now." Depressed, jobless, uncertain where my next stop is in life. I don't need to focus on escape. But speaking of . . . "We haven't heard from Fay since she took off. It would only be the two of us and Zin anyway, who, last time I checked, wasn't in the right headspace for a girls trip either," I say, and start walking again.

"Actually, Zin is totally down. We even discussed Italy!" Val calls out, running to catch up.

I shove my hands in my pockets, shoulders up to my ears to fight the gusts of wind as I forge ahead. "Those days are over. Time for us to move on."

"Hold up, wait for me!" Val is hustling to keep up with me. "First of all," she holds up her thumb, and I know a list of arguments is headed my way, "Fay loves you." I keep walking, ignoring her millionth reminder that Fay's silence is not about me. "Second, I will not accept that those days are over." I shake my head at her, complete with eye roll and sarcastic grin. "Fine, maybe today's not the best day to make any decisions. Let's just leave it for another time."

"Whatever you gotta tell yourself." We continue to walk in silence until we reach the coffee shop. Once at the door, I stop.

"You coming in?" Val asks, her hand on the handle.

"Val?" I cry.

"Okay, no trip." She puts her hand on my shoulder. "Sorry for even bringing it up. Bad timing."

"No, it's not that, it's just . . ." I stagger a bit, overwhelmed by what I'm about to say. "Is it wrong that even though I really wanted my baby, I'm also relieved by what happened, relieved that I'm not tied to Wren for the rest of my life?" There it was: a layer of emotion I'd resisted exploring. It found its way out. Val rhythmically caresses my back to steady my breath one *shh, it's okay* at a time.

"He hasn't even reached out once," I finally say as I wipe my cheeks.

"The world works in mysterious ways, Keeks." Val pulls me toward her and holds my shoulders square, so we are face to face. "He was a jerk," she says. "In some bittersweet way, this was a blessing. You're just processing it all. You're gonna feel all the things, but Frankie and I are here for you."

I chuckle.

"I just feel like I'm in an emotional washing machine. It's a lot."

Val pulls me in for a hug, then looks at me with compassion in her eyes, a mirror reflecting the confusion I can't put into words yet.

"Yes, it is," she confirms. "But we'll get through it, one spin cycle at a time."

"'Kay, enough." I smile through my tears. "Can you order us some breakfast sandwiches, please? I'm withering away."

Val smiles as she pulls opens the shop door.

"Wait," I stop her. "I don't think I've ever truly thanked you for how you swooped in and saved me, no questions asked."

"You're my person—it's in the job description." Val waves me away, undercutting the incredible and unwavering friendship she's always given me.

"It's just, you got me out of that relationship, out of that condo, out of Miami . . . you let me live with you, you're there for me—always. Thank you for everything—" I pause, and she smiles, hand on her heart "—and also, for the bagel you're buying me, 'cause I'm broke and bordering on hangry." We laugh, and Val disappears into the shop to line up at the takeout counter.

I feel my phone buzz in my back pocket. I pull it out and see that I have a message on Instagram.

What are we watching tonight?

It's Frankie. I respond: Eat, Pray, Love?

I love me some Julia, Frankie replies with a smiley emoji.

Val's right, maybe there is a bittersweet blessing in all this. As I type, a glimmer of hope flickers inside, reminding me that love can bloom in even the harshest of climates.

Fay

TORONTO, DECEMBER

Dear Zinnia,

I've been going back and forth as to whether I should write you. I don't want you to get the wrong idea. I'm not opening a channel of communication here. That's not what this is. I'm writing because I have feelings, and I want to get them off my chest because, Zin, it hurts. You hurt me.

A lot.

I can't quite wrap my head around why you chose Adam, why you left your whole life behind to move to California, why his dreams matter more than yours. More than us. So I won't even go there.

Here's where I'll go: How could you not even show me the decency of telling me you were moving? How could you, of all people, have done this to me? To us?

You're not who I thought you were.

You know, when you left me in New York, I thought, well, you were young, you were pregnant, you were scared.

But now?

You robbed me of believing our love was real.

Don't answer because I'll just delete it.

Fay

I hit send before I have a chance to reread what I've written. I don't want to lose my nerve. I have to be done with Zinnia, put that chapter of my life behind me and move on. I can't hold on to hope that she'll come back and choose me. Instead, I have to choose me.

I lean back to stare at my screen.

It's really over.

In the last four months since I've spoken to or seen Zin, I've kept tabs on her life out in California. It's been painful as all hell to see the photos she posts on socials every day. But I just couldn't imagine a world where I wouldn't know what's going on in her life and still feel connected in some way.

Some of her photos are so profoundly beautiful. I can just picture her standing behind her camera, inspired by a tree or a city light, extracting a full narrative from the world around her.

The last one she posted was a close-up of her fingers. One hand pulling the cuticles off the other. It was fragile and vulnerable, with a unique dimensionality that made it almost unbearable to look at. The caption underneath read *Parts of me*.

But her photos and captions provoke something in me—like a call to action—a raw offering that speaks straight to my heart.

With my decision to choose myself comes a whole slew of changes. First and foremost, no more checking her socials. It shakes me up with anxious energy, the same chronic sense of unease I've felt ever since my return from Europe.

Istanbul was great, but it was all work, no play. It was a last-minute trip that came up at the perfect time. An artist I agreed to show had her pieces hanging at a gallery there. She flew me in for a week so I could select which ones I thought would sell best to my clientele. I extended my stay to check out the area and look into further opportunity, maybe even to settle there permanently, but my heart wasn't in it. Nothing inspired me. Instead, my time in Istanbul helped me realize something.

I had nothing to come home to.

Toronto is lifeless without Zin.

I sent out an email to the long list of trusted collectors and art community members I've come to know in the past seven years to announce that I'll have my last show the night before Christmas. I will be closing my gallery doors forever. It was a hard decision to make, but, in the end, it was the right call.

Getting out of my lease wasn't easy, but my landlord made an exception; he knew how much I've been struggling this last year. I also found someone to sublet my apartment, so for all intents and purposes, my life here is done. I have nothing anchoring me to Toronto, so I'm ready to fly free. Move on to the next chapter. Whatever that may be.

My savings have dwindled to enough for one last plane ticket, and if this last show sells at least half of my leftover pieces, I should be good for about two-ish months on a shoestring budget. Enough to find a waitressing job or something.

I click out of my email and into a new window. I key in beach town cheap warm all year and hit enter. A few places pop up: Penang, Malaysia; La Paz, Mexico; Hội An, Vietnam. But only one catches my eye: Cascais, Portugal. I've never been, but looking at the pictures online I can already smell the turquoise sea and lush mountain air. I don't speak any Portuguese, but I'd be an asset to the tourists since I'm fluent in English and French. I click around, looking for Airbnb rentals in the area, and I feel my stomach doing flips already. I don't know the last time I did something this exciting.

Scrolling some more, I slip into a daydream of what life would be like living in Portugal. Even in the dead of winter, I'd be wearing a thin layer of clothes, soaking in the sun by the Atlantic coast. Seafood by the pound and nata pastries every night of the year. The more I let it sink in, the more sure I am that this is the right decision.

I check on flights for after my exhibit. The first flight out leaves Christmas morning, which means I can't go to Val's Christmas dinner like I planned.

I take a deep breath as I hover my finger over Val's contact. There's a small chance she understands, but there's an even larger chance she gives me hell. After not returning her calls, texts, or emails since the day I ditched her when she was in Toronto—to pack up Zinnia, lest I remind her—I finally reached out to her and Kiara when I got back. They said they'd accept my apology under one condition: join the de la Vega family dinner in Montreal.

Who am I kidding? She's ten thousand percent going to give me hell.

"You what?!" Val shouts when I break the news to her over FaceTime. "What's in Portugal?"

In the background, I hear Kiara say something about how I flee whenever things get hard. Her words come through loud and clear. "Like a rolling stone. That's our Fay."

"Shh, Kiara." Val tries to muffle Kiara's condescension. "I will not tell her that. Although," she redirects her attention to me, raising her brow. "She has a point."

"You know I have a point. A sharp, pointed, truer than true point." Kiara's matter-of-fact tone tells me I'm in for an earful. I'd be lying if I didn't say I secretly hoped Val would be alone. She'd let me off the hook way easier than Kiara.

"Val, give Kiara the phone, please." There's an unintended growl to my voice. Kiara's face appears on the screen; she's feigning indifference and half-smiling.

"What?" she says, provoking me.

"You know what. You know better than anyone else that when you're done somewhere, it's time to pack up and go. So don't sit there all high and mighty and replay an old narrative like I'm running, or whatever. I'm not running. I'm choosing to start a new life." That's the truth. I'm choosing not to live in the wake of sadness. To not sit around like some day-old leftovers.

Kiara stares at me, completely unimpressed, but then says, "Here's the thing. When we spoke, we promised each other that we wouldn't back down from telling each other the truth, even if it hurts to say or hear. That's how we are." I nod. "Well, you said you regretted not saying anything when you saw how things were playing out with Wren and me."

"Right? What's your point?" I ask defensively.

"You want to make me say it?" Kiara exchanges a glance with Val, who pops her face onto the screen.

"Say what?" I ask, my heart starting to pump harder.

"We know about you and Zin!" Val blurts out.

My face falls.

"We know everything." Val waves her hand to make a big circle. "Like all of it."

I don't know what they think they know, but I'm not falling into this trap.

"Yup," Kiara goes on. "One might say you aren't running toward this new life in Portugal." She air quotes *new life*. "You're running as far away from Zin as possible. If we don't call you out on it, you'll go. And then what?" She cocks her head. "Have you thought about what happens next?"

"Thank you for your concern," I start, letting her little speech roll off my shoulders. "But, although you two may think you know, you really don't."

"You're right," Kiara continues. "We don't know what it feels like to fall in love with your best friend only to have them etch you out of your life like you were—"

"—an afterthought," we say in unison.

Maybe they do know.

"What did she tell you?" I ask, pursing my lips. "You know what, it doesn't matter. You're right." Those words coming out of my mouth sound like a foreign language to me. "So what if I'm running? There are worse things I could do than move to a stunning beach town and, I don't know, maybe start painting again. Live a simpler, slower life, surrounded by water and good food."

"Sounds like a dream, actually," Val says with a smile. Kiara shoots her a look, and Val just shrugs. "What? You're saying that doesn't sound good?"

"Not. The. Point," Kiara says through gritted teeth. "Even if Portugal is a good idea, which it isn't," she puts up a finger, "come here first like we planned. Leave from Montreal. You promised." She starts to cry.

That's the thing about Kiara. One second she's this fierce scary human, the next she's this soft Squishmallow I just want to hug. I envy how she can access her emotions and show them so unfiltered. So raw.

I can see in her eyes that this isn't just about her being a good friend to me and showing me a mirror; it's that she needs a friend. I don't think I realized this visit meant that much to her.

When we spoke last, we went through all our issues with a fine-tooth comb. Nothing went unteased. We got through it all: How sorry I was that I failed her when she was at rock bottom. She apologized to me for how triggering it was to watch her drink so belligerently. I begged for forgiveness for how callous and self-centred (and heartless and unreliable and the list went on) it was for me to not reach out when she lost her baby. She completely broke me when she said that what hurt her the most wasn't that I wasn't there for her, it's that she didn't expect me to be.

That hit hard. What does it say about me that my best friends don't think I'll be there for them when they need me most? That's when Val told me I could make it up to them if I promised to visit for Christmas.

"I'm sorry, Kiara," I say, tears welling in my eyes. "Please understand." I hang my head low. "I'm not in a good place. Not in here." I point to my heart. "Not in here." I point to my head.

Val hands the phone to Kiara and disappears off-screen. Kiara and I sit staring at the screen, less than a foot away from each other's faces, yet worlds apart from understanding one another.

Val returns, swipes the phone from Kiara, and fills the screen with her smiling face, paper rustling in the background.

"Hear me out," she starts. She looks at Kiara and then back at me. "Both of you." She clears her throat and continues, "What if you don't come here next week— Ow!" Val turns to Kiara. I imagine she must have kicked her because Val bends over and appears to rub her leg or foot off-screen. "May I finish without being violently attacked, please?" She tilts her head toward Kiara, and Kiara rolls her eyes. "As I was saying, what if you don't come here for Christmas . . ." She winces, bracing herself for more violence. When Kiara remains still, she goes on. "But you agree to meet us in Rome for a redo of our tenth annual girls trip. You'll be like an hour away, so no excuse."

"I already told you I'm not going," Kiara says, and she folds her arms and leans back on their couch.

"Yeah, me neither." I shake my head. What are they not understanding? I will not come within two feet of Zinnia, and there's nothing that either of them can say or do to make me change my mind.

"Just drop it, Val, these trips are done as far as I'm concerned," Kiara adds.

"At least we agree to that," I say to Kiara with a nod.

"Okay, so . . ." Val props the phone up and lifts her hips to pull something out of her back pocket. Then she sits back down and says, "I hate to pull out the big guns, but our trips are far from over. It's in the contract."

"What contract?" I ask.

"When I was at my parents' the other day, I found an old scrapbook with a bunch of tickets and photos from past trips." The call pauses for a moment, and then Val and Kiara are back again. "I just sent you a photo of it by text. Did you get it?"

"Hold on one sec, I'm pulling it up . . ." I click open the photo, and Val's fancy cursive handwriting jolts me back to that afternoon in her yard, the night before Zin left for Juilliard and I left for Emily Carr. "I can't believe you kept this."

Kiara and I listen as Val begins to read:

> We promise that no matter where we are in the world, no matter what job we have, or how many babies we are collectively raising, that we, Valentina de la Vega, Kiara Campbell-Rothstein, Marie-Francine "Fay" Gauthier, and Zinnia Saad, will meet once a year, for a minimum four days, for an epic girls trip somewhere in the world. We solemnly promise that the last week of February is

reserved for the aforementioned trip, no ifs, no ands, no buts—except our fine butts. The rules are as follows:

1. The trip must take place in a new location every year.
2. The total cost of the flight and room must be no more than $1000 per person.
3. Every year, someone else picks the destination and that person is in charge of booking accommodations and city excursions.

We will make the world our own personal playground and stay friends forever and ever and ever. TILL DEATH DO US PART!!!

"See? Friends forever. We all signed it. You have to come," she declares, holding up the contract like she has just read out something that's actually legally binding.

"Val," I scoff. "You can't hold us to something we wrote over ten years ago. Things have changed."

"Let's just figure all this out when you come for Christmas, okay?" Val goes on. Obviously, she didn't hear when I said I'm not coming. Or if she heard, she's chosen not to register it. "My dad's making his famous turkey dinner, and Keeks and I will bring you to Le Jasmine, the best club ever." Val pouts her lips and nods her head.

Kiara's on my side. She sees the pain in my eyes. She knows that a two-day pitstop in Montreal, swept away by festivities and parties, is not what I need.

Because that's the thing. Running to or from isn't how I'm framing this. I'm going so I can be still for a while. Plant roots somewhere and create my own life, one where I choose myself.

"How about this," Val says. "Think about it." Her voice softens. "My dad always says, 'Don't make permanent decisions about temporary problems.' That's what this is, Fay, temporary."

"Sure," I say to appease her. "I'll keep that in mind."

"Promise to call while you're there!" Kiara grabs the phone. "Like, a weekly check-in." She's crying again. "Don't run from us too."

I hang up as the words *I love you* fade in the background.

Zinnia

LOS ANGELES, JANUARY

THE STORY I SOLD MYSELF WHEN WE MOVED TO CALIFORNIA WAS that it was the right choice for us as family, but the truth is, after almost five full months of living here, it was the right decision for me too. I can breathe better: the air is cleaner, the spaces are bigger, endless, even. Each never-ending boulevard makes my soul vibrate; there's room to grow here, for me to matter.

So, with a New Year comes new resolutions.

Resolution number one: Run every day. It's a commitment to my health, and it sets aside time for me to connect with myself. Which leads to my second goal . . .

Resolution number two: Don't sign up for every parent committee at Darla and Saul's school. I still do what I can, volunteering for the Halloween dance set-up and organizing book drives, but I resist the urge to then chair events and chaperone field trips. I throw my hat in the ring to get involved when it's driven by my desire rather than my guilt for not working. It also allows for more time to explore photography.

Resolution number three: Devote more time to my passion. I don't have a clear outcome in mind in my pursuit of photography. I mean, I know it's not to become the next Ansel Adams or Max Rive. I'm done being someone else; I only want to be me (that's another resolution).

But for now, photography is an outlet of self-exploration, a path to finding myself and slowly becoming that person.

Resolution number four: Figure out what to do about Adam.

Back in the Bahamas when I told Kiara about my affair, she said something that stuck with me: an affair is a symptom of something missing in your marriage.

At the time, I hated the thought of Fay being a symptom. She was love. My true love. No, Adam and I weren't the perfect couple. And yes, we let our lust for each other fade away like a forgotten blankie. Our relationship took a back seat not only to child-rearing but to my selfhood, something I didn't just resent him for, but for which I blamed him entirely. Now I realize those were convenient emotions to justify my affair.

When we moved to California, I stupidly thought that with Fay no longer in the picture, I could focus on Adam and rebuild a relationship where I might find happiness. But so far, that hasn't happened. Because while I may not have wanted to believe that Fay was a symptom, there's no denying she was a response to my unhealthy marriage.

Adam and I barely spend time together; his energy goes outward—to work and colleagues—while mine is focused inward on the home and our children. Our lives are delineated by the roles we play. Perhaps that works for some couples, but for us it just exacerbates my loneliness and this feeling that I don't matter. Where I used to blame him for holding me back, I've now reconciled that it's not his fault. He's still showing up the same way he always has, and it's on me for never saying anything. I've never made it known that I'm unhappy.

So, yes. Fay *was* a symptom. Not of my strained marriage but of my inability to access my voice. To communicate my needs.

So, I'm spending time reflecting on the changes I need to make. Combining resolution number four (figure out my marriage) with resolution number one (run) has been a practice of intentionally clearing my head so I can let the answer come to me.

Some days, when I run, I can reach a meditative state, my mind completely blank, just me and the sand beneath my feet. And some days, like today, each step is an active way to untangle the thoughts that consume me, the mess I created. Breathing in and out steadily as I run along the shoreline, salty air sticking to my skin, I try to empty my mind and allow myself to be fully immersed in the emotional landscape of my senses: the sun, the smell, the sound of waves crashing, birds flying overhead, my gaze fixed forward as I run. *Out here, I am untethered*, I tell myself. I have the freedom to feel my body unfettered by the elements, unbound by time.

I pull my phone out of my legging pocket to check my pace. Just as the screen lights up, my toe catches on a protruding rock, and I end up flat on my face.

My cheek is bleeding, my hands are chafed, and my mouth is filled with sand. I try to get up, but my legs are throbbing, so I sit still, panting, letting the ache wash over my body. I look around, and there are two young girls, one with a small frame, short, jet-black hair, and smooth, dark skin. High cheekbones and intense stare. Looks just like Fay. I smile at her.

She returns the friendly smile, walking over to me. "You okay?" she asks. The resemblance is uncanny. I must be imagining things.

"I'm fine," I smile again at not-Fay. "Thank you." She walks away, but Fay's face is still staring at me in my mind's eye.

Maybe this is a sign that I should reach out again—like how Val saw versions of me, and then *poof!* all was right with the world.

Nah, I think with a sigh, and I push the thought out of my mind.

I look back at the sand beneath me, lay back, and let my head rest against the ground. The thought of Fay being right here, ready to help me get back on my feet is exactly what went wrong with our relationship. It wasn't on equal footing. It was all about me. I don't want her to come back to me when I'm down—even if it is just a fall on a run—to help me. When Fay and I reconnect—if she'll ever talk to me again—I don't want it to be because I need her, but rather because I want her. She deserves that.

But still, I can't figure out if I miss girlfriend Fay or best friend Fay, and I don't know that it matters. I just miss her.

When Fay sent that final email telling me not to reach out, of course my first reaction was to reach out. I hit reply and started drafting my response, typing faster than I could think. But that was impulse. That was guilt. That was fear and loneliness. It wasn't respect, and that's what she was really asking for: for me to see her, to finally see her and respect her wishes. So, after I got my response out of my system, I deleted my draft in hopes that my silence would speak louder than my words.

But if I could fill those silences, it would be to tell her about everything I've learned in the months between us. Especially how right she was about pursuing photography. It's helped me get in tune with myself. Because behind my camera, I feel invigorated. Asserting myself every time I click the shutter closed, bridging this new self with the old self I had once known en pointe. I'd get in front of an audience, and the whole world knew I existed. On stage, I was present, people saw me, felt how powerful I was, how my body filled a room. I took up space.

In some ironic reality, I feel that same force behind the camera. Only my presence is known from my necessary absence. Two forces simultaneously at play, and that simple paradoxical truth fills me with strength and self-assurance. I don't have to be seen to know I am here.

I've been experimenting with movement the last couple of weeks. Trying to capture the energy and noise of the beach, but I've limited myself to black-and-white. It's easy to show the blue of the water—I want to feel it. The way the sea wraps around the world, expansive, perilous, unsuspecting, generous, fraught with a history that only the depths of the ocean floor will ever truly know.

Adam wouldn't get it. Fay would, though. She'd see how my images not only create my story but *are* my story. How each image is constructing myself, in every sense of the word. I hope she sees my feed and feels that my photos are talking directly to her.

This coffee reminds me of you.

This is where I fell and gazed up at you.

I push myself off the ground and make my way to standing. I dust off my legs and shake out my hands. I'm scraped up, wet, dirty, and bloody, but nothing that won't heal with time. I start to run again, this time with newfound conviction. Movement. Forward drive. Pounding the wet sand, kicking up water, I take out my phone and snap a photo of the path ahead. I try to capture the speed, people blurred in the background as a symbol of my movement and shaky focus—clarity in motion. Black and white, with just enough depth to give a point of view.

I post my photo to socials as an invitation, and I caption it: *resolution in progress: the road I travel is the one that calls to me.*

On my jog home, I smile at the commitment I've made to myself and I realize there's one major thing I need to do in order for my path to be completely clear.

I just don't know if I can fully commit to myself while I'm still half in with Adam . . .

I run faster and faster, and with every step, I find more and more conviction that I know what I need to do. If I want to live my truth, live a central role in my life, then I can no longer be a supporting character in Adam's.

I pull out my phone and text him: We need to talk.

"You look serious," Adam says as he walks down the stairs, joining me in the kitchen. He pulls out a chair and sits across from me.

I'm sitting, waiting with hands folded in my lap, two cups of tea in front of me. I slide one over to him.

"Thanks," he says as he reaches for the tea. He takes a sip and sets the cup down on the table. "I feel like I know what you want to talk about, and I just want to start by saying we can't leave California." He places his hands in prayer position. "You haven't given it a fair shot yet, Zin, and we said at least a year, maybe even two. I know you haven't made many friends, but it'll come. A few buddies from work have been saying that they want to get the wives together for, like, a dinner or something. That could be good." He nods reassuringly. "Geoff says his wife has a book club, you could joi—"

"No, it's none of that." I shake my head and pull at a dry cuticle on my thumb. "I appreciate that you're looking out for me. I like it here more than I thought was going to. It's . . ." I take a deep breath.

"What? What is it? Is this about Darla's speech therapy? Because I went to HR, they said that my insurance should cover it. I don't know why they sent that invoice. I'll put it on my list for tomorrow." He lifts up slightly to reach into his back pocket, pulling out his phone to take a note.

"Adam?" Another deep breath, but this time I close my eyes. There's no simple way to say what I'm going to say, and I know the second I say it out loud, it's going to change everything. Our relationship, our family, the way he sees me. It's time I come clean. I can't carry this lie around anymore. I open my eyes and look my husband in the eye. He's waiting for me to speak, scanning my face for the reason why I asked him to talk. Why I look so solemn. "I cheated on you," I say softly.

I watch as he processes what I said. His eyes search mine, and I stare back, waiting for it to sink in. That's when the colour drains from his face.

"Come again?" he says.

I scratch at a dry patch of alfredo sauce on the table, missed after last night's dinner cleanup. "I cheated on y—"

"Never mind, I heard you." He watches as I keep scratching. One patch, then another.

"Stop it," he says as he extends his hand and lays it on top of mine. "Stop cleaning and start talking. When?"

"Where do you want me to start?" I look him straight in the eye. I knew he would want the whole story. And I'm prepared to tell it. I just wasn't prepared for how overwhelmed I'd feel. My throat feels constricted, like I'm choking on my breath. My mind feels hazy and grey; everything I practised is gone, and all I see is a dirty table in front of me. I swallow and lower my shoulders away from my ears. "I'll tell you everything. But first—" I turn my palm up to hold his hand, but he pulls away "—I'm sorry."

"We're not there yet." We're not at apology; we're at anger. "Who? When? Start at the beginning, and don't stop until I say so." He stands up and walks over to the couch. He nods at the empty spot beside him, signalling I should join him.

I walk over to sit on the couch, leaving a good amount of space between us. I press my hands into my face, rubbing up and down. I stop, I let my hands fall to my lap, and I look up. In front of me is our mantle with several framed pictures of our kids displayed. I point to one of Darla at a dance recital. Tutu, pink leotard, sparkly tiara. "We could start there," I say. "I was twenty-two when we had her. Just a kid. I had a whole career ahead of me, or the promise of one at least." I turn to face him, pulling my knee onto the couch.

"I was only twenty-four when we had her, Zin, I know that part of the story. I was there, remember? Spare me the history lesson." His voice flares with anger, only not the screaming kind, the kind that is used to hide pain.

I'm shaking my head, trying to hold it together. I don't want to sound like I'm making excuses, but I don't know what else to say. I catch a tear as it rolls down my cheek, swiping it away as I attempt to start over.

But when I open my mouth, Adam interrupts. "I had to build a career while juggling a baby too, you know." He grabs my phone from my hand and shows me my screensaver. Our kids on Venice Beach having a picnic the weekend after we moved. He slides the screen open and starts scrolling through my camera to show me more pictures of our children. He thinks he's proving his point; little does he realize, he's proving mine.

"It's not the same, Adam." I try to pull my phone away, but he yanks it closer to his chest. "You got to focus on your career because I focused on this." I motion to our home, the pictures of our children.

He stops scrolling and clicks on a picture of me and Fay in cottage country. The photo fills the screen. From the look on his face, I can tell that all he sees is two best friends doing their best-friend thing. I grab the phone before he has a chance to realize that what he's really looking at is the two of us in our bathrobes, nuzzled up to each other while eating spaghetti in bed after making love for hours.

I shove my phone under my leg. "Adam. I—I love our family. It's not about them. I shouldn't have brought that up, it's just that you said start at the beginning, and I, I . . ." I'm fumbling to find my words. I take another deep breath and try again. "I had nothing growing up. I had a mother who bailed and a dad who gave up on me. I never in a million years dreamed that I could have all of this. Our beautiful family, two cars, a five-bedroom home. This is more than I could've ever asked for. But it just—"

"It wasn't enough," he says, lowering his head; anger disengaged, defensiveness in full swing.

"Please, let me talk." I lower my head down and take a deep breath, watching as my chest rises and falls. "What I'm trying to say is that I got lost in all of this."

"So, it's my fault you cheated?" He folds his arms across his chest.

"No, it's mine. I was so busy being Darla and Saul's mom that at some point, when I stopped to look up, I realized I was gone." I hold my hand over my heart as I let the tears flow freely. "But it's not your fault. None of it. I didn't know how to balance it all. How to be a mom without losing myself in the process. It's not you, Adam. I mean, yeah, for a while I blamed you. I thought maybe if you pushed me to do something or helped out more at home . . ." I wipe my tears and look at Adam. "But it's not your fault," I say again as I reach for his hand. This time, he lets me hold it. "You couldn't have known because I never told you."

I take another deep breath and reach for my phone. I open it back up to the photo of Fay and me and lay the phone face up between us.

"What are you showing me?" He looks at the photo and then looks up at me. Then it clicks. Me and Fay in bed not as friends: as lovers. "Fay?!" He grabs the phone to look closer. He's staring like he can't believe it. It was right under his nose, and he never saw it coming. He stands up and starts pacing. His wheels are turning as he rubs his temple, staring at the photo in disbelief. "With Fay? Your friend Fay? A woman?! The woman I welcome into our home? I break bread with? Our kids' godmother, for fuck's sake?! Zin! Fucking Fay? How long?

How long has this been going on? All those trips—wait, is this cottage country? When you went away to tell Fay we were moving?" He slumps back down on the couch, farther away from me. "I'm so fucking dumb."

"It started a little over a year ago, I guess." He looks at me. "But it's been over for months." I shift over to move closer to him, but he moves away and crosses his arms.

"That makes it better. Glad it's over," he responds sarcastically.

"I'm sorry." I take another deep breath. "I fell in love with my best friend. I didn't intend for that to happen. It wasn't my plan to hurt you. You think I wanted to ruin our family? To lie to you?"

"Poor you," he says bitingly.

"No, I didn't mean it like that." This isn't how I wanted this to go. "Adam, I'm sorry I cheated. I want you to know that. You're a great man, and you don't deserve this. I'm also sorry I didn't stop right away. I knew it was wrong, I knew it would hurt you, although, at the time I don't know that I thought about that. I was just thinking about how utterly broken I was inside. I tried to put it behind me. I ended it with her and, well, I don't know. I chose this, I chose us, I chose California and our family. I wanted to give us a second chance."

"And?" he asks with a deflated look on his face.

My chest swells with sadness as the tears fall slowly at first and then all at once. Adam is crying too.

"I thought maybe I'd find my way back to you, but I don't know, I feel like maybe we're even further apart now than before." I take a beat. "Adam, please know that it was never about not loving you. It's about learning to love myself."

"I stopped you from loving yourself? Is that what you're saying?" He's staring at me like the floor just caved in right under him. We sit in silence for a moment, and then he finally asks the question to end all questions: "So, we're done?"

I nod.

He pushes himself off the couch and walks away, moving slowly toward the kitchen. I watch as he takes a glass from the cupboard, steps toward the fridge, and pours himself water. He brings the glass to his mouth, drinking in gulps. When he's done, he sets the glass on the counter, pauses, and walks back toward the couch. He stops in front of me.

"You're leaving me for Fay?" he asks, looking for confirmation.

"No! No, Adam." I reach out to touch his hand, but he pulls back. "No. I'm not leaving you for Fay." I clarify one last time: "I think we should separate. But not for Fay." I stand up so that we're face to face. "If we're honest with each other, this—" I motion between us "—has been over for a long time."

I see a little tinge of compassion break through his face. A softening of his brow, his mouth starting to relax. Honesty, as it turns out, might save me a lot of heartache.

"I love you, Zin." He cups my face. "I don't know that I feel the same way." I take a step, closing the gap between us. Reaching my hands behind his neck, he inches forward, letting me hold him. He cries into my shoulder, me into his chest.

"Fay?" he asks as he pulls away. This time when he says her name, he's processing the information rather than resisting it.

I nod.

He walks back to the couch and sits down again. I join him, our cups of tea in hand.

"I don't think your life stopped by the way," he starts as I sit down. "It just became about someone other than you. You say it like it's a bad thing that you gave your time to those kids."

"Not a bad thing, Adam. But it consumed me completely."

We keep talking like that for hours: Adam asking questions—not with prosecution but with curiosity, trying to figure out where and why things went wrong—and me, doing the best I can to string my story together so I can give him the information he needs to catch up. And, hopefully, to move forward . . . separately.

Adam and I have had multiple conversations over the last few weeks about how to proceed. We know a few things for sure—like we are going to get divorced, and it's going to be friendly—but there are still so many details to iron out—how to tell the kids, when and where one of us will move, how all of this is going to play out.

We also decided that it's best that he sleep in the guest room. A piece of information I forget every morning when I wake up and roll over to his empty, cold side of the bed.

The real impact of my mother leaving and how I've been on an eternal search for happiness, for home, has come up a lot during some of my and Adam's discussions. I thought, simply, that home was where the heart is, and I always interpreted that as being in love with someone. But it's more complex than that. In theory, it would be beautiful to find home in someone else, the heart of another, but that can only happen when you create a home within yourself.

My focus for the next few months needs to be on me and my family. Together, Adam and I will get through this and find a healthy balance where all of us—Adam, Darla, Saul, and I—can matter.

Tonight, to show his support, Adam is attending an event my photography instructor is throwing. My self-portrait will be exhibited along with the work of a few other of her standout students. It took me weeks of hard work and many failed attempts to finally finish my self-portrait, but I'm proud of how it came out. It's shot from above and has two pairs of baby shoes, worn-in pointe shoes tied together, a pair of sneakers flung on their sides, and my bare feet. It reflects a perspective I didn't realize I'd been searching for—a grounded view of all that makes me who I am.

A small four-by-four-inch canvas that reminds me I have my whole life ahead of me to figure out who I am becoming.

I walk downstairs and Adam is already awake; he's helping out with breakfast, which is a commitment he's made to me. He wants to be more present so that we can share the load.

"Good morning." I smile as I walk over to the coffee machine. I press the button and watch it flash green. "Can I help with breakfast?"

"No, I'm all good. But your phone's been blowing up, by the way," he says over his shoulder as he flips an omelet.

"Sorry," I say as I reach for it. "Probably my instructor. She wants me to help hang some pieces."

Or maybe it's Fay. I know Val told her about the split, so maybe, just maybe, she's reaching out to see how I'm doing. Stranger things have happened. I shake out the thought as I turn my phone over and see that I have eleven missed calls from Kiara.

"It's Kiara," I say to Adam, smiling as I kiss the tops of my kids' heads and walk over to the couch to call her back.

Why would she call eleven times at seven in the morning? I know she's worried about me, but this is excessive, even for her.

I sit down on the couch and click her number.

She picks up before it even rings.

"Zin?" she says, her voice trembling.

"Is everything all right?" I ask, immediately concerned.

"No," she replies. "Eduardo died last night."

PART 3

Home

Valentina

MONTREAL, FEBRUARY

WHEN THE PERSON YOU LOVE MORE THAN THE WHOLE WIDE world dies, a part of you dies too.

This past year, I've confronted life in so many ways. I've scrutinized its purpose, dissected its significance, and challenged its boundaries. I lost all my friends, only to rediscover each relationship in a more profound way. I ruined my chance at true love, but ultimately I learned that love is as much about timing as it is about readiness. Jack may have been the right person, but I was the wrong version of myself. I peeled back layers I didn't know I had when I took over Valentina's, and it taught me that with enough passion and tenacity, I can forge my own path and make my own dreams come true. Yet despite the whirlwind of ups and downs I've gone through this year, today, as I sit at my father's funeral, I'm confronted with life in a whole other way. How do I begin to make sense of my life, my world, without my father in it?

With my father gone, my life feels completely empty, devoid of meaning; I feel like I'm free-floating, uncertain, unanchored, falling into the abyss.

Nothing can prepare you for the void.

Like a flash storm, it floods right in and pulls you under. Just like that, you're drowning—water all around you, arms flailing, gasping for air—and all you want to do is fight, swim as hard as you can to find a way back to shore, but no matter how hard you kick, you aren't moving. Adrift, all sense of direction is lost in an endless sea of grief.

How could he be so alive only to go to sleep and never wake up?

A week ago today. That was the last time I saw him. I kissed him goodbye on his cheek as I left his house to grab a cab home. I teased him for acting like the neighbourhood watch as he stood in the doorway waving to me. "Let me know when you get home, mi'ja." He stood there, door wide open in the freezing cold, making sure I got into the car safely.

"Of course, always. ¡Te amo!" I yelled from the cab as I closed the door behind me.

"To the far side," he replied, waving happily.

I texted him as I promised, letting him know I was home, and he replied with *un beso*. How was I to know that would be his last kiss?

When I woke up the next morning, my mother called to tell me he was gone.

My dad was gone.

The funeral is beautiful, exactly how my dad would have wanted it. The whole room is filled with loved ones: aunts, uncles, cousins, business associates, employees, and so many friends from different pockets of his life. Right by his coffin is a photo of him in our living room. It was taken eleven years ago. I had just finished my summer interning with Zin at Valentina's, and my dad threw us a celebratory dinner. We were having one of our after-dinner dance parties, a de la Vega tradition. My dad leading the conga line, as always. He's smiling in the picture, exactly how he'd want to be remembered: the life of every party.

My mom, as expected, has not been in her right mind all week. So I had to find a way to push past my pain and muscle through to plan the funeral. But planning how to honour my dad has felt like a nearly impossible feat. I had to choose the coffin he would be lowered in, the bed where he would lie, the flowers that would adorn the funeral home, and the photo to display beside the coffin. I found the deference within to get through it all. Then came the decision of what music to play during the ceremony. That was the hardest decision of all. My dad would've wanted the music to be perfect.

It took me three full hours to go through his music library. It was nearly impossible to choose between something up-tempo and full of life—because that was Papá—or something elegiac, more poetic, something that could capture both the magnitude of his life and the weight of the loss. Over the years, my dad had given me countless golden tokens of wisdom—Eduardo-isms, that's what he called his adages—but the one that I'll keep closest to my heart is *instead of thinking about living, mi'ja, just live. Baila, baila, baila.* He knows more than anyone that I can get stuck in an endless loop of overthinking, can get paralyzed by the weight of decision. So his advice to me was to dance because, in his mind, the only way to savour this life is to move through it moment by moment. That's why I finally decided on the Gipsy Kings. It's the last concert he went to with my mom where they spent the night wrapped in each other's arms dancing the night away. His favourite song is the one about how the moon lights up the dark sky, an instrumental flamenco rumba, a rhythmic beat that carries both hope and yearning, love and grief.

While listening to it play during the ceremony, I can hardly contain the gut-wrenching thought that my dad would have loved his funeral. He would've wanted to be there.

Kiara ensured everyone got the news. Fay got here a few days ago, and Zin flew in today. They are both staying for the entire novena, nine days of mourning, to honour Eduardo. This is the first time they're seeing each other. They're on their best behaviour for my sake, but I know they're both itching with the discomfort of being this close. They are huddled around each other at the after-service reception, each with a face longer than the other as they watch me. Kiara's using her body as a physical buffer between Zin and Fay.

My mother and I are sitting on a pale yellow couch at the back of the room, waiting as people line up to wish us their condolences, sharing memories about my dad, and filling in gaps in our knowledge with stories, stretching his life past the thirty-one years I've known him. More memories to hold on to, more context of who he was outside the home, more tearful, sombre faces to prove how many people loved him.

Eloise is next in line. She holds my mother's hands, kneeling by her side. She looks over to me and says, "Your eulogy was beautiful," and the look in her eye makes me burst into another wave of tears.

From across the room, Fay mouths *you okay?* I shake my head slightly, chin quivering. I don't think I'll ever be okay again.

After Eloise and I hug, I decide it's time for a break. I lean into my mom to tell her I'm going to get us something to drink, but when I stand up, I bump into the next person in line.

Jack.

He grabs my shoulders to keep from knocking me over, and without exchanging so much as a word, he pulls me in. Like a silent movie, he slowly, but firmly, wraps his arms around me, squeezing me tight. My arms lay limp by my sides at first, but then, once I settle into his embrace, I feel my chest deflate, and I wrap my arms around his waist. He smells like Cool Water. Familiar and comforting, just what I need right now.

When we finally peel apart, I keep my head down, avoiding his gaze. A million thoughts run through my head, but none of them makes sense. It's all mush. I stare at the carpet beneath my feet like I'm being paid to count the flowers in the pattern. Eventually, I ask, "How'd you find out?"

"Kiara," he says softly.

She really did rally the troops.

"Thanks for coming," I whisper. I look up and breathe him in. "I didn't think you'd—"

"I know what you thought." He places a hand on my shoulder, the sides of his mouth curling up in a tiny smile. "But this is your dad." His attention veers toward my mom behind me, and his face falls again. He bends over and whispers something to her, then he takes my hand and weaves me through the crowd of people.

"He would've loved this," Jack whispers once we get to the back corner of the room.

I nod. "Yeah." I look around. "So many people are here. It's a little overwhelming." I cup my face in my hands. No tears left to cry, I stand there quietly and try to calm my breath. Jack places a hand on my back and caresses me gently. "I can't believe he's gone. Sixty-four . . ." I choke back my tears.

Jack mumbles, "But he lived the life of ten men." My dad used to say that like it was his badge of honour.

"Jack? You wanna go for a walk?" I look down and straighten out my merlot crepe midi dress.

Without hesitation, he grabs my hand and says, "Sure." He leads me out of the room through the side door. Neither of us has a jacket on, and even though it's well below zero, neither of us flinches from the cold when we step outside. The crunch of snow underfoot echoes in the wide open field.

"How you been?" he asks sincerely as we walk side by side.

"Honestly? I've been pretty okay up until this." I take a deep breath. "How are you?" I ask, staring in front of us. "How's Poppy?"

"We—" He shakes his head as if to say it's over.

Oh.

He stops walking and turns his body toward mine. Reaching out his arms to hold me, his face is filled with longing. "Val? I read—"

"My letter?" I finish. He nods, and I'm all of a sudden overly aware of my face. I want to cry, but my cheeks betray me. I'm blushing for sure because I can feel I'm on fire.

"I heard our song the other day," he starts. "It came on while I was in line at a coffee shop on my way to work. When I heard Stevie Nicks hit that first note, the image of us at Zin's wedding came to my mind. Remember?" He smiles.

I do. We should have been on the dance floor celebrating my best friend's nuptials, but instead Jack and I were fighting outside the hall. It was the biggest—and only—fight we'd ever had. University was done, we both had jobs lined up, and he wanted to move our relationship to the next level. He was ready to move in together, but I wasn't. The timing just wasn't right. I remember the precise moment I turned to walk away from him, our song came on. Tears welled in my eyes, I tried to run, but he caught me by my wrist and whipped me around. "How's that for timing?" he said with a smile so charming, so romantic . . . He took me in his arms, right there, and we rocked back and forth for six and a half minutes.

I sigh. "Jack—"

"No, let me finish." He lifts his hand for me to stop. He takes a step closer to me and goes on. "I pressured you to move faster than you were ready. I did it at Zinnia's wedding, and I did it again when I proposed." He pauses, and we hold each other's gaze. I open my mouth to speak, but he continues. "I knew it was bad timing when I proposed, I mean," he combs his fingers through his hair, "this is bad timing too." He chuckles self-consciously. I shake my head to urge him to continue. Breath bated, I'm waiting for him to say what he came here to say. "I never stopped to think that maybe that's all it was. It hurts like hell that you thought you needed to lie about cheating just to get out of a life with me, but I wish I had paid more attention to what you were going through and how maybe, like you wrote, it was all a cry for help. I didn't understand how much you were hurting; I just saw my desire to forge a life with you. Maybe even a part of me was scared I was losing you, so instead of giving you space, I held on too tight. I set myself up to get hurt, and I've spent every day regretting it because, Val," he cups my face, "I realized that life means nothing without you. You wanted more sparkle, or whatever it is you said we lacked, but to me, you've always sparkled. You dazzle me. And if I can promise you one thing, it's that I can do more than sparkle. Sparkles are an optical illusion. A trick of the eye. They flicker, and then they fizzle out. What I'll give you is something that lasts forever." He takes a step closer to me and puts his hands on my arms. "Because try as I might to move on, try as I might to etch you out of my heart, you're there. You're always there.

I've never loved anyone like I love you, and I never will. And I know today, today of all days, is not the time to be telling you all this, but seeing you there, in the pew, looking lost and filled with grief, I knew where I needed to be sitting, and it wasn't at the back of the room, it was by your side, holding your hand. That's where I belong. Being strong for you, holding your pain so you can fall apart. That's what I want to do. That's who I want to be for you."

The cold wind brushes along my exposed skin, sending a shiver down my spine. Jack continues to hold my arms as he finishes speaking to me, and I just stand there, shocked, statue-still, gazing into his eyes, feeling every word he speaks rush through my body. He loosens his hands and slides them up my back to draw me closer to him. I'm frozen in place, no clue what to think, too numb to form a coherent sentence.

He stares at me expectantly and adds, "You don't have to have an answer now—" he points to the chapel "—not here, not like this—but I'd like to see you again."

I take a deep breath. There are so many things I want to say, but my head is spinning. I want to tell Jack that he's right, it was never us I said no to, it was the timing. It's what keeps coming up for us, and maybe there's a reason.

I feel stretched emotionally beyond what any human can handle, too overwhelmed to speak. Even if I tried, I'd probably stutter and blubber and fall to pieces.

Instead, I place my cold hand on his cheek, look him in the eye, and say, "I should check on my mom," and I start to walk away.

"Of course," he says despondently.

It's 5 p.m. and pitch-black outside when we finally leave the funeral home. All I want to do right now is climb into bed and make the world disappear, but instead, I'm standing in the freezing cold, listening to Kiara explain to Zin why sleeping at a hotel is not an option. Everything from *Val needs us* and *you two need to kiss and make up* to *it's freezing, so get in the car or I'll leave you here.*

I love her so much right now.

"You guys fight all you want, but I'm getting in," I say, and I break up our little huddle to get into the car. "Kiara," I say as I look at her from the passenger seat, "drop me off at my parents', please. Zin, you take my room, and Fay, you sleep with Keeks."

"I'm fine on the couch," Fay says. She walks around the car and climbs into the back seat. "What?" She looks at Kiara who is giving her a Wild West stare-down from the driver's seat. "You snore."

Kiara and I both roll our eyes and smile. "It's true, you do," I say, and I look back to Fay. "Either way, I think I'll stay with my mom tonight. She'll be all alone. I want to be there."

"Are you sure?" Zin says as she finally climbs into the back too. "I don't want to make you—"

"I'm very sure. Now, let's go." I should be more annoyed by their shenanigans, but it brings juxtaposition to my day, balancing heaviness with the absurd.

Everyone buckles up, and we start down the road, which means I'm one step closer to my bed. I turn back and glimpse Fay and Zin both glued to either end of the back seat.

"Let's put on some music," Kiara says, scrolling through her playlist. "We Are Young" by Fun comes through the speakers. "Nothing like a good rallying cry." She winks at me.

Even though my world has undoubtedly been altered forever, in some ways, some things never change. Just four friends driving through our city streets as we hum along to music. Despite the ache in my heart, I feel undeniably grateful. In my moment of need, my friends are here by my side, surrounding me with love. Each one of my girls brings me a glimmer of hope that my dad was right: live in and for the moment—that is all we have.

"Love you girls." I blow kisses to each of them as Kiara pulls up to my parents' house. "We'll have breakfast together tomorrow? We can go to Sweetie's?" Kiara nods, and Fay and Zin echo with a yes from the back seat.

"Pick me up for nine?" I lean over to kiss Kiara on the cheek. "And don't park illegally. My mom'll kill you if you get her car towed. Love you." I close the door and send kisses into the visible winter air.

When I walk into the house, there's an eerie feeling. Normally when I go over, both my parents are there to greet me, the scent of dinner wafting from the kitchen, music playing, all signs of life being lived in this shared space. But today I'm surrounded by darkness. The lights are off, no one is home, it smells stale, and it's way too quiet. It feels strange. Maybe it was a bad idea to separate from my friends. I don't want to be alone tonight.

I pull out my phone and open a new message box.

Want to come over? I'm at my parents'

A reply comes in instantly: I'm just around the corner.

I go over to the front door and peek out through its small square window as I wait.

Under the street light, a shadow emerges and spills across my snowy driveway.

Jack's here. He steps onto the walkway, and before he has a chance to knock, I swing the door open.

Without a word, I pull him into me, my hands on his frozen cheeks, his arms wrapped around my waist. We stand like that, in the doorway, lips so close I can feel his breath on my face. The magnetic charge of our touch surges through my body and creates a shock as our lips crash together. Jack's right: it's not sparkle, it's fire.

I want to pull away to tell him that if we spend our lives waiting for the right timing, then we'll miss the chance to write our love story. I want to tell him I love him, and I will love him forever, unbound by the rules of any clock. I feel alive in his arms and can't stop kissing him.

In this moment, where I'd normally want words and reason, plans and promises, I let it all go and just live.

Kiara

"YOU GUYS HUNGRY? SHOULD WE ORDER PIZZA?" I LOOK IN THE back seat at a red light, and the two of them have grown even further apart, if that's possible. They are sitting slammed against their respective doors, at opposite sides of the car, staring out their windows. You could fit a family of eight between them. Neither one answers me. "Or, maybe not . . ."

I whistle to amplify the awkwardness, but after a few more seconds of non-response, the discomfort compels me to pull over. I swerve the car to the side of the road and turn around to face them.

"Okay, listen up, this is uncomfortable for all of us, so why doesn't one of you hop in front so I don't feel like the Uber driver, or you can get out here and walk your cold asses home."

I flick the unlock button so they know I'm serious.

"For real, get out," I say.

They exchange a look as Zin makes a move to open her door, letting a biting cold enter the car. "I'd like to talk, if you're ready." She swivels around so she's facing Fay, but Fay doesn't answer. "Fay?" A gust of wind sweeps the car at avalanche speed, shutting the door.

Startled, Zin jumps forward. "Fuck this city!" She pulls her coat—or, more precisely, the coat Val lent her—more tightly to her chest and rubs her hands together. "Or we could sit in this freezing car, and

I could just listen while you yell at me." Fay looks at her, and the two of them stay locked like that for a moment. "Just talk to me, please," Zin implores.

"Fine," Fay surrenders, but through tight lips. "But you're dropping us off at a restaurant," she directs me. "It's like minus thirty and squalling outside. I'm not walking. Taj isn't far, good?"

"Okey-dokey," I say and smile. I can't believe that worked. "Next stop, Taj." I drive a couple more blocks to the side street where the best Indian restaurant in town is tucked away.

When we get there, I hand them a key to the apartment. "See you *both* at home," I warn, as though there was a chance only one of them would return.

They nod, throw their hoods over their heads, and then, swiftly, make a run for it, braving the elements all the way to the front door of the restaurant.

I watch as Fay opens the door for Zin, and when they've both vanished from sight, I drive off. If I had to place bets on what I think will play out tonight, it's this: Fay's anger has dissipated under the Cascais sun, so she may show Zin more compassion, but it's only skin deep. Because she's still very hurt. It won't be taking the moral high ground, and it won't be a burn-me-once attitude. No, instead I think she'll do and say whatever it is she needs to in order to get through this meal—and the next eight days—and then they will return to their separate lives, drifting further away from true reconciliation.

If Zinnia had her way, they'd both apologize, kiss, and make up. She's changed a lot these past months and truly grown into herself. She's got a self-assuredness that I don't recognize in her, and although she may shoulder most of the blame, in an effort to keep moving forward, she won't let Fay trudge the past into the present. At least, that's what I hope.

If I've learned anything this past year, no one person alone can create a dynamic. Although one side may trigger a situation, it's all reaction from there. We act as foils, matching energy with energy, tension with tension. Only when one side lowers their guard can the cycle break and maybe, just maybe, a new dynamic take shape.

What I would give to be a fly on that restaurant wall right now.

Actually, there's also the chance that they jump down each other's throats and naan goes flying, in which case, I'd rather be curled up in bed watching movies.

When I get home, I step into my kitchen, my hands finding their way to my hips as I take a hero's breath. With a deep exhale, I allow the weight of the day to move through me and release.

Today has been relentless, and keeping it together for Val is no small feat. Especially since, inside, I'm crumbling too. Eduardo's love showed no bounds, which is partly why his death cuts so deep. He was a great man, so great in fact, that sometimes I forgot he was a mere mortal. But that's not why his loss is so profound. I think it reminded me that life is fragile. You can make plans for the future, you can dream of tomorrow, but just like that, a snap of the finger, from one second to the next, it can all be gone.

I brush my fingertips to my belly and let out a long, weighted exhale.

In a commitment to indulge in the small pleasures in life, I walk over to the fridge to grab sustenance: leftover Chinese, a bag of chips, and a pint of double chocolate caramel ice cream. I set myself up on my bed, flick on the TV, and spend the better part of an hour watching trailers, which, undeniably, is as much a form of entertainment as a two-hour movie. Just as I'm about to click into *Honey*, my phone buzzes in my back pocket. It better not be one of the girls asking me to come get them at the restaurant. I'll die if I have to go back out into the cold.

It's Frankie. I smile as I read his short but apt message:

Movie?

You read my mind, I reply. Video or text?

Within seconds, my phone is ringing, Frankie on the other end.

"Hey beautiful, how you doing?" His soft, syrupy voice envelops me instantly. He's sitting on a lounge chair on his balcony, and I can see from the shoulders up that he's got his shirt off.

"It was a hard day, but I'm here now, so . . ." I smile.

"Val's dad's funeral was today, right? We can talk about that, if you want. No need for a movie. You know that's just my excuse so I can see you."

I blush and shake my head. "There's nothing to say, really. But if I did wanna talk, you'd be the person I'd want to talk to."

"Back atcha." He winks. "So, what are we watching?"

"Nothing serious. Funny and light. I was thinking *Honey*."

"Hmm, how about something with a little romance?" He raises his brow, and my stomach flips. Even though we've become real friends over the past months, there's no denying that every time we talk he makes me swoon like a teenage girl at a Shawn Mendes concert.

"Okay." I look up at the ceiling to scan through the menu of movies in my head. I've got them better sorted than Netflix. "We could do *Dirty Dancing*?" I raise a brow.

The mere thought of trying to sit through some of those steamy scenes with Frankie on my screen watching my reaction might be too outside my comfort zone. I feel a tingle between my legs just thinking about it. I quiver and shake, pushing the thought out of my mind.

"Damn!" He throws his head back and lowers his phone. I catch a glimpse of his bare stomach . . . all abs.

"Maybe *Step Up* instead," I suggest.

"How about you tell me more about what just happened over there?" His hoarse voice lowers into a whisper, luring me back into my illicit thoughts.

His perceptiveness is bang on. So attentive. I barely have time to process a little body quiver, and he's already pointing it out, with flirty energy no less. I take a deep breath and sigh. Biting my lip, I lower my head, keeping my eyes focused on his face. I pull out my hair tie and let my curls fall loose. "I was thinking about how it might be uncomfortable to sit through the scene when Baby goes to Johnny's room and finds him there, shirtless, like you are now, music playing, candles going, all sexy and steamy. Kissing his bare back and moving together in perfect synch . . ."

"Sexy and steamy, huh?" He dips her back and kisses her chest, his hand leading the way to her back, slipping down to her pants. "I know the scene well." Now Frankie is licking his lips.

My breath quickens as the pulsing between my legs gets too hard to ignore. I close my eyes and smile faintly, thinking about Frankie's hand caressing my body and finding its way to the heat throbbing in my pants.

"Kiara?" he asks softly.

"Mmhm?"

"Can I tell you something that's been on my mind ever since that first day I met you at the pool?"

I nod. The piercing look in his eyes penetrates right through my soul.

"I really like you." He stretches out *really*, working his lips and tongue around each drawn-out syllable.

I never thought I'd hear those words. I mean, he called me exquisite way back when we first started talking, but we friend-zoned somewhere back in September. He's become someone I look forward to spending time with in a platonic way. I mean how else can it be when our relationship depends on whether his Wi-Fi will hold up? Not to mention the ocean between us.

Something feels different tonight though.

The energy . . .

"Why don't you show me where Johnny puts his hands?" I surprise myself at the suggestion, but just as the words leave my mouth, I know there's nothing else I'd rather do right now than share this moment with Frankie.

I lick my lips to entice the offer, but he doesn't need luring. He sets his phone down and adjusts the lens so I can see his whole body. He could double for Apollo he's so hot.

I prop my phone up as well, leaning it against the lamp on my nightstand so he can see my face and the top half of my body.

He slowly moves his hands toward his pants and says, "Then, as he kisses her chest, he lifts her arms and takes off her white shirt."

As instructed, I remove my sweater and unclip my bra. I move my hands slowly and softly around to remove the straps and cover my breasts. He's watching me, eyes squinting with intensity and focus. Shyly, I begin to caress myself, fingers tracing the outline of each nipple. "And then?" I stare into the phone as I slowly let one hand move down.

"And then, he kneels at her belly . . ." I reach down and raise my hips as I slip my hands down my pants. "Kissing every inch of her along the way . . ." My head falls back, and I take a big, deep breath.

"Are you joining me?" I ask.

He stands up, and his face disappears from the screen. All I see is body. He pulls at a string, and in one swoop his linen pants drop to the floor. His relaxed beach attire is way sexier than my cozy Roots sweatpants and tube socks, but that's off-screen. He can't see those. I manage to stop staring just in time for his face to reappear. He sits back down and the screen is filled with his bronzed naked body, blue sky all around.

"Where were we?" he asks as he gently begins to stroke himself.

"Right. Here," I reply, letting my jaw open as I reach between my legs. Dripping with wetness, I part my lips and start with two fingers in a circular motion. He is stroking himself slowly. We find a synchronized rhythm, and it feels like we are moving together, almost as though we are touching each other, despite the fact that there is a screen between us.

Our eyes are locked. I can feel him inside of me as I clench with ecstasy. I move faster to keep up with his pace, and I can tell he's getting closer, stroking with growing intensity. I get wetter and wetter from the pressure of my fingers. I slip inside and gasp for air as I orgasm. Then he moans out. We are both panting, bodies tingling and quaking. My breath slows, and I sigh softly.

"Wow," I whisper.

"Wow," he repeats.

"That was . . ."

"You are exquisite."

I smile. There's that word again. I look into the screen and see him looking at me. Through his eyes, I see what he sees.

I am exquisite.

"I can't believe we just did that!" I say sheepishly. Not an ounce of regret, just release and connection.

"I can. I've been waiting to do that to you since we met." He takes the words out of my mouth. "Well, I've been waiting to do that to you with my own hands. Touch your lips on mine . . . What do you say?"

His question is like an invitation, but I'm not sure if he's asking me for round two right now or if he wants to meet up. "What do you mean?" I ask so I don't jump the gun. Although, my facial expression is certainly not hiding my excitement.

"How cold *is* Montreal?" He pronounces it *Mon*-treal, just like a non-*Mon*trealer would.

He means meet up. The invitation both frightens and exhilarates me.

"Freezing!" I exclaim, then, instinctively, I add, "But I would keep you warm."

"I bet you would."

We stay locked in what feels like an unending staring contest. A long pause, bloated with possibility.

My heart is pulling me toward Frankie. This man who lifted me out of the trenches with his kindness and compassion. My gut is telling me I need more time. It's hardly been six months since I left Wren, and I don't feel whole yet.

Wren eroded so much of who I was. He chipped away at me, and rebuilding myself—to break the *toxic bond*, or whatever my therapist called it—has required much more conscious effort than I had anticipated. I lost myself in that relationship, and I'm only now in the process of putting Kiara back together. Despite my unquestionable feelings for Frankie—this incredible specimen of a man who is not only a feast for the eyes but chicken soup for the soul—I'm not ready to *like him* like him. Sharing a movie at a safe distance, that's what feels right for now.

I've learned the hard way that a broken heart breaks hearts; I'm in no condition to give myself to someone else yet. Although doing what we just did through the safety of our screens, each in our own homes, in different countries, is definitely something I'd like to do again.

"I'd love that, Frankie." I pull the blanket over my bare body and bring the phone closer to my face. "But it's still too soon." Saying no is the right thing to do. "Is that okay?" I wince, holding my breath waiting for him to be upset and tell me that I led him on. Maybe call me a few names and hang up on me.

But in true Frankie form, he smiles and clicks his tongue against his teeth. "I like you Kiara. I'll wait forever and a day for you to be ready."

My whole body tingles.

Fay

AS WE WALK INTO THE RESTAURANT, THE INTENSE SCENT OF CURRY and cardamom hits me in the face, dulling all my other senses, which is good because until this moment my eyes have been burning a hole in the back of Zin's head, my mouth is drier than the Sahara, my fingers are tingling three notches from numbness, and my brain is going berserk.

In the thirty seconds it took us to step out of the car and into the restaurant, I've played out multiple boxing match scenarios, each ending with a knockout. Me hitting the mat. Not Zin.

I've had months to process how things went down between us. Months to forgive and move on. Months to sift through my memory and see where it all went wrong. If there were signs I missed them all. In every version of the past, I'm the fool who leaves the ring two teeth shy of a set.

It still feels so raw. Even with all those months to mend my heart, it all went out the window the second I saw her.

I look at Zin, who is standing a foot in front of me, reticently picking at her cuticles.

"You want to find another place?" I ask as I take a step forward to stand by her side. Indian food is not really her jam, but if the smell is too much for her, she doesn't show it.

Zin shakes her head and gives me a half smile. "It's fine." She swallows.

"For two?" the host asks.

"Yeah, just us," I confirm. "Could we maybe sit at the back there?" I point to a two-person table in the corner of the restaurant, way out of earshot from the next closest table. The only thing more uncomfortable than our impending conversation is the idea of having an audience.

"Great. Follow me." He grabs two menus and leads us to our table. "Your waiter will be right with you," he says as he rests the menus on our plates. He helps Zin out of her coat and pulls out her chair for her. He makes his way to my chair to help me in, but I wave him away, placing my coat on the back and sitting down.

The clatter of cutlery and murmurs fill the dining room, amplifying the silence between us. I reach for the glass of water, anxiously keeping my hands busy.

Zinnia's eyes dart around the room and come back to her menu, her nervous energy manifesting in napkin fussing, cuticle picking, minor chair adjustments, and fake menu reading. I try to interpret the emotions displayed on her face. Is it guilt? Regret? Remorse? I can't tell.

I know what she's going to say. I know it's going to be a mélange of *I shoulda this, I shoulda that, please forgive me*, which only further exacerbates the unbearable tension manifesting in my neck.

I shouldn't have agreed to this, yet here we are.

We start talking at the same time.

"Thanks for—" she says.

"Go ahead, say—" I begin.

"Sorry, you go," she says and tucks a curl behind her ear.

"No." I purse my lips, my voice calm but tinged with a hint of bitterness and steely resolve. "You have the floor. Go ahead, explain yourself."

With a pained expression in her eyes, shoulders hunched, she rests her hands in her lap and takes a deep breath.

More silence ensues.

"Well?" I huff. "Don't just sit there. Say something." A mix of victim and martyr all at once, her taciturn demeanour is amplifying my frustration.

"You're so mad at me," she says.

I nod and reach for my water again. Way to state the obvious.

"I'm sorry, Fay." She keeps her head hanging low, though she's looking up at me. "There's nothing else for me to say. What I did was abhorrent. Not a day goes by that I don't regret it. Regret leaving you. Regret not telling you. Regret all of it." Her voice is shaky, and I can tell she's being sincere, but owning up to what she did isn't enough. I want to know the *why* of all of it. Why she kissed me that night. Why she changed the terms of our friendship. Why she kept secrets from me. Secrets that would inevitably break us apart and break me into a million little pieces.

"So why'd you do it?" I ask. "Why'd you let me love you?"

"I dunno." She shakes her head and begins to cry.

She's had months to think about it, to think about what she would say to me. The best she can come up with is *I dunno*?

"You know what? I don't think we should do this." I push my chair out and nearly topple over the waiter who is now at our table.

"Are you ready to order?" he asks, pen and paper in hand.

Zin tilts her head to look at me, her face begging for me to stay. "Please, Fay. I have a lot I want to say to you. I'm just nervous. Sit down. You must be famished. The least we can do is eat together."

Before I decide whether I'll stay, Zinnia orders for us: one tikka masala, one lamb curry, and one sag paneer. Two naan and some mango chutney with papadum to start.

"Fine." I pull out my chair to sit back down. "I'll stay."

"Did you enjoy Istanbul?" Zin asks, placing a napkin on her lap.

"Wow, Zin. You really asking that?"

"Yeah, why? Didn't you have a good time?" She's acting dumb, but I know exactly what she's after.

"I did. It is beautiful. Lonely." I place my hands on the table. "Does that answer your question?"

"That's not . . ." She looks down at her hands. "You didn't see Aiyla then?"

"Zin, what the fuck? Of course I didn't. I didn't travel halfway across the world with a broken heart for a one-night hookup. Is that what you think of me?" My voice is louder than I intended, calling attention from patrons at tables around us. I take a breath. "I went there for work. A decision made easier because my girlfriend and best friend in the entire fucking world up and left me like I was yesterday's trash and didn't have enough fucking respect to look me in the eye and let me know that she was leaving. How about that?"

"It was a stupid question. I'm sorry." She looks at me, eyes downturned. "And Portugal?"

I take a few calming deep breaths. She said she has so much to tell me; meanwhile, she's giving me the run-around and masking it as two old friends catching up.

"Zin, can you tell me whatever it is you came here to say? No, you know what?" I fold my arms and place them on the table as I lean forward. "Let's start with why you didn't tell me you were leaving." She tightens her lips and looks down. "You didn't even give me the chance to come with you." Which is exactly what I would've done, and she knows it. Uproot my life and follow her anywhere. I see from the look on her face that that's the reason she didn't tell me.

"I didn't want you to come with me," she says, and the words hit me like a ton of bricks. Thinking it is one thing, hearing it is entirely something else. I eye the exit and think about how long it would take me to dash for the door. "I didn't want you to come with me because I didn't want you to give up your whole life. I know what that feels like—I did it with Adam—and I loved you too much to ever make you do that, not for me. I couldn't live with myself knowing that you'd given everything up, and then what? Be beholden to the invisible strings that bind us? I'd blame myself for stunting your future, and—"

"Stunt my future? Are you serious?" I'm stunned. In the span of five seconds, I've felt every emotion possible. Anxiety, frustration, anger, shame, and now, utter confusion. How could she not know that *she* was my future? I would've followed her to the depths of this Earth if she would have let me. Because for me, that's love, and I never would have ever felt beholden or stunted. But that's my way of loving and never had it crossed my mind that any form of compromise to Zinnia feels like sacrifice. In her heart, she was protecting me from feeling the way she'd always felt, stifled by love, because in her world, that's what love is: so consuming that it threatened to erase her.

Was this her twisted way of loving me?

"Zin," I start. "Up until a few months ago, you were my entire future." As I say the words, more lights go off. Maybe that was part of the problem. Is that where the pressure was coming from for her?

I start to cry, letting each tear hit the empty white plate in front of me.

She reaches her hand across the table. I feel her skin against mine and an electric shock courses through my arm.

"I left Adam," she states point-blank.

My heart thumps.

"I've moved out."

Double thump.

"It's over."

Thumpity thump.

"I wanted to tell you, but I didn't want you to think that's why I was reaching out. Like some desperate attempt to get you to speak to me." Her fingertips caress my skin, and with every stroke, a shiver shoots up my arm, up my neck, behind my ear, down my spine. "It's real, though. It's over between me and Adam." She takes a deep breath and brings her chair closer to mine. No longer face to face, we are sitting side by side.

Now I'm the one fidgeting, biting the inside of my lip, the pulse in my body so loud I hear it in my brain. What does this mean? She wanted me to know, but she wants to give me space? She left Adam and what? What is she saying?

"It's you, Fay." Her words pull the tears out of my eyes, tugging at my heart. "It's always been you. I always knew we belonged together, but I ran from it. I was stupid, and I'll have to live with that for the rest of my life if you don't forgive me, but it's you I love. I've loved you from that first day I walked up to you in the cafeteria, that strong face you wore to hide how lonely and nervous you were. I used to accuse you of running from your emotions. But I was wrong. I was the one who had walls around me. You were only ever trying to find your way in. I see that now, and I realize how much I fucked this up when I left without telling you." She sits up straight. "I screwed up majorly when I chose California over us. Not because I shouldn't have gone or because you might've followed me, but because I kept you out. But you have to know it wasn't easy for me. It wasn't as simple as you or California. It was way more than that. You know that all I've ever believed is that sacrificing my happiness for my children was what would make me a good mom. But I realize now what you've always known and tried so hard to teach me: it doesn't have to be either or, it can be both and. But at the time, that's what choosing us meant for me. It was more than me and you, it was my mom and my baggage and my half-formed identity and my stupid way of sabotaging my life, holding myself back from true happiness because I was scared. But I've done the work. I'm not the same person who lied to you back in August and I'm not—" Her breath catches. "You know me, and you only ever pushed me to be my true self. You're the one who believed in me when I was dancing yet never lied to me if I asked for critique. You're the one who pushed me to pursue photography, which I have, by the way, and I love. You're the one I want to sit with in the park, looking up at the sky to watch clouds form, calling out every shape from Greek statues to hot dogs. You've never tried to make me something I'm not, because you see me, you always have. And Fay, I see you. And I'm sorry I ever accused you of bottling up your emotions, because I finally realize how filled to the brim those emotions have to be to explain the outpouring of love you've always shown me. You give your love so unconditionally and so freely—" Her voice breaks. She pauses to catch her breath, extending her hand out to touch mine again.

She leans in and takes a deep breath. I lean over and glide my fingers across her forehead, sweeping a curl away from her face. I leave my hand on the side of her head, and I feel the weight of it as she releases into me.

Somewhere along the way, somewhere between being her best friend and being her lover, I forgot that Zinnia came with her own backstory. One that I watched first-hand as it unravelled her at the seams. How could I have thought that Zin was capable of deliberately trying to hurt me? She was only ever trying to survive. I was too caught up in our love story to see that my friend would never cause me pain. *She* was in pain. That's what I'm realizing as she continues to explain to me what I already know.

"You finished?" I ask firmly, because if I don't stop her, she could go on like this forever, and I've had about enough.

The waiter interrupts with our meal and trolleys over another small table to lay out enough food for a family of four. He takes his time, setting down each dish carefully as Zin and I sit staring, watching as he slowly cleans dripping sauce from the side of a copper bowl, his movements painfully slow, like a snail making its way through molasses. When he's done, he lowers his head and opens his hands to show us our food, motioning to us that everything is now ready to be enjoyed. Zin and I bow our heads in thanks.

"Yes. I'm finished. That's all." She stops and continues to look at me. "Except, also—" she places her hand on mine "—I'll do whatever it takes to prove to you that you can trust me. Just say you still love me, or that . . ." her voice trails off. "Just say something. Anything."

"Anything?" I raise my eyebrows.

"Yes, anything. I mean, within reason. I can't move back to Toronto. My life is in California now. My kids are in school and finally adjusting. And Adam, I mean, he won't move back, and shared custody isn't possible when you live in two countries, but—" She's rambling.

"I don't want any of that." I hold my hand up. "So you can just stop."

Her face falls. She swipes the napkin off her lap and folds it neatly beside her plate. "I'm sorry, Fay." She stands up. "I'll stay somewhere else tonight."

She pulls her jacket on slowly, and I watch as she begins to walk away. I let her take a few steps before I finally put her out of her misery.

"Let me show your art," I say, holding my hand out to her.

Zin takes a step back toward the table, and in full rewind, she removes her jacket, places it on the chair and sits back down.

"What? What art?" She looks at me, confused.

"Your photos. Let's show them. You said anything, right? Well, let's find a place in LA and show your work." She continues to scan my face for the punchline. "Listen, despite my attempts to unfollow you on social media, I couldn't. Your stuff is too good. Plus, I know you well enough to know that each photo you've posted has been for me. I felt like you were trying to speak to me through your photos. The black-and-white one? 'The road I travel is the one that calls to me.'" I repeat her caption verbatim. "It's sensational. I could feel the movement under your feet set against the power of stillness. Like the log you captured up at cottage country."

A smile forms as she wipes away a single tear from her cheek.

"You have a gift, and I want you to show your work," I insist.

"Done!" she agrees. "Where do I sign?" Her chest puffs up and down in excitement. "I'll let you show my photos. Art. Whatever. But is that really all you want? What about us? Everything I said?" She fidgets with her hands.

"Listen, Zin, I sold my gallery, which I'm sure you know about, and I moved to Portugal. I set a life up for myself there because I had nothing left in Toronto." She lowers her eyes. "I thought it was the right move. I thought if I was far away from you, I'd be safe from getting hurt again. But I was wrong. Because the only thing that hurts more than loving you is loving you from afar." She lifts a brow. "To be clear, I had zero intention of forgiving you tonight. But I don't know, you've changed my mind. Open hearts open hearts, right?" I smile as I pay homage to Eduardo, his words lending themselves perfectly to us in this moment. I squeeze Zin's hand lightly. She squeezes back.

"So, we show your art?" I ask. We're both smiling like two giddy schoolgirls. "It's not too much pressure?"

She shakes her head.

I lean into her as I take her face with my hands, holding her close so I can speak at a whisper. "You really left Adam?"

Zin nods and bites her lower lip. "I missed you like a part of me was missing. But I also realized I had to become whole before this could ever really work." She motions between us. "I want to be with you, but not because you fill a hole in my heart, but because my heart is finally whole and I want to share it with you."

My cheeks hurt from smiling so hard. Never in my wildest dreams did tonight play out this way, and yet, here we are. Locked in a moment where the road finally leads back to us. This is it. And I know she feels it too. I can see it in her eyes.

The whole restaurant is watching us, but I don't mind the audience. We both laugh, tears rolling down our faces.

"I love you, Zin. And now I have until the end of time to show you just how much." I twirl my ruby ring around my finger and pull to slide it off.

I push away from the table. My chair rubs against the wood floor and makes a loud noise, attracting a few eyeballs. I adjust my pants as I begin to kneel at her side. Holding her hand in mine, I make my way to the floor, keeping her gaze the entire time.

"Zin, I love you. I will always love you," I start.

"What are you doing?" she asks.

"Showing you my love. Choosing you. Holding my hand out and asking you if you'll choose me one final time, Zinnia Saad. Will you marry me?"

"Is this crazy? Are you for real?" She looks around like she's searching for a hidden camera and then comes back to me, locking her eyes on mine.

I nod. I am crazy. It wasn't but thirty minutes ago that I was thinking of spiking her curry with extra hot sauce just to watch her suffer, and now, here I am, down on one knee, proposing.

"Yes! Yes!" She nods frantically. "A million times yes! Fay, oh, Fay!" She jumps out of her seat with a shout of joy and pulls me up for a kiss, causing the entire restaurant to now catch on to what's happening. Cue applause. It's so corny, but I don't care.

She said yes.

Zinnia

I ROLL OVER, AND FAY IS RIGHT THERE BESIDE ME. I'M OVERFLOWING with euphoria as I glide my toes up her leg and wrap my arm around her waist, shifting the duvet so our bodies touch, skin to skin, nothing between us. Pressing my chest against hers, I breathe in the vanilla scent of her skin as I kiss her shoulder.

Fay's back.

My Fay.

My fiancée.

I nudge her softly and hear her sigh a gentle morning exhale, then a happy moan when she feels me pressed up against her.

How did I get so lucky?

"I love you," I whisper into her ear, brushing my fingers through her hair.

She wraps her arm around my neck and flips over to face me. "I love you too."

We are going to create such a beautiful home together. One home, two hearts. Because love is that simple.

I tent the blanket around my body as I climb on top of her. I lower myself onto her and kiss her lips.

"Are you guys kidding me?" Kiara yells, knocking loudly on the door. "I told Val we'd pick her up at nine to go to Sweetie's!" She bangs a few more times to make a show of how annoyed she is. "Hurry up! Let's go!"

"Merde!" Fay mutters.

"I haven't heard you speak French in a while," I say with a giggle.

Kiara knocks like she's about to break down the door. "If you don't open this door, I'll huff, and I'll puff—"

"Calm your horses!" I jump off of Fay, and we both rush to get our clothes on. I search the floor for my pants, but the bottoms are still soaked from our walk home. I rip through my suitcase to find a fresh pair of jeans, pull them on, and throw on the first sweater I see.

We're both dressed at marathon speed. I'm still zipping up my jeans as I make my way for the door, but Fay stops me.

"Hey," she says, cupping my face. "We don't have to tell them if you're not ready."

"Are you kidding me? No more secrets, I want everyone to know!" I hold my hand up, and her ruby on my finger catches the sunlight, creating a red reflection on the walls. I slam my mouth onto hers and kiss her hard as I squeeze her cheeks together. "Come on, we'll be late," I say as I swing the door open. "So sorry, Keeks. I'll call Val from the car and tell her it's all my fault."

"We're barely late." Fay holds her phone up to show Kiara the screen. It reads 8:55, which, for all intents and purposes, makes us five minutes early.

"Well, you two seem happy," Kiara winks at me as I brush past her and race down the stairs, pulling my jacket on as I go. "Guess my little plan worked last night worked?"

"You have no idea," Fay yells over her shoulder. "Tell you at Sweetie's."

Kiara gets into the car and starts the engine to let it warm up. I'm outside with Fay, brushing off the snow, when Kiara lowers the window to tell us there's been a change of plans. "Val just texted. She prefers if we just pick up coffee and meet at her parents' house. We'll grab Bijou—it's close."

"Ugh, I want some good old Italian coffee. I get enough of that

Third Wave shit in California," I protest as I toss the snow brush behind the back seat and step into the car.

Fay gets into the front seat and slams the door, sending an avalanche of snow onto the windshield. She looks at Kiara, shrugs her shoulders and turns up the heat, rubbing her hands in front to warm up.

"Bad coffee is a fair trade-off for sun year-round."

"Agreed. Plus, Val loves the latte at Bijou, and they have amazing scones," Kiara insists. "Buttery, flaky, mmm, I'm hungry."

"In Cascais, I'd have a nata with my latte every afternoon around three," Fay adds. "Life is so different there. Europeans really know what they're doing."

"Tell me about it," Kiara says with a sigh.

Fay takes that as an open invitation to start on a diatribe about Cascais. As we head to Bijou, she fills us both in on her experience there. The job she took at a smoothie counter by the beach, the surf yoga she did every morning, and all the travellers she met.

After we pick up Bijou—five blueberry lemon scones and five lattes, one for each of us and an extra for Paula in case she's awake—we head toward Val's. When we pull up to her house, Kiara puts the car in park. We're about to jump out when Fay hits Kiara across the chest, holding her back from moving.

"Yo, is that Jack?" Fay points across the street.

I look out of my window and see Jack kissing Val at her front door. "It is, it is!" I squeal as I duck down so he doesn't see me. Kiara and Fay do the same.

"Oh snap! Yes!" Kiara claps loudly. "Holy, what's in the water this week?!"

Fay looks back at me, and we giggle. Guess we weren't as quiet as we thought.

"Should we pop out and yell surprise?" Fay suggests.

"Yeah," I reply as I roll my eyes. "Let's ambush him on his walk of shame. That wouldn't be awkward at all."

Like three little spies, we sit and wait in the car, popping our faces up just enough that we can watch Jack pull his hood up and walk down the street.

When he's out of sight, none of us reaches for the door handle. Instead, we remain there, motionless. No one says it, but I know we're all thinking the same thing: we're about to walk into the de la Vega home, but Eduardo won't be there to greet us.

"Are you coming in?" Val bangs on the rear window, startling all three of us.

Kiara turns off the engine as I step out of the car, bag of scones in hand. "Sorry, we needed a second to compose ourselves before we came in." I wrap my arms around a coatless Val.

"Get inside! You must be freezing," Fay insists, slamming the car door behind her. "We're coming. Keeks? You got the coffees?"

"Sure do."

When we step into the house, it's exactly as I remember: warm and welcoming; it feels like home. Each corner of this house holds another memory. I see us, four teenagers, in our pajamas, singing into wooden spoons, watching music videos, dancing in front of the TV. I see us huddled around Kiara on the bathroom floor, crying from her devastating breakup with Martin, her grade-nine boyfriend, the one who dated her simply so he could get closer to Val, his true crush. I see us jumping up and down when I got my acceptance letter to Juilliard. I see us, high out of our minds from having smoked our first joint, ransacking the fridge and pantry, thinking no one would be the wiser, only for Eduardo to find us in uncontrollable fits of giggles, packing our faces with Lays and with Froot Loops covered in chocolate milk. He for sure knew but let on like he didn't. He just walked into the kitchen, made himself a cup of tea, and said *I hope you're all sleeping here—I'm making arepas for breakfast*. That was his way of telling us no one drives high.

I can't believe he's gone.

On the mantle are photos that capture everything I've missed this past decade. Snapshots of parties, anniversaries, holidays—photos to mark every occasion. Eduardo and Paula's true love displayed one still shot at a time. There's an older photo amongst the new ones; the sunlight has faded some of the image's colour. I pick up the frame and trace the photo's edges with my finger. It's the one of Eduardo sitting on a dock, feet dangling in the water, and Paula lying on her side, head resting on his lap, legs curled up on the dock. I can feel the heat of the summer sun, the blue sky blanketing the green mountain tops. The lake looks calm, yet there's a little ripple around where Eduardo's feet tickle the water's surface. He's leaning on one hand, and the other rests on Paula's bare back. The photo is taken from behind. So much is being conveyed in this image. So much intimacy and closeness: the proximity of their bodies, the soft touch of his hand. We can't see their faces, but I imagine they both have their eyes closed, soaking in the warmth, at peace and restful. They could probably fall asleep just like that, in the comfort of each other. This image tells the story of love. No need to exchange words, just a simple moment where two people sit together in stillness, looking out onto the bucolic landscape, surrounded by nothing but the elements. The time stamp reads 2003.

"Who took this photo?" I ask Val. "It's absolutely beautiful."

"Oh, that one? That was the weekend we went up north for Saint-Jean-Baptiste. We rented that summer house, remember?" She comes over and grabs the frame from my hand. "I think you took this picture, actually." She hands it back to me. "Pretty, yeah?"

"Yeah." I stare at it and travel back to that day. All of a sudden I remember standing on the dock holding a disposable yellow Kodak. I did take it. "You think I can keep it?"

Val shrugs her shoulders. "My mom loves that photo. But I'm sure she'll let you make a copy. We can ask her when she wakes up."

"Maybe we blow it up and hang it for your show?" Fay clips the photo from my hands and stares at it. "You had an eye, even back then." She traces her finger across the centre. She winks at me and replaces the frame back on the mantle.

Kiara's on the grey loveseat, covered in crumbs, halfway through her scone. Fay and I make our way over to sit on the couch across from her. Fay reaches for the scones and hands me one as I pull a blanket over our laps. I miss this house. So many memories here. It's strange to think Eduardo isn't in the other room making his famous arepas or putting a playlist together for a dance party.

"You think your mom will move?" I ask Val, who has found a cozy spot next to Kiara.

She stares off pensively and takes a sip of her latte. "I don't know." She looks around. "It's a lot of house for one person."

We stay silent, each of us taking in the space. We spend the next hour or so reminiscing through the years, travelling down memory lane, laughing about the good times, and crying as we remember the days when we were there for each other through the hard ones.

"I've been a bad friend this year. I'm sorry for that," Fay says to Kiara as Val and I watch the exchange. "I wish I had checked in with you back when you got pregnant. And you—" she looks at Val. "When your dad first got sick. I loved him very much. I'm sorry that I didn't get to see him before—"

"I know," Val says, reaching across the coffee table to take Fay's hand in hers. "You've apologized enough."

"She's right. Why are you bringing this up now?" Kiara asserts, devouring the other half of her scone in one bite. "We've moved on. Forget it."

"I know, but still . . . I need to say this," Fay insists. "No excuses, I should've been there." She releases Val's hand and then leans back onto the couch. She looks at me and continues, "A wise person once told me that real love knows no conditions. And I think that's where we went wrong. We let some contract we wrote when we were kids dictate how we show up for each other rather than just being there when and how we needed. We let it symbolize the strength of our friendship as if this once-a-year gathering was enough instead of actively showing up for each other every day. Real friendship isn't about a weekend getaway, it's about the daily micro-moments of being there for each other, making space in our lives and showing up regardless of how busy we are. We held each other to impossible standards.

We stopped listening to one another, yet we all expected to be heard. We wanted to be prioritized without reciprocation. So I'm sorry for the part I played in that."

We're all crying and nodding along in silent agreement.

Val smiles as she breaks off a small corner of her scone. "Sorry not sorry, because I don't know . . ." She shrugs, popping the piece into her mouth. "It's sort of been like a hard reset."

"You know what Eduardo would've said?" Kiara starts. She looks at the mantle of pictures across from us and continues, "A true friend doesn't make your problems disappear, but a true friend doesn't disappear when there's a problem."

"Didn't he also used to say that one should always carry stamps because you never know when you need to mail something?" I tease as I wipe away a tear.

We all erupt into laughter.

"Shh, my mom's still sleeping." Val brings her finger to her mouth to quiet us down.

"Oh! Can I have her scone?" Kiara motions to the bag on the coffee table.

"Off!" Val slaps her hand away.

"Have you been eyeing that since you finished yours?" Fay laughs.

"You know it," Kiara jokes. "What? If no one's gonna have it—" Kiara reaches for the bag again.

"Here, have mine. I'm stuffed," I say, passing her my last corner of scone. Val's eyes widen as my hand reaches in front of her, and Fay's ruby ring glints on my finger.

"Are you kidding me?" Kiara beams, the realization hitting her immediately. She sets my scone down.

I nod vigorously, and Fay grabs my hand to hold it up. "Oh, yeah, we meant to tell you—she said yes!" she declares with no further explanation, then cups my chin and lays a big, sloppy kiss right on my lips. Our first public display of affection in front of our friends, and it feels so good.

Val and Kiara shriek with excitement and we launch into the details of how it all went down. The fight, the makeup, the proposal. "So maybe we do Rome next year after all?" Val looks at us, insinuating that perhaps a destination wedding is the next girls trip.

"I was thinking more of a summer wedding, actually," I say.

"Oh yeah?" Kiara asks. "Like, the Laurentians? Lakefront?"

"Oohhh! Maybe we all rent a place together, and you can bring the kids?" Val squeals. I can see by the expression on her face that she has the whole thing planned already. Right next to her title as CMO of Valentina's, we could add Wedding Planner Extraordinaire.

"I'd love that," Fay says and wraps her arm around me. I rest my head on Fay's shoulder, and we stay there like that for a while.

"That would work for me," Kiara adds. "Close drive from Ottawa."

"You got the job?" Val grabs her arm forcefully. We all watch as her face transforms from excited to forlorn as she realizes that if Kiara got the job in government as an education consultant, that means she's moving.

Kiara nods. "My program was approved. They're moving me out there in the spring. I didn't want to tell you while all this was going on . . ."

"What are you talking about?! Friends are there for the bad times but also for the good! And this is *good*!" Val beams with joy.

"Congratulations, Keeks, that's a big coup for the school system," Fay says with a smile.

"I'm so proud of you." I beam. "You're gonna blow them away."

"We'll find you another roomie." Kiara pets Val's head. "Perhaps a certain gentleman caller might be interested?"

Val shoots straight up and looks at the three of us, realizing that we saw Jack this morning on his walk of shame.

We all erupt into laughter again.

"You see, this . . ." Val nods, reaching for a tissue. Her laughter has summoned tears, a combination of joy and sadness. "You guys, this is why I need you."

Looking around the room at my three best friends, I know now that if I ever feel lost again, I just need to look in their eyes, and there I'll be.

"I miss him," Val says tenderly, wiping a tear from her eye. The weight of shared loss sits heavy on all our hearts. "He'd be so happy you guys are here. You know what he told me when he drove me to the airport last year?" Val asks, glancing at each of us. "When you're with your friends, they make your heart feel whole."

"Oh great," I say through blurred vision. "I'm gonna cry again."

Kiara reaches for the tissue box on the coffee table and plucks four, one for each of us.

We stay cuddled on the couch for hours: Fay and I cozy under a blanket while Val and Kiara snuggle together on the loveseat beside us.

We've each experienced one of the worst, undeniably hardest years of our lives, yet somehow, we made it through the other side. Closer than ever, if that's possible.

No contracts needed.

Acknowledgements

NAN, YOU WERE THE FIRST PERSON TO EVER READ THIS BOOK. I loved that you toted the very first draft around New York City on our weekend away. I watched as you snuck moments in coffee shops to flip pages, marked up the margins while we lay in bed, and looked up to ask me questions as we walked through the streets. Watching you engage so deeply with my manuscript was a gift and one of the greatest highlights of this journey—matched only by your astute advice and insight into my characters and their friendship dynamics. You helped make them more real, and you made me feel like a real author.

To Mel and Phil, and our whole big, beautiful family, thank you for supporting me and filling my life with story. I hope I've learned from you how to show up with the same generosity, attention, and care—for other writers and for the people I love.

Laur, you are my biggest cheerleader and, bar none, my biggest fan. Your support and encouragement are a lifeline. As I continue to write, I imagine you waiting with open arms for each new story. That's how special you make me feel. Our friendship is one of the great privileges of my life.

Andrea and Vienna, your feedback, encouragement, and literary nod as avid readers gave me the confidence I needed to keep going. Your kindness has become part of the way I move through the world.

Lesley, Yaffa, Moranne, and all my friends—thank you for inspiring me, believing in me, and championing my success. Your faith in me has taught me how to be a better friend in return.

Ali, only you entertain the endless hours of my craziness: the anxiety, the doubt, the fears about my writing career. Thank you for indulging my overthinking and for also telling me when it's time to take a beat and shut the eff up. The way you show up for me is truly everything. Thank you. If I could show up for you with half the grace and steadiness you effortlessly show me, I would still only be a shadow of your greatness.

Geri, Celia, Molly, and my early writing group members—there would be no book without you. Those nights spent discussing characters, tension, plot, and line-level writing in our amateur, figuring-it-out way meant everything to me. Hearing your thoughts on my girls shaped *TIWINY* in its earliest form and made me a better writer. I can't wait to walk into a bookstore one day, pick up one of your novels, and say, "I know her!"

Noreen Nanja, fellow early writing group member and dear friend, thank you for your continued support. Amy Jones, thank you for your invaluable feedback—before you, *TIWINY* was all tell and no show.

Alex D'Amico, thank you for believing in me and helping make this book happen. Whenever I doubted myself, you were there to champion me. Your industry guidance and friendship have carried me here. Thank you a thousand times over.

A massive thank you to Kenna Barnes, who shared my vision and helped keep this book safe. Over the years, I've come to rely deeply on your expert editorial insight. I will forever be grateful that you believed in this story.

Thank you to the entire team at ECW, including Sammy Chin, Jess Albert, and Jennifer Gallinger, as well as Thomas Hayman for a stunning cover and Ulka Simone Mohanty for reading my novel for audio.

Mom, I loved watching you read my manuscript—and when I say watching, I mean I literally stared at you out of the corner of my

eye as you turned all 300-plus pages, waiting for the good parts (and squirming through some of the sexy ones). I held my breath for the verdict, and then you cried—and I knew I had you. Thank you for reading my book and handling it with such care.

Dad, you may never read this book, but just know, you are everyone's Eduardo.

My kiddos—Azalea, Ivy, and Brighton—you inspire everything I do. The cheers and hugs we shared when I got my book deal still make my heart burst. You were so proud of your mama, and I hope to keep making you proud today and always. More than that, I hope I show you—by how I live and love—what it means to honour the people who believe in you. I won't turn this into a life lesson—but hey, I'm your mom, so here it is: Follow your dreams. They really do come true.

To all the writers out there working toward their dream book deal, drafting late into the night, imagining their stories in readers' hands around the world: I'm right there with you. I believe in you. And if you need to hear it directly, reach out—I'll be in your corner, always.

And lastly, to Val, Kiara, Fay, and Zinnia: each of you is a part of my life now. You are creations of my heart—pieces of my past and hopes for my future. Your friendship holds the complexity of time, the depth of love, and the respect true friendship requires. You are so real to me. As you move out into the world, I hope others love you as fiercely as I do.

Living a life filled with meaning is the work of a village. My community fills my heart—and will continue to fill the pages of the books to come.

This Is Why I Need You is my first book—of many, I hope. My characters always existed in some form. Like something out of Pirandello, they were simply searching for their author. In that way, I wrote this story—and it wrote me too.

Entertainment. Writing. Culture.

ECW is a proudly independent, Canadian-owned book publisher. We know great writing can improve people's lives, and we're passionate about sharing original, exciting, and insightful writing across genres.

Thanks for reading along!

We want our books not just to sustain our imaginations, but to help construct a healthier, more just world, and so we've become a certified B Corporation, meaning we meet a high standard of social and environmental responsibility — and we're going to keep aiming higher. We believe books can drive change, but the way we make them can too.

Being a B Corp means that the act of publishing this book should be a force for good — for the planet, for our communities, and for the people that worked to make this book. For example, everyone who worked on this book was paid at least a living wage. You can learn more at the Ontario Living Wage Network.

This book is also available as a Global Certified Accessible™ (GCA) ebook. ECW Press's ebooks are screen reader friendly and are built to meet the needs of those who are unable to read standard print due to blindness, low vision, dyslexia, or a physical disability.

This book is printed on FSC®-certified paper. It contains recycled materials, and other controlled sources, is processed chlorine free, and is manufactured using biogas energy.

ECW's office is situated on land that was the traditional territory of many nations, including the Wendat, the Anishinaabeg, Haudenosaunee, Chippewa, Métis, and current treaty holders the Mississaugas of the Credit. In the 1880s, the land was developed as part of a growing community around St. Matthew's Anglican and other churches. Starting in the 1950s, our neighbourhood was transformed by immigrants fleeing the Vietnam War and Chinese Canadians dispossessed by the building of Nathan Phillips Square and the subsequent rise in real estate value in other Chinatowns. We are grateful to those who cared for the land before us and are proud to be working amidst this mix of cultures.

ecwpress.com